Dedicated

to

THEM

Sitting or standing, as the mood or the ritual occasion dictated when they posed for the royal sculptors millennia ago, they stare pleasantly out upon the long green snake of Egypt—which they called Kemet, "the Black Land"—and the desert wastes of "the Red Land" beyond.

They have been there, some of them, five thousand years and more.

If there is an Earth five thousand years from now, some of them will doubtless be there still.

Smiling, happy, confident, serene, ravaged no longer by the fierce ambitions and violent passions that often moved behind those deliberately impervious formal masks, they have a satisfaction, not given to many, which they will never know but seldom doubted:
They always said they would live forever.
And as forever goes in the lives of men, they have.

THE ROYAL HOUSE OF THEBES—SUPREMELY POWERFUL . . . FATALLY FLAWED . . .

HOREMHEB—the bold and popular General who hungered for the sacred crown of the Pharaoh—and would do anything to make it his.

TIYE—the Queen Mother and Great Wife who ruled Egypt for decades behind the façade of her husband's leadership. She had already lost one of her children to the merciless demands of power—now she would have to sacrifice her beloved Akhenaten for the good of the Kingdom.

NEFERTITI—the most beautiful woman in the world bred from birth to be the Pharaoh's devoted slave—and follow him into whatever tortured obsession his restless mind conceived.

AKHENATEN—the dream-filled King of Egypt who dared to challenge the ancient order of his people and dethrone the jealous deities of his land for the glory of one, almighty God . . .

A God Against the Gods

BY ALLEN DRURY

Fiction

ADVISE AND CONSENT

A SHADE OF DIFFERENCE

THAT SUMMER

CAPABLE OF HONOR

PRESERVE AND PROTECT

THE THRONE OF SATURN

COME NINEVEH, COME TYRE

THE PROMISE OF JOY

A GOD AGAINST THE GODS

RETURN TO THEBES *

Non-fiction

A SENATE JOURNAL

THREE KIDS IN A CART

"A VERY STRANGE SOCIETY"

COURAGE AND HESITATION, *With Fred Maroon*

* *A Dell Book*

A GOD AGAINST THE GODS

ALLEN DRURY

A DELL BOOK

Published by
DELL PUBLISHING CO., INC.
1 Dag Hammarskjold Plaza
New York, N.Y. 10017
Copyright © 1976 by Allen Drury
All rights reserved.
For information address Doubleday & Company, Inc.
New York, N.Y. 10017.
Dell ® TM 681510, Dell Publishing Co., Inc.

ISBN: 0-440-12968-0

Reprinted by arrangement with
Doubleday & Company, Inc.
Printed in the United States of America
First Dell printing—February 1978

INTRODUCTION

IN THE GREAT BEND of the River Nile at present-day Tell-el-Amarna in Egypt, where some thirty-three hundred years ago the Pharaoh Akhenaten built his city of Akhet-Aten, there remains today nothing but a great empty plain broken in a couple of places by a few low lines of crumbling mud-brick wall—all that is left of what was once the capital, under "the Heretic," "the Criminal of Akhet-Aten," as his own people came to call him, of Ancient Egypt.

As recently as the turn of the present century much more of the city was visible and quite a few excavations were made. Today the desert has reclaimed it, awaiting a time when Egyptian and foreign archaeologists may have the opportunity, and the money, to dig again.

For the present it is desolate, empty, haunted, brooding. Boundless and bare, the level sands stretch far away.

Yet there is here, of course, much more than a poetic cliché from Shelley. There is here the mystery of the man who was either "history's first idealist," as he has been called, or history's first great royal madman. It is entirely within the bounds of human possibility that he was both. I have my own ideas, developed herein. But the chances are good that we will never know for sure.

Who was he, what was he—unhappy Akhenaten, whose hooded, self-defensive eyes stare out of his long, pain-filled face in the colossal statues that now stand in the Cairo Museum? Over and over in these pages you will find the men and women of his family, the men and women of his Court, asking themselves and one another these questions. None ever finds the final answer, as no Egyptologist or novelist has ever found the final answer. One version is in these pages, the one that seems to me most logical out of the fragmentary, conflicting evidence that Egypt's secretive sands have so far yielded up to us. But it is only one. . . .

It is necessary for the novelist of this magnificent but misty time to do exactly what the professional Egyptologist does: assemble the few scraps of known fact—try to reach conclusions as logical as possible about them— take a deep breath—and make a firm and arbitrary decision.

So it is with dates, spelling of names, familial relationships, personal motivations.

For instance:

Estimates of how long Ancient Egypt had been an entity prior to the events of this novel and its sequel, *Return to Thebes,* range from a minimum of one thousand to a maximum of almost three thousand years. I have chosen arbitrarily, on what seems the main burden of the evidence, to put it somewhere approaching two thousand years. We do not know: only the sands of Egypt, which cover all, know; and until there is time and money to dig to the full beneath them (assuming that might be physically possible, in itself an optimistic conjecture), we will never know with any degree of certainty. Somewhere in the neighborhood of two thousand years would seem to encompass logically and comfortably the earliest beginnings, the seventeen dynasties recognized by the Egyptian historian Manetho (who himself did not come along with *his* arbitrary guesses until 305 B.C., more than a thousand years after the events of these novels), and the so-called "Hyksos invasion," which preceded the Eighteenth Dynasty.

In the same fashion I have chosen 1392 B.C. as the birth year of both Akhenaten and his wife and cousin, Nefertiti. It was somewhere around that time: there are as many guesses as there are Egyptologists. I have grounded my time frame on that arbitrary date and have anchored it at the far end to the year 1330 B.C., which allows sixty-two years for Akhenaten's birth and adolescence, his co-regency with his father Amonhotep III, his co-regency with his younger brother Smenkhkara, the reign of his youngest brother Tutankhamon, the reign of their uncle Aye and much of the reign of Horemheb, last Pharaoh of the Eighteenth Dynasty. Some professionals may dispute this, but anyone who delves into Egyptian history soon finds that his own guess is just about as good as anyone else's—providing it allows sufficient elbow room for the generally agreed-upon lengths of these various kings of the Eighteenth Dynasty. This I have sought to do.

Similarly with names. Horemheb, for instance, is "Harem-hab" to the brilliant present-day Egyptologist Cyril Aldred; "Harmhab" to the first great historian of Ancient Egypt, James H. Breasted; and appears elsewhere variously as Horemheb, Horemhab, Haremhab, Haremheb, Harmhab, Harmheb, Heru-em-heb—somebody has to make a decision, and in this case I'm it. "Horemheb" has a solid ring to me, so "Horemheb" he is herein.

This decision, as with many other names, is based on what to me seems easiest and most euphonious for the present-day reader to articulate and understand. Akhenaten's father was known to the Greeks, Romans, and to modern-day Egyptians who follow their lead, as "Amenophis III." Aldred renders him "Amon-Hot-pe." I have chosen the third most popular version, "Amonhotep," as the simplest for the modern reader's purposes. Similarly the Sun God himself appears in many texts as "Re," pronounced "Ray" or "Reh." I prefer the simpler rendition "Ra," pronounced "Rah," which seems to fall easiest on the tongue. He is also "Amon," "Amun," and "Amen." "Amon" seems the simplest, both when standing alone and when used as part of a name.

I have also adopted the practice of breaking down into their components, for the first three times they appear in the text, the more difficult names of the Eighteenth Dynasty. If one gives to *a, e,* and *i* (which were unknown to the ancients and only introduced in Greco-Roman times for much the same purposes of convenience that I am striving for here) the sounds "ah," "eh," and "ee," it becomes relatively easy. The name of Akhenaten's (Akh-eh-*nah*-ten's) third daughter, who appears here as a young girl and will play a major role in *Return to Thebes,* is a real jawbreaker—Ankhesenpaaten. But if the reader will take a moment to sound it out slowly—"Ankh-eh-sen-pah-*ah*-ten"—the going becomes much easier and the name quite beautiful. And so with Nefer-Kheperu-Ra, Ankh-Kheperu-Ra, Neb-Kheperu-Ra (the brothers Akhenaten, Smenkhkara and Tutankhamon), and the rest.

For easy reference by the modern reader I have also, in common with many Egyptologists, adopted certain recognizable locutions. For Amonhotep III to refer to his family as "the Eighteenth Dynasty," for instance, is a complete prolepsis, since Manetho and his list did not come along until more than a thousand years later. And yet the Ancient Egyptians were a time-minded and orderly people and undoubtedly (to use a word beloved of the professionals) had some sense of what went before, and in their own minds must have had some cataloguing of the royal houses that preceded theirs. Accordingly I have them refer to their own "Eighteenth Dynasty" and their own "House of Thebes," because this makes it easier for us to understand what they are talking about.

By the same token, they did not know the terms "Valley of the Kings" or "Valley of the Queens," although they did have some general way of referring to the royal necropolis on the west bank of the Nile opposite Thebes. "Beneath the Peak of the West" is one with some historical foundation, and I have used it fairly often; but, for us, "Valley of the Kings" is more instantly recognizable, and so I have often used it too. "The blood of Ra" is a locution for the blood royal that they may not have used, but it is understandable here. They did not know the terms "mother-in-law," "brother-in-law" and the like. They did not know that millennia later we would refer to the oddly elongated skulls of Akhenaten's family as "platycephalic." But we know that, and it simplifies understanding in the text.

One name I have retained in its original form is "Akhet-Aten," the name of Akhenaten's new capital. We know it more readily as "Tell-el-Amarna," yet it seems fitting to keep the name he gave it—and to syllabify it throughout, so that it will not be confused with his own.

We do not know how the King was addressed by his intimate circle, particularly by family members, and so I have assumed that, as with all royal families, a certain human informality must have existed behind palace doors, especially in moments of stress. Thus I have freely interchanged "Majesty," "Son of the Sun" and occasional direct personal use of names such as "Neb-Ma'at-Ra" (Amonhotep III), "Nefer-Kheperu-Ra" (Akhenaten) and so on. To Nefertiti's father, later the Pharaoh Aye, I have given the all-purpose title of "Councilor," because that seems to best represent what he was to the four kings of his immediate family prior to his own assumption of the crown. Virtually all other names, titles and terms I use come directly from the ancients, without change. Akhenaten's mother, Queen Tiye, *was* "the Great Wife," Nefertiti *was* "the Chief Wife'" and so on.

Certain things that Egyptologists have made a great mystery of, I have chosen to believe were exactly what logic indicates they were on the basis of the records that have come down to us.

There is, for instance, the matter of Akhenaten's relationship with his younger brother Smenkhkara. He made Smenkhkara his Co-Regent, gave him Nefertiti's name, conferred upon him the formal title "Beloved of Akhenaten," and had his sculptors portray them together in poses that are considerably more than fraternal. Yet there are substantial Egyptologists who refuse to admit the clear implications of all this. Instead they go off into some mystical realm of rationalization in which they claim that this relationship was purely platonic. Simple logic would indicate that the facts were exactly as Akhenaten, who prided himself on "living in truth" in all things, publicly and unabashedly proclaimed them to be.

And there is the mystery about Horemheb, who, prior to his own assumption of the crown, refers to himself as "Son of the Living Horus"—in other words, of the then reigning Pharaoh, Aye. The logical probability is that Horemheb, being a practical and pragmatic man, styled himself the son of Aye because he was indeed just that;

and the Mutnedjmet he married was his own half sister, last surviving bearer of the legitimacy of the throne, whom he married to secure his own claim to it.

Much is made of the fact, also, that Akhenaten apparently suffered the deformities of what we know as Frölich's syndrome, which usually results in impotence. Therefore, some argue, he could not have fathered the six daughters (to say nothing of the three daughters by three of his daughters) whom historically he did father. Yet it is not impossible for Frölich's syndrome to be arrested prior to impotence, and I have assumed that it was in his case, for the simple reason that this is the only logical way to explain both his deformities and the daughters he made such a show of—as if to say, "You thought I couldn't do it, didn't you?"—which, as I understand him, is exactly how he would have felt about it.

And there is the famous mystery of one of his colossal statues, which stands now in the Cairo Museum devoid of genitals. Much has been made of this. Yet over the empty genital area there is a large irregular plaster patch, noticeably darker than the surrounding plaster, and there is a very definite difference in texture between it and the rest of the statue. Now, undoubtedly this has been noted by others, and perhaps the difference means nothing: and yet, again, the simplest and most logical explanation is the very strong possibility that someone, probably Horemheb, ordered the statue emasculated as a sign of contempt for Akhenaten and his rather wide-ranging sexual activities. Great mysteries are made of things like these by the professionals, and great battles rage.

My approach has been to stick to the simple facts of what we know and follow them as nearly as possible to their logical conclusions. Thus you will find herein what is, I hope, as reasonable a reconstruction as can be devised of those ancient, bloody days when Akhenaten was rising to power and beginning his attempt to overthrow the gods; and when his family, unhappy and greatly disturbed, was reaching the reluctant conclusion that he must, in some fashion, be removed from the throne.

Allen Drury

A GOD
AGAINST
THE GODS

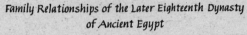

THE HOUSE OF THEBES
Family Relationships of the Later Eighteenth Dynasty of Ancient Egypt

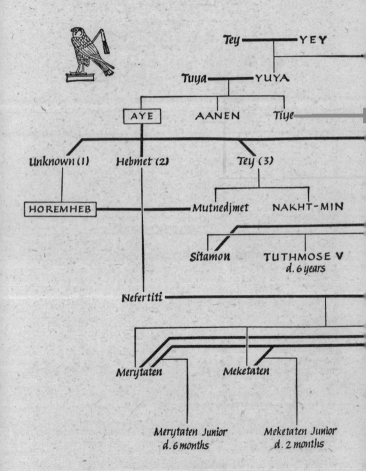

Tey ——— YEY

Tuya ——— YUYA

AYE   AANEN   Tiye

Unknown (1)   Hebmet (2)   Tey (3)

HOREMHEB ——— Mutnedjmet   NAKHT-MIN

Sitamon   TUTHMOSE V
d. 6 years

Nefertiti

Merytaten   Meketaten

Merytaten Junior
d. 6 months

Meketaten Junior
d. 2 months

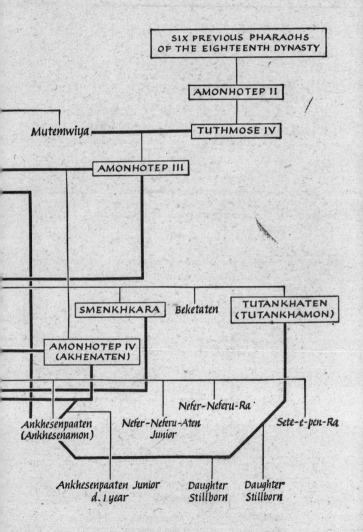

BOXED CAPITALS : PHARAOHS   CAPITALS : MALES
Italics : Females   ▬▬ MARRIAGES   ▬▬ ISSUE

SIX PREVIOUS PHARAOHS
OF THE EIGHTEENTH DYNASTY

AMONHOTEP II

Mutemwiya ──── TUTHMOSE IV

AMONHOTEP III

SMENKHKARA   *Beketaten*   TUTANKHATEN
(TUTANKHAMON)

AMONHOTEP IV
(AKHENATEN)

Ankhesenpaaten
(Ankhesenamon)   *Nefer-Neferu-Aten*
Junior   *Nefer-Neferu-Ra*   *Sete-e-pen-Ra*

Ankhesenpaaten Junior
d. 1 year   *Daughter*
Stillborn   *Daughter*
Stillborn

PRINCIPAL CHARACTERS IN THE NOVEL

The Royal Family of the Later Eighteenth Dynasty (Pharaohs in capitals):

AMON-HO-TEP III, ninth King and Pharaoh of the Eighteenth Dynasty

Queen Mu-tem-wi-ya, his mother

Queen Tiye, his Great Wife

Queen Gil-u-khi-pa of Mittani, his second wife

Queen-Princess Sit-a-mon, his daughter and wife

AMON-HO-TEP IV, later AKH-EN-ATEN, tenth King and Pharaoh, his son

SMENKH-KA-RA, eleventh King and Pharaoh, his son

TUT-ANKH-ATEN, later TUT-ANKH-AMON, twelfth King and Pharaoh, his son

Princess Bek-et-aten, his daughter

Queen Nefer-ti-ti, Chief Wife of AKH-EN-ATEN

Queen Kia of Mesopotamia, his second wife

Meryt-aten, Meket-aten, Ankh-e-sen-pa-aten, Nefer-neferu-aten Junior, Nefer-neferu, Set-e-pen-ra, daughters of AKH-EN-ATEN and Nefer-ti-ti

AYE, older brother of Queen Tiye and father of Nefer-ti-ti, thirteenth King and Pharaoh

HOR-EM-HEB, fourteenth and last King and Pharaoh of the Eighteenth Dynasty, his son

A-a-nen, younger brother of Queen Tiye, Priest of Amon

Others in the Court:

Amon-ho-tep, Son of Hapu, scribe, sage, builder, adviser to the Royal Family

Ra-mo-se, Vizier

Bek, chief sculptor to AKH-EN-ATEN

The Lady Anser-Wossett, chief lady in waiting to Queen Nefer-ti-ti

Hat-sur-et, Priest of Amon

RAMESSES, lieutenant to HOR-EM-HEB, later first King and Pharaoh of the Nineteenth Dynasty

Amon-em-het, a peasant

Allies:

Bur-na-bur-i-ash, King of Babylon

Tush-ratta, King of Mittani

Gods:

Amon, "King of the Gods" at the start of AKHEN-ATEN's revolution

The Aten, AKHENATEN's Sole God

Horus, Ptah, Hathor, Sekhmet, Thoth, Anubis, Isis, Osiris and many others

Amonhotep, S.H.

So DO I SIGN MYSELF, remembering the small, wizened, modest man who gave me life, thinking thereby to give him in return a fame of which he never dreamed in all his sixty humble years as a farmer:

Amon-ho-tep, Son of Hapu, risen very high and destined, as we all declare so stoutly on our tombs and monuments, to live forever and ever. . . .

Now that I too am very old, I sometimes question this. It is not in the children of Kemet, the Black Land, to question such things, but now and again some of us do . . . when we are very old . . . and very secretly. . . .

It would never do for one who has passed most of his life in the Great House, most of his life as the willing and, I like to think, useful servant of Pharaoh, the Good God, the One-above-all-others who lives there, to have in public a thought so unsettling. But sometimes, as I say, I do have such thoughts. I am a little more independent of mind, and no doubt of demeanor, than most. It is possibly the reason why the Good God has always chosen to favor me, and why I have been able to survive these recent years and remain, as I do to this day, a famous and honored man upon whom he still smiles with favor when he sees me—even though the One who smiles upon me now is many years away from the One who smiled upon me first. It is not his fault that he profited from the troubles of the House of Thebes; indeed, having his nature, he could do no other. Particularly when those who were of that House so grievously lost *ma'at*—the sense of *the fitness of things*—and allowed such evil days to fall upon the land of Kemet.

I went down the Nile a month ago, leaving from the

1

never ending clamor of the docks at Thebes in the old
familiar way, watching the pleasant life of the eternal
stream passing by on all sides—the excited shouts and
chatter of the pilots and sailors, the greetings called out
cheerfully from the banks, the barges laden with goods
going up and down between Thebes and the cities of the
Delta, the small papyrus boats carrying families on business or pleasure, the occasional state barge of the high
official parting all before it. I no longer travel like that
save on the greatest of occasions when I am sometimes
called back to the Great House to participate; but like all
the sons and daughters of Kemet, I love the river. As we
should, for from it comes our past, present, future, our
reason, our purpose, and our life.

So I traveled down, being poled by two of my slaves,
taken captive by my namesake, Amon-ho-tep III (Life,
health, prosperity!), on that expedition to Nubia upon
which I accompanied him so long ago, when we were
young. He never made another, though on his monuments
you will find him telling you how he subjugated Syria,
Naharin and wretched Kush. They all say things like that,
the Ones who live in the Great House, and sometimes you
cannot tell who has done what, or indeed who is who. But
does it matter? They are all gods, they are all eternal, they
come and go unchanging in the endless story of Kemet,
always conquering, always victorious, always all-knowing,
always all-powerful, always, essentially, the same . . .
save one. And although the One who sits in the Great
House now has done everything he could to obliterate his
name and his memory, from the life and deeds of *that*
One the land of Kemet will never really recover. Him she
will never forget, though forgetting is official and always
will be official, forever and ever. . . .

I passed by his city on my eighth day on the river. It
was nearing dusk and along the banks in the little villages
the humble folk from whom I come were cooking their
evening meals. Across the water floated laughter, happy
voices, the comfortable noise and bustle of family concourse. It was so until we neared the great bend against

the eastern cliffs where he decreed that his city should be built, and where it rose, complete, in two furious fantastic years. Then all habitation ended, a great silence fell, and on the soft winds blowing out of the Red Land came no sound save the ghostly sounds an old man heard in memory:

The high, imperious cries of Akh-en-aten (Life, health, prosperity!) . . . Nefer-ti-ti's firm yet gentle voice . . . the happy gossip of their daughters . . . the eager boyish voices of his two younger brothers, Smenkh-ka-ra and Tut-ankh-amon (Life, health, prosperity to them both!), innocent of care before they too became God and Pharaoh . . . the calm, unhurried phrases of his uncle and father-in-law Aye (Life, health, prosperity!) as he waited patiently for the day, when he, too, would so ascend . . . the soft, unyielding tones of his mother, Queen Tiye . . . the weary complaints of his father, Amon-ho-tep III (Life, health, prosperity!), not to be saved by divinity, doomed soon to pass to the West and knowing it . . . the sibilant comments of the other uncle, Aanen, Second Priest of Amon, bitter and unforgiving, working ceaselessly toward the day when he dared challenge the God who worshiped the Aten . . . and all the others, myself among them, younger then, confident, certain, perhaps a little contentious in the power I still held in the Palace . . . and my friend Hor-em-heb (Life, health, prosperity!) who holds the Palace now and who, for Kemet's sake, had to join in silencing, finally, the most dangerous of the many voices of the House of Thebes . . .

Ghostly they are now, ghostly and yet curiously alive for an old man dreaming on the river. I could hear them as clearly as I hear you, see them as clearly as my eyes see you. When I returned up the river to Thebes from Heliopolis, where I had gone on the business of one of my sons, just dead, it happened again.

I stood for a long time by the rail but I do not think I will go that way again. I am very old, now, and there is little chance that I will again have business on the river even if Amon were to give me strength, which lately he has not. I think it better, perhaps, that it should be so, for there is no profit in it for me, and certainly no satisfaction. I cannot find it in my heart to condemn that One even though I understand why my friend in the Great House now feels he must. And I agree with that. I agree with that. Make no mistake, I agree, it must be done. But I do not want to hear their voices any more.

All, all are gone, the House of Thebes. A year ago his sister, the Queen-Princess Sit-a-mon, to whom in these later years of my retirement I served a comfortable time as High Steward, died at her own great age: the chapter closed. Already in so short a time, twenty-six racing years since his death, nothing remains of his city but a few half-finished tombs in the cliffs; piles of rubble; the crumbling outline of a mud-brick palace here and there. The wind from the Red Land blows gently over them, the sand piles ever deeper. Men stay away, it is a haunted place. I do not want to go there again. But it was a wondrous city once and he was a wonder, too. And while few men in the land of Kemet understood him or will ever understand him, the fact of his living cannot be denied by the One who rules now or by anyone, no matter how determined the attempt. That fact, I truly believe, will live forever and ever, whether or not men ever really know why it all happened.

It did not seem necessary to know, then: we were, for a time, swept away by it. I doubt if we shall ever know, now. He was strange, very strange. I can see him as a child, far back before his city, before he became Co-Regent, the strange, gangling, malformed, horse-faced boy, walking the painted mud corridors of the Palace of Malkata at Thebes with his awkward, painful, shuffling gait, child of a god and soon to be God himself. What was he? Who was he? Why did he come our way? Why did he savage so the land of Kemet?

These are questions the river does not answer as it runs

forever through the Black Land and the Red, through the Two Kingdoms, the narrow, winding corridor of life and green, past Thebes, past Abydos, past Memphis, past all the rest . . . past the terribly lonely ruins of Akhet-Aten-Amarna, his city.

Those were troubling days in the land of Kemet. We did not know their like before. I suspect we shall never know their like again. I pray we never shall. But I am glad that I was there.

It began, as many things do in a royal house, with the birth of a child—two, actually, for she had much to do with it also—and the death of a child. . . .

BOOK I

Birth of a God

1392 B.C.

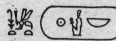

King of
the North
and South

Neb–Máat–Ra,

Son of the Sun

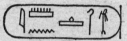

Prince of Thebes,
AMONHOTEP III

Royal Spouse

Great Wife

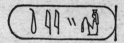

TIYE

Kaires

I AM KAIRES, as men properly say Kah-*ee*-race, named by my father, after he brought me finally from my birthplace to his beloved city of Thebes, for the great scribe Kaires who lived during the time among men of the God Nefer-Ka-Ra (Life, health, prosperity!) of the House of Memphis, one thousand five hundred years ago.

I, also a scribe, write this in the twenty-second year among men of the God Amonhotep III (Life, health, prosperity!) of the House of Thebes. Even do I live in his house itself, in the Palace of Malkata, for I am young, well favored and, I think, intelligent; and such are needed for the governing of the empire of the Two Kingdoms that stretches now south to the Fourth Cataract of the River Nile, north beyond Syria to the land of Mittani, and east and west to the Mountains of Light beyond which the Red Land begins and only the wretched Crossers of the Sands dare go.

Together with my friend Amonhotep the Scribe (he who comes of humbler birth and a father named Hapu, both of which he flaunts from time to time when surrounded by the scions of noble houses who find themselves unequipped by nature to match his lively brain), I am entrusted with the taking down of the words that fall from the lips of those in the Great House; and being of inquiring mind and still something of a stranger here, I have much cause to ponder upon the curious world in which I find myself.

For instance:

In my birthplace, while we have the same formal writ-

ten language as all Kemet, we have a dialect that falls
much easier on the ear: at least when we speak it has a
flowing sound. There are places in it, as in my name
when properly pronounced, where a gentler emphasis
comes, as: K*ah-ee-ra*ce. Not so in Upper Kemet and
stately Thebes. Here the language is harsher and more
abrupt. The name of the Good God may be *written*
"Amonhotep" (Life, health, prosperity!) but when they
say it in their slurred, birdlike speech it becomes something like: "Mnhtp." Try that, if you will!

They write the Great Wife thus: "Tiye." But they pro-
nounce her name, as nearly as I have come to understand
them: "Ttt." And I, Kaires? "Krs," if you please!

If you would listen to a weird, amusing clamor, come
with me to the docks here in Thebes where the unending
boats come and go, or walk among the pillars and temples
of Karnak when the worshipers gather for festival, or wander in the market any morning. Shrill, twittering, a constant
rush of sibilants, gutturals and swallowed syllables overwhelmed by the quick gulps and hurried intakes of air
that are only designed to keep the speakers alive until
one statement can be completed and another slithered out
like a snake—it is enough to make the foreigner shake
his head in bafflement when he does not laugh outright.

Since no one laughs outright at the ways of the land of
Kemet or at the immortal ancestors of the Good God in
the Great House who ordained these ways many, many
hundreds of years ago, I decided early to shake my head
and offer a helpless smile. This technique will produce
gales of friendly laughter and a patient attempt to assist
the stranger. Eventually one learns: and I am now already
becoming quite proficient. As a result, Amonhotep the
Scribe thinks that I will go far. My father has taken no
notice of me yet, so I do not know what he thinks. But I
agree with Amonhotep the Scribe.

"Foreigner . . . stranger." I note that I use these words
almost automatically even now, when I, who am fifteen,
have been here already three months. With my blood, I
am neither foreigner nor stranger—though I have promised my father, on pain of banishment (or possibly even

death, for he is a very determined and righteous man), that this is something no one will ever know. It does give me, however, a greater interest than most in the land of Kemet. It is my observation that I respect its ways and traditions rather more than do some of its own—not including, of course, my father, who guards and cherishes the peace and order of Kemet above all things. In that I find that I am already becoming like him: more careful of Kemet, let us say, than some others who live in the Great House, whose interest in the order and stability of the Two Lands is not quite what it should be: as I see it.

Again, for instance:

Today, everywhere, in the streets, in the shops, in the common houses, on the farms, in the little towns and the great cities, all the way along the river from the Delta to the Fourth Cataract, there is light and jubilation in the land of Kemet.

Yet all is hush and tension in the Palace of Malkata.

Another child is about to be born to the Great Wife, Queen Tiye—a son, say the priests of Amon.

Here, if anywhere, it should be a happy day.

Yet it is a somber one.

Why?

I do not know, and it puzzles me; and although I spent the better part of half an hour at our sunrise meal, trying to discover from my friend Amonhotep the Scribe, Son of Hapu, what causes the Palace to lie shrouded with secrets, he turned me off with sly jests and laughter. But he did not fool me. The jests were half-hearted, the laughter did not ring with his usual confident air. Something is on his mind today, and I take this to be very significant, for he is very wise and knows many things. I am convinced he knows the inner troubles of the House of Thebes. But he will not tell me.

"You are too young for such weighty matters," he said airily. "And, after all: who says anything is wrong? You sound like the girls gossiping in the harim. Abandon such pursuits, little brother. There are better things for you to worry that busy head about."

Now in the first place, as he well knows, I detest this

arch "little brother" business, which sounds patronizing
in the extreme to one with my background and intelligence. It annoys me.

And in the second place, while I may be somebody's
little brother, so casually do the royal gods and goddesses
of Kemet breed with one another, I am quite certain I
am not his. I told him as much in no uncertain terms.
But again he only laughed.

"Be patient and keep your eyes open," he said finally.

"Very sage advice," I said sarcastically. "Worthy of a
great scribe."

But he did not respond with his customary half-
affectionate, half-acrid joshing. Instead his face fell suddenly somber, and he sighed. An elder's sigh can be rather
devastating, particularly if the recipient is fifteen: who
knows what awful things it may portend?

We finished the meal in silence, the slaves cleared the
simple utensils away. He was off to Karnak, two miles
down the river, to witness the formal arrival of Amonhotep
III (Life, health, prosperity!), to seek Amon's blessing
on the child about to be born. And I have been delegated
for the day to assist Mu-tem-wi-ya the Queen Mother
with the many letters she continues to send to her royal
counterparts in the Middle East, even though her son has
been on the throne for twelve years and she has long since
ceased to have any influence.

"It keeps her happy," I heard him explaining just the
other day to Queen Tiye; and since there is no harm possible from it—since her letters are all intercepted as they
leave the Palace, are read by her son, and are then destroyed—it continues. Occasionally she expresses some
mild surprise that she receives no answers; but the Good
God merely asks her dryly, "What can you expect of the
barbarians beyond our borders?" And since she has never
thought very much of them this agrees with her own ideas
and she accepts it with a shrug and a contemptuous, knowing little smile.

I think, myself, that the old lady—she is now forty-two,
I believe, quite a great age for the royalty of Kemet—is
remarkably well preserved, aside from the slight mental

vagueness that permits her to believe this little charade. Or does she believe it? Sometimes the glance she gives her son is just a trifle too bland. He never appears to let it bother him, but it would make me uneasy, I think.

This morning I find her, too, to be in a mood that disturbs me. Normally with me she is very affectionate, very light, very fond, very motherly. She accepts our blood relationship tacitly, we never speak of it, but I know she knows: we gossip a bit. Already, in three months here, I would say I have become one of her most trusted confidants—indeed, a genuine friend. Normally, as I say, my hours with her are fun. Today she too is gloomy, restless, uneasy. Her words are sharp, impatient. There will be no letter writing this time. I discover she too is going to the temple of Amon: she tells me they are all going.

"You had better come with me, boy," she says, clapping her hands sharply for the ladies in waiting, who come scurrying up, twittering and chattering nervously, with the kohl for her eyes, the heavy gold rings for her fingers, the pectorals of lapis lazuli, carnelians and turquoise to hang around her weathered neck, the thick black wig to cover her shaven skull and surround her small sharp face, the royal gold circlet with the uraeus, the poised jeweled cobra above her brow which she still wears on state occasions. "You might as well see us all in our finery asking the blessing of the priests on this new child. We put on quite a show."

And so they do, and today, as I too arrive at Karnak as the hour nears noon, seeing my friend Amonhotep the Scribe already well situated just by the entrance to the temple of Amon—he waves with a cordiality that asks forgiveness for his earlier sharpness, and I, naturally pleased at this public sign of favor from one so influential, wave back vigorously across the shoving, jostling, amiably colorful crowd—I realize that they will all be here, the House of Thebes and those who serve them most closely. They will be dressed in their finest—and I have learned already that it can be very fine indeed—for the edification of the people, for whom they are no more nor less than the embodiment of a dream, a fixed, unchanging and eternal dream in the unending story of Kemet, the great, the favored, the one and only land.

Today it appears they are all coming by water, straight down the river from Malkata, instead of crossing to the east bank, taking chariots, and arriving with a great jangle and snorting of horseflesh, which is what Pharaoh has lately taken to doing.

It seems better that they use the river this day. The Family and the river—they belong together on great occasions. It is more befitting. This I feel and so, evidently, does the crowd, for its response to them all is wild, excited, reverent—and loyal. Whatever troubles the House of Thebes, it has nothing to do with its relations with the people. The people are cheerful, happy, satisfied with their world, obviously worshipful and loving of Pharaoh, his family and his servitors. I must continue to look elsewhere for the answer to the undercurrent of unease that lies within the Palace, for certainly it is not carried over openly, here among the crowds.

Listen to them shout! I ask you: was there ever such an awed—such a loving—such a *satisfied* sound?

Mu-tem-wi-ya is the first to arrive, myself crouching inconspicuously, almost concealed, at her feet. She stands in the prow of the barge, which is painted with electrum, the mixture of gold and silver so popular with the highborn in Kemet. Her right hand rests lightly but firmly on my shoulder, just enough to steady herself, not so obviously that anyone along the shores can see. A great shout of greeting, deeply affectionate and respectful, begins as her barge puts out from the landing at Malkata; it continues steadily all down the river to Karnak; it reaches crescendo as she relinquishes her hold on my shoulder with a quick, affectionate squeeze, and is handed to the dock by the Vizier Ramose, glittering from head to foot in his robes of gold, his great black wig gleaming down each shoulder, his staff of office held reverently at his side by a slave from far-off Naharin, north near Syria, come to his service through who knows what happenstance of friendly tribute or conquest of war.

Ramose keeps his face stern and grave toward the

Queen Mother, although these two are good friends. I have noted that no one of royalty or rank—with the single exception of Pharaoh, whose smile is fixed—ever smiles in public in Thebes: it is all very stern, very proper, very forbidding. At first I found this somewhat offensive, accustomed as one is in other places to a more natural way of conduct, even among the great. But it has not taken me long to see the reason, to understand it and approve. These are gods and those who serve gods: and such do not smile. Gods are not human or they would not be gods. Many centuries ago they learned this: how much easier it is to govern through love if love includes a very healthy share of awe and fear. This too is befitting. Pharaoh's ritual smile is benediction, but it is so remote and inward-turning that it is also promise of great retribution if things do not move in ways pleasing to him.

So Mu-tem-wi-ya arrives, accepts Ramose's grave greeting with a nod of even greater gravity, then walks alone along the processional way, hot in the eternal bright sun of Kemet, that leads from the river to the cool dark entrance to Amon's temple. The avenue is empty of people. It is guarded along each side by soldiers rigidly at attention. At their backs the crowds fall suddenly silent as she passes. She pauses for just a moment at the entrance (I having already slipped through the massed thousands to squeeze in beside Amonhotep the Scribe, who gives me an affectionate smile of greeting); two white-clad priests of Amon step forward to assist her; she bows low, gives each a hand; and so flanked, back rigid and erect, eyes straight ahead, disappears inside.

A curious exhalation, low, sustained, tremulous, gentle, as though the whole respectful breath of a people were being simultaneously released, comes from the crowd. Then instantly they turn away, excited and happy again, back toward the river, as in the distance comes another rolling wave of roars and cheers. The next members of our royal gathering are about to reach us. Amonhotep and I strain eagerly to see who it is. The racing gossip of the crowd tells us before we can make them out: it is the two principal wives of Amonhotep III (Life, health, prosperity!) after Queen Tiye—his oldest child, and so far only daughter, the eight-year-old Queen-Princess Sit-a-mon; and the Queen Gil-u-khi-pa, daughter of King Shuttarna of Mittani.

The Princess Sit-a-mon is a small, dark, laughing girl whom I have seen several times in the Palace. Today she too wears the customary frozen mask, though from time to time a little genuine excited smile breaks through, which the crowds love and greet with an extra cheer. So far I have not had a chance to speak to her, but in private she appears to be very sweet, very jolly, very trustful and loving of the world. She is obviously adored by her father though I am told by Amonhotep the Scribe that Pharaoh made her his bride solely and entirely to legitimize his own succession to the throne, and that he (Amonhotep the Scribe) is quite sure that he (Amonhotep III, Life, health, prosperity!) has no other desires or intentions toward his own daughter. Quite often, I understand, these father-daughter relationships in the royal House are not that innocent: quite often children result. This case, my friend assures me, is different, although of course as the daughter grows older and more beautiful the father's self-discipline may grow less.

Basically, however, the marriage came about simply because in this land of Kemet succession to the throne passes through the eldest daughter. Therefore Pharaohs often marry their oldest sister to secure their hold on the throne. This Pharaoh had no living sisters at the time of his accession. His marriage to Queen Tiye, who was not royal (he was then about ten years old), was arranged by Mutemwiya, his mother, and by Mutemwiya's brother and sister-in-law, Yuya and Tuya, parents of Tiye and her two older brothers, Aye and Aanen. As Pharaoh and Tiye grew older their marriage developed into a genuine love match, so that now the Great Wife, Queen Tiye, sits almost equal with him on the throne, goes with him everywhere, is consulted on everything, in effect rules Kemet almost as much as he does. Love in itself, however, was not enough to provide the legitimate succession that Pharaoh needed. Therefore when Queen Tiye bore her first child, Sitamon—eldest daughter of a Pharaoh and, therefore, carrier of legitimacy—her father promptly married her to settle once and for all his claim to the throne.

Nothing like producing your own legitimacy, as my friend remarked dryly in one of those confidential remarks with which he has already come to trust me; but in this case it solved the problem, was accepted joyfully by the country, and now Queen-Princess Sitamon is fully as popular as her parents, whose joy and delight she obviously is. She will never be permitted to marry elsewhere, of course, and as if to compensate, they shower her with constant attention, gifts, her own small palace and court within the complex at Malkata; and the people, understanding, seem to give her extra love whenever she appears—a small, bright, cheerful symbol of the strange contortions the needs of the throne sometimes impose upon the rulers of our strange land.

At her side today stands Gil-u-khi-pa of Mittani, a bride of state married for political reasons by Pharaoh a couple of years ago in his tenth regnal year. He issued a commemorative scarab about it, recounting how she arrived with "a retinue of 317 women." Many of these have been quietly married off to deserving nobles around the country. Gil-u-khi-pa also has been given her own palace within Malkata, but apparently, aside from an occasional rumored visit, as perfunctory as any he makes to the countless anonymities in his official harim, Pharaoh never goes near her.

This would fully suit a stupid woman, but Amonhotep tells me that Gilukhipa is not stupid. Instead, she is quite intelligent, alert, informed. Official neglect therefore has made her jealous, turned her inward, made her bitter, waspish, vindictive. There is no sharper tongue in all Kemet, my friend tells me, than Queen Gilukhipa's.

"Stay wide of Gilukhipa unless you can use her to advance your own ends," he said the other day—a rather odd comment, since if I have "ends," at this point, he seems to be more conscious of them and more knowing about them than I am—"and if you do use her, be very sure you never give her anything she can hold over you. Because she certainly will."

I don't know what prompted his warning, but of course as with all I learn, I shall not forget it.

Now she rides along in the second royal barge beside little Sitamon, the latter's popularity concealing Gilukhipa's lack of it: the shouts seem to rise equally for them both, which is probably why Pharaoh decided they should ride together. It is obvious to Amonhotep the Scribe and to me that she knows this exactly and is, therefore, probably even more embittered than usual. Her back seems extra rigid, her eyes exceptionally fierce, her demeanor more than necessarily stern and aloof. It is not until their barge is nearing shore that she shows the slightest sign of human feeling. At that point Sitamon looks up at her, tugs excitedly at her hand, points at the great snakelike crimson and gold flags snapping from their standards all around the temple, and says something with an eager, delighted grin. Not even Gilukhipa can resist Sitamon, and for a second she smiles back, reaching down with a perfectly natural gesture to adjust the child's gold circlet with uraeus, which has slipped a bit to one side. The crowd rewards them with an extra roar. As if in reproval, Ramose greets them with an extra solemnity. They both become suitably severe again, walk together hand in hand down the glaring empty avenue, are met in their turn by the priests of Amon, and disappear inside the vast stone structure.

From up the river comes another welcoming roar, and for a moment Amonhotep the Scribe and I speculate as to who it can be. The ranks of the House of Thebes are rather thin, at the moment: Pharaoh has his mother, no brothers and sisters, Tiye so far has produced only two children, and all in all it is rather a shaky house. Tiye's delivery later today (it is generally understood that she began labor just before noon, and is progressing well: how these rumors sweep through a crowd no one knows, but they do, and with an air of great authenticity, too) is expected to add one more son. But it will be several years more before the Good God can feel really secure in the midst of an abundant family. So who can this be coming now?

For just a moment Amonhotep and I speculate, though we know it cannot be so: can this be the Crown Prince, Tuthmose, named for his late grandfather Mutemwiya's husband Tuthmose IV (Life, health, prosperity!), and the other three brilliant Tuthmoses who preceded him?

The Crown Prince is six now, and only two weeks ago was installed by his father as High Priest of the god Ptah, five hundred miles downriver in the northern capital of Memphis in the Delta. My friend professes to see something significant in this—he regards it as a direct defiance of the priests of Amon here in Thebes—and yet why should Pharaoh have to "defy" his own priests? All the temples, all the priests, all the people, all the land, belong to him; he is the Good God who carries the word of all the other gods to us mortals. He is supreme. *He is God.* What need for him to "defy" anybody? Nonetheless, my friend becomes very mysterious and deliberately uninformative, I expect I shall have to probe for more, as time goes by.

Right now he says excitedly, "Wouldn't it be something if he has had the boy brought down to sacrifice for his new brother right in the temple of Amon! Wouldn't that be something!"

And for a second he almost hugs himself with excitement. Then he remembers abruptly where he is, pretends to be scratching his sides, relaxes and looks away.

"It couldn't be," he mutters out of the side of his mouth as we turn again to stare together up the river. "He wouldn't dare."

It comes as a profound shock when I finally realize, after a couple of disbelieving moments, that by "he" my friend means Pharaoh. It is the first, though I am beginning to suspect that it may not be the last, time that I have heard subversion spoken aloud in the hard bright sun of Kemet. Whom does Pharaoh have to "dare"? Again, I make a mental note to probe further.

For the moment, I myself do not dare to catch my friend's eyes or indicate in any way that I perceive his meaning. We add our voices to the roar that now mounts steadily as the next great electrum-gilded barge approaches the landing. My friend gives a little grunt as we perceive who it is: not Tuthmose at all, of course, but the Councilor Aye, brother of Queen Tiye, son of Yuya and Tuya, nephew of Mutemwiya, member of that powerful family from Akhmim whose destiny seems to have become increasingly entwined, in these recent years, with the destiny of the House of Thebes. And will so continue, I hope for several reasons—not least being the welfare of Kemet, to which I already know all of them to be deeply devoted.

Aye is unusually tall for a man of Kemet, nearly six feet, where most are rarely more than five; in this he resembles his aging father, Yuya. He is a man whose visage in ordinary circumstances is almost as stern as it is on ceremonial occasions such as today; a man austere and somber—a man of state. I have talked to him directly only once, but even on that occasion, which one might have expected to be reasonably relaxed and friendly, there was no diminution of his remote and solemn manner. My immediate impression was that he simply adopts at all times a forbidding and indeed "stagy" aspect, seeking thereby to evoke an awe and deference men might not give him otherwise. I very soon concluded that this was too facile an explanation. Aye is solemn and thoughtful, careful and remote, because that is really the way Aye is; and the evidence of this is borne out by the fact that, of all men at Pharaoh's Court, none wields more influence, both openly and in secret, than he.

Already he has succeeded Yuya as Master of the Horse; already he too refers to himself in his formal titularies as "one trusted by the Good God in the entire land . . . foremost of the companions of the King . . . praised by the Good God." This flowery rhetoric, which I perceive to be standard in our land when men of importance refer to themselves, in his case recognizes no more than fact. He is indeed foremost of the companions of Pharaoh the King, he is indeed trusted, praised and given power in some ways equal, though often more indirect, to that of the Vizier Ramose himself. In relation to Ramose and all the rest, he has one paramount advantage: he is brother of Tiye and brother-in-law to Pharaoh. But in Kemet, where men are amazingly well judged on what they can actually do, and where the lowliest in origin can rise upward rapidly through the society if he has the ability, this would not be enough to take Aye so far if he did not deserve it. He is, I have concluded respectfully already, a very wise, very perceptive, very farseeing and very patient man.

Today he gives no sign whatsoever of the fact that intrigues the whole land: that his wife also lies in labor in their modest villa inside the Palace walls. Should it be a son, the House of Thebes will someday have another good servant to thank, along with Aye and Yuya, for its successes. Should it be a daughter, a destiny much greater may await. Twice, in Mutemwiya and in Tiye, the family of Aye has produced queens for Kemet. May it not do so sometime soon again?

None of this shadows the thin face, high cheekbones and level, intelligent eyes of the Councilor as he stands like a statue in his barge, nearing the dock at Karnak in front of the avenue of priests. For him, too, the people call out, and the sound that accompanies his progress is great. But for him there is not the affection they gave to Mutemwiya, the fond reception they accorded Sitamon and, with a good-natured generosity, extended also to unhappy Gilukhipa. There is more of solemnity in the cries they give for Aye. He is not liked in the way others are liked, for no man so austere and so obviously enwrapped in his own thoughts—Aye's thinking, as my friend Amonhotep the Scribe put it to me, is louder than most men's conversation—can ever evoke quite the unrestrained popular response given to others. He thinks, and he makes people think when they see him: in the presence of such an obvious intelligence, a deep respect, tinged not a little with awe, is all that he can expect. It is what he gets, in a greeting that accompanies him to the landing and then ceases, as abruptly and as dutifully as it began when his barge took water fifteen minutes ago upriver at Malkata.

And then suddenly, far off but heavy and insistent like the noise of some great reverent sea, a sea whose waves sound for no one else so profoundly, solemnly yet joyously as they do for him, the unmistakable noise begins and grows until it seems to envelop the universe. From Malkata the final barge has set out, and no one anywhere in all the world could have slightest doubt of whom it carries.

The One Who Lives in the Great House, Strong-Bull-Appearing-As-Justice, Lord of the Two Lands, Establishing-Justice-and-Causing-the-Two-Lands-to-Be-Pacified, Horus of Gold, Mighty-of-Arm-When-He-Smites-the-Asiatics, King of Upper and Lower Kemet, Lord of Truth Like Ra, Son of the Sun, Ruler of Thebes, Given Life, the Pharaoh—Amonhotep III (Life, health, prosperity!) comes.

Now the world splits wide with sound, the earth trembles, the skies are rent, the Sun looks down upon his Son with happiness and all of Kemet rejoices, united in one heart, one mind, one dream of unchanging order that has already managed to survive for nearly two thousand years and will go on into the future, as we say, forever and ever.

I find my eyes are wet with tears, I am shouting like the rest, at my side my friend is similarly overcome. It is impossible not to be moved as Pharaoh approaches. Yet even as I tremble, some cold, small machine inside continues to observe: I too am perceptive, farseeing and patient, and soon I too hope to be wise with what I learn in Thebes.

So as his barge—not plated with electrum like the others, but, as befits Pharaoh, all in gold—comes slowly, slowly down the Nile, the oarsmen aiding the current with deliberate cadenced strokes in response to the rhythmic cries of the helmsman, the six trumpeters along each side of the craft sounding triumphant blasts from their long golden instruments at regular intervals, the long thin streamers, scarlet, blue and gold, flying from the golden canopy over the golden throne, everything glitter, everything gold, I study Amonhotep III (Life, health, prosperity!), ninth Pharaoh of the Eighteenth Dynasty to rule the land of Kemet.

I am thrilled by the presence of the God: but I analyze the man. In this I think my father might be proud of me, though he could never admit it, of course, for to analyze the God aloud, or to let it be known to anyone that you are doing it, is treason and sufficient to bring death if discovered. Only Amonhotep the Scribe, noting my shrewd eyes searching through their emotional tears, realizes, I think; and already I think Amonhotep the Scribe is a true friend of mine, who will not tell. He thinks I have "ends" to seek in Kemet, and already I feel he is beginning to take an active and encouraging role in them, though I myself am not even sure yet what they might be.

The great barge begins its final approach down the channel to Karnak. And all the world cracks wide with sound . . . for what?

I see a small, brown, stocky, round-faced man in his twenty-second year, his height, perhaps five feet two inches, more characteristic of the country than Aye's tallness.

To cover his naked skull he too wears the formal wig, its two pendant flaps descending on each side to rest upon his chest, the whole draped with a striped cloth of gold bound around his head. On his chin he wears the narrow-cut, false beard of ceremony, a traditional regal anomaly in clean-shaven Kemet. Over all is the round, domed Blue Crown of the Two Kingdoms, made of leather and studded with gold sequins. It is encircled by the uraeus—in his case, not one but three cobras, poised to strike his enemies—the cobra being the emblem of the goddess Buto, patroness of Lower Kemet, who in turn is associated with the vulture goddess Nekhebet, patroness of Upper Kemet, thereby symbolizing the union of the Two Kingdoms. (The gods and goddesses of Kemet are another subject. Intelligent though I am, I shall have to study that one for quite some time before I can even begin to understand its endless ramifications!) Behind the cobras is the disk of the Sun, which is known here under various names in its various forms—as "Re," "Ra," "Re-Herakhty," most importantly, "Amon"—and of late, with increasing emphasis, particularly in the royal House, "The Aten."

Pharaoh's body is clad in the pleated kilt of royalty, also of gold, held at the waist with a broad belt of gold encrusted with jade, amethyst, malachite, garnets, lapis lazuli, jasper, turquoise and pearls. Lodged in the belt is a wicked-looking jeweled ceremonial sword.

Loosely yet firmly he holds the traditional crook and flail, also gold, which, stretching back into the remotest antiquity of Kemet when kings first came out of the fields, symbolize his role as kindly yet all-commanding shepherd of his people.

On his face he wears a fixed smile, an expression stiff but more pleasant than the others. To the Good God it is permitted, as it is to his young daughter, to smile just a little, but for different reasons: she because she is a child . . . he because he is the supreme ruler of all men and all things, Son of the Sun, head of the Empire, servant yet co-equal of the gods, center and mover of the universe.

How must it feel to be born to such a place!

How must it feel to sit there?

I study his face closely as the golden barge approaches. Nothing speaks to me from its careful blandness but an opulent, youthful, self-satisfied, self-indulgent divinity. Yet there must be more behind: he, too, I am sure, must be affected by the unease that grips the Palace. But of course he cannot show it, and perhaps, buoyed up by the deafening happy scream that accompanies him, he does not feel it now, has forgotten it for the moment, thinks only of the excitement of the occasion, thinks only of another son being born—thinks only of being God.

Standing to the left and just behind the throne, solemn and stern, wearing the traditional high priest's leopard skin, is his other brother-in-law, Aanen, younger brother of Aye, older brother of Queen Tiye, Second Priest of Amon in the temple at Karnak—second only to Pharaoh himself as ruler of the priests of Amon whose temples and holdings, fanning out up and down the river the length and breadth of Kemet, in farms, granaries, thousands of cattle, hundreds of smaller temples, minerals, gold, all kinds of wealth, equal in some ways the power and influence of Pharaoh himself.

What does Aanen think, too, and what does it mean to

stand in such a place? He is not the man his brother is, and yet he holds great power.

Gently the barge touches land. As if by magic all sound stops. The ears still ring with it in the great hush that descends as Aanen steps first ashore, exchanges grave greetings with Ramose, turns and bows almost to the ground. With a stately slowness Pharaoh rises from his throne, hands to Aanen his crook and flail, steps ashore, reclaims them, crosses them again upon his chest; bows gravely to Ramose, also almost prostrate before him; and then proceeds, not looking to right or left in the absolute silence, to follow Aanen with slow and measured tread into the dark, mysterious entrance of the temple.

Once again comes that curious, quivering tremulous exhalation, as of a whole people breathing its soul in one great all-embracing sigh, which followed in lesser degree his mother. And then behind the soldiers the crowds begin to move, swirl, change. Voices break out, children cry, dogs bark; all becomes happiness and chatter as the people prepare to settle themselves more comfortably to await the return procession. None wish to leave, for all pray with Pharaoh for the safe deliverance of a strong son pleasing to Amon; and besides, now the pomp is over for an hour or so. It is time for picnic, before they must silence themselves to greet again, in suitable love and reverence, the Good God.

Amonhotep the Scribe asks me to hold his place for him while he goes and relieves himself in the public place behind the temple. I promise lightly: if he will return the favor. Being closer to the Palace, we are both still a little more under the spell of Pharaoh's passing than the amiable crowds. We laugh but we are still moved, still thoughtful; our minds still race with many speculations, many things.

As I watch his compact little figure go scurrying off on nature's business—the crowds making way for him respectfully, for it is well known that Amonhotep the Scribe, Son of Hapu, is a favorite of the God and exercises much influence in the Palace—I think about the pageant I have seen.

In this first great public ceremony I have attended in Thebes, I have been moved, touched, stirred: the mystique of the God has reached me, I will not deny it. Yet still the cold little machine inside keeps wondering: what lies behind, what does it all mean, what does it add up to? If the Two Lands are really well ruled by this solid little figure in the golden clothes, what means the unease in the Palace of Malkata?

I have seen him pass, glittering, glittering, and I wonder what he thinks.

I know what *I* think, though I take much care to conceal all trace of it when Amonhotep returns refreshed to keep his part of the bargain and release me so that I, too, may hurry back to stand in place another hour to see the golden figure go.

I think that I care more already, in my heart and mind, for the land of Kemet than he does. I do not know how I sense this, but I do. And I wonder if I will ever have the chance to give to her the devotion and the prudent husbanding which she deserves.

Amonhotep III (Life, health, prosperity!)

I PASS THEM, exuberant and welcoming along the river and in the streets, or solemn and respectful as I come to worship in the temples, and I wonder what they think.

Do they think? Do they have any comprehension at all of the world I live in? But quickly I answer my own question: of course not, how could they? I am the God, and gods are not understood by mortal men because as everyone knows, they do not live like mortal men. Gods are not worried about their families, concerned for their

power, surrounded by shifting shadows that may be
friendly one moment, hostile the next. . . .

I live with other gods, hundreds of them: strange figures of men with heads of falcons, rams, baboons, dogs,
crocodiles—women in the form of cows, lionesses, scor-
pions, vultures, cobras . . .

I am their equal, their companion, their master and
their slave. They surround me in all I do.

They surround me. . . .

Today began, as all days in Kemet begin, with my
awakening. When Pharaoh awakes the world awakes, for
I am the incarnation on earth of Ra the Sun, and of Ra's
son Horus as well; and no life starts, and no life lives,
without me. All things start with me. So it has always
been in Kemet, and so it will always be, forever
and ever.

I arose and went into my House of Morning, the small
private chapel in the Palace of Malkata—and at once I
was surrounded. Amon-Ra was instantly with me in the
persons of a dozen white-clad priests led by my brother-
in-law Aanen. Amon-Ra is the greatest of gods, the god
of Thebes, the god of my House, the "King of all the
gods" of Kemet and the Empire. He is also the god who
owns half my kingdom: he is the god who surrounds me
most of all.

Thus he surrounded me this day, as on all days since
I inherited the throne, to watch me take the ritual bath in
which I duplicate the way in which Ra bathes each morning in the ocean of heaven. As I bathed, I restored the
life force that flows from me to the Two Lands, just as
Ra's bathing restores the life force that flows from him to
the universe. When I finished, the priests, some wearing
the falcon mask of Horus, others the ibis or baboon mask
of Thoth, the god of wisdom and learning, anointed,
robed and invested me with the crook and flail, the
uraeus and other insignia of office. They gave me the
most important of all, the "Ankh," or symbol of life,
which comes each day from the God Amon to the Good
God, myself, so that I may in turn pass it on and thus
give life to the Two Lands. Then I said the words that I

say every morning to start life on earth going again after
the night, just as Ra says them in heaven. And simultaneously, from the Fourth Cataract to the Delta, in all the
many temples of Amon-Ra, priests representing me representing Ra received the Ankh and spoke the same life-
giving words.

And so, in Kemet and in the whole world, life began
again.

Now of course I would not have you think that in
Kemet we actually believe that all life ends at nightfall
and does not resume until dawning when Pharaoh-as-Ra
says so. We are, so those who observe us tell us, a practical and pragmatic people, and we know, naturally
enough, that many things go on at night—beasts, busi-
nesses, arrivals, departures, birth, death, love, robbery,
murder—many things, while Ra is making the journey
in his sacred boat back under the earth from west to east,
passing through the stomach of the sky-goddess Nut so
that he may be born again at dawn.

We know life goes on while Ra makes his journey.
But we also know that ritual and order hold Kemet together, and we know that without them Kemet would
not be the great kingdom and powerful empire she is.
And since we wish to preserve her so, we preserve the
rituals that preserve her order. Even on days when I am
ill, the people never know that I do not rise and say the
words for Ra. Aanen or one of his fellow priests of
Amon says them for me, and it is announced, as it is
every day, that I have done it. Thus the ritual is preserved—and the order is preserved.

Thus it has been for almost two thousand years, and so
it will be, forever and ever.

So: I worshiped, I said the words, I discharged the first
daily obligation of my divinity, and then, like mortal men,
I ate. Priests and servants hovered, anxious to seize for
themselves whatever sacred scraps I left. I took satisfaction in fooling them, this morning: I was hungry and I
ate it all. Then I returned, still accompanied by Aanen,
to my private rooms. At the door I told him firmly,
"Brother, I would be alone with my wife." "But she is

my sister," he protested sharply, looking as angry as he dared. "You may see her later in the day, if she wishes to receive you," I said evenly, and gave him a firm but pleasant stare, both of us knowing that she would be receiving no one but the absolutely necessary this day. "Well—" he began, still sharply; but even now he does not quite dare defy me openly, and so after a moment his eyes dropped, his voice trailed off in a mumble: "Well . . ." "Go, Brother," I said. "Make yourself ready to attend me to Karnak, for I go there to worship for her and our new son. I shall be departing in the fourth quarter of morning. Be ready." And then finally he did say, "Yes, Son of the Sun, I go as you desire." But it did not come easy to him, and I thought again as I have thought many times in the last two years: he is grown too great.

And I thought further, as I have also thought: *They have all grown too great.*

Struck by this knowledge, which haunts me too often nowadays, I paused where I was with my hand on the edge of the door. I watched his back, its lines indignant, as he hurried off down the long corridor, pretending to himself that his departure was his own idea, that he really had other business and had to leave me of his own accord. At the distant turning in the hall he met Amonhotep the Scribe, Son of Hapu, and with him the new young scribe, Kaires, whom I have glimpsed a couple of times, always in the distance: he has not attended me yet, though I understand Amonhotep is training him with great care and has assigned him principally to my mother. She likes him, he is a bright lad apparently: I must keep an eye on him and promote him to higher service if he deserves it. I need "King's men," loyal to me above and beyond the fear-loyalty that is given the God.

As I watched, Amonhotep the Scribe returned Aanen's hasty and almost contemptuous greeting with a grave air, followed by a grim little line of amusement around his lips which Aanen, hurrying away, did not see. Then Amonhotep saw me and paused, so abruptly that young Kaires, tumbling along behind like an eager puppy, bumped into him. They laughed together—I could see from Amonhotep's lack of annoyance that he too already thinks well of this youth who has been added to the household staff at his father's request—and then, abruptly grave and suitably respectful, they bowed low to me. I bowed also, and then smiled. Emboldened by this, Amonhotep smiled back. So too did Kaires, which for just a moment produced a somewhat shocked expression on Amonhotep's shrewd and amiable face. But the boy meant no harm, so again I smiled. Amonhotep relaxed, they bowed again and withdrew; but not, I am afraid, before they both perceived the unhappy expression that recaptured my face as I sighed and turned back toward the door. I did not mean for my unhappiness to return so rapidly and so openly, but against my will, it did. I must be more deeply concerned than I admit to myself.

Must be?

Of course I am.

Within the private apartments all was hushed and quiet. Doctors, nurses and the inevitable priests of Amon stood huddled about, attempting with their earnest expressions and low-murmured talk to convince me of a depth of knowledge which is limited by spells, incantations, and foul-smelling poultices on the one hand, and by the hoped-for kindly interventions of Bes, the guardian of childbirth, and Hathor the cow goddess, deity of motherhood, on the other. There is no reason to believe that Bes and Hathor will not attend Tiye kindly today, as they did with both Sitamon and Tuthmose. Both births went smoothly, Sitamon being delivered in three hours, Tuthmose a little more slowly, but with no great difficulty, in four.

Tiye is a very healthy woman, and a very determined one; and also we have both prayed long and faithfully for this new son—prayed, ironically, to Amon, who does not know that in this birth he faces yet another challenge to add to those I have already given him.

For this reason I worry, of course: Amon does not take kindly to challenges, and those that are given him must be given with subtlety and with skill. I think the challenge of Tuthmose has been so given. I am hopeful I may

in time give the challenge of this new son in the same
fashion.

These thoughts were mine as I entered the bedroom
where my love lay, and saw the pert little face that conceals such a loving heart and such a fiercely protective
and determined will. She stared at me with great dark
eyes; a welcoming smile, sweet, patient, indomitable,
touched her lips. "It is beginning," she said. "May Amon
give us a strong and healthy son," I said. For a second
a gleam of amusement that was for me alone flashed into
her eyes. She beckoned me close and I leaned down. "He
would not if he knew," she whispered; and I, who know,
unlike my people, that Amon does not know all things—
only those that his priests overhear for him—whispered
back, "He will not until it is too late." A sudden fear
came into her eyes, shielded by my body from the doctors, nurses, and priests standing respectfully silent against
the wall at my back. "Is Tuthmose . . . ?" she whispered.
"Tuthmose is well and on his way. He should be here in
the third quarter of morning." "He is all right?" "He is
all right," I said firmly. "He is escorted from Memphis
by Amon," she said. "But for every priest of Amon there
are two of Ptah," I said. Her eyes stared into mine for a
long moment. "I will feel better when I know he is safely
here." "Do you think I will not?" I demanded with a
sudden naked honesty. She started to say something, then
was cut off by pain. After it passed she managed a smile
and gripped my hand tightly for a second. "We must not
be afraid," she said. "We are not," I whispered fiercely.
"We are not."

I leaned down and we kissed as desperately as though
we were youthful lovers again, attempting to reassure one
another that the world is not full of shadows threatening
happiness. She grimaced once more and turned her face
so I would not see. I stepped back. Doctors, priests,
nurses hurried forward, hissing like geese who would im-
press me with their diligence. I uttered a silent prayer to
Bes and Hathor, that they might be kind to my wife, to
me and to our son; and withdrew to walk alone through
the painted mud corridors of Malkata to the robing room

where I was to consult, as I do every morning, the Vizier Ramose, and then be made ready for my departure, shortly before noon, to Karnak.

Thus the conflict intruded, even there—there, perhaps, more than anywhere, for it is through my sons that it will be expressed hereafter.

You may ask why it must be so: why does not Pharaoh, the all-powerful, the omnipotent, the owner of all things and all men in the land of Kemet, put down the overweening priests of Amon, reduce their power to manageable proportions, break up their holdings of land, cattle, granaries, gold, jewels, swollen beyond conscience—say the magic word, and return them overnight to the influential but reasonable status they held up to the time of my great-grandfather, the brilliant Tuthmose III (Life, health, prosperity!)?

I will tell you why: because, starting with my great-grandfather, Amon-Ra has become so inextricably entwined with the fortunes of my family, with its foreign conquests, its empire-building and its steady accretion of wealth and power, that it is now impossible to remove the growth on the House of Thebes by some simple, ruthless surgery. It must be done, if done at all, by the most delicate and skillful of excisions. It is to this that I have increasingly devoted my thoughts and my talents as I have matured from the ten-year-old child who came to the throne on the death of my father, Tuthmose IV (Life, health, prosperity!) to my present status as the Good God who has already worn the Double Crown for twelve years.

By now I am sanctified not only by blood but by custom. Kemet is used to me. Each year I can do more. But each year, of course, Amon has grown stronger too. And so it is not a simple matter.

When my family came to the throne there were great intrigues between Tuthmose I, his two sons, Tuthmose II and Tuthmose III, and his daughter, the great Queen-Pharaoh Hat-shep-sut (Life, health, prosperity to them all!). Suddenly, one morning in this same temple of Amon to which I am about to depart to pray for my new son, Amon intervened. At that point Tuthmose I was on the throne; but Amon, even as Tuthmose I was offering prayers, suddenly turned (his golden image carried high by the usual band of white-clad priests) and bowed low to Tuthmose III, then only a minor princeling of the royal House. At once Tuthmose III displaced his aging father, assumed the crown, and began the struggle with his half sister Hat-shep-sut which was to give her some years of independent rule but resulted ultimately in his own supreme power, the deliberate obliteration of her name and memory, and the start of his great conquests through the Middle East that created the empire to which I am heir.

Thus, as you can see, our House owes much to Amon, for his priests deliberately intervened to settle a dynastic conflict that was gravely threatening the existence of the Two Lands. Thereafter, though Hat-shep-sut for a few years managed to keep both the priests and her half brother and co-regent, Tuthmose III, under control, they worked ceaselessly to confirm Amon's choice, which they had so dramatically and skillfully arranged that morning in the temple. And when Tuthmose III came finally to full power, it was Amon who was responsible, Amon who encouraged, sanctified and thus guaranteed popular support for, his military conquests. And it was Amon, naturally enough, to whom in gratitude he gave the power, the influence and the actual physical wealth, drawn from his conquests, which was the start of the priests' overweening power today.

I was not aware of all this until I began to study the records of my House in greater detail after my formal education was completed. Pharaohs receive a rigid schooling: we are scribes, we are skilled in military arts, we are readers—we are well-equipped men, the equal of any in the Two Lands, by the time we leave the hands of the tutors in the Palace school. This fits us for rule. It also makes some of us think—particularly those of us, like myself, whose eyes do not look outward from Kemet because they do not need to look outward: because all out there belongs to me already, so that I have no need for conquests to keep me busy or to distract me from my thoughts.

From the Fourth Cataract, far to the south in Ethiopia, to the land of Mittani, far to the north in Syria, I rule over the Empire of Kemet. My garrisons are stationed in a dozen vassal kingdoms. A handful of armed men, an annual appearance of my representatives to collect tribute, an occasional dynastic marriage, a routine gift of gold to those whose lands do not produce it in the abundance that Kemet enjoys—such are all that is necessary now to hold the Empire. The alliances must be kept up, the symbolic appearances must be made, the correspondence and the gifts must be faithfully delivered. With a diligent attention to these relatively minor and painless requirements, the Empire today virtually runs itself.

Kemet stands at the peak of her glory. I stand at the peak of Kemet. It is as simple as that. Only one thing shadows the comfortable equation—the fact which has now become with me almost an obsession: Amon is everywhere and into everything. And in the past two years or so this has become, for me, too much.

I do not know exactly when I began to realize this; one day, I believe, in a conversation with Tiye, who keeps me company in all things and possesses, in that small round head I love to cradle in the hollow of my arm, ten times the wisdom of most men. Tiye is my delight and my great good fortune, the one adviser above all others whom I trust, admire, respect and listen to. The shy ten-year-old boy who found himself being married to the shy ten-year-old girl from the house of Yuya and Tuya has grown up to find himself the husband of the perfect wife, lover, companion, friend—and equal partner, though we must maintain the outward forms of my personal supremacy, in the rule of Kemet.

To me she gives love, understanding, support, children —and advice shrewder than any I receive from anyone with the possible exception of her brother, Aye, and, lately, from Amonhotep the Scribe, Son of Hapu. These three I trust above all others, and Tiye above the other two. It is for this that I have issued a scarab, that small, gleaming beetle whose form we have transferred to jewelry and masonry and used to proclaim our worship or our praise, telling of her glories and making clear to my people that she sits at my left hand, almost as great as I. It is for this, also, that a year ago I ordered made for her in her town of Djarukha a "pleasure lake," or basin, its length being 3700 cubits and its breadth 700 cubits. And it is for her that I issued a scarab showing myself rowing in my state barge on her lake, piercing the dikes so that the Nile might flow in and enrich the land and thus provide fine crops for her private wealth.

And it was at her urging that I named the barge *Radiance of the Aten.*

For Aten likes not Amon, nor does Tiye, nor do Aye and Amonhotep, nor do I.

When I first published the scarab, in fact, there was much muttering in Amon's temple. It was led by my brother-in-law Aanen, he whom I elevated to be Second Priest of Amon in a burst of generosity (never to be reversed, once done) when at fourteen I first began to be so deeply in love with his sister, thinking it would be a kindly gesture to her family, and also give me better control of pushing priests. This was my mistake. He even dared challenge me openly one day, here in the Palace. "You pay too much tribute to the Aten," he said, his tone carrying, as always, its sharp little edge of criticism and impatience. I shrugged. "Amon has a hundred thousand priests throughout the Two Lands and owns as much of them as I do," I said. "The Aten has only a barge—" "And the temple you have built for him at Karnak!" he interrupted. "That little thing!" I said with an equal sharpness. "Are you comparing that to the vast halls of Amon? Come now, Brother! You make too much of too little." "We would have preferred the barge to be named for Amon," he said with a prim pursing of the lips. "Well, it is named for the Aten," I said, "and published so to the people, and so it stands." "They will be confused," he said, his tone becoming uncertain in the face of my obvious determination. "Amon will no doubt set them right," I said dryly. "Do not worry about such a little thing, Brother.

Amon reigns, forever and ever." And I turned and walked away, and presently the grumbling in Amon's temples subsided, though I know they still resent it whenever I use the Aten's barge to sail the river. But since for the time being I have done nothing further, they have perforce subsided; though they watch. Always, they watch.

Amon is the hidden essence of Ra the Sun, which is secret, forbidding, unreachable, unknown. The word "Amon," indeed, *means* hidden. For this reason his sanctuary at Karnak, like his sanctuaries everywhere, is shrouded in darkness: massive, dim, mysterious, frightening. Passage leads into passage, hall into hall, secret chamber into still more secret. Far inside, in the murky depths, mystery of mysteries, holy of holies, stands his gleaming golden statue in its sacred barque, lighted by a single ray of his father Sun, falling through a cleverly angled hole in the ceiling in such a way that his eyes are sunken, brooding, distant, terrifying in their somber depths. He is a god worshiped in fear by the people. He is supreme. And he is very cold.

The Aten is the disk of the Sun, its open, natural essence, its golden rays, its light, its joy. The Aten is everywhere, beaming down upon the Two Lands and all the people. The Aten is open, candid, lovable, the giver and benefactor of all things, which all men may see whenever they wish to look upward. Amon hides: the Aten gleams. And slowly, slowly, ever so carefully, my House has begun in recent years a patient and cautious shifting of emphasis to the Aten, as counterweight to Amon, who needs control but is too strong to be openly challenged, even by us who are the Sons of the Sun in all his manifestations.

Rekh-mi-re, Vizier of my great-grandfather Tuthmose III (Life, health, prosperity!), wrote of my great-grandfather that he "saw his person in his true form—Ra, the Lord of Heaven, the King of Upper and Lower Kemet when he rises, *the Aten when he reveals himself.*" My great-grandfather, like earlier kings of our dynasty, was officially said to have "rejoined the Aten" when he died; before that event he had constructed a temple to the Aten at Heliopolis in the Delta, seat of the cult of Ra-Herakhty, the Sun-God. Under my grandfather, Amonhotep II (Life, health, prosperity!), the disk of the Aten became prominently displayed. At his command it carried a pair of enveloping arms to protect the *ka*, or essence of being, of the land of Kemet, the royal House and the people. In the reign of my father, Tuthmose IV (Life, health, prosperity!), the Aten became officially the god of battles who makes Pharaoh supreme and gives him power over all his dominions—a great universal god whose exalted position in the sky entitles him to rule over the empire of all that his rays shine upon.

Thus slowly but surely the Aten became recognized as a deity separate from Amon. I in my turn have continued the process. I built the modest temple which so incenses Aanen and his fellows. I named Tiye's barge. I built my palace on the west bank of the Nile near the necropolis, becoming thereby the only Pharaoh ever to defy and prove empty the warnings of Amon and the cult of Osiris, god of the dead, that the west bank must be reserved only to the dead. I have started a new complex of buildings at Medinet Habu, near Malkata, among them another shrine to the Aten. From time to time I make public display of my worship of him; and contemplate, in due course, some further things upon which Tiye and I agree.

In the same spirit and with the same motivation, I have more recently moved against Amon on another front. You note I say "moved against" as though it were a military campaign. So it is, for me, and to it Tiye and I give the thought and care that we no longer have to give to foreign battles, for they have all been won. . . . It will be a while before the battle against Amon is won.

Three months ago, acting on a decision reached some time before but known only to Tiye and to Aye, I announced the appointment of my son, the Crown Prince Tuthmose, to be High Priest of the god Ptah at Memphis, the capital of Lower Kemet. The boy is now six years old, a fine, sturdy child, always laughing and happy like his sister Sitamon. He is very bright, very perceptive: already he understands something of the burden that will someday be his when I have rejoined the Aten and he in his turn has become Son of the Sun, God, King and Pharaoh. So he listened willingly and eagerly when his mother and I explained to him that we wished him to fill this post for us, highest religious office in the oldest, and in some ways still the most powerful, of the Two Lands.

Millennia ago, before the kingdom was united by my unutterably remote ancestor, Menes (Life, health, prosperity!), each of the Two Lands developed its own gods and goddesses and its own theology. That is why we have so many, many gods and goddesses, and that is why, even though Amon is the god of my House and Upper Kemet, the principal god of Lower Kemet, Ptah, still has his own powerful priesthood and still occupies in both lands a high and honored place. And that is why it occurred to us that there, too, might be a shrewd way to reduce the power of Amon.

Having the Crown Prince as High Priest of Ptah would certainly give that god an enormous surge of popularity and prestige; close behind comes, for those who will grasp it, power. It is our thought that, by the time he becomes King and Pharaoh, Tuthmose will have strengthened Ptah to the point where that god will be an adequate balance for Amon—for that is what we seek. Not the destruction of Amon, as Aanen and some of his priests seem to think, but a balance for him, which will make both gods more manageable and keep either from becoming an insuperable burden to the dynasty and the people.

So I announced the appointment of Tuthmose, and before there could be any protest or outbreak—indeed, what outbreak could there be? I hold Amon in checkmate as he does me, and none of his priests dare oppose me openly—the boy and I had boarded the *Radiance of the Aten* and sailed away downriver to Memphis, leaving Tiye in charge at Malkata. Our progress, as always, was triumphal and slow, but in two weeks' time we had reached the ancient capital. A week after that, in my presence—and you may be sure, the presence of the leading priests of Amon in Lower Kemet for I requested their presence and they did not dare refuse—the child became High Priest of Ptah.

And today, even as they begin to robe me in my golden clothes, he is on his way secretly from Memphis, scheduled to arrive here within the hour, to accompany me to the temple of Amon at Karnak and there worship with me in honor of his new brother.

And that new brother? For him, too, I have plans. Him I will dedicate to the Aten, and so balance will become counterbalance, and counterbalance again, and ultimately the power of the priests will become diffused, softened, reduced. Where many grasp, competition will cancel itself. Less will be taken by the temples and more will return to our House.

And Pharaoh, in my sons' time if not in mine, will again become what he traditionally was before Amon came to stand at his elbow: a god without equal, a ruler whose servants no longer subvert him, even as they serve.

Such is our plan, and momentarily I expect the Crown Prince. I have had my talk with the Vizier Ramose, that excellent if humorless man who supervises for me the day-to-day administration of the kingdom. The task needs someone humorless: I do not mind that he has no small talk, worries about details, frets and nags at things he conceives to be wrong. Usually they are, usually I can count on him to straighten them out for me—drastically, sometimes, but always fairly. He is a man of rigid honor, absolute loyalty, endless devotion. Were it not that it would totally shock his sense of fitness to the point that it might give him a nervous breakdown, I might tell him, too, my plans for Amon, because certainly he would assist them without question. But, as I say, in his mind it would not be fitting; and in Ramose's world, all things must fit. So I leave him untroubled as he is, privately worried about the situation, I know, but not permitting himself to think about it; concentrating instead on all the thousand details that are necessary for the efficient functioning of a modern and progressive kingdom, which is what I believe we have.

They drape about me my golden kilt, they fasten the golden belt. On my feet they place the golden slippers. The wig, the plaited cloth of gold, the golden crook and flail, the gold uraeus, the blue Double Crown: one by one, with infinite care and many incantations, they place them on me. And by now Tuthmose should be here.

I clap my hands sharply, a slave leaps forward, I say: "Bring me the Councilor Aye."

Grave and dignified as always, that good man who is his sister's equal and his brother's infinite superior comes. I know that he is deeply concerned that his own dear wife, Hebmet, also lies in labor in the compound of Malkata. But his thought now is all for me.

"Has the young ibis reached the nest?" I ask, in the simple code we use.

"Not yet, Son of the Sun," he says, the worry in his eyes determinedly hidden, but clear to me.

"There is no word of his flight?"

"It was good as of last night's reporting," he says. "But I have had no word today."

"We must leave in ten minutes," I note. "My mother is already on the water. Sitamon and Gilukhipa leave in a moment. You are next."

"Then we must go," he says calmly; and steps forward, with a familiarity I permit only him, and places a hand lightly on my arm. "The ceremony must go forward," he says, softly so that the attendants and priests, who have fallen back at his approach, cannot hear. "Do not worry."

"Easy words," I say, more sharply than I intend, for a fear is beginning to grow in my heart, as in his.

"He will come," he says gently, though I can see he too is beginning to imagine the unimaginable. He bows formally, raises his voice, says firmly, "Majesty, I will see you in the temple," and backs out, to go to the landing and board his barge.

Silently I pray for a moment—to Hathor, to Ptah, to Thoth and Geb and Nut and Ra-Herakhty and Isis and Harmakis and Buto and Sekhmet, to all the human-bird-and-animal-headed deities who surround me; and finally, in a desperation whose irony even in that moment does not escape me, to Amon-Ra himself, to his wife Mut and his son Khons, for *my* son who comes from Memphis, and who should by now be here.

I hear the roar of greeting, enthusiastic but respectful, that greets Aye. I know it is time for me to leave. I stand back, survey myself in the full-length mirror held before me by two slaves; find all in order; grasp the crook and flail firmly, compose my face into the pleasantly smiling, serenely untroubled expression it must carry always in public; and proceed, in the midst of slaves, priests and attendants, to the dock, and so into the state barge, which today of necessity is not *Radiance of the Aten* but its sister vessel, *All Is Pleasing to Amon.*

All down the river I barely hear, barely see, the hundreds of thousands who roar their greetings as I pass. Aanen stands at my shoulder. Our eyes have met once, as I stepped aboard. His were expressionless and fathomless. So do I hope mine seemed to him. He bowed very low and assumed his post slightly behind and to the left of the throne; we have not exchanged word or look since.

Confident, satisfied, happy and serene—for so they must believe me to be—I move slowly down the river before my people. In my mind I am desperately praying —for my son who is coming from Memphis, and for my son who is coming from the womb. No word comes as yet from either. Yet it must from both: it must. And from both it must be good.

It must.

It must.

Aanen

HE WORRIES, my arrogant brother-in-law: something in the set of his shoulders, which only I can see as I stand behind the throne while we move slowly down the river past the screaming throngs, tells me so.

He worries, and so he should. . . .

He is not alone.

To tell you the truth, so do I.

It is no small task to challenge Pharaoh, not something to be undertaken lightly. Death, instant and cruel, may await us all—if he lets impulse rule where only the cold and careful mind can be of any help. He may do so, for he is spoiled beyond his twenty-two years, heir to all the hard-won empire of ancestors stronger than he. Hatshepsut, the Tuthmosids, his grandfather, Amonhotep II (Life, health, prosperity to them all!), have left him a mighty heritage. He presides over it with three wives, two harims, infinite wealth, endless gold and a populace that obviously adores him. This sound coming from both banks of the river is hardly a human sound: it surpasses welcome, it transcends loyalty, it rises into realms of love and worship given only to the Good God, and to few Good Gods with the absolute fervor accorded him.

This little Pharaoh is supreme in all things, and above all in the love of Kemet. But he is not supreme over Amon, though he thinks he can be. But he cannot, and today he will find it out.

Our brief exchange this morning was typical of the way his attitude toward the temple of Amon and those who serve it has changed in these recent months. Always, now, there is contempt, scarcely hidden, in his voice when he speaks to me. Always now there is as much ignoring of my wishes as he dares, an attempt to exclude the priesthood of Amon-Ra from its rightful place and rightful honors.

Most insulting of all to me personally, there is an open dislike for his own brother-in-law, whom he seems no longer able to separate from the god he has evidently come to despise.

Well. He put me here and here I shall stay. And we shall see who is the stronger, the God Amon-Ra or the God Amonhotep III (Life, health, prosperity!).

This morning he could not even separate the brother-in-law from the Priest of Amon, he has come to dislike me so much in both capacities. My blood gives me the right to see my sister; my office gives me the right to attend her accouchement. Minor priests of Amon are at her side: it was the grossest insult to prevent the attendance of the highest, next to Pharaoh himself. Yet neither as brother nor as priest would he let me in. Contempt was in his tone, contempt in his action. It was flagrant in all degrees, and I shall not forget it. Contempt for me I could possibly stand, but not contempt for the god I represent.

When we return to the Palace from the ceremony, I shall again demand entrance, and this time in the presence of those he fawns upon, such as my high and mighty brother Aye, and that pompous little scribe who scuttles about listening and learning all the secrets he can, Amonhotep, Son of Hapu.

We shall see then what he does . . . unless, of course, by that time he has other things to think about.

I believe this will be the case: and I perceive as we near the landing at Karnak that he too considers it a likely possibility. His shoulders are rigid with tension. It cannot be the tension of ceremony, because the Good God is the child and prisoner of ceremony: he does little from one year's end to the next but follow ceremony. He has been on public display from the age of one, thousands of ceremonies have come and gone. It is not ceremony that bothers him now: it is worry for his son. And it is not the son perhaps even now entering the ranks of the gods in my sister's bed at Malkata. It is the son who has already entered, and who comes from Memphis, at his father's wish, as High Priest of Ptah to assume command of Amon's ceremony, and thus be his father's pawn in the dangerous game he plays with Amon.

This would be sacrilege, outrageous, unthinkable, unforgivable—if it happens. But I do not think it will.

My brother-in-law thinks—or rather he did think, up to a few minutes ago: now he is not so sure, and every second grows more worried—that his secret plans for my nephew have passed unnoticed by Amon. But Amon-Ra is king of the gods and all things are known to him.

A slight but not quite normal stirring in the palace at Memphis—the ordering up, quite casually, of chariots for a "hunting party" to take the little Prince for a few days along the boundaries of the Red Land—the gathering of supplies and provisions for an expedition much longer than that—and it occurred to our temple in Memphis that something we should know about was under way. A few judicious bribes were dispensed from Amon's vast wealth, a little judicious torture was administered in two or three cases by our special corps of protectors of Amon, and soon we had the whole story.

The Crown Prince was to be secretly brought to Thebes, was to displace me and my fellow priests, and was to be given control—the High Priest of Ptah in Amon-Ra's own temple!—of the ceremony of prayer and greeting for his new brother.

It would have been a direct insult that Amon could never forgive. It would have meant a constitutional crisis of such magnitude that one or the other must go down before it.

It could not be permitted to happen.

For all our sakes, the mad plan of my arrogant fool of a brother-in-law had to be thwarted.

When word reached me, brought by a courier who had ridden two of his three horses to death along the way in his frantic haste, I made up my mind at once. I went directly to the Good God. I was received with the usual undertone of scarcely veiled insolence. I was pleased to see that it vanished, very soon.

"Son of the Sun," I said, after bowing almost to the ground and rattling off his titles according to the prescribed ritual, "I understand the Crown Prince comes from Memphis to attend his brother's birth."

I had the satisfaction of seeing a look of blank dismay touch that round, smug little face for a second. But I will give him credit: he has will power, and with it he mastered his expression almost instantly and returned it to its usual bland serenity.

"Oh?" he said. "Is this what you hear, Brother?"

"It is not true, then," I said promptly, and though he concealed the struggle inside, I knew it was going on. He decided to be honest.

"Such is my desire," he said calmly.

"And plans are well advanced for his journey?"

"Well advanced."

"Would it be too much to ask," I said, and I am afraid I could not keep a certain dryness from my tone, for contempt breeds contempt, "that Amon-Ra be permitted to do suitable honor to his noble brother Ptah by accompanying the Prince in suitable numbers on his journey?"

"It is kind of you to ask, Brother," he said, "but it is not necessary."

"Not necessary," I agreed, not revealing that I knew the monstrous plan behind the journey, "but fitting to the order of things in Kemet—that order which has existed unchanged for thousands of years and will continue for thousands of thousands, into eternity. It is right that Amon-Ra pay respect to Ptah, it is right that priests of Amon as well as priests of Ptah accompany the Prince. To do otherwise would be to violate *ma'at,* the eternal order of things. The land of Kemet would be puzzled and dismayed were the order of things to be so disarranged that Amon could be deliberately ignored and egregiously offended."

He hesitated, and for a second looked uncertain. My brother Aye stepped forward, and whatever his thoughts (and it is not the first time that I have suspected him of plotting secretly against Amon), his voice was grave and decisive as it always is, thereby lending a spurious air of deliberation and authority to one whose ambitions are no secret to me, his brother, however he attempts to dissemble.

"Majesty," he said, "Son of the Sun: my brother the Priest of Amon speaks sense. It would be only fitting that Amon, too, accompany the Prince from Memphis. However," he said, raising his hand a little at my instinctive movement of gratification, "since the Prince is High Priest of Ptah, it would seem right that for every priest of Amon there be two of Ptah; and that in any event there be no more than fifteen priests for such a journey. Otherwise it would become unwieldy and a slow public progress, instead of the speedy journey made necessary by Her Majesty's imminent confinement."

"They should come by water, then," Pharaoh said. "Ramose"—the Vizier stepped forward, bowed low—"do you send word at once that the Crown Prince be accompanied as the Councilor Aye suggests, and that the company for safety's sake be given also an escort of a hundred soldiers from the garrison at Memphis."

Ramose bowed low again and withdrew. We three were left alone.

"Thus," my brother-in-law said, staring at me with insolent eyes, "will my son be safe."

"Thus will Amon be suitably honored, even as Ptah is honored," I replied, staring back.

"Thus will the peace and order of Kemet be kept," my brother Aye said quietly, "as it is the duty of all of us to do."

This was a month ago, and in that month spies went to Memphis (my own, and Aye's on Pharaoh's service), plans were revised, supplies were increased; the agreed-upon number of priests and soldiers was assigned, two barges—*Ptah Is Satisfied* and *Amon Is Gracious*—were outfitted; and two weeks ago my nephew and his company set forth upon the river, heading south into the northward-flowing current.

And so now Pharaoh and I are arriving at the landing at Karnak, and no word has come from the High Priest of Ptah and his flotilla. Last night they were encamped within half a day's journey, as my spies told me and Aye's, I am sure, told him; but nothing has been heard today, though they were expected in the fourth quarter of morning, in time for the boy to accompany his father to the temple.

We had to leave without him: how sad.

I see in my brother-in-law's carefully veiled eyes and tensely held posture as he steps ashore, smile fixed and eyes straight ahead while he takes back his crook and flail from Ramose and prepares to follow me into the temple, that his worry is now beginning to consume him.

My eyes do not meet his, I make no slightest gesture,

bargain. I give him children. I give him counsel. I give
him love. I give him strength. I know now, after twelve
years in his bed, that I have sufficient strength to give
him what he needs and still keep within, in some secret
place known only to me, enough more to meet for us
both whatever the gods may bring. I am not weak. I am
stronger than he. This I know now.

I did not know it when we married. Then I was as shy
as he, pushed forward by my parents, Yuya and Tuya,
and by my aunt Mutemwiya, when there was no sister
he could marry, no heiress to the throne. We were ten,
and pawns.

We are not pawns now.

At first it was a children's game: Kemet loved us, we
were taken everywhere, for months we were on constant
display. Of Kemet's five million people, probably two million at least came out to see our triumphal progress up
and down the river, from Nubia to the Delta. Everywhere
we went, all day, all night, crowds lined the banks of the
Nile on both sides: the cheering never seemed to stop.
Even when we were sleeping, when we were in our private quarters, when they could not see us, it continued.
We were their dolls, two little figures clad in gold who
held Kemet in our hands.

So do we hold it still.

Then came growing up. The marriage became real,
passion woke, we were lucky: real love followed. In com-
memoration he gave me the small cartouche of royal blue
porcelain, bearing on both sides his given name, Neb-
Ma'at-Ra, which I wear always on a gold chain around
my neck. The dolls were dolls no longer. The Good God
began to take more and more power unto himself. My
aunt the Queen Mother Mutemwiya, my parents Yuya
and Tuya, aided by those court officials whom they
trusted, aided by the priests of Amon who then were
friendly to our House, gracefully yielded authority into
his hands. They perceived that he was growing into a
clever boy who could handle it. They perceived that I,
Tiye, could handle it too. They perceived more than that:
they perceived that I was becoming as astute at state-

craft as he. They did not object when he raised me to be always at his side, when he published scarabs in my honor, when he listed my titles with his on our monuments, temples, palaces, such as had almost never been done before with a Great Wife in all of Kemet's history —such as had never, ever, been done with a commoner Queen.

They knew he needed me. They knew that without Tiye, the Great Wife, he might weaken and falter. They knew I would keep him strong, because I am strong.

Our first child came, Sitamon the laughing and happy: another doll for Kemet. He married her immediately, with my acquiescence, indeed at my urging, for thus was the royal succession established once and forever, beyond all challenge. Relieved of his worry about that—for until then, in the eyes of the people, he was somehow not quite legitimate, though they loved him—he loved me more. The great years began. And presently, too, began the struggle, and the pain.

We could understand why our House needs a strong priesthood at its side, we knew the history of Amon-Ra and how he had become so entwined with us. We could not understand that he should be our equal, that he should own as much wealth as we, that he should attempt sometimes to override our wishes and flaunt our orders, in ways silent, secret, subtle, apparent to us if not to the people. We made clear our displeasure in ways as silent, secret and subtle, but unmistakably. A mutual hostility was born. Presently we could imagine another such intervention as had lifted Tuthmose III from obscurity and toppled his father Tuthmose I (Life, health, prosperity to them both!) from the throne. We did not see where the threat might come from, for no one else had the royal blood, but we felt that Amon might be ready and capable, should the chance arise. Then the God brought me to bed again, and this time we had a son, Tuthmose. Now there was a Crown Prince. Now Amon had his weapon.

But so, of course, did we.

Aiee, aiee, aiee! May Bes and Hathor help me! I shall

not cry out, I shall not let them see my face! I shall be strong. I shall be . . . strong . . .

Tuthmose is a sunny child, like his sister yet with an instinctive gravity that indicates awareness of his position, which we have explained a little, in simple terms. We have educated him at Memphis as much as possible, using as our excuse the fact that many of the Pharaohs had been educated there when they were princes. To placate Amon, and—he foolishly thought—to give our House control of his priests, my husband decided to name my next older brother, Aanen, to be Priest of Amon, second only to Pharaoh himself, in the temple at Karnak. It was perhaps the only time he ever went directly against my advice: some instinct told me to beware of this dour, impatient older brother. The Good God disagreed, but within a month he knew, too late, that I was right.

Aanen liked the power of Amon. He became loyal to it. Never quite daring to oppose us openly, he nonetheless took the side of the god. He became a threat; and now his nephew, our son, was the pawn.

We could not turn to Mutemwiya, growing somewhat vague as she becomes older, or to my parents, retired now and living in our ancestral home of Akhmim, capital of the ninth province of Upper Kemet, near the Nubian border. It was a problem we must solve ourselves. Soon I saw the way.

For centuries the Aten, the sun's disk, has been a secondary deity, one of the many forms of Ra. In the past hundred years our House has raised him gradually to a greater prominence. The purpose of the Good Gods before us has been the same as ours: not to eliminate Amon but to balance him.

This is our only purpose.

We have no quarrel with Amon: it is his grasping priests who concern us.

We ordered a temple built to the Aten near the temple of Amon. At first my husband wished to make it huge and grand, "a message they cannot miss." Both I and my oldest brother, Aye, who is very wise and very close to me, cautioned against this. Pharaoh scaled down the plans, made it more modest: even so, the message, as Aye and I had known, was not missed.

My husband gave me the "lake" at my favorite town of Djarukha. He decided to publish a scarab. I suggested that it show him riding in a barge to open the dikes of the Nile to flood my land and bring me wealth. "What shall I name the barge?" he asked. I laughed: "You know." He nodded and smiled with sudden comprehension. *Radiance of the Aten* sailed the Nile. We built other small temples to the Aten, as far north as the Delta. We built Malkata on the west bank of the Nile, bringing life to the land of the dead where no Pharaoh, defying Amon, had ever dared build a palace before.

Four months ago Aanen appeared before us both in the throne room. Aye was also there. It was a frightening conversation, for Aanen wanted nothing less than our son.

"The Crown Prince," he began cautiously, "is now six years of age."

"Yes?" my husband said, an ironic puzzlement in his voice. "We, his parents, are aware of that."

"It is time," Aanen said, "that he should be brought more fully into the life of Kemet."

"Is that not something for us to decide?" Pharaoh demanded sharply; and my brother Aye added quietly, "Surely, Brother, you presume too much when you seek to instruct the Good God and the Great Wife on how they should handle their son."

"He has been too long at Memphis," Aanen said stubbornly. "He should be here in Thebes."

"Why?" I asked. "He will come to Thebes in due time."

"The people want him here," Aanen said, and my husband snorted.

"Are you saying they do not want him in Memphis? I am told he is enormously popular there. Why should he be brought to Thebes right now? He is not educated yet. He is just beginning scribal school, he has much to learn."

"Cannot your favorite Amonhotep, Son of Hapu, teach him?" Aanen asked, not bothering to conceal his sarcasm. "I thought *he* knew everything."

"He may not know everything," my husband said with a dangerous quietness, "but he is wise enough not to defy Pharaoh."

"I am not defying Pharaoh, Son of the Sun," Aanen said with a sudden obsequiousness that fooled no one. "I am only telling Your Majesties what Amon hears the length and breadth of the land: the people would like the family reunited."

"I know what the people think as well as Amon!" my husband snapped; and for just a second there was a sly, sardonic amusement, instantly banished, in my brother Aanen's eyes.

"We do not dispute that, Majesty," he said with a sudden gravity. "But if you know, then you know that the people also wish the Crown Prince to spend more time with Amon. He has reached an age when he should be included in our ceremonies here. It is time for him to pay his respects to Amon-Ra and take his rightful place in Amon's house."

"And what is his 'rightful place in Amon's house'?" Pharaoh asked, again the dangerous quietness in his voice; and again my brother Aye followed softly with, "Yes, Brother, what is it you are proposing here?"

"I propose nothing," Aanen said quickly. "I suggest only that if"—and he dared say this, not using our son's title as he should have—"if my nephew is to be brought down to Thebes, then in addition to his other studies he should rightfully take his place among the acolytes in the temple of Amon. And he should be given, as befits his rank, a suitable title and suitable duties there."

"And then, I suppose—" my husband began angrily—and then he stopped. But suddenly in all our minds was the same picture: the golden statue of Amon leaning down a hundred years ago to touch a priest in the ranks named Tuthmose III and raise him thereby instantly to the throne at the expense of his father.

For a moment no one said anything further: it was as though Pharaoh and I could not draw breath, so vast and fearful was the abyss that seemed to open at our feet. But the insolence of my brother Aanen had not yet run its course, for presently he shifted a little and asked softly:

"Surely, Son of the Sun, you do not fear that Amon will mistreat or miseducate your son? Surely you know that we will treat him as tenderly as you yourselves, during those hours when he is with us? On what grounds can you object?"

Again there was silence while my husband and I, too astounded and dismayed by such effrontery and such danger, sought vainly for words. My brother Aye came to our rescue.

"On what grounds do *you* insist?" he asked our brother Aanen, a sudden harsh bluntness in his voice: and now it was time for Aanen to give way, which he did at once, smoothly and with just the right degree of affronted surprise.

"I do not 'insist,' Brother!" he exclaimed. "How could I possibly 'insist'? I make a suggestion only, one so obvious and natural that it is desired by all reasonable people who have at heart the welfare of the Good God's throne and the House of Thebes. And that means all the people of Kemet, and the Empire as well. What is so treasonous about that?"

"No one said anything about 'treasonous,' Brother!" Pharaoh snapped, recovering speech and determined now, as we all could see, to end this ominous conversation. "We are pleased to hear your suggestion, we shall consider it, but I do not think I can promise you that anything will be done about it."

"Amon and the people will be disturbed and puzzled," Aanen said in an elaborately aggrieved tone.

"I would not advise Amon," my husband said in a remote and chilling voice, "to disturb and puzzle the people too much, Brother. That might lead to trouble. And none of us wants that."

"Oh no," Aanen agreed hastily. "None of us wants that, Son of the Sun." He bowed low and began to back out. He paused at the door. "Am I to tell Amon, then, that for the time being the Crown Prince will not come to do him honor?"

"You may tell Amon," my husband said, and his voice

grated with anger, "that the Crown Prince does him honor daily in his temple at Memphis, and that there the Crown Prince will remain until such time as the Great Wife and I deem his schooling to be sufficiently advanced."

"Very well," Aanen said, his voice a regretful sigh as he left us. "Very well, Son of the Sun, if that is your desire, and my sister's."

After his ostentatiously worried face had disappeared and the curtain of beads across the door had ceased to sway from his elaborately humble departure, there was silence again in the room.

Pharaoh broke it at last in a firm and decisive tone.

"I see," he remarked to my brother Aye and me, "that we are going to have to move much sooner than I had thought. Your sister has an idea about this, Brother. Tell us what you think of it."

And so three months later Tuthmose became High Priest of Ptah at Memphis, and in Amon's temples my brother Aanen and his friends muttered and were furious. But it was done, and we had captured the pawn, not Amon.

Ah! Ah! Ah! Aiee, Bes and Hathor, help me! I will be strong! I will be strong! Bes! Hathor! . . . help . . . me . . . ahhh . . .

But now I worry. And Pharaoh worries. And Aye worries, though he has worry enough, with Hebmet in her usual difficult labor scarce half a mile from here, across the Palace compound. May Bes and Hathor help her to safety, too, and give them a healthy child to serve our House.

Why is Tuthmose not here? Why have we not had word this day from his party? All was well yesterday, they were making good time, our son was well and happy, excited by the journey. Where is he now?

I will not imagine that he is not well. I will not fear Amon. I will think only that there has been some natural delay. Perhaps a barge has run aground, there may have been a small collision, often these minor accidents happen on the river. Or the current is proving stronger than they thought, and the slaves are tired from rowing up-

Something moves within the House of Thebes. I watch respectfully, I listen, I wait. Presently it will become clear to me, though I suspect already what it is. Pharaoh is displeased with Amon, and seeks a way to lessen his power. Amon also is displeased. Out of such displeasure, who knows what things may come for the land of Kemet?

I watch, I listen, I wait. This morning I saw the Priest Aanen, that creeping man, fling furiously away from his brother-in-law the Good God. This morning I saw the Good God for a second look profoundly worried, profoundly sad. Just now when he passed, I, who know him very well by now, saw behind the frozen smile and fixed, official aspect of his face something else, some trouble deeply hidden, deeply felt. Things appear to be nearing crisis. I watch, I listen, I wait.

Such is the advantage of the scribe, and such is the advantage I am arranging for my young friend Kaires, who bounces beside me like a puppy, yet beneath his outward innocence carries the weapon of an extremely intelligent mind becoming daily more shrewd and skilled in the ways of Kemet. There is some mystery here too. He appeared suddenly from nowhere, suddenly was assigned, with no explanation to anyone, to work with me in the Palace of Malkata. At first I resented this, was cautious, withholding; then his natural charm won me over—and something else. I suspect he has sponsorship from somewhere very high. I suspect he is here because someone sees him as a potential future actor in the game we all play in the Palace. Much that they never dream goes on behind the golden spectacle that awes and delights the people. I suspect it will be well for me to be his friend. So I have become, and quite genuinely, too. The charm and innocence still predominate: the shrewd intelligence and carefully analytical mind, potentially ruthless, potentially hard, come now but cautiously and rarely to the surface. But they are there, if he ever needs them. And as the years spin out for the House of Thebes, he may.

I intend to be his friend on that day, as I am on this. Today, however, we are concerned with today; and al-

though he conceals it cleverly, thinking I do not notice
after my uninformative conversation at breakfast, I can
see that he, too, is still worrying the fact that all is not
well in the House of Thebes. He does not know exactly
why, but he is at work upon it. Soon it may come to him.

Indeed, soon it may come to us all, if what I suspect
is true. Appointing the Crown Prince to be High Priest
of Ptah was slap enough in the face of Amon. That act
alone guarantees Amon much loss, for now many of
Amon's riches will be diverted by Pharaoh to Ptah at
Memphis, and Ptah will grow great and powerful at
Amon's expense. It is no wonder Aanen and his fellows
are frantic and aghast.

I suspect—and I think Pharaoh now suspects—that
they may be vengeful too.

And yet what else could he and the Great Wife expect? Amon-Ra has grown so great in the last hundred
years that he will not give up without a struggle. And he
will enlist many other gods and goddesses too, for most
of them hold their temples and their more modest wealth
solely at his sufferance. Amon's priests have worked out
their web of alliances with the priests and priestesses of
lesser gods as astutely as Tuthmose III (Life, health,
prosperity!) worked out the alliances that form the fabric
of his great-grandson's empire. Amon has great abundance: he permits some of it to spill over to Thoth,
Sebek, Ra-Herakhty, Nekhebet, Isis, the Mnevi Bull of
Heliopolis, Bast, Sekhmet and the rest. Amon, in effect,
has bought himself over the generations many friends.

It is not one god that Pharaoh and the Great Wife
have challenged: it is all the gods, led by the greatest of
them all. A formidable phalanx, to be brought low
through the instrumentality of one small, six-year-old boy.

I do not underestimate the will of Pharaoh, however;
and as I have come to know them both in the past ten
years during which I have moved gradually into a position of high confidence in the Palace, I particularly do
not underestimate Queen Tiye. Behind Pharaoh's bland
and pleasantly smiling face lies a strong determination to
protect his power and his House; but behind Tiye's lies

that determination plus an even fiercer and greater: to
protect the land of Kemet, which her family, like mine,
has served so well. And of our two rulers, though it is
treason to even think so and I would never breathe my
thoughts to anyone save possibly, someday, young Kaires
when he grows older and has need of the knowledge, it
is the Great Wife who has the greater strength and the
stronger character. The Good God rules Kemet, but the
Great Wife rules him. This, after studying them both, do
I sincerely believe.

They take a fearful gamble with their little High Priest
of Ptah, and obviously they are aware of it, for he comes
up the river from Memphis today heavily guarded by his
own priests and a hundred soldiers. Yet he is accompanied by the priests of Amon, too, and guards cannot
always be on guard. I do not know whether his parents
intended him to arrive in time to conduct the ceremonies
here—what an exquisite and unforgivable insult that
would have been to Amon!—but I suspect it may have
been so. If it was, it has already been thwarted: Amon
himself, or one of his lieutenants—perhaps Hapi, god of
the Nile—has already caused sufficient delay to prevent
him from attending. What else may Amon have con-
trived?

"Amonhotep!" Kaires cries suddenly at my side, his
hand anxious on my arm. "Who comes there?"

Instantly, for no reason I know, my heart jumps, my
face sweats, something cold and freezing grasps my body.
One of the gods speaks to me, I know not which: I *know*.

Quickly I spin in the direction he gestures, around us
the crowd falls suddenly silent: a small boat crashes
against the landing, a young soldier, pale, terrified, gasping for breath, staggers, against all the rules of Kemet,
into the empty avenue before the temple. Harshly the
guardsmen spring upon him, as quickly I shout, "Make
way for Amonhotep the Scribe!" Stunned and obedient
like the cattle they sometimes seem to be, the people
move swiftly out of my way. Kaires racing behind me, I
dash for the little group in the middle of the empty street
in the pitiless blazing sun. The guardsmen, who know me,

hesitate at my shouted command, then give way. The youth is shoved roughly toward me. Kaires and I support him on both sides a little farther along the now terribly empty and desolate way. A fearful silence falls on the crowd.

"*Whisper!*" I order in a fierce whisper of my own. "*Tell me!*"

And he does, and the world of Kemet changes forever in an instant's dreadful time.

"*Come with me!*" I order, still whispering; and, Kaires still assisting—his face, I note with approval, as rigid and unrevealing as I am forcing my own to be—we take him rapidly to the door of the temple.

Tall priests, selected for their forbidding height from among Kemet's normally small-boned population, glare down upon us. But I know one who stands taller than they.

"*Bring me the Councilor Aye!*" I command; and when they continue to hesitate, still glaring, I repeat in a vicious whisper, so savage that they actually blink and step back a pace, "*Bring me Aye or I will have Pharaoh take your heads!*"

And after a moment of what they consider necessary bravado—I memorize their faces and if I can do it I *will* have their heads after this dreadful day is over—they take us inside.

Even as they do, from upriver at Malkata there begins a great, sustained, joyful roar that races along the shores and over the water until it fills the world with overwhelming happy sound.

The Great Wife is apparently safely delivered of her son.

Aye

SHARPLY ON THE STROKE of noon, when the sun abandons his youthful form of Horus and emerges in his full
maturity as Ra, the Good God entered the temple. Standing respectfully aside in the shadows, we who had preceded watched him walk in slow, deliberate procession
behind my brother Aanen to the great pylon gateway
which he ordered erected in Amon's honor four years ago.
This vast structure, surmounted by eight flagpoles carrying long thin streamers painted with symbols sacred to
the god, was created of the stones torn from a charming
little pavilion built by Amonemhat I (Life, health, prosperity!) one thousand years ago. Thus do the Good Gods
pirate one another, tearing down each other's monuments
in order to build their own. There is a lesson here for
them in the transitory nature of man—even men who are
gods—but I doubt that they perceive it. Certainly I do not
think this one does. But in any event, why should he?
So it has always been in Kemet. And what has always
been in Kemet will always be in Kemet.

To dare to think otherwise is to begin the cracking of
the universe.

He passed through the gateway into the main courtyard, and instantly the hushed silence all around was
broken by the clash of cymbals, the sound of castanets,
the rhythmic metallic jangling of sistrums and the sweet
flutter of harps. Twenty of the young priestesses of Amon,
naked as always save for their intricately woven bead col-
lars, danced forward and back, forward and back, in
their standard ritual dance. I noted that he watched it
politely but without his usual interest. Normally he will

catch my eye, designate one or two; they will be sent to
the harim, he will enjoy their variety for a week or two
before he returns to my sister, and then they will be sent
back to the temple carrying suitable gifts—unless, if they
are lucky, they have caught the eye of some noble and
find themselves transported to some other harim—or, if
really lucky, into marriage, motherhood, domestication,
respectability, that solid family life which in royal House
or peasant's hut is in many ways the life's blood of
Kemet.

Today he looked neither right nor left, eyes straight
ahead, smile fixed. The girls danced as close to him as
they dared; some of them even dared to look disappointed
when he showed no interest. He remained unmoved. Soon
they withdrew, whispering sibilantly among themselves.
He proceeded. Mutemwiya, Sitamon, Gilukhipa and I followed, with solemn paces, into the inner courtyard.

There he paused, bowed low to the statue of Tuthmose
I (Life, health, prosperity!), turned and bowed low to
the giant statue of himself which he caused to be erected
three years ago. He has already begun the process of
self-deification, itself an indirect but somewhat more
customary challenge to Amon, of the sort Amon has managed to absorb before and no doubt could do again—
were that the only challenge.

Dutifully we followed as he led us past the copper-
sheathed obelisks of the Good God Hatshepsut, not entirely defaced despite the savagely vengeful efforts of her
half brother Tuthmose III (Life, health, prosperity to
them both!) after her death. So we came into the third
courtyard, past the unending jumble of statues, paintings,
obelisks, monstrous men, monstrous women, monstrous
animals, that glorify the dead Pharaohs and the living
gods of Kemet. And so presently, through a hallway suddenly narrow, suddenly so dark we could hardly see, we
came to the inner sanctum where the single ray of light
from Ra falls upon the golden head and hooded, brooding
eyes of his son Amon.

There his other son paused, as did we all. Aanen sang
the traditional chant of supplication for blessing on the

new child; Pharaoh formally offered the incense, wheat, gold and jewels he had ordered sent earlier from the Palace, which the priests had placed on the altar before the somber figure in the gloom.

Then in a clear voice he said:

"May my new son, the god, be safely delivered of his mother's womb; and may my older son, the god, be safely delivered of his journey to my side." He paused for a second and when he spoke again a certain cold iron was in his voice: "Your son, the Good God, expects your help in this, O Amon."

There was an audible gasp from the priests. Gilukhipa, a curious sometime ally of mine, shot me a sudden sharp glance, then instantly resumed her masklike look. Mutem-wiya for a second looked openly dismayed, then also became impassive. Little Sitamon, moved by who knows what childish thought or impulse, suddenly gurgled with laughter, a clear, delighted, silvery sound.

There followed absolute silence.

Pharaoh bowed to Amon-Ra and, walking backward as mortal men walk backward away from him, moved toward the entrance. Watching, I saw hastening forward in the inner courtyard a tall, white-robed priest, face drawn and agitated. He stopped abruptly, stepped to one side, bowing low, to let Pharaoh pass. Then he hurried to my side as I too prepared to bow, back out, and follow.

"Amonhotep, Son of Hapu, wishes to speak to you," he hissed. *"At once."*

And at once, for the wisdom and discretion of Amonhotep, Son of Hapu, I know and respect, I went to him, slipping out a side entrance and hurrying to the temple door. There I found a white-faced Amonhotep, a white-faced Kaires and a terrified young soldier gripped firmly between them. Pharaoh approached, walking forward now, not seeing us, his eyes far away and troubled as they have been all morning. We bowed almost to the ground, waited respectfully for him to pass. Then Amonhotep gave the young soldier a savage shake.

"Tell him!" he commanded. And the soldier did.

Would that I were not Councilor to the Good God

now! Would that I could return with him happily to the Palace, kiss my sister, return swiftly and peaceably to my own quiet house where my own dear Hebmet undergoes her hard and difficult labor. *There* is where I am needed now! Not here, standing dazed in the glaring sun, staring dazed at Amonhotep, Kaires and the young soldier, while all around the world is filled with the wildly happy shouts that attend my sister's safe delivery.

But there is no rest for councilors to the Good God: there are so few he can trust. There is no rest for Aye, who must bear always upon his shoulders the care of Kemet. There is no rest for anyone who challenges Amon. For now Amon has struck back, in a way terrible to contemplate.

What Amon does not understand—and even as I try to comprehend it all in one staggering moment, I find I must try to analyze, I must try to be generous, I must try to be fair, for that is Aye's curse, that he is doomed to see all sides and yet be called upon to act—is that he has reacted out of all proportion to the challenge. The elevation of the Crown Prince to be High Priest of Ptah was not intended to be a threat to Amon. We recognize Amon's necessity to the House of Thebes. We have desired only a check, let us say: a balance. A counterweight. A control. A lever with which to reduce insufferable priests, my brother Aanen chief among them, to their right and manageable level.

And now Amon has turned and exacted a terrible revenge. And how am I to tell the Good God?

"How will you tell the Good God?" Amonhotep whispers, and without answering him directly—for indeed I do not as yet have the slightest idea, so awful will be his anguish and so terrible the vengeance he is apt to let slip upon the one who brings him word—I respond instead with those other details that must be attended to at once.

"Kaires," I say, and he looks suddenly terribly young but absolutely determined, so that I am proud of him, "do you take the soldier to the house of Amonhotep. Stay there until I send word. Do not speak to anyone on the way. If this one tries to speak to anyone, silence him. Kill him if necessary."

"Oh, sir," the young soldier cries, "I will be silent! I will not speak! Oh, believe me, Your Mightiness!"

Even in this awful moment I cannot refrain from a slight smile at his peasant ignorance of titles, and in a more kindly tone I say, "My boy, I know you will not. But just be aware that if you do my young friend here will kill you. Understand?"

"Yes, Mightiness," he says humbly, and I know we will have no trouble with him.

"Good," I say. "Kaires, be off!"

"Yes, sir!" he says, tugging at the soldier's arm, and together they go hurrying away, to be lost immediately in the ecstatically happy crowd that shouts for Pharaoh's departure, simultaneously honors my sister, and knows nothing of horror.

I turn to Amonhotep, who, I can see, is being restored to reasonable composure by the necessity for careful planning, just as I am.

"What about the other members of the party?" he asks, anticipating my words.

"Exactly," I say. "Ramose will emerge from the temple in a second. Tell him. The two of you get a boat and go instantly to the place. Command everyone to stay there until I send word."

"Excellent. And you, my poor friend? How will you do your difficult job?"

"I shall think of something."

He nods quickly, hurries forward to Ramose, speaks a rapid sentence. Ramose visibly staggers, then instantly recovers, shrugs off his golden robe, tosses it to a nearby priest. They hurry forward through the crowd to the waterfront. Mutemwiya emerges from the temple, and I have found the solution. But first I must have a word with my brother Aanen, who has now seen Pharaoh safely to his barge and is returning to the temple.

I can tell that so far he has heard nothing; but I now understand much about that curious air, as of some secret inward knowingness, that I have observed in him all day.

I step directly in his path so that he almost bumps into me before he manages to stop, and say in a cold and level voice, "Brother, I would have a word with you."

An instant alarm, as instantly gone, flickers in his eyes.

"Later," he begins impatiently. "Later. I must help the Queen Mother—"

"Others will help her," I say savagely, and I grip his arm with a terrible grip that makes him almost cry aloud with pain. "*Now*. And in the presence of Amon. We are going back into the sanctuary, Brother. We are going to speak truth before the god. Come with me."

He comes—reluctantly, looking angrily about, desperately seeking some excuse to break away. But there is none. Priests part before us, the ceremony is over. We are alone as we retrace our steps. There is no excuse. He comes.

Somber and hooded, the gleaming jeweled eyes of the golden statue stare down upon us in the single shaft of light.

"Look well upon the god, Brother," I say softly, "for you have murdered our nephew and the Good God will take a terrible vengeance upon Amon. This golden statue, the gold in your temples, your jewels, your cattle, your swollen granaries, your rich, abundant fields—all, all may fall before the vengeance of Pharaoh. How could you and your fellows ever be so stupid, Brother? How could you ever be so mad?"

"I do not know what you mean!" he replies angrily, and though our argument is furious our voices still are whispers in the presence of the god. "I have no knowledge that anything has happened!"

"You have had knowledge that it would happen, Brother," I say, still softly, "and you may believe me when I tell you that now it has. An unexpected sand bar, carefully selected—a tipped boat—a little boy—your nephew, Brother, our flesh and blood for all that he is— *was*—Crown Prince and High Priest of Ptah—struggling and crying in the water. And who goes to the rescue, Brother? Not the priests of Ptah, for they are ruthlessly shouldered aside in the mad rush of the priests of Amon to save the boy. They surround him, they tug at him, they cry out and shove and haul. And somehow, Brother, he slips from their grasp and sinks before their eyes *in three feet of water*. They try—how they try!—but it is too late. Alas, Brother, how sad. How sad for everyone. But most of all, perhaps"—and I turn and exchange somber stare for somber stare with the golden figure who looms above us—"how sad for you, O Amon-Ra!"

"He will strike you dead!" Aanen hisses, but I shrug with an indifference I do not quite—not *quite,* for old awes die hard and I have been reared in the cult of Amon—feel. Nonetheless, my voice is unmoved when I reply.

"He will strike dead him who does not tell the truth, Brother." And suddenly I fling up my arm toward the god and shout into the musty dust of centuries, "Now! *Now!"*

And my brother Aanen falls in terror, cringing and crying at my feet. And so we stay for some seconds until gradually the color returns to his face, some resurgence of determination to his jaw, a new and dangerous hatred in his eyes.

Slowly he gathers himself together, slowly rises. When he speaks it is in a whisper filled with savagery and no longer afraid.

"If Pharaoh takes vengeance upon Amon he will split asunder the land of Kemet and destroy the world. *We* may be destroyed, Brother, but he and his House will also be destroyed in such a battle. *That w*ould be the madness, not the disciplining of a Good God who has grown too great."

"And what of Amon who has grown too great?" I demand bitterly. But I see that my brother is lost to us forever.

"There is no solution for it, Brother," he says with a returning confidence, "except this: that we have to live together. So let us do so peaceably and as friendly equals."

"But Amon does not wish to be an equal, Brother," I say. "He wishes to rule."

"Tell the Good God," he says, and now he has recovered sufficiently that it is his voice which holds the menace, "that he would be most unwise—most unwise—to seek to topple Amon. For Amon lives. Amon lives!" And turning his back to me, he raises both arms to the god and begins to chant: *"O Amon-Ra, O King of the gods, O highest of the high, mightiest of the mighty, maker of the world, spanner of the horizons, terrible in strength, awful in vengeance, O Amon, Amon, thou who art forever—"*

And so I leave him as the eerie babble continues, supplicating his idol who looks down from above unmoved by mortal men. But it is not mortal men he deals with now. It is a god like himself.

I leave my brother alone in the gloom, chanting madly on beneath the golden figure, and I go to find the Queen Mother. And in my heart of hearts I know, for Aye is honest with all men and above all with himself, that my brother—may Anubis, welcomer of the dead, and the forty-two judges who bar the gates of the afterworld deny him entry to the Field of Rushes where the Westerners live on into eternity beneath the guardian gaze of Mert-se-ger, the Lover of Him Who Makes Silence, the goddess of the Western Peak!—I know that my brother is right.

We *do* have to live with one another, and if Amon is to be defeated, it must be done with more caution and more care than my poor sister and brother-in-law have lately shown.

Alas! I cry for them, and for the boy, who was an intelligent child and might have been a great Pharaoh! But the needs of the world press on.

I go to find her who must carry the news and comfort them in their anguish.

Mutemwiya

HORROR, HORROR, for the House of Thebes! And I, an old, frail woman, must now be strong enough to help them all.

Well: so I am. It has been my son's custom in recent years to humor me, to pretend that I am beginning to wander in my mind, to assume, pleasantly but firmly, that I am leaving behind all interest in affairs of state. But he knows this is not so. He knows I write constantly to all our allies throughout the Empire. He knows I continue the great work of his father, Tuthmose IV (Life, health, prosperity!), without which, and without the work of his ancestors who went before, his present state would be nothing.

He is an odd mixture, my son. He cares for Kemet, he makes the little show of interest necessary to hold together the Empire, he loves and adores the Great Wife and their children, he is very jealous of the authority and continuation of our House—but I think he is beginning to become obsessed with Amon to the point where it is clouding his judgment. Obviously so, for it has now produced the tragedy we face today.

I have seen many sorrows in my time: behind the public masks we wear, things do not always move so happily for the kings and queens of Kemet. They have not moved so for me. Six children stillborn, four dead in infancy, my husband gone early, my sole surviving child come to the throne a boy of ten amidst intrigues that only my strong will put down. It has not been easy. No wonder I am old before my time. But, like all the women of our family, I am strong—*strong*. Were it not so, things would have gone hard with the House of Thebes.

My grandson Tuthmose, that dear, laughing little boy! Hapi, god of the Nile, has taken him. And Amon-Ra, enraged by my son and Tiye, has been the instrument to put him into Hapi's hands. Hapi can be kind and Hapi can be cruel. Today Hapi has been cruel, for he is a friend of Amon, and perhaps is enraged at the way my son has treated Amon.

My nephew Aye came to me as I was about to enter my barge for the return to Malkata. Something in his desperate face made me step aside as he beckoned me to do. My nephew is a staid and solid man, conservative in all things: when Aye is agitated, there is reason. And so he told me, with much bitterness against his brother, my nephew Aanen. And he told me what he and the other wise man, Amonhotep the Scribe, Son of Hapu, had done to keep the news away from the people until Pharaoh and the Great Wife could be told. And he told me I must be the one to tell them, for my son could not take vengeance on me for bringing the news, and only I could soothe and help them through the agony.

All of this was true, and so I thanked Aye and said I would do it. But I told him I needed help, and so he stands beside me now, my hand upon his arm as the barge moves out into the current, steadying me as he always steadies the House of Thebes. He is a good man, my nephew, and we will see this sad task through together for the sake of Kemet, whose order and safety must be preserved.

We turn into the downflowing current, the oarsmen grunt and strain, for a second we veer sharply. Both Aye and I almost lose our balance: Hapi is still angry for his friend Amon. But then he relents, the barge rights itself and takes the river smoothly, we begin the slow progress upstream to the Palace. On both banks, as warmly as before, the people roar their adoration. Why cannot our feet be more certain when they stand upon such love?

I have discussed this subject many times with my principal friend abroad, King Shu-ttarna, of Mittani, father of

our dour Gilukhipa. He has not answered my letters in
recent years—I am not too sure my son is sending them
to him, though I do not know why, for I do not interfere
in statecraft, only attempt to make sure that all is attended to, and that relations remain good between us—
but when he did, he confessed to being as baffled as I.
Once, in an apparent fit of melancholy, he asked me:
"What is love? Particularly when it comes from the people? How can they possibly love us, who are so high
above them?" I wrote back, I am afraid somewhat tartly:
"Love is what keeps us on our thrones, and without it
we fall. So do not ask what it is. It is there. Be thankful
we have it, otherwise there would be a great tumbling in
Kemet and Mittani." He did not respond for quite some
time after that, but he deserved my sharpness. "What is
love?" indeed! If one has to ask, particularly in relation
to the people, one might as well not write. They are there
—it is there. They go together. At least they do for the
House of Thebes, and as long as they do, we need not
worry for our throne, however much may happen to disturb us.

Eh, well. Those were pleasant days, of correspondence
and philosophy. Things are grimmer now.

We move steadily on upstream. The wave of love
washes us along, mingled now with the happy excitement
of my niece's successful delivery. She has a son—one son,
poor girl. It is well that she too is strong, for strength
will be needed when I reach the Palace.

We swing right into the channel, see the Palace dock
ahead. Sitamon and Gilukhipa are just landing. Sitamon,
relieved of the burden of ceremony, dances off the barge
with a little girl's abandon, laughing and merry. The
crowds give her an extra roar, and even Gilukhipa smiles
and appears more relaxed. Sitamon does this to people.
Later on tonight, when her parents are clutching one another in the grip of sorrow, her sunny nature will be of
much help to them.

My barge touches wood, I step ashore, still on Aye's
arm; with instinctive agreement we turn and I bow low
to the people, first to the right, then to the left; raise my

right arm in salute; and, for the first time, smile. The sound of affection outdoes itself as we turn and start walking slowly along the broad, stone-flagged approach to the Palace, between the rows of gently swaying palm trees and the soldiers standing on perpetual guard.

Hardly aware I am doing it, I utter a long-drawn, heavy sigh as we near the massive gate to the compound; and gently Aye, always perceptive, always understanding, says, "Be of good cheer, Aunt. Your Majesty can do nobly and well the difficult task that lies before her."

"Can I?" I ask quizzically. "I am only an old, frail woman."

"Not old," he says, "and not frail. I am beside you. Come."

And still gently, but firmly, he leads me in, past the bowing nobles and the humble slaves and the doctors and nurses and somber, white-robed priests of Amon, until we come to the door of my niece's room. It is guarded by two tall priests of Amon, who will not, I wager, be standing there in another ten minutes. They will, in fact, be lucky to be alive. Their last task on earth, in fact, may be to open the way for me, who may possibly carry their deaths along with my news. It is an ironic thought, and grim, and I see it in Aye's eyes too as we exchange glances at the threshold.

Grandly the doors are flung open, grandly the older priest announces, "Her Majesty the Queen Mother, She Who Is Gracious and Shining in the Eyes of Amon!" And grandly I go in, Aye releasing me and stepping back a pace as the doors close behind us.

Startled, my son and my niece look up. He is seated on the bed, holding both her hands, worship, infinite love and happiness in his face. In a cradle before them squirms and squalls the newborn god.

We bow low and come near. I stoop first to kiss the Great Wife on a cheek still wet and fevered from her labor, then kiss Pharaoh, and then turn for an instant to smile down upon their new and only son. Aye gravely does the same, then takes my arm with a strengthening grip. Something in the action gives us away. Both Pharaoh and the Great Wife turn pale.

"What is it?" Pharaoh demands in a tight, constricted voice; and somehow, steadied by Aye's blessed grip upon my arm, which does not shake or falter but sustains me word by word, I manage to tell them.

After I have finished there is a dreadful quiet, broken only by the occasional tiny mewlings of the new god in his cradle.

Then suddenly my son gives a terrible howl, Tiye a ghastly shriek. He buries his face in her breast, she cradles it in her arms, her head falls forward to rest alongside his as they rock in agony together. Outside there is the sound of startled voices, people running, exclamations, worried cries, a growing tumult.

"What is it?" someone shouts, pounding on the door; and presently my son lifts a ravaged face that stares at me without seeing. Then with a terrible, deliberate slowness, he rises and crosses the room to the chair upon which he has laid his razor-sharp, jeweled ceremonial sword.

"No!" Aye and I cry together, and Tiye, grief suddenly giving way to horror as she watches, echoes frantically, *"No!"*

But he is beyond listening as he goes softly to the door and cries out, in a harsh, commanding voice,

"Enter, O priests of Amon standing guard at the Great Wife's door!"

And obediently the doors swing open and they come in, side by side. And with what appears to be a single stroke, so swiftly and with such frightful vigor is it administered, the sword flashes like a snake in the light; a cry of horror goes up from the crowding watchers outside; and bumping and slithering across the reeds upon the floor, two bloody balls that once were heads bounce along until they come to rest, still twitching, at the farther wall.

"Take them away and clean up this mess!" he shouts in the same strident voice. And in ten minutes' time, while Tiye, Aye and I watch in horror and outside the trembling crowd shrinks back, slaves have entered and done their work, the bodies are gone, the heads bundled away, whitewash has been splashed on the bloodied walls, new sand and reeds cover the floor. The doors are closed. All is neat and orderly as before.

And again the room falls silent, and again the only sound is the tiny, fitful caterwauling of the newborn god.

Presently Tiye, her face still a mask of desolation but nature coming fast to her rescue, reaches down toward the child; and Pharaoh, coming gradually back to his senses, reaches down with equal tenderness, lifts him up and hands him to his mother. Tiye begins to nurse him and softly, gently, begins to cry, her tears falling unchecked on his pink, unknowing, oddly elongated little skull as he busily sucks. And so at last Pharaoh cries, too, and I cry, and Aye also; and for a few minutes we weep fiercely together, yet with a family tenderness that is somehow greatly strengthening. And so a semblance of peace returns.

But it is elusive, as we learn when my son finally speaks.

"I will have his temples," he says in a voice so soft it is almost crooning. "I will have his jewels and his gold, his cattle, his granaries, his farms and fertile lands. I will have his statue, which is richer than mine. I will melt it down. I will chisel out his name in all its places. I will drive him from the land of Kemet, and his memory shall be an execration, forever and ever and ever, for millions of millions of years. Go you, Aye, and tell Ramose I wish him here to carry out my order. Rouse up the army, prepare the generals, make ready all things. Amon is dead in Kemet, though he knows it not. Go, before he rallies. *Go!*"

And never have I admired my nephew Aye more, and never have I quite understood the infinite integrity and courage of his character as I understand it now: for quietly and simply, without bravado, dramatics, unnecessary emphasis or fear, he replies gently:

"No, Son of the Sun, I will not go. Nor will I let you perpetrate such madness."

Instantly Pharaoh is on his feet, his eyes wild again with rage. He starts for the sword, Tiye and I scream out our protests.

The sword lifts high but Aye does not move. Calm and unflinching he stares with a patient acquiescence, a curious innocence, into the eyes of Pharaoh; and it is an innocence that defeats him, for after a moment of terrible tension he suddenly flings the sword across the room and, dropping his head in his arms and wrapping them so tightly across his eyes that it is as though he is trying to obliterate the world, he bursts into great, wracking sobs that shudder through his body from some infinite well of despair that has no bottom.

And so we are again quiet for a time, until the storm is over.

At last it is. He lowers his arms, looks at us all from devastated eyes; steps forward and embraces Aye, kissing him on both cheeks; kisses me; returns slowly to Tiye and the child, still suckling peacefully; kisses them both; and presently asks, in a voice which, praise Amon—or whatever god may be guarding our House at this dread moment—is shaky but normal again,

"What, then, shall I do?"

Aye looks gravely at me, defers, and waits. My thoughts cease whirling, concentrate, coalesce.

"My son," I say, "the first thing—the very first—is to send an immediate offering to Amon in penance for the slaying of his priests. It must be generous and unstinting, and with it must go your humble apologies. Blame it on a sudden fit, a mad sickness, anything—but do not admit the real reason, and do not be hostile. That way you will appease the priests and lull them until you can find another day."

At this his expression, which had begun to turn stubborn as I spoke, becomes relaxed again.

"Then you think there will be another day? You approve, that there should be?"

"There must," I say firmly, and Aye and Tiye both echo with equal certainty: "There must."

"But you must wait," Aye says. "You must be careful.

This time you underestimated Amon. You must never do so again."

"It has cost me a son," he says with a dreadful bitterness. "I have learned my lesson."

"And I mine," Tiye says; and abruptly, as the full realization of what has happened strikes her anew, she begins to weep again. Pharaoh holds her tightly, murmurs broken, muffled, soothing words. Aye and I exchange glances, I nod: it is time to go.

"Majesty," Aye says quietly, "do not give up. You are right about Amon. He must be controlled. But indirectly —cleverly—shrewdly . . . I shall send the offering to the temple at once."

"Gold," he says, not lifting his head from Tiye's. "He loves gold. Not too little—not too much. I shall trust you to decide."

"It will be done," Aye says. "I shall see Your Majesties tomorrow, or when you need me."

"Thank you," he says. He leaves Tiye for a moment, embraces us both again.

"Mother," he says defiantly, "our House will survive."

"I have never doubted it, my son," I say. "But carefully—carefully."

"Yes," he says, and from the bed Tiye, her expression suddenly determined through her sorrow, nods firm agreement as we go.

Outside the door we find two soldiers now on guard, others standing rigid at attention all down the corridors. Priests of Amon are nowhere to be seen.

"The offering cannot arrive too soon," I say, and Aye nods grimly. He claps his hands. An aide to Ramose appears from a room down the hall. Before he can start forward, a woman whom I recognize to be from Aye's house comes hurrying in. She is crying, and instinctively, now, it is I who place a strengthening hand upon the arm of Aye.

"Master—" she begins in a breaking voice. "Master—"

"Hebmet!" he cries sharply, and dumbly she nods.

"But, master," she says through her tears, "you still have a daughter—a beautiful girl—"

"*Hebmet!*" he cries again, and it is the only time I have ever heard, or ever expect to hear, such naked emotion in the voice of my nephew Aye.

For a moment all is still in the hall. The woman withdraws, weeping; the soldiers stand sympathetic but not daring to be other than rigid and unmoving; the scribe hesitates.

Slowly my nephew lifts his head and speaks to the scribe in a voice husky but firm.

"Go, you, to the temple of Amon. Take with you a thousand in gold. Tell them Pharaoh apologizes humbly for the deaths of Amon's priests. Tell them he was seized with a madness, but it has passed and will never happen again. And then"—his voice breaks a little but he makes it firm and goes on—"find Ramose and tell him to announce to the people what he already knows. Tell him to send word to all the cities of Kemet and all its farms and all its people that the Crown Prince Tuthmose has been drowned accidentally in the Nile on his way from Memphis"—a startled groan goes up from the soldiers and is quickly carried out into the compound—"and that beginning at sunset the land of Kemet will be in seventy days' mourning for His Highness, who has returned"—he hesitates the tiniest second, then concludes strongly—"who has returned to the Aten, and will presently go to lie with his ancestors in the Valley of the Kings beneath the Western Peak. Go!"

The scribe, white-faced, bows and rushes away. I increase the pressure of my hand upon Aye's arm, as now, finally, after his work is done, he gives me a dazed, far-off glance and then nods and begins to move. We walk through the hushed corridors. Outside a new sound, uneasy, unhappy, disturbed, comes distantly: the soldiers have spread the news, and the word of Tuthmose's death is out.

"My dear," I say as we reach the place where our paths diverge to his villa on one side of the compound, and to my small palace on the other, "let me come to your house and keep you company tonight."

He cannot speak, but only nods. And so we walk hand in hand along the empty pathway while Ra glares pitilessly down in the blinding afternoon, and in the land of Kemet the people both mourn and rejoice for the House of Thebes, which this day has known great joy and great sorrow and has seen the world change, to move in new directions no one yet can foresee.

Ramose

TONIGHT I AM TIRED and I am sad, but I must not admit it.

For look you, what a great man I am and what a great office do I hold!

My distant predecessor Rehk-mi-re, Vizier to Tuthmose III (Life, health, prosperity!), described himself thus:

"There was nothing of which he was ignorant in heaven, in earth, or in any part of the underworld."

I do not claim quite such omnipotence, being kept sensibly modest by many things including my own nature and the constant advice of my busy half brother, Amonhotep, Son of Hapu: but I do much, and know much.

This is what the Good Gods advise those of whom they appoint Vizier:

"Look after the office of the Vizier and watch over everything that is done in it, for it is the constitution of the entire land. As to the office of the Vizier, indeed, it is not pleasant; no, it is as bitter as its reputation. He is one who must give no special consideration to princes or councilors nor make slaves of any people whatsoever. . . . Look upon him whom you know as on him you do not know, the one who approaches your person as the one who is far from your house. . . . Pass over no petitioner without hearing his case. . . . Show anger to no man wrongfully and be angry only at that which deserves anger. Instill fear of yourself that you may be held in fear, for a true prince is a prince who is feared. The distinction of a prince is that he does justice. But if a man instills fear in an excessive manner, there being in him a modicum of injustice in the estimation of man, they do not say of him: 'That is a just man.' . . . What one expects of the conduct of the Vizier is the performance of justice."

This is my office and my charge: to do all things evenhandedly, and all things well; to assist Pharaoh in all the daily details of the kingdom and Empire; to hear litigations over land, to establish and enforce the laws by which herds, flocks, harvest, fish, game, trees, ponds, canals, wells are taxed; to determine justice in civil cases; to dispense the common law, which is not law as it is written in books, but law as it falls from the lips of Pharaoh, derived from his three divine qualities of *hu*— authority; *sia*—perception; and *ma'at*—justice. And derived also, of course, from the *hu*, *sia* and *ma'at* of all his predecessor's, back into the mists of time to Menes (Life, health, prosperity!), first ruler of the Two Lands and fountainhead of all the wisdom of all the Good Gods since.

Such is my position: overseeing all, guiding all, knowing all.

For the first time since Pharaoh appointed me Vizier of Upper Kemet, I wish tonight I did not hold this post. Tonight I know too much, of death and birth and tragedy. Tonight for the first time I feel old. Intimations that Anubis and the judges of the underworld are waiting surround me in my silent room, in this palace sleeping uneasily now in strange mixture of jubilation and sorrow. I would not mind being back with Amonhotep, my half brother, in our home town of Athribis in the Delta, playing innocently along the mudbanks of the Nile, long before our native brilliance called us both to the attention of the Great House and started us upward on our rise to power in the land of Kemet.

Tonight the Palace sleeps: all is quiet. The family, with all its heavy burdens, has long since gone to rest. In the painted corridors and down the long palm-lined ave-

nues the soldiers stand at attention; in hushed tones the
guard is changed at the usual four-hour intervals.

The savage heat of Ra's full vigor in the afternoon has
faded into the gentle yet still oppressive exhaustion of
the summer night. A soft wind blows off the Red Land.
High above, Khons in his silver boat transports the souls
of the dead across the sky; his cold white light shines down
to cast strange shadows on pillar, cornice, tree and massive temple, on obelisk and monstrous statue. Even the
river is quiet now, only lapping gently at the dock: all
boats tied up, all sailors snug ashore in their stopping
places. Once in a great while the soft hooting of an owl
breaks the silence. Which god or goddess inhabits his
furry form tonight? I do not know, but bow my head and
wish well whoever it may be. For it is not wise to antagonize the gods of Kemet, who are everywhere, in everything, most present when we see them least.

It is not wise to antagonize the gods: but it has been
done, and now I suspect, as I patiently write down the final
records of the major happenings of this one day in
Kemet's eternal history, that tonight the Palace sleeps but
its principal residents do not. I can imagine, for I know
them well, how the Good God and the Great Wife still
lie weeping in one another's arms, even as the gentle fret-
ting of the newborn god at their side reminds them that
life does not stop when one life stops. In her little palace
in a far corner of the compound, Gilukhipa probably lies
awake, staring at the ceiling, not knowing whether to be
pleased or sad at the strange events of the strange House
to which statecraft has assigned her, unwilling but helpless, for as long as she may live. In the house of Aye
in another quarter, the good man, yielding to open emotion
for once in his life, weeps for gracious Hebmet, dead too
young in giving birth, while at his side the Queen Mother
from time to time wrings out cloths in cold water and
places them with loving tenderness across his eyes. In
another room the young wet nurse Tey suckles the baby
girl, whose occasional gurglings remind them, too, that
continuity survives in change. Only Sitamon in her little
doll's palace will be soundly asleep in the innocence of

childhood: troubled while awake but instantly forgetful of it all the moment her head hit the pillow.

Sitamon and one other rest soundly tonight. Down the silent river behind the secret walls of Karnak, cold Aanen presides in the vast stone room, dimly lit by tapers flickering in the Red Land's breath, where on a catafalque the body of a little boy lies sleeping. The priests are preparing to place a heart-scarab on his breast to preserve the seat of life, to draw out his brains through his nostrils, to remove his entrails and other organs, to place them in four canopic jars in which they will be preserved forever, and to fill all his cavities with natron, that resinous material which for the next seventy days will mummify his body and make it ready for its final journey to the Valley of the Kings.

Is Aanen satisfied this night? I suspect not, for Amon-Ra won this battle, but both Aanen and I know this Pharaoh and the Great Wife. The war will go on.

And the five million people of Kemet, in all the cities, towns, villages, farms and empty places, all up and down the life-giving river where Hapi holds sway? Many sleep, I suspect, innocent and unknowing as yet of what has happened here, and destined, perhaps to be uncaring, save in a remote and general way, when they do know. But many others will be lying awake as Khons' silver boat passes slowly overhead, and in its lovely and impersonal light they will be greatly aware and greatly disturbed, and they will be wondering, as I wonder: What will this day mean for the House of Thebes? What does it portend for Kemet? What will the gods weave for us all as this day's ripples extend and spread outward in their slow, inexorable development down the years?

Eh, well. I do not know. I know only that the Vizier must continue his work, whatever. So I take my writing brush and my roll of papyrus, and on it I inscribe:

That on this day, on his way from Memphis to Thebes, there died:

Tuthmose V, Crown Prince, High Priest of Ptah.

And there was born, in the Palace of Malkata, to the Great Wife Tiye:

Amonhotep IV, the new Crown Prince.

And also in Malkata, to Hebmet, wife of Aye, a daughter, named by her mother, just before she gave up her life for the child:

Nefer-ti-ti.

Which means: *A Beautiful Woman Has Come.*

BOOK II

Education of a God

1377 B.C.

  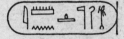

King of the North and South   Nefer–Kheperu–Ra   Son of the Sun   Prince of Thebes, AMONHOTEP IV

Royal Spouse   Chief Wife   NEFERTITI

Gilukhipa

Now ALL IS POMP AND CEREMONY in the Palace, and once again, as on so many boring occasions in the past fifteen years, we must all troop ourselves out to see and be seen. Today the strange horse-faced boy is to become both God and married. It is almost too much for one glorious day in this glorious household. Can I stand the ineffable joy and excitement? Or shall I swoon completely away, as I have often thought of doing in the midst of some ceremony, just to find out what my marvelous husband and his smug Great Wife would do about it? Probably order me summarily swept into the Nile, there to become the plaything of Hapi and the speedy meal of Sebek the crocodile god. A fitting end, they would tell one another, laughing the while. Poor old Gilukhipa has finally brightened somebody's life for a few seconds, anyway!

Well: it is not as though I have not tried. When I first came to this country, a girl of fourteen, political pawn of my father, I did my best to please the little brown man who greeted me. He was God, supreme ruler, Pharaoh, the living Horus, Lord of the Two Lands, the King, the Great Bull, and all the other mighty things his titularies tell us he is. It was not my fault that I was almost a foot taller than he and plain in the bargain. The contrast brought immediate titters, hastily suppressed, when I disembarked at the landing of Malkata from the elaborate state barge on which I had spent almost two months coming down from Mittani. First my three hundred and seventeen ladies and I had been obliged to travel overland two weeks by donkey caravan, to the sea which they call in Kemet "the Great Green." Then I had been hidden away

behind curtained doorways while my ladies were free
to gambol about on the decks of our flotilla enjoying the
fresh air and sunlight. I was forced to stay inside, away
from the eyes of the impious, while we hugged the coast
slowly down past Phoenicia, Palestine, Edom and Sinai
to the Delta, and so into the onrushing currents and slowly
winding passages of the great river with which even I
have come to feel a mysterious bond, in my years here.
Still I was not to reveal myself, for I was to be a surprise
to the people of Kemet.

Certainly I was a surprise to him: I could tell from
the instantly suppressed flash of anger in his eyes that
somebody was going to hear about it, and not in a friendly
way. Obviously they had not told him of my height and
my plainness, though it was clearly the height that rankled
most. "You are tall!" he blurted out—the first and last
time he ever said anything purely spontaneous to me. "The
better to see Kemet, Majesty," I replied calmly, for I
am not a daughter of Mittani for nothing, and was no
more impressed with all their fuss and feathers then than
I am now, though I soon came to see the necessity as a
method of statecraft. "This," he said, and already his
tone dismissed me, "is the Great Wife Tiye. I commend
you to her friendship, and she to yours." Another little
figure, not so brown as he, much prettier than I, stepped
daintily forward and held out her hand. I did not know
exactly what to do, so I bent low and kissed it. This proved
to be right, for she smiled graciously, drew me close,
and kissed me on both cheeks in return. "All hail Queen
Gilukhipa!" she cried in that deceptively soft and silvery
voice that nonetheless rose with a startling power and
carried clearly over the river to the massed thousands on
the eastern bank. A great answering shout dutifully went
up. Flanked by the two of them, I was escorted into the
Palace.

Next day the formal marriage ceremony took place.
That night he visited me dutifully, and dutifully he continued to do so, sporadically, for the next three or four
years. I never conceived and bore him a child, and presently our relations lapsed into a grudging informality in

which I have been neither consulted nor confided in by them, and also not mistreated, either—neither fish nor fowl, neither friend nor enemy—just Queen Gilukhipa, paraded at ceremonies, given my own small palace and court within the compound of Malkata, attended by the small handful of my ladies who did not soon marry and melt away into the ranks of the nobility. Left to my own devices, principally. And bored— bored—bored.

So to amuse myself I have made my lifetime study the House of Thebes. There are many about who have done the same—the Councilor Aye, for instance, constantly gathering new honors, titles and powers as the years go by . . . the Queen Mother Mutemwiya, at fifty-seven gradually shriveling into a little wizened gnome like a scarab beetle in the sand, but faithfully prodding and pushing the dung ball of her family up the hill of years . . . Amonhotep the Scribe, Son of Hapu, into everything as always, working closely with Aye and gathering almost as many honors . . . faithful Ramose, growing gray but still Vizier of Upper Kemet . . . the bitter, ever watching priest Aanen and his white-robed, twittering cohorts in the temples of Amon . . . the soldier Kaires, now serving far up the Nile near the Second Cataract as chief scribe for all of Pharaoh's armies in Upper Kemet—an unusually high post for a man of thirty, but he is an unusual man and a friend of mine (not lover, though the gossip claims it. Pharaoh's queens do not have lovers; some of them do not even have Pharaoh) . . . and the Queen-Princess Sitamon, also my friend and somehow managing to be her usual placid and cheerful self even though her life too is one of boredom as she leaves girlhood and moves on into her twenties and a future as empty as my own. (Gossip never touches her and Kaires, thanks to the shield I provide them willingly with my well-known friendship for him. I wish them well, feeling sorry for them, too, because of course nothing can ever come of it save a few scattered, furtive meetings over the years—and Pharaoh's terrible vengeance should he ever find out. But we are all clever people. We have a pact that he will not. And he will not.)

The study of the House of Thebes, then, is the lifework
of Gilukhipa of Mittani, third Queen of the Two Lands
after Sitamon and the Great Wife Tiye—who remains
all-powerful as always, as much the ruler of the Two
Lands and the Two Lands' ruler as she has always been.
She is supremely shrewd, that one, though she no longer
has quite the air of serene assurance that she wears on
their joint colossal statue that stands at the entrance to
the temple he is building to Amon at Luxor, just up the
river from the vast complex of Karnak. She has given
him three more children, now, two of them princesses
stillborn, the third the boy Smenkh-ka-ra, who is so beautiful he might as well be a girl and already, to my mind,
gives some indications that he probably is. He is too
delicate and cloying for my taste: I find him sticky, like
the sweets with which all in Kemet love to complete their
meals. But he is of course very popular with his parents
and with the people, so one dissembles in this instance
as one does in so many others. And he has one virtue,
I suppose, at least in his parents' eyes: he tags along
after his brother like a little shadow all the time. So the
Crown Prince has at least one unthinking, uncritical, absolutely devoted follower, in any event.

That he does not have many of these, aside from
Smenkh-ka-ra is, I suspect, one of the things that has
brought the lines of tension and care that are beginning to
mar noticeably the heretofore smugly placid and untroubled countenance of his mother. For most of her life, particularly since her parents, Yuya and Tuya—both now
mummified and resting peacefully in their sarcophagi in
the Valley of the Nobles a couple of miles north of here
—cleverly maneuvered her forward to become the wife of
Amonhotep III (Life, health, prosperity!), everything
went exactly as she wanted it . . . until the day she gave
birth to Amonhotep IV. And that has become another
story.

For the boy's first nine or ten years, everything appeared normal. He was a handsome and well-formed child,
obviously intelligent; quick to perceive, quick to understand, quick to learn. At age five he was placed in the
hands of Amonhotep, Son of Hapu, who has supervised

that intensive and thorough education that is given all heirs to the Double Crown. Kemet's Pharaohs are working rulers, and with few exceptions most have been able men, educated far above the average run of their subjects, excellently trained for future duties and responsibilities.

So it was with the Crown Prince until at some point—coming on so gradually and unexpectedly in his tenth year that, looking back, none of us can say exactly, "This was the day"—there began those curious physical and psychological changes which set him apart from ordinary men as all Pharaohs are set apart by their divinity; I mean set apart in ways strange, unpredictable, unprecedented, impossible to hide and, to the superstitious, almost terrible.

I have said that he was physically well formed and handsome as a child, and so he was, aside only from the enlarged, almost platycephalic skull which seems to have crept, for some unknown reason, into the line of Thebes. Although hardly anyone (certainly not I) saw the two stillborn princesses, so quickly and secretly were they whisked away to the mummifiers and hustled to their tombs, word gets around in the Palace, particularly to those like myself who listen carefully. Their skulls, too, had the odd enlargement; and so too—though Tiye keeps the sidelock of youth carefully wound around the top of his head in an unusual fashion she refers to with a challenging laugh (yet who could possibly challenge her?) as "my new style for sons"—does that of Smenkhkara. Throughout Kemet I hear the whisper goes, in the mud-brick villages, the busy bazaars and crowded cities, that Amon is angry with the House of Thebes; and though he dismisses the idea with a scornful laugh, I think my husband suspects so, uneasily, too . . . as so he should, considering everything.

Greater change than this, however, had been reserved for the Crown Prince; and were he intrinsically a more lovable child, which I do not consider him to be, I should feel a genuine sympathy and sadness for him. As it is, I feel some, though his attitude toward me has always been remote and no real communication exists between us.

But it is impossible not to have some regrets for his sake
—and a secret and profound gratification for my own.

For the first time since I came here I have been glad
that I have been unable to bear Pharaoh's children.

Almost imperceptibly, as I say, yet still so swiftly that
within two months we were all aware of it, there began in
his tenth year a curious transformation of the child
Amonhotep IV. His hips began to broaden, grow heavy,
sag like an overweight woman's; his belly began to spill
forward over the edge of his kilt like a middle-aged
man's; his genitals, I am told, almost disappeared in rolls
of fat; his arms became spindly; his neck and face
seemed almost hourly to elongate. "Horse-faced" I have
called him, and such is the common description—only
whispered, never, ever, stated in his parents' presence—
used by everyone in the Palace and throughout Kemet.

Tragically, out of this increasingly strange body, his
fine, intelligent eyes have continued to stare; and gradually, as he realized how different he has become, there
has entered into them something veiled, secretive, self-
protective, withdrawn—yet at the same time harsh, imperious, arrogant and commanding.

Kaires, I think, was the first to put his finger on it, one
time three years ago when he was in Thebes on official
business and had come, under the guise of our friendship,
to my palace to be alone with Sitamon. Later they came
to my bedroom where I had dismissed the servants and
prepared with my own hands a nourishing meal. The talk
turned, as it inevitably does in the Palace, and I am sure
all over the Empire wherever thinking people gather, to
the Crown Prince. Kaires frowned, deeply troubled.

"I think we have here," he said slowly, "the makings
of a fanatic. May Amon and the gods help us if this proves
true when he becomes Pharaoh."

"My brother may never become Pharaoh," Sitamon said
in a voice equally troubled. "The disease may continue, to
his death. Which," she added, and her voice became both
pensive and sad, "might be better for him—and for all
of us."

But her forebodings—unfortunately, I agree, for both

him and the Two Lands—have not been borne out. The
disease did not go on to his death; soon after our conversation, as mysteriously and suddenly as it began, it was
arrested. After a year of discreet but intensive observation
by everyone, it became apparent that there would be no
more changes. A grotesque—but highly intelligent and, in
some curious way, not unattractive grotesque—was destined to live on as Crown Prince.

And today, at the command of his father, the second
part of his sister's prophecy also fails. Today he becomes Co-Regent, Pharaoh, God—and, of all things, husband. For I was not entirely accurate when I said that
his only devoted follower is little Smenkhkara. Nefer-ti-ti
loves him also, and apparently quite genuinely so. She
must have done from a very early age, not to be repelled
by the changes. If anything, they seem to have made her
more protective and more tender toward him. It is, as
Kaires, Sitamon and I agree, the thing that may prove his
salvation and that of Kemet. Much rides on the lovely child
whose dying mother Hebmet, with a prophetic accuracy
greater than most mothers are capable of at such a time,
named her "A Beautiful Woman Has Come."

For she *is* beautiful, Nefertiti: there is no denying it.
She too is different—a trace of platycephalic skull there
also, carefully hidden under wigs and the oddly shaped
"crown" she affects. (Could that particular flaw have
come down through her father Aye to his children, through
his sister Tiye to her children, a last bequest of Yuya and
Tuya lying quietly in their tombs?) But in her the difference is a refined and beautifully structured beauty almost
unique in the land of Kemet; at least, in the rarefied
world in which we live. Now and again, in some mud-
brick village along the river, in some crowded market
place in Thebes or Memphis, I have seen a girl, a boy,
a startling vision of perfection, gleam suddenly from the
crowd and as swiftly disappear. Such beauty does exist in
Kemet, here and there, most unexpectedly; but it is very
rare in royal and noble houses. Where it exists among the
peasantry, it will swiftly wither and be forgotten with all
the anonymous millions who till the soil and grow the

food and build the temples and do the work that supports the royal world. But in Nefertiti, I believe, it will live forever.

Soon after her mother's death, Aye married the wet nurse Tey, who I understand will today be officially designated "nurse, stepmother and tutor to the Queen" as soon as Nefertiti is married and crowned. She is a pleasant woman, not overly bright but placid, comfortable, completely devoted to her husband, her stepdaughter, and the two children she and Aye have had together, the girl Mut-nedj-met and the boy Nakht-Min. She is also friendly with Kaires, which gives me a conduit of information from that household. Aye encourages Kaires' familiarity with his family, as he has encouraged most things having to do with Kaires and his career. Indeed, were it not for Aye, Kaires himself acknowledges he would not have risen so far so fast in Pharaoh's service. He has a quite genuine liking for the Councilor, who is a forbidding man in many respects but a most worthy one; and the Councilor and his family reciprocate.

So we have watched, Kaires, Sitamon and I, the growth of Nefertiti and the predestined ways in which she and the Crown Prince have been directed together by the shrewd if not always subtle hands of their parents. Born on the same day—that day fifteen years ago when the first Crown Prince, Tuthmose V, was murdered by the priests of Amon, thus hardening the feud between my husband and the priesthood into the pattern it has followed ever since—the children were obviously fated to marry should they both reach marriageable age. Aye, Tiye and Pharaoh, in fact, must have decided this within hours after the two were born; and all their actions have looked to that objective since.

In keeping with the unprecedented pattern established by Pharaoh when he raised the Great Wife to a position virtually equal to his own on the throne of Kemet, Nefertiti and the Crown Prince have been treated with the same equality in their education, their training and their general upbringing. Both have sat at the feet of Amonhotep, Son of Hapu, that busy man whose infinite wisdom, so fervently hailed by others, I sometimes fail to perceive. Both have been thoroughly schooled in the history of the Eighteenth Dynasty and of all the dynasties preceding, back to Menes (Life, health, prosperity!) of the First. They have been taken to Sakkara to see the vast city of the dead where many of their ancestors lie. They have been taken to Giza to see the pyramids and Harmakhis, the Sphinx—one thousand, four hundred and fifty-six years old this year, majestic and moving as always in his ancient grandeur and mystery. They have been given instruction in the rights, duties and responsibilities of Pharaoh and his consort. They have been shown to the people together time and time again. They have even had a joint "household" set up for them, with nurses, servants, personal attendants, even their own cook.

Is it any wonder that since the age of four they have wandered about the Palace hand in hand, or that between them an indissoluble bond of love and trust should have grown?

For a time we thought, Kaires, Sitamon and I, that the changes in the boy might frighten Nefertiti, drive her away, make the fulfillment of her destiny an intolerable agony instead of the natural outgrowth of the years of careful intimacy arranged by their parents. We underestimated the work of Pharaoh, Aye and the Great Wife. We knew they doubted, too, and worried frantically. (Tiye's wrinkles and strained expression, begun with Tuthmose's death, grew deeper. By now they are so indelible that she will never lose them, for all her pride and cleverness.) For a time the parents were as uncertain as we all were. But the Crown Prince only gave his bland, enigmatic smile and Nefertiti only clung to him closer. Sympathy and pity have given an even deeper dimension to her love. And so, today, all comes right for the planners—in that sector, at least.

In others, I am not so sure. Certain aspects of the children's education have been highly secret, yet one speculates with some accuracy after having had as many years as I with the freedom to observe. My husband's feud with Amon has grown more embittered with the years, even if he has constructed a new pylon, a massive ornamental gate, at the entrance to the temple of Amon at Karnak; the start of a new hypostyle colonnade leading to the ancient mystery; new temples to Amon's wife Mut and their son Khons; and even though he is now into the seventh year of building a huge new temple to Amon along the riverbank at Luxor, a mile to the north of Karnak, with a new avenue of ram-headed sphinxes to lead to it. These are gestures, engaging thousands of workmen, costing millions: but I suspect his heart does not forgive Amon, any more than Amon forgives him. I wonder what the children have been told about this, and what it will mean when the Crown Prince inevitably acquires, along with his status as Co-Regent and his new title of Pharaoh, a power and influence that will be, in many ways, the equal of his father's.

Equal—and perhaps greater. For my husband is not a well man these days, and there is more behind the co-regency than the simple desire to confirm his heir in the authority that will someday be fully his.

It has become the fashion in recent years to refer to Pharaoh as "Amonhotep the Magnificent," and so he is; but aside from the care he has devoted to the upbringing of the children, an increasingly listless participation in necessary ceremonies, and an occasional languid passage down the river to Memphis and back, the magnificence has become mostly self-indulgence, the crown an excuse for selfish inattention to duty. Were it not for Tiye—who must be given credit, for all that I do not like her—for Aye, for Ramose, for Amonhotep, Son of Hapu, and for such rising younger functionaries as Kaires and his friends, the Empire would be in parlous shape today. My father King Shu-ttarna writes me from Mittani, warning of disaffection in this place, unease in that: there is a sense of things coming unloosed at the center. Self-indulgence may have gone on too long, selfishness and languor may have been permitted to gain too much the upper hand. And yet none of us in the Palace can find it in our hearts to blame Pharaoh too much, because he is not, as I say, a well man.

Lately he has begun to suffer occasional intense pain from abscessed teeth; a growing corpulence has blurred and engulfed the small, tightly muscled brown body I first knew; a near paralysis sometimes seems to hamper the movement of his limbs. He no longer hunts: more and more he is carried about on litters and covered thrones, when he shows himself at all. He is only thirty-seven, yet already Amonhotep III (Life, health, prosperity!) shows troubling signs of becoming an old man. It is the hope that the co-regency will correct this, that it will provide the necessary youth and vigor to prop up a flagging man— that it will restore the center.

And yet what kind of a co-regency will it be?

A grotesque to help a cripple!

Is this to be the salvation of the House of Thebes?

I must linger no more on such gloomy thoughts. It is nearing the third quarter of morning. Soon my ladies will be here to help me dress (warmly, for it is a chill winter day) for the twin ceremonies of the Crown Prince and his lovely love. Once again we must all go down the river, as we have so often in these empty, endless years. This time it will not be to the ancient temple at Karnak: this time my husband wishes the ceremonies to take place at his new, half-finished temple at Luxor. Again, it is a defiance of Aanen and his fellows, who wish all ceremonies to be held at Karnak, always.

The body wastes, the mind at times seems wandering: but the hatred remains.

We shall see how it flowers in the son and in the daughter-in-law.

Grotesque or no, Amon may yet have met his match in our strange Crown Prince.

Aanen

My SISTER ASKED ME—nay, commanded, in her imperious way which becomes more overbearing as Pharaoh becomes less interested in the necessities of governing and permits more and more power to slip into her willing hands—that I make the ceremonies this day "absolute perfection."

Other than this, she gave me no instructions. I concluded that it was simply another challenge, another testing. For me, "absolute perfection" means the highest reflection of the power and grandeur of Amon. For her, I know it means the less to do with Amon the better. She was simply giving me another of those endless challenges they always fling at me from the Palace, to see whether I would dare glorify Amon, whom I know they fear and despise. She obviously thought I would be afraid to do so, and so would devise some empty show of pomp and frivolity in which Amon would be forced to take a secondary place to meaningless spectacle. Once again she underestimated me, as they all have all through these years when the Palace has been unrelenting in its indirect but incessant pressures against the god I serve.

I have ordered "absolute perfection," and it is a perfection that will cry "AMON!" and "POWER!" in tones so loud that even the Great Wife, my ailing brother-in-law and all their sycophants of a sickly Court will bow down in awe before the great god's majesty.

One thing they obviously thought would be a handicap for me. Pharaoh roused from his slothful lethargy (brought on by all these years of dissipation, luxury and self-indulgence) to add his own command: the ceremonies of co-regency and marriage for their monstrous boy should not be held in the ancient holy of holies at Karnak where Ra first stood upon the hill and created life by spilling his own seed when the great waters receded. They should be held in the new half-finished temple Pharaoh is building for Amon at Luxor.

"Building for Amon."

Busily he runs about, adding a hypostyle column at Karnak, it is true, but spending far more to add endless bits and pieces to the complex at Medinet Habu, which now includes not only Malkata but a vast mortuary temple to himself, to be guarded by two vast colossi of himself, and which he has now formally named—Amon, note this!—"The House of Neb-Ma'at-Ra Shines Like Aten."

And Amon is supposed to believe he worships Amon!

"Building for Amon," indeed!

A bitter jest, in my estimation, employing thousands who should be devoted exclusively to glorifying the only true temple, at Karnak; costing millions that should be going directly into Amon's coffers, if tribute is what he wishes to pay—which of course he does not, as we all know in the Family, however much the show may persuade the people of Kemet. The people of Kemet by and large are ignorant fools, fit only to till the soil and cultivate the annual bounty of the Nile. But they have one great quality which the House of Thebes will not destroy in them, does not dare destroy in them, could not destroy in them, no matter what. They worship—they venerate— they love—*they fear*—the god Amon. And nothing from the Palace can change that fact, or will ever change it. Amon, raised to his pinnacle by the House of Thebes, at once their creation and their creator, has been supreme too long. His power, his temples, his lands, his gold, his cattle, his priests, his spies are everywhere.

It will take more than my disloyal family, more than their weirdling son, to change that fact.

So I have accepted the Great Wife's challenge. I have devised the ceremony this day to reflect what Amon truly is, the extent of his influence, the magnitude of his power.

Not forty, as is customary, but three hundred white-robed priests will greet the Family when they land at Luxor—and not just priests from Amon, either. I have enlisted friends from Ptah, from Sebek and Buto and Ra-Herakhty and Isis and Osiris and the rest. We are all threatened: we must all stand together. Not ten or twenty trumpets, gongs and cymbals will herald their coming, but two hundred. Not ten or fifty flags will fly from the half-completed pylon proclaiming Amon, but a thousand from every pillar, every cornice, every stage in the progress from landing to inner temple, proclaiming Amon and all the gods. And after they land, before the ceremony can begin, we will delay them and hold them up and make them wait, while still more hundreds of priests of all persuasions, to the blare of still more trumpets, gongs and cymbals, bear the sacred barque with the golden statue of the god down the sacred mile-long avenue from Karnak to Luxor.

Only then, when everyone has been suitably impressed with Amon and his fellow gods, only then, when they have had to wait—and wait—and wait, shivering beneath the chill winter skies which today look down upon the sacred precincts, threatening rain—and may Amon deliver even that upon them!—only then will they be allowed to proceed within and hold their ceremony.

Only then will my misshapen nephew become Co-Regent, Pharaoh and God; only then will my luckless beautiful niece take to her side for life her deformed, her ludicrous love. Only then will they be able to imagine, poor fools, that they can finally do to Amon what they have secretly dreamed of doing all these years.

And only then will Amon have proved once again that the dream is hopeless and that only he, borne high on the people's love, and aided by his fellow gods, is really supreme in the land of Kemet.

I stand here in Luxor in the uncompleted hypostyle hall, beneath the dark and lowering sky. My high priest's leopard skin flaps against my shivering thighs in the sharpening breeze. About me hundreds of priests of all per-

reliable, highly intelligent, highly informed, aware of all that moves in the land of Kemet, even from my distant post at Semneh near the Second Cataract. I make it my business to know: I have my friends in the Palace, throughout the army and in the temples. I travel, I come to Thebes often on army business, now and again I am permitted to go as far north as my favorite Memphis on special inspection trips. I keep an eye on things.

Pharaoh—Queen Tiye—Aye—my oldest friend and mentor in Kemet, Amonhotep, Son of Hapu—all rely upon me. So, too, does Gilukhipa, whom I dare to trust and who, in gratitude for faithful friendship in her lonely life, trusts me as well. So, too, does Sitamon, whom I love but can never marry. This does not diminish the love, which, thanks to Gilukhipa, flourishes. I take great risks in trusting Gilukhipa with this, I know; but I discovered long ago that to beget trust, one gives it.

The daughter of Mittani and I have struck a good bargain. It has been as my friend Amonhotep said to me on that day fifteen years ago when so many things began that we are all still playing out: "Stay wide of Gilukhipa unless you can use her to advance your own ends." I did not think then that I had "ends" in Kemet—or if I did, they were vague, unformulated, hardly suspected by me— half-dreamed, half-glimpsed, swirling and unreal.

I see many of them more clearly now.

One thing I see very clearly indeed on this brisk and uncomfortable morning when the wind blows sharply off the Nile and we all shiver in Kemet's coldest winter in recent years: I have been very wise to make two other friends, as well. My big-brotherly companionship when they were tiny—my little notes and gifts and visits as they grew older—my subtly changing attitude, moving deliberately from big-brotherhood to the friendship of equals, to the still easy yet dutifully respectful humility of the trusted servant-familiar, as they grew into adolescence and moved inevitably toward power—all have been exactly right. The Crown Prince and Nefertiti have served my ends, too; and so, I trust, they will continue to do after today's ceremonies when he becomes Co-Regent, Pharaoh, and God, and she becomes the new Chief Wife, second only to Tiye and destined, I believe, to wield in time an even greater power.

As they rise, so do I intend to rise: because, to put it quite simply, Kemet needs me. The misgivings I had about this House of Thebes when I first arrived have been borne out. It is a difficult House, uneasy at the apex of the power of the Eighteenth Dynasty. Its head is already an ailing man, though only thirty-seven; its heir is a tragically misshapen youth, deformed by who knows what vengeance of ancestors or of Amon; its real ruler is an indomitable woman who yet cannot control her brother Aanen and his priests, nor keep intact without Pharaoh's help, a society and an Empire which seem to be suffering from a growing internal decay. Order in the land is increasingly challenged by many who escape unpunished, order in the world tips erratically as Kemet tips. How much longer can it continue thus without true disaster coming upon us?

These are most secret thoughts I do not discuss with Gilukhipa or with Sitamon, nor with Amonhotep, Son of Hapu, nor with the Councilor Aye, though I know these last two in particular share them fully. They are not the thoughts one dares speak except to one's closest intimate. Fortunately I have one, and we engage in much thought and discussion as to how Kemet may best be saved. He is my second in command, my friend, my almost-brother, whose fortune is now committed for life to mine, who will rise or fall with me as Amon ordains. We are bound together inextricably by our love and respect for one another, but even more by our love and concern for Kemet. Together, I think, we will save her, working with all others—and I know they are many—who feel the same.

You will remember the young Theban soldier, scarcely a year younger than I, who stumbled exhausted into the midst of the ceremonies at Karnak on that fateful day to bring word of the death of Tuthmose V. You will remember I took him to Aye's house for safekeeping. There we became friends, encouraged by Aye, who quietly encourages so many things. The Councilor perceived in him the same careful, diligent qualities, the same deep love

for Kemet, as existed in myself. It was Aye who saw to
it that the young soldier was assigned to me as my principal assistant when I completed my training as scribe and
received (also with Aye's help) my first assignment with
the local garrison in Thebes. It was Aye who suggested
to Pharaoh that he keep us together as a team when I
moved on to my happy years with the garrison in Memphis,
my following assignment in Aswan, and now, in these
past three years, my major office as chief scribe of all
Pharaoh's armies in Upper Kemet.

"You and your friend," the Councilor said to me once,
"are two sides of the same coin. Kemet needs you, and
you must stay together so that you can help her."

So we have, and it is to Ramesses alone that I confide
these thoughts I have, which today, in spite of the gloomy
overcast while Ra withholds himself and makes us shiver,
are somewhat lighter and somewhat brighter than they
have been in recent months. For we are two who do not
regard with misgivings the rise of Amonhotep IV and
Nefertiti. We are among those who, despite his handicaps, regard the Crown Prince as the great hope for a
resurgent Empire and a glorious new era of strength and
stability for Kemet.

Despite his handicaps—or because of them? Who is to
say exactly? He was such a handsome and well-favored
child to begin with: and then the horror descended. There
are some, like Gilukhipa, who say that this has turned
him inward, made him dangerous, a potential fanatic who
might do harmful things to Kemet. I remember an occasion three years ago when I myself once voiced such
fears. Yet with them I expressed the qualification that
this might not occur were Amon and the other gods to
come to his aid, and to Kemet's. Gilukhipa still holds to
her original fears, but Ramesses and I, watching closely
as has everyone around him, have gradually changed our
opinion. I am not so worried now, for I think the burden
he has to bear, while naturally making him shy, and
suspicious to some extent of those better favored, has also
strengthened his character in ways most subtle and most
profound. It has seemed to us that in the past few months,

as his father's intention to make him Co-Regent has become known and published throughout the land—on another of those handsome large stone scarabs Pharaoh is so fond of, and so loves to scatter broadside to his people on major occasions—the effect has been to make the Crown Prince more steady, more secure, less bothered by his physical deformities, more inclined to embrace necessity as virtue.

"You still have pity in your eyes," he said to me during my last visit a month ago, unfortunately catching me at it. "You still shrink a little. You must be stronger than that, Kaires: I am. These hips, this belly, these arms, this neck, this long, brooding, solemn visage my countrymen love to call 'horse-faced'—oh yes, they do, I hear these things!" he interjected sharply at my raised hand of protest—"these will be my principal means of governance. I am set apart already by divinity: how much more impressive I am now that there is no one—*no one*, Kaires, in all of Kemet—who looks anything like me. I am unique. All Pharaohs are unique among their fellows by divinity. I am unique in addition because I *look* unique. It gives me an extra strength. You will see."

Bravado, desperation, compensation—what? I could not tell, carefully though I examined his expression as he spoke. I do not know now, for sure. But I prefer to think, and Ramesses agrees, that he is finally at peace with himself, that he is no longer intimidated by his deformities: that he is ready to go ahead.

For this, great credit must go to his parents, to Aye, to all of us who have loyally supported and encouraged him. Most of all, it must go to Nefertiti, who has most loved, supported and encouraged him. We live in a time of strong women, in the Eighteenth Dynasty: Hatshepsut—Tuya—Mutemwiya—Tiye—Sitamon—Gilukhipa. This frail little girl who bears in her way, too, a burden, the burden of great and unusual beauty, may yet prove to be the strongest of them all.

I think there was a time, quite brief, when she doubted; when the habit of childhood love, growing slowly into adolescent adoration and then into something more mature, almost broke under the strain of the changes we could all see occurring before our concerned and helpless eyes. But she never spoke of it to anyone, so far as I know, and least of all to him. Her love only became fiercer, more protective, more profound, her sympathy for his ideas more adamant and unyielding. A few of those ideas they have expressed to me, in very guarded fashion. As nearly as I have been able to gather, they have something to do with "strengthening Amon by strengthening the other gods."

This seems to me a paradox, and one that frankly has worried me to some degree. But again, I have resolved my doubts in their favor. It will be good if the feud between Amon and this House can come peacefully to an end, for it has sent through the land in the years of their growing up a secret current of restlessness, uncertainty and unease which has not been good for Kemet. It has increased that sense of subtle but insistent decay that has so disturbed Ramesses, myself, Aye, Amonhotep, Son of Hapu, and many, many others. It has sprung from Pharaoh and from Tiye, who have seemed to placate Amon with the one hand while giving him many subtle and insistent challenges with the other.

I am sure sour Aanen thinks of it as nothing but an unmitigated feud, despite the new colonnade and pylon at Karnak, despite the new avenue of ram-headed sphinxes, despite the vast new temple to Amon still building here at Luxor, despite the frequent gifts of gold and jewels that find their way regularly to the altar from Malkata. Aanen of course has a guilty conscience: he cannot forget the murder of Tuthmose V. Neither of course can they, which makes me as suspicious as Aanen of all these favors, which so often have a double edge.

Nonetheless, the whole thing is bad. The royal House and Amon *together* maintain the order of Kemet, *together* hold society stable, *together* rule the Empire. They have been partners for centuries, never more so than in this Eighteenth Dynasty which Amon did so much to help restore after the evil Hyksos were driven from the land. This is the right and immutable way of Kemet, which nothing should be allowed to alter because it was ordained in the Beginning that it will last forever and ever.

It is this which we look to the two children, who today become no longer children, to refurbish and restore. Then all will come right again in Kemet and we will go forward to a future increasingly glorious.

He *is* unique; so, in considerable measure, is she. Neither has any memory of the murdered brother and cousin, neither has any reason to carry on the feud. Amon, it is true, needs some chastening—it is not the House of Thebes alone which has been guilty of upsetting the balance, by any means. But all we need and pray for is that the balance be restored, that the partnership again be made equal, that trust again flow from Palace to Amon and from Amon to Palace. Then all will be well for us, in all things, again.

Soon they will be coming down the river under the leaden sky, the pomp and color even brighter by contrast, the trumpets and cymbals and loyal shouts of welcome even more ecstatic and impressive against the grayness of the day.

I believe him to be at peace with himself.

I believe this means peace for Kemet.

I resolve my doubts in his favor, and I hold myself ready, as he knows I am, to serve him loyally and faithfully in every way I can.

Amonhotep III (Life, health, prosperity!)

I FAIL. I do not know what it is. Sometimes I think Amon is indeed taking vengeance upon me; yet what have I done to Amon that can possibly match what he has done to me? But I fail: there is no mistaking it. Each day I hope for permanent improvement, each day, tongue in cheek, my brother-in-law and his anthill of priests pray to their god that I grow better. Each day, tongue in cheek, Amon gives them the only answer they dare to have him give and Aanen relates it to me: I will get better.

It is a game we play. But wearisome—wearisome. At least to me. I am sure Aanen and his white-robed hordes enjoy it, as they watch me die.

For dying I may be, I sometimes think. Other times I am not so sure. Quite often I think I may have many years ahead of me. Then come days when my teeth pain, when my body, which has lost its trimness, groans, when arthritis blows into my bones with the wind off the Nile. Some days I can hardly walk, hardly talk. Then comes an easing, a resurgence, a restrengthening. It, too, may last for days, weeks, even months. Then the malaise creeps back. I hobble in misery and think I may die.

I too pray then, though it has been years, now, since I prayed to Amon when I really pray. I pray to Amon in his temples, which are growing bigger and better every day as many thousands of workmen labor under the command of my namesake, Amonhotep, Son of Hapu, to add new hypostyle columns, new statues and the new third pylon at Karnak, additional buildings at Medinet Habu, and, at Luxor, the entire new temple which I have dedicated to the god and to his wife Mut and his son Khons. In private I pray to other gods, principally to the Aten. The Aten understands and, in his beneficence, is kind. Sometimes I pray to him in public, too, and here and there along the Nile and throughout the Empire I have built new temples to him, as well. They are not as magnificent as Amon's but they are pleasant, light and airy things. They give me pleasure when I worship in them, and they infuriate Aanen and his fellows. This, too, I think, improves my health: or at any rate, my good nature.

The Aten's temples are not yet, however, popular with the people. I have conceived of the Aten as, among other things, a symbol of universal unity, drawing all the diverse peoples of the Empire together. But even there Amon still holds the upper hand, for he does not see the need of another to assist him. There is little I can do about it short of an open confrontation, and this I am not well enough to do. Nor am I, indeed, in any position. I have supped too long at Amon's table, and he at mine, for me to challenge him openly. And I, in any event, am already too old.

Fifteen years ago, when Amon killed my son Tuthmose, the Great Wife and I swore that we would, in time, have vengeance. Now and then in the years immediately following we thought we saw the chance. But each time caution prevailed: sometimes through the intervention of Aye the ever patient, sometimes through my mother, sometimes through Amonhotep, Son of Hapu, and, more lately, through the diplomatically offered but calmly assured and self-respecting opinions of young Kaires, rising fast in my service. And there have been occasions even these did not know about, when Tiye and I might have struck out with fearful force at Amon but were restrained by our own common sense, which also exists.

The moment has never seemed quite right, the opportunity never quite ideal. So we have compromised with stick and carrot, expending vast sums for Amon on the one hand, favoring the Aten and becoming increasingly formal and remote with Amon on the other; hoping meanwhile that sufficient of the populace would begin to follow our lead so that the small priesthood of the Aten we have established might grow in size and influence to a point sufficient to balance Amon. So far it has not happened. Amon is too ingrained in Kemet, too intertwined with our House, too much a habit, too loved—and too feared. Loved and feared among the superstitious, I am unhappily forced to acknowledge, perhaps even more than I.

While Kemet has a ruling overlay of the educated, the mature and the sophisticated, I am afraid the ignorant and superstitious still form the great bulk of our population. The older I grow the more I realize that our royalty rests, our ruling classes rest, on the foundation of the great mass of the illiterate, there below. The aristocracy governs Kemet, but the peasant mass in its mud-brick villages *is* Kemet. And thus, to them, with all their superstition, ignorance and habit, the battle with Amon appears no real battle at all, because it is inconceivable to them that Amon could ever be shaken. Amon, and the fellow gods whose priests he has been able to purchase, subvert or enlist, is a part of the universe as immutable as I am. How can my people possibly conceive of a break between us, when I am not strong enough, and did not realize at an age young enough, that break there might ultimately have to be?

This, of course, was because I did not really realize, though instinct and concern for my authority made me restive, how determined Amon was to rule both king and kingdom. I wanted only to restore the balance, I did not want all-out war. When I made Tuthmose—that sweet, innocent little boy!—High Priest of Ptah, it was only to seek a balance. Amon chose to regard it as a declaration of war, and so Tuthmose died, the war's first but most sensational casualty. Too late then the Great Wife and I realized what we confronted. And, as I say, it has never come right to gain revenge.

Until, perhaps, today.

Today, using the excuse of my health and the desire that he become fully educated in the methods of government should the Aten decide suddenly to call me to the Valley of the Kings, I am making the Crown Prince Amonhotep IV my Co-Regent and am simultaneously marrying him, as I was married myself, into the sturdy house of Yuya and Tuya which has already given Kemet two strong queens in Mutemwiya and Tiye, and great public servants such as Aye. This is good, strong blood, which has been of great benefit to the House of Thebes. It will continue to be so, through Nefertiti. And in due course other purposes will be achieved.

It is quite true that the growing uncertainties of my health make it vital that I have someone young and vigorous—or if not "vigorous" in the usual sense, at least determined—beside me. I find ceremony increasingly burdensome, increasingly hard: yet there are times, ordained on the calendar from the Beginning, when I must participate, no matter how I feel. It is true that three years ago I delayed by one day the start of the Festival of Opet—which I myself established—that ceremony in which Amon in his sacred barque is carried up the river from his temple at Karnak to visit his new temple at Luxor which I am building for him, there to remain for two weeks while all of Thebes gives itself up to carnival, and then be returned with similar pomp to his ancient resting place. But only once have I been so ill. All other times, even when I have had to be carried in a litter, I have attended the various ceremonies required of me. But particularly in these recent years it has been a major ordeal. I shall be glad to let the new Pharaoh share the burden.

I shall also be glad to encourage him in what I believe will be his determined attempts to bring Amon back within reasonable bounds.

For he is very determined, my second son; and the determination, if anything, has become even more deepseated and adamant as his mysterious and tragic ailment has bent and twisted him out of the shape of ordinary men.

Sometimes I almost fear for him, in fact, so headstrong does he seem. His mother discounts this, serene in the certainty that we have educated him in statecraft and guile beyond all danger of misjudgment. Yet sometimes I am not so sure. Those bland, intelligent, self-protective eyes stare at me without expression, the huge flabby lips draw up in a slight and enigmatic smile.

"Do not worry, Father," he says calmly. "I shall know what to do."

But will he?

Tiye is convinced of it, but Tiye always is convinced that she can foresee all things, bend anything to her will, conquer everything even when events prove her wrong— and that anyone trained by her can only acquire the skill of governance she has herself. Yet it need not be necessarily so. And therefore I wonder . . .

We have trained them both, of course, with equal care,

knowing from almost the day of birth that we would
marry them to one another someday should they survive.
Aided by Aye and Tey and Amonhotep, Son of Hapu,
and also, in his casual yet careful way, by young Kaires,
we have explained to them patiently the situation with
regard to Amon, our hopes for the Aten, our desire that
they might succeed in redressing the balance we have
failed to achieve. It has been our impression that the lessons have gone home, though both are extremely close-
mouthed and skilled at keeping their own counsel. Kaires
has told us that they talk to him vaguely of "strengthening Amon by strengthening the other gods," which we all
interpret to mean basically the Aten. Yet they do not say
so specifically, and they do not tell us how they plan to
go about it. It is imperative that Pharaoh keep his counsel except with those he absolutely trusts: yet not to absolutely trust his own parents—! It has hurt us deeply,
but we have learned not to pry, for we know it will avail
us nothing.

Only once since his ailment changed him from the direct, outward-going, happy lad he was into the brooding,
withdrawn, almost unknowable figure he has become has
the Crown Prince shown open emotion and that was two
weeks ago when his mother and I finally revealed the fate
of his older brother.

At first he looked absolutely horrified. Then he dropped
his ungainly head into those long-fingered, bony hands
and began to weep as deeply and bitterly as though his
brother had been his dearest friend, not an almost mythical figure who died on the day he was born. Instinctively
both Tiye and Nefertiti went to him and offered comfort
with gentle hands on the narrow, shaking shoulders, the
bald, elongated skull.

Finally he grasped their hands in his and looked up at
me with a haunted look.

"He will pay," he said, as determinedly as I once did
myself. "Amon will pay."

Then the storm seemed to pass, he relinquished their
hands, wiped his eyes on a corner of his kilt, subsided
into the empty, brooding look he often has. Only an oc-

casional, gradually diminishing sob broke the silence. Presently he stood up, shrugged off our still-murmured sympathy. The bland veil dropped again over the eyes that so often look hurt inside when you catch him in unguarded moments.

"Thank you for telling me," he said gravely. "It is well that I should know everything."

And everything he now knows, so we shall see how he proceeds as Co-Regent. He is trained, knowledgeable, educated, equipped—greatly intelligent, shrewdly perceptive, at once moody, introspective, decisive—and determined.

Determined.

May it be to Amon's humbling, the good of our House and Kemet's good that I elevate him to my side this day and give him a wife as determined as he. I should like to continue ruling alone, but I have lost the vigor of my *ba* and *ka*, the very soul and essence of my being, and by myself can do no more.

Tiye

I RULE, as surely as ever Hatshepsut (Life, health, prosperity!), though I do not wear the Double Crown. I rule through an ailing man, who looks to me increasingly to carry the burdens of Kemet and the broader burdens of empire. I rule with the help of Aye, Ramose, Amonhotep, Son of Hapu, Kaires, my mother-in-law, our other trusted intimates: but above all, *I rule.* And so I intend to do after this day, for together we have trained a Co-Regent who will do for Kemet and the Empire what I have done in these later years of my husband's failing health. He will consult me, as he often does now. He will take my advice, as I have accustomed him to do. Together we will do what needs to be done.

Kemet senses Pharaoh is not well. It has made it difficult for me to maintain the ceremonies, the contacts with allies, the needed regular show of force along the boundaries of empire that keep the whole intact. I have managed to do so, with great diligence, strength of character and the help of friends—but without the strong figure at the center that made it all so simple in our earlier days. He tries still, my poor husband. But something—perhaps, though we never admit the thought to one another, the vindictiveness of Amon—weakens his will and steadily saps his strength.

It was for this reason that I decided six months ago that he should make our son Co-Regent. Pharaoh, as always when I make up my mind to something, was easy to persuade. The thought, he said, had occurred to him also, and indeed perhaps it had: it carries its own logic, given the state of his health, the needs of the country and the necessity to be always on the alert against the insatiable greed of Amon. I forget which of us coupled the idea with the thought that it would also furnish the perfect occasion for the wedding; probably I did, but he may have, for it too has its logic. My son, intelligent, educated and decisive as he is, yet needs the strengthening Nefertiti can give him—the same strengthening I have given his father. It has always been inevitable: why not do it now?

So it was decided. We told them, they were delighted—we thought. We sometimes find it hard to divine exactly what the Crown Prince is thinking, particularly since his ailment changed his personality so drastically from the candid child he was to the brooding, enigmatic adult he is becoming; and taking her cue from him, Nefertiti often is equally aloof and unknowable. Together they seem to inhabit a private world into which outsiders, even parents, do not win easy admission. Sometimes Pharaoh and I try, now and again Aye will have a long, confidential talk with his daughter; but from these discussions we all bring back to one another the same story. There has been polite respect, solemn attentiveness, apparent agreement on many points—but after it all, nothing really solid, nothing you can put a finger on and say with confidence, "Here they stand."

It has been most frustrating and most hurtful. We have only their best interests at heart: surely they should accord us that, and treat us with candor accordingly. It baffles us, but after several frontal assaults in recent years (which has always been my way when, through Pharaoh, I have held supreme power), I have learned to back away and approach it indirectly. Not that this has done me much good, either, to tell the truth; but at least it has restored our relations to one of easy mutual reliance and familial compatibility, if not the complete trust we as their parents would desire.

Yet we have, I think, done our best to train them for the hard tasks they begin to assume today. Invaluable Amonhotep, Son of Hapu, who has so many responsibilities of building temples, supervising armies, acting as Pharaoh's chief scribe and one of our principal advisers, was given the additional job of directing their education. He managed it brilliantly. We all assisted. Extensive education in the history of Kemet, a thorough knowledge of the royal House, reading, writing, the endless details of government, the problems of empire—they have had them all, plus the necessary training in ceremonies, the study of the gods (with particular attention to Amon and the way in which he became so entwined with our House), the duties they owe to Kemet as well as the rights they have inherited—there is little they have not learned in fifteen years . . . except, of course, the practical, day-to-day, human side of running the government, which I have had on my shoulders so much in recent years, and of which they must now relieve me—that is, to some degree.

I expect it will be some time before they are sure enough of themselves, confident enough of their new powers, to govern without me. Indeed, as long as Pharaoh lives and I remain in good health, they cannot have complete power anyway. They must still consult us, final decisions will still rest with my husband and so, in ultimate fact, with me. I shall still rule Kemet. Which is just as well.

I love my son. Like Nefertiti's, my love if anything has grown deeper, more compassionate, more tender, as his terrible ailment has run its physical course upon his body and worked its inevitable transformations upon his personality and his mind. I love him. But I think he needs, for a time, a restraining hand, and one not quite so near, nor quite so blindly devoted to him, as Nefertiti's.

Now and again it has occurred to us that perhaps we have done our work too well with those two. We have trained them to be lovers from their earliest days, done everything to make their union inevitable, created a devotion so strong it stands like a great bridge between them, defying the world. But it must not defy the world too much: and there, perhaps, we have gone too far. For there will be great testings of such a one as my son. And sometimes, if bridges do not bend a little, they break.

We have only been able to guess at what has gone on inside that quick, intelligent mind as it has witnessed its formerly handsome body spread and sag, elongate and become grotesque. It was a horrible thing to watch, which we did, helplessly, though all of the temples and all of the gods were appealed to, and even Amon, I think, tried sincerely to assist. (I am not one who thinks my brother Aanen to be quite so malevolent as others do, though of course I can never forgive him for the death of my first son, who would have been the ideal ruler. But conflicts are conflicts and it is not the first time in Kemet that a prince has died. It has often been a matter of who struck first. Amon did, that time, and looking back with some dispassion, now, over fifteen years, I can see that it was our fault that we were so stupid as to let him seize the advantage. In the past two weeks since he got over the initial shock of the knowledge, we have tried to instill in the Crown Prince the lesson to be gained therefrom: delay your vengeance as long as possible, but when it becomes inevitable, strike first and strike hard. His father and I have never really recovered the advantage we lost that day.)

As I say, we could only imagine what went on inside while the outward shell was being transformed into something larger than, more awful than, and in some strange fashion more attractive than, life.

I can remember him sitting in his room in Malkata for hours on end—days, even—staring, with a sort of brooding wonder that was heartbreaking to see, at his body as it grew steadily more malformed. I think in the beginning he thought it was some awful punishment we had visited upon him for some unknown reason, and I can only imagine the dreadful inner hours this must have given him. But when he finally let us know this thought, giving a pain that cuts me still, blurting it out suddenly in his high, shrill voice—*"Why have you done this to me?"*— we were able to convince him with tears and love and earnest lamentations that it was none of our doing, that we felt as stricken and as helpless as he. And thank the gods, he believed us.

So he would sit, staring for hours without a sound as his body changed. Now and then I would come into the room without warning and there would still be no sound —only tears, welling up and falling unheeded down the inexorably enlarging cheekbones. Welling up and falling unheeded down . . . welling up and falling unheeded down . . . welling up and falling unheeded down. And always silently, helplessly, with no word of complaint any more, just a sad, hopeless acceptance that broke my heart and breaks it still, though eventually that phase passed and he seemed to become reconciled to it and, as we all sensed, even strengthened by it.

Out of such adversity there could have come, in a character less strong and less determined, something touching upon, or perhaps going beyond, the far reaches of sanity. We could have had a royal madman, who would, for the sake of Kemet, have had to be either hidden permanently away, or killed; or we could have had a royal suicide; or we could have had a vegetable driven mindless by horror. But he survived: he survived. His father and I were powerless to impede or control his illness, but one thing it could not take away from him—what we had given him at birth: character—strong character. He would not have survived, else.

When the storm finally passed, leaving behind the ravaged body, there began, aided by Pharaoh and myself, by Nefertiti, by Aye and Amonhotep, Son of Hapu, by Kaires, by Sitamon and even, in her odd, begrudging fashion, by Gilukhipa, a process of rebuilding which we all found easier than we had anticipated. Secretly we all dreaded what the end result would be, did not know what response we would receive when we tried to help him re-enter the world of ordinary men. We forgot—in fact we did not know, for when the disease began he was only ten and had been given little opportunity to show it—that we were not dealing with an ordinary man. We were dealing with one quite extraordinary, made even more so by the ordeal through which he had passed.

At first he did not wish to emerge from the confines of Malkata, where we had kept him with his willing acquiescence, away from the general eyes of Kemet during the three years in which the transformation occurred. Word of course went out through all the slaves, servants, soldiers and visitors who constantly pass in and out of the compound that something most strange was happening to the Crown Prince. But we did not expose him to the people as a whole. We simply let them gossip, knowing there was nothing we could do to prevent it.

There came a day, some three or four months after we were beginning to conclude that the disease was arrested and would savage him no more, when Pharaoh and I decided we would go down the Nile to Memphis, to open several new temples to the Aten that we had ordered built, to worship at the chief temple of Ptah and to spend several weeks there in our northern capital, worshiping at the tombs of our ancestors in Sakkara and seeing to the general business of Lower Kemet.

We asked him if he would like to go with us. His response was to shuffle—not stride as he used to do, how beautifully and how swiftly as a boy, but shuffle, breaking our hearts all over again—to the full-length mirror which he had insisted that we leave in his room all during his illness.

"Looking like *that?*" he demanded in a harsh croak, heavy with emotion.

"Yes, my son," Pharaoh said gravely. "Like that."

"Mother," he said, and he turned to me in an almost frantic desperation, "do I have to go? *Do I have to go?*"

There ran through my mind in a second many things. But the main one was: *we can help, but his recovery is principally up to him.*

"No, my son," I said as gravely as Pharaoh, "you do not have to go. But remember that you are Amonhotep IV, that you are the Crown Prince, that the day is coming inevitably when you will be Pharaoh—even," I added gently but fearfully, not knowing what the response would be—*"like that.* Will Pharaoh hide away from his people? His people love Pharaoh. Will he answer their love by being afraid to look them in the eye and let them see him?"

"Trust the people, Nefer-Kheperu-Ra," my brother Aye said softly, using the name my son will have at coronation with the familiarity of love and caring. "Trust them. They will not abandon you."

"I must think," he said then, covering his eyes with his hands and rubbing them wearily like an old man. "Let me think."

"Yes," Pharaoh said gently. "Think, my son. And then, we hope, you will come with us."

We withdrew quickly and left him; and within the hour, asking only that Nefertiti be allowed to go with us, which of course fitted perfectly with our plans in any event, he came to us and said firmly:

"I will go."

After that, for a few minutes, we all cried together in one another's arms in sheer relief and love for him and for each other; and after that he never looked back from the road he had chosen, the only road open to a Pharaoh if Pharaoh he was to remain.

We sailed the next morning in full flotilla, my husband, our son, Nefertiti and I housed in the golden ship of state in the center of the line of seven vessels that formed our expedition.

A vast concourse had gathered on the eastern bank, for word of our journey had of course been sent out by mounted messengers as soon as he announced his willingness to go.

When we appeared on the landing we were surrounded by a group of soldiers, staff and dignitaries headed by faithful Ramose. They bade us farewell, then stepped aside. A great gasp went up from the other side as we walked, the children close behind, up the ramp and prepared to mount the double throne.

For a second my son looked completely panic-stricken. We tensed in fearful anticipation that he might turn and hobble back.

Then his shoulders straightened, he moved to the railing and with something we did not know he had, but discovered in that instant, a very real and very great dignity apparently born of his ordeal, he lifted both arms, thin and spindly as they had become, and with a generous and sweeping wave seemed to embrace all of our tensely watching people.

At once a roar of love and approval went up, repeated again and again as he continued to bow and wave gravely to them.

Again the tears were not only in his eyes but in those of all of us. He had come through. He had survived.

So it went all down the river as we moved slowly through Upper Kemet and so on into Lower Kemet and the Delta, reaching our objective three weeks after setting sail from Malkata. Crowds were everywhere, every village we passed was filled with welcoming, loving, happy people. The private word that sometimes seems to travel faster than light preceded us the length of Kemet: the Crown Prince was changed, but well again. He was still the Crown Prince. And he was theirs.

At one particular spot, I remember, a vast bend of desert on the eastern bank of the river about halfway between Thebes and Memphis, so many thousands had gathered from the countryside about that they seemed to stretch almost as far as the low, rocky ridges that bounded the sands. Here he asked that the flotilla be halted so that he might greet them more intimately, proposing that he and Nefertiti be permitted to disembark and ride among them in one of the two ceremonial chariots we had brought along in the supply ships. With considerable misgivings his father and I looked at one another, but the two children were so radiant, so excited and so happy that we did not have the heart to say no. We asked Aye and Amonhotep, Son of Hapu, to ride with them, gave our blessings and waved them off.

For almost two hours, while we stayed aboard and strained our eyes to watch their progress, they rode back and forth across that enormous plain, their passage marked by a constant wave of excited and happy cheers.

Finally, exhausted and almost drunken with delight, they returned to us and we set sail again. But long after we began to move they stood together at the railing looking back at that vast plain and its throngs which still shouted distantly after them.

"That was the best of all," he said to us as the river turned away and the plain passed finally from view. "That was best of all."

"It was," agreed Nefertiti, her eyes alight still with the glow of it. "Oh, it was!"

But in Memphis, of course, and indeed everywhere, it was the same: acceptance, understanding, loyalty, love. We stayed three weeks, returned in the same triumphal way. This time we did not stop at their favorite river bend, but again they stood at the railing to wave and stare back, long after the loving crowd had again roared its greeting.

"Still the best," he said with his little enigmatic smile as the plain once again slipped from view. "Still the best."

"Yes," Nefertiti said, holding close to his arm. "We must come here someday again."

"We will," he promised gravely, "when I am King."

After that trip there has been no turning back. He took his place once more with the Family in all our public appearances, presently began to go accompanied only by Nefertiti: lately, sometimes, even alone, when his father and I for one reason or another have been unable to attend. Since the co-regency and marriage were announced, he. has traveled with her again all the way to Memphis and back, to the same acclaim. They have accepted him. He has survived.

Now on this chilly day that threatens rain he is about to take his place on the throne-beside-the-throne. I am satisfied as a mother with his remarkable recovery, satisfied as a ruler with what we have all accomplished with the two of them. Under my guidance he will be a good Co-Regent and she will be a wonderful helpmate.

I, the Great Wife Tiye, Pharaoh in all but name of the Two Lands, welcome the new Pharaoh and his Chief Wife to power beside me. Should the Aten call away me or my husband, which will effectively end my power whichever it is, Kemet will rest in good hands.

I, the Great Wife Tiye, Pharaoh in all but name of the Two Lands, have so arranged it.

Aye

I HAVE MISGIVINGS: but events proceed.

Soon we will be leaving for Luxor, and nothing at all can now reverse the course that all our lives are taking.

I have done much to decide that course, I am as responsible as any, I have desired nothing more than this. Why, then, should I have doubts now, when it is much too late to change anything at all? When what I have dreamed and planned for fifteen years is about to come true?

The reason is, I think, the boy, and, in equal extent, my daughter, whom we have trained since babyhood to be his mirror image—if I may use such a term, knowing what the mirror now reflects . . . yet this, I suppose, is a cheap shot and unworthy of Aye: for the mirror not only reflects grotesquerie but a brilliant mind, a dreamer's imagination, an idealist's heart—and a will which is, I suspect, of iron.

He has confided much in me in these recent years, more than his parents have ever suspected, more than I have ever told. So has she, though her thoughts have usually paralleled his so closely that I have needed to know only the one to anticipate the other. I do not believe this has happened with Amonhotep, Son of Hapu; I am sure Kaires, for all the relative closeness in age and all the easy intimacy he was shrewd enough to establish early with them, has never been taken into their confidence so deeply. It has imposed on me a great burden, one more of those I have always carried for Kemet. Much of the molding of those two minds which now are about to acquire such power over the land has been done in the quiet private talks we have managed to have out of sight and sound of the rest of the Family.

From the others they have received all the standard things. From me they have received not so much instruction as sympathy and a patient ear. This they have apparently considered of greater value. Certainly to it they have given greater response, even though their response to the others has been impeccable. They have been dutiful children in all respects, moving with an easy grace to acquire the knowledge and the skills needed for government.

To the others they have revealed the formal results.

To me they have revealed the inner questionings.

These began, as did so many things in the minds of my nephew and my daughter, with the illness. That watershed in his life, whose consequences, still only partially revealed, still mysterious and not yet fully knowable, will obviously become part of the history of Kemet, apparently started many wonderings in his mind. They seem to revolve basically around the gods.

Why it should be that after almost two thousand years of recorded history there should appear in the land a Pharaoh who questions the gods, who have been ordained from the Beginning and are eternal, I could not say, un-

less it is that none came to his assistance when he prayed
to them for help. But question them he does—not only
Amon the obvious, whose relationship to the Family makes
us all uneasy, but all the rest as well. Ptah . . . Ra-Atum
. . . Ra-Herakhty . . . Mut . . . Hathor the cow . . .
Sekhmet the lioness . . . Isis . . . Osiris . . . Nut . . . Geb
. . . Khons . . . Thoth the ibis or baboon . . . Horus the
falcon . . .

There is not a one whose existence and justification he
has not challenged in our private talks these past two
years. Dutifully his little echo my daughter has parroted
him. What am I to make of this?

I have tried to tell them how our belief in the gods began: how the first unification of the Two Lands came with
Menes (Life, health, prosperity!) of the First Dynasty,
which believed in Ra, and so gave Ra—the Sun at the
height of his noontide glory—an initial supremacy over all
other gods. I have told them how our ancestors—those
dim and distant folk whom we call, across the haunted
valleys of two thousand years, the Ancients of Kemet—
initially worshiped the deities they saw in the major ele-
ments about them, in the earth, the sky, the waters of the
River Nile, the wind, the rain, the scarab in the sand who
symbolizes the formation of the earth as it forms tiny balls
of dung in which to house its eggs and thus shelter and
bring forth life. I have told them how the spreading unification of the land after Menes—psychological and mental unification, as well as physical unification—gradually
merged Ra with all these other deities, yet kept him supreme, so that the sun cult always remained the dominant
religion down to the time of their own immediate forebears
of the Eighteenth Dynasty, when Amon (even he still
retaining Ra in his formal name) became through circumstance and politics "the king of all the gods."

I have told them how each town and locality had its
own god, how each developed its own priests and temples,
how all were absorbed finally by Ra and Amon, yet how
each has still to this day retained its separate individuality
in the hearts and minds of the people, who worship, fear,
or love many gods.

I have told them why we worship certain animals and birds—not because we actually worship *them* but because we worship certain attributes they have which we associate with the gods they represent: the falcon, fierce and protective of Pharaoh and the land, as Horus; the ibis and baboon, shrewd and quick and full of shining wisdom, as Thoth; the lioness, stern and punishing to those who transgress, kindly and protective of those who obey, as Sekhmet; the crocodile, who guards longevity in the good and takes it away brutally from the bad, as Sebek; and all the rest. I have told them how we worship ritual because ritual each day reaffirms the order of things as it existed from the Beginning, and enlists each god anew in the service of the land and of Pharaoh—and in turn, of course, enlists Pharaoh himself anew in the service of the land and of the gods.

And from two shy yet stubborn eyes, and from two sparkling yet equally stubborn ones, there has looked out the one question I cannot answer if they cannot comprehend:

Why?

I have told them *why*, many times over. And so I think it is not a matter of "cannot" comprehend but a matter of "will not" comprehend.

And this, I tell you frankly, much disturbs me.

For if Pharaoh himself does not believe in the gods, then what will happen to the land? What will happen to the ancient order of things which, save for the unhappy subjugation by the Hyksos and one or two other relatively brief chaotic periods of our history, has always kept Kemet a happy, prosperous and stable country, a marvel to the nations and a beacon to the world? What will become of all of us, when the Co-Regent and the new Chief Wife pick up the power that already trails listlessly from the hands of my brother-in-law, that needs only time to fall forever from the strong, indomitable hands of my sister?

What will happen to Kemet then?

I can only hope: I can only hope. I have done my best to listen sympathetically, to try to understand, to try to end their questioning and bring them back. If they have an alternative to offer, they are not telling me. If they are not telling me, I know they are telling no one.

I cannot believe—*I cannot believe*—that they really contemplate any serious attempt to change the immutable order of things which has come down to us from the Beginning. I must tell myself, as I have told myself constantly since this most disturbing irreverence began, that it is simply the exuberance of young minds, simply the game of youth running free from a few last independent hours before it goes under the yoke of discipline and joins in the task with which all in the Great House are charged, the preservation of the eternal order of this eternal land.

I have to believe this, but I am not sure I do. The wind blows cold off the Nile, but it is not only the weather that chills my bones: the cold goes deeper, it strikes my heart. I love them both most dearly, yet if they really feel as they hint they do—if they really attempt to challenge the very soul and being of the Two Lands—then there can be only one ending.

And in that ending there can be for the Councilor Aye, in love and fear and horror, devoted always and only to the good of Kemet, only one role he can possibly play. And he will not be alone.

The cold strikes deep, it ravages my heart. I dress to go to Luxor now, but I go in a growing fear I hope I may succeed in hiding from them all.

They must never perceive it, for there is the possibility I cling to as desperately as every sailor tossed unsuspecting into the arms of Hapi clings to the floating palm branch.

I may be mistaken.

I pray to all the gods that this is so.

Nefertiti

THE DAY IS HERE, the day is here! It is *here*.

I, Nefertiti, shall be Queen. My cousin, my love, will be King. We will rule Kemet with the Good God and the Great Wife as long as it pleases the Aten to let them live.

Then we will rule alone.

And things will change.

My noble ladies in waiting have washed me thoroughly with scented waters softened with salts of natron. Now they dress me, here in the main Palace of Malkata. They bring me warm woolens against the windy cold. They bring me, to go over them, a sheath of gold, pectorals filled with many jewels, rings, bracelets, golden sandals for my feet, my own special conelike blue crown which I designed and which is like no other, rising high and drawing back from my face to reveal it in all its beauty.

There is no one in Kemet as beautiful as I. There is no one in Kemet—I hesitate, but I am strong and fearless, and I say it—there is no one in Kemet as strange as he. He believes this gives us great advantage. I believe it too. What he believes, I believe. For he is always right.

The ladies in waiting flutter about me, exclaiming and awe-struck by my beauty. They increase it with kohl for my eyes, powders and rouges for my cheeks, tints for my hair. I hold my head very still, examining myself over and over in the bronze jewel-ringed mirror which he gave me on our last birthday. (I gave him a small scarab which he wears as a ring, showing on its reverse Horus the falcon representing Pharaoh, standing on Sebek the crocodile representing longevity, and flanked by two cobras representing the goddess Buto of Lower Egypt—thus,

Lower Egypt protecting Pharaoh and giving him long life. These are things we no longer believe in, but it is a pretty conceit. And it symbolizes something for us: we seem to feel more at home in Lower Egypt, away from the intrigues of this city, though it is here in Thebes that we will chiefly rule.)

I study myself in the mirror, and slowly, carefully, with infinite delicacy, my principal lady in waiting, An-ser-Woss-ett, draws rings of green kohl, made from ground malachite, around my eyes, heavily shading my eyelids, drawing out the fine lines at the end of each eye to exaggerated lengths to make me seem glamorous and mysterious—not that I need much of that, for I *am* glamorous and mysterious: but it is the custom. Then from another little pot she takes powdered red ochre, which she applies to my lips and cheeks to heighten their already lovely color. My hair (which will be seen briefly when my unusual crown is removed after the wedding and then formally returned to my head by my uncle Aanen to signify my coronation as Queen of the Two Lands and Chief Wife of the Co-Regent) she tints lightly with henna—again, a custom, for it shines with a beautiful dusky red color, as it is. Custom also calls for it to be shaven after I become Queen, and for me to wear heavy wigs thereafter; but this I think I will not do. I have classic features, a long, lovely neck; why hide them under an ugly thatch of someone else's hair? I will permit them to be covered with cloth of gold for certain major ceremonies, but for the rest I shall wear my crown and look as nature intended me. This will be treat enough for Kemet, I think, and while there may be a little grumbling that I break tradition, what of it? It is not the only tradition we intend to break.

Now An-ser-Woss-ett is preparing to drench me with perfumes, which I must admit I like. Myrrh and frankincense, cinnamon, bitter almond, sweet wine mixed with honey, sweet rush, cardamon—they all blend together in a delicious jumble which I thoroughly enjoy. I shall smell lovely when I come to his bed, though it will not be the first time: we have had each other many times in the weeks since our marriage was announced and no one, save possibly Kaires, has even suspected. We have become very clever at concealing what we do—and concealing what we think. Only my father suspects our thoughts a little, and even him I think we have succeeded in confusing. It is vital that we do so, until we have the power. There will be time enough then for the world to exclaim.

I said "many times" but actually it has only been twice, for it has not been easy to arrange: but it has been enough to prove to me that I can be his wife, as he can be my husband, willingly and joyously in every sense. I was not at all sure of this, for you must understand that his terrible illness imposed a strain on me greater than it did on anyone save himself: and of course I did not know what final damage it might have done to him. For a long time I was uncertain on all counts, even though I have known almost from the time I knew anything that someday we would marry. I knew that this would still be true if he should survive the change, no matter what he looked like, or what, if any, his powers might be—for from the first our marriage has been considered necessary for Kemet. But I really thought for a time that it might have to be a marriage complete with all the love, affection and support I could give him, but incomplete in the one thing that matters most to us and to Kemet—that we should be able to love one another in all ways, and that we should also be able to have many healthy sons to strengthen our House and continue the Eighteenth Dynasty forever and ever.

Since the continuation of the House and the Dynasty are so important, I was even prepared if necessary to accept the fact that I might have to submit myself to some substitute father (undoubtedly Pharaoh himself, ailing as he is), so that my sons could be produced for Kemet behind the public screen the marriage would provide. But now I know that this will not be necessary. It is the one thing I had to know to be able to go through this day with genuine joy and happiness I should feel, and show the people.

Therefore I persuaded him to join me in the experiment, which at first he was a little reluctant to undertake—not for any moral reasons, for since the age of eight we have witnessed what happens in Thebes during the Festival of Opet, from peasant hut to royal Palace (two weeks of drunkenness and couplings of all kinds everywhere, even in the streets), and nothing about the morals of Kemet shocks us now. Indeed, the morals of Kemet do not exist in the sense, for instance, in which morals seem to exist in some heathen lands beyond Mittani which we read about. It is the order of things which exists in Kemet, and the order of things can be stretched to include almost anything as long as the order of things remains the order of things. This is a lesson we have learned and will not forget.

So we would both, I thought, have acquiesced, as a matter of simple practicality, had it been necessary for me to lie with his father to beget our sons: but we would neither of us have been happy about it. I explained this to him gravely, while he watched me with those calm eyes which can be sometimes almost hypnotic in their steady, deliberately expressionless gaze. I did not allow his lack of response to shake me. I did not stumble or falter. I continued to the end. But I realize now that I should have carried away inside a hurt from which I would never have recovered had he not studied me with silent intensity for a moment when I finished and then said quietly:

"Any Sons of the Sun who are begotten on your body will be begotten by me and by no one else. I will kill myself before I will let my father or anyone else profane the only woman I will ever love."

After that, it all went easily; and I found out what I had to find out: that the illness by some miracle had stopped before it destroyed him altogether as a man; and that I, out of the love I have known since our babyhood and the compassion that has joined it since his illness, was capable of taking to myself his misshapen body without revulsion, without reservation, without anything but what I have always known for him, a love so deep that it can never change.

So we are one entirely, and so the day will proceed as happily and fittingly as it should. I needed only to know about his body to be to him in all things the great Queen I know I have the ability to be. It has been many, many years since I needed to know about his heart, for it has belonged to me always, as mine to him. And for his mind I have known, as early as I knew anything, trust and respect and utter confidence in all he says and does. For he is always right.

He is quick, very quick, though now this is hidden behind the shy, veiled eyes, the deliberately bland expression, the customarily unsmiling face. It is best that this be so, for he and I have many thoughts and many plans that Kemet must not yet know.

An-ser-Woss-ett applies the final trace of powder to my cheeks, the tiniest final touch of rouge to my lips, one more lightest tracing of kohl along the eyelids, a swift final shower of many perfumes. She stands back and studies me. I study myself. All the ladies flutter. She likes what she sees, I like what I see. We exchange the smiles of two women working in harmony to achieve the result both desire. I take a large carnelian ring engraved with the head of Horus (she is a sweet but very superstitious woman) from the box I have concealed beneath the table and, reaching for her hand, place it upon her finger. She drops to her knees, kissing my hand and praising me. All the ladies do the same. I stand, go to the mirror, turn this way and that: I gleam with gold and jewels from head to foot. My beautiful face is perfect, my lovely long neck is white as the whitest sand and soft as the softest linen. My eyes are dark and mysterious—and as intelligent as his, which few in Kemet know. Which is just as well.

I feel radiant.

I look radiant.

Very soon now they will come for me and I will go in my own special ship of state down the river to Luxor. And all along the banks of the Nile amid their wild hysterical shouts of love and loyalty, the people will say to one another, and I will hear them say it, "Lovely, lovely! Oh, she is beautiful, she is beautiful! A Beautiful Woman Has Come, and now she is ours!"

And he will greet me with the smile that lights only for me, and in the brooding eyes that conceal so much of pain and hurt there will today be only happiness.

And I shall be content.

Amonhotep IV (Life, health, prosperity!)

THE PALACE HUMS WITH LIFE, activity, excitement, the constant comings and goings of slaves and nobles, the clank of metal as the soldiers assemble for my honor guard in the center of the compound, laughter, happy outcries, joking, frivolity, eager anticipation of the cere-monies to come. But here in my room, three doors down the painted mud-brick corridor from my love, all is hushed and quiet, all is business.

Solemnly they are dressing me, solemnly I am submit-ting. As always, they do not know what I think, and as always it is making them uneasy. I give them my stare, which is basically shyness but which they think is some-thing more, something deliberately challenging and forbid-ding, and they move awkwardly, embarrassed by my gaze. Even my parents and my uncle Aye, who come in and out from time to time to observe our progress (themselves be-ing dressed early for, I suspect, exactly this purpose), are a little taken aback by me, a little nonplused, almost, you might say, a little fearful.

Until today I have been their son and nephew, their problem child whom they have been able to treat with love (I have never doubted this) and compassion (for which I have often been grateful, though more often it has only made me feel even more agonizingly helpless in the grip of my malady).

But suddenly, today, it is upon us.

Suddenly it is all about to become different—forever.

Suddenly I am about to become no longer their problem child but in many ways their equal and, if time and—I almost said "and the gods," which would have been ironic, but such is habit—health are on my side, their supreme successor, who will rule long after they have returned to the Aten and gone to lie beneath the Peak of the West.

Today I will become Co-Regent and King, Son of the Sun sitting beside my father. Today I too will be Pharaoh, and none of us will ever be the same again . . . nor will our land of Kemet.

This would be true even if I were to conform to what they expect of me and fit myself into the immemorial pattern which stretches back almost without a break two thousand years to Menes (Life, health, prosperity!). Amon will crown me, and even if I no longer believe in Amon, that fact alone would set me apart in the eyes of my people and change me irrevocably . . . except, of course, that there is no need for me to be changed irrevocably, now.

That is something which has already happened to me.

The proof is before me, because I am standing now in front of my mirror—that dear friend and enemy who has kept me company so many hours, so many days, so many weeks, so many months, so many years. When I first began to change, they wanted to take him away: I would not let them. They did not want me to watch myself undergoing terrible things, but I knew better: I had to know. I had to watch it all. I had to understand myself, as I have had to understand them in their constantly shifting attitudes toward me. I have had to know what it meant to them to see me become a monster.

I also had to know what it meant to me to see myself become a monster, if I was to survive and live long.

I have survived. And I like to style myself "He who has lived long," because for three years they did not expect me to live at all. They expected the gods, if it was the gods, to twist and wring my body until it could no longer exist among the living. They expected to escort me to the Valley of the Kings long, long ago.

But I did not give up.

And I survived.

Do you have any concept at all of what it has been like for me? I do not expect most of you do, for how could you? Few if any of you were born a normal child, grew to the age of ten a handsome, lithe and favored lad —and then began to see horrors happen to you that no one could explain, no one could understand—and no one could stop. Few if any of you have been in the grip of so horrible a disintegration of what was once a most beautiful and most lovely Prince. Few if any of you can look back, to this day, and see him running along the pathways of Malkata, happy and carefree and sturdy in the sun. My family can see that: I can see that. *I can see him!* I will always see him. Sometimes I try to speak to him, to exchange messages, to call out to him as he races by: "Stop, stop, do not hurry so! Tell me how it was then! Remind me how it was when you and I were young and strong, for I do not want to forget!" But increasingly with the years, I do: his voice grows steadily dimmer on my ear, his words are getting lost . . . he does not hear, he races on.

But I shall always see him, happy and sturdy and carefree and young, always running, running, running, on the sunlit pathways of Malkata.

And what does he do now? He shuffles. If he has to hurry, he hobbles—so he has learned never to hurry, The voice which gave promise of becoming deep and manly has a tendency to become either high and shrill or, when filled with emotion, a heavy croak that is sometimes almost unintelligible. So he has learned to be silent, for the most part, speaking little and seeking to have the little mean much. His family and his servitors apply to him such words as "brooding" and "enigmatic." They do not know he is so only because he feels a fool, and does not wish to sound one.

Most of them do not understand how I hide inside this

ungainly shell that has been left me after the storm passed by; most do not see the desolate *ba,* the lonely soul that hurts and hurts and hurts, deep in the long, narrow eyes that cast upon the world that proud and speculative gaze. They think pride is all it is: pride and arrogance.

It may be pride, but it is only pride so that they will not see how I suffer, and arrogance so that they will not dare come close enough to guess.

Of course there are those who do: Nefertiti knows, my parents know, dear Sitamon, Aye, Kaires and Amonhotep, Son of Hapu, know; Smenkhkara, who loves me but is still almost a baby, senses if he does not understand; even Gilukhipa, in her tart, standoffish way, suspects and, as much as her dislike for her situation permits, sympathizes. Some few are perceptive, but not many. My station in life keeps most of them away; the defenses I have had to erect around myself make sure the rest will never venture further within the barrier.

It is just as well, for they would be shocked and terrified by what they would find there.

If Amon and his fellow gods created, ordained and caused all things, then they created, ordained and caused the heir to Kemet to be as I am today. If they are responsible for everything, they are responsible for me. If they have the power to correct all things offensive to *ma'at* and the eternal order of things, then they could have corrected me. If they can answer the prayers of the lowliest superstitious peasant along the Nile, then they could have answered mine.

But they did not.

They did not.

Have you any idea how terribly I prayed, in all those endless days and months and years? Can you conceive of my dreadful agony and my dreadful humbled prayers to them?

But Amon and his fellows never answered me.

They never did.

Often and often I have asked myself why. I was a good boy, I offended no one, I did no one harm, I was always polite and happy and smiling and kind. I did my lessons faithfully, I co-operated eagerly with everything my family and tutors did to prepare me to be a good King. I loved my family, my teachers, my country, my people, my life. I was a good boy.

But the gods struck me down; and when I begged of them, over and over and over again, so many times—so many times—with terrible weeping and frantic appeals in the privacy of my room, to rescue me, to restore me, to make me whole and healthy again, they paid no heed. My friend and enemy on the wall gave me proof of that. My mirror said, day after day, "You see? They ignore you, poor abandoned youth. You cry out to the great gods of Kemet, but they refuse to answer Kemet's heir."

Day after day, month after month, year after year, my mirror told me true. And in all the length of Kemet priests and other men jeered and laughed and called me "horse-faced" and whispered of my helpless surrender to deformity.

I still do not know why. I am sure I will never know. It might have been Amon, angered by my father's subtle but stubborn resistance: yet was not Amon sufficiently appeased when he took my brother Tuthmose? And what other gods have we offended, in the House of Thebes? It seems to me we have been generous and respectful to all. And of Amon we have asked only that he be again what he was always intended to be by our Dynasty, our partner and our friend.

I know this has offended Amon, who, like my uncle Aanen, wishes to rule all. But to take such vengeance upon a child innocent of these intrigues?

It was, in any event, a way to guarantee him an indelible education in the ways of the gods. The gods may be sure he will never forget the lesson, for it is always before him, on the wall.

So I began to question—secretly, I know, much disturbing my uncle Aye, that good man who counsels me in all things—though he would never admit it to me. Why all these gods, who are supposed to be so marvelous and all-powerful, yet who first take vengeance upon an innocent child and then ignore his abject, bewildered cries for help?

What purpose do they really serve, except to keep the poor peasant comfortable with his lot and encourage the superstitious to look to some power beyond themselves to rationalize their own shortcomings or the blows of fate they cannot understand? What do they really do, save prey upon the people and steal away from the House of Thebes the power and the wealth which should rightfully all be ours?

I am not hostile to Thoth, who has the worthy duties of presiding over writing, wisdom and the arts; he is a somewhat severe but generally kindly-looking god as our artists depict him, standing beside Pharaoh with his ibis or baboon head on his human body. I find Sekhmet, particularly as she sits in the eternal twilit silence of the little temple to her husband Ptah along the north wall at Karnak, a most stunning and impressive figure, and I am not afraid of her, for I know she too has much wisdom. Sebek the crocodile grants long life (when he is not moved suddenly to chop it short, of course), and in most cases, as long as they are blessed with continuing good health, men seem to consider this a good thing. Horus the falcon represents my divinity and that of my father, as of all Pharaohs, in a most dramatic and emphatic way: he makes a wonderfully commanding symbol in statue, pectoral, pendant, ring and temple carving. Buto the cobra speaks for Lower Kemet and is believed to protect Pharaoh, as in my ring from Nefertiti, and there is no great harm in that. Nekhebet the vulture does the same for Upper Kemet: so be it. Great Ra moves across the skies in all his many aspects, and if the ignorant wish to worship him in many aspects instead of one, that too does little harm. Ptah began the first creation of all things in Memphis before the kingdom spread to the Two Lands, and still deserves respect for that. Isis is the universal mother symbol. Hathor is full of joy, kindly to women, and she and Bes aid them in childbirth. Osiris presides over the kingdom of the dead, with vast elaborate rituals for the deaths of Pharaohs and of lesser men who can afford it, and this gives much wealth and employment to many who might otherwise have neither. It is costly, but harmless.

So you see: I do not feel hostile to the gods in general, though I cannot forgive them for not answering my prayers. The basic thing is that I simply do not see their necessity, particularly when Amon, as their leader, directs them in attacks upon me and my House and so divides and plunders the people of Kemet, who yet do not object . . . which, of course, is another mystery to me.

Why do the people like so many gods? Why do they not see the simple advantages of one?

This I ask my uncle Aye, whom it horrifies. Apparently never, in all our two thousand years of history, has anyone, let alone a Pharaoh, questioned the gods. Apparently never has anyone, let alone a Pharaoh, thought out for himself the advantages of one single, universal god to channel the worship of all men, to simplify the gathering of all tribute, to serve as instantly recognizable, universally accepted unifier of empire, if Empire we must have.

Apparently I am unique: though of course I might not have been had the gods not seen fit to change me out of shape and then refuse my prayers that I be restored to health again. We will never know, though the gods may live to regret that they did not permit me to find out.

Certainly I promised them everything in my awful desperation.

I should have been so grateful.

They could have had whatever they desired from me.

But they chose otherwise.

And so, therefore, have I.

My parents have attempted to direct me toward the Aten, and I find him a most pleasant god, as light and open and friendly as the little temples they have ordered built, no doubt as a hint to Amon, up and down the Nile. Were I doing it—as of course I soon will be—I might make the hint a little stronger, for I think the Aten would indeed be a good counterbalance to Amon and the other gods.

I think, indeed, he might be more than that. I am studying him far more deeply and carefully than my uncle knows. I have many thoughts, half formed, half hinted, half dreamed, about the Aten. I find he comes to me often: it is getting so he is always with me. (I have even designed, secret from all but Nefertiti, a representation of him: a kindly disk from which descend many little hands holding the ankh and conferring Aten's blessings upon Pharaoh and his wife.) I do not know, yet, where he may be leading me, but in some fashion I do not yet understand, I have a feeling that I am in his hands. I do not know what will come of this, but I am beginning to sense that it is a process that is under way and may not stop.

Sometimes this frightens me, for challenging Amon and the gods is no light thing. But already the Aten speaks to me when I pray to him, and his words are encouraging.

He says:

"Do not be afraid."

And I think, under his guidance, I am beginning not to be afraid.

For the first time since my ailment began, I think *I am beginning not to be afraid.* And for this I thank the Aten. He was not strong enough—yet—to withstand the other gods when they wished to destroy me. But perhaps, with my help, he will be stronger than them all someday. I feel he is good to me, and I have determined already: I will be good to him.

And so perhaps the day will come when, thanks to the Aten, I will not be afraid of anyone or anything . . . and of Amon and his fellows least of all.

I have discussed this with Nefertiti, as I discuss with her all things, and she, too, says:

"Do not be afraid."

I expected this, for she agrees with me and supports me always. She is my love, who has never failed me from our childhood on, even when the awful sickness fell upon me. Always when we were children she followed me, believed in me, looked up to me. (The boy who runs forever down the paths of Malkata in my mind does not run alone: a small, dark, laughing, lovely ghost keeps him always company, hand in hand.) And when the sickness came, she never wavered, never flinched. And lately she has proved to me—and to herself, as it was necessary for both our sakes that she do—that our love can achieve physical expression and thus grow greater for the good of Kemet and our House.

I am almost dressed now: the knobbled feet are

sheathed in their golden sandals, the twisted legs, the bulbous stomach and the swollen, hateful woman's hips are
swathed in the golden plaited kilt that only Pharaohs wear.
The jeweled bracelets adorn my arms, the jeweled pectorals my chest, the staff and flail are in my hands, the ceremonial beard is strapped to my chin, the great wig covered
with cloth of gold enswathes my forehead and drops down
beside the long, unsmiling face to rest upon the narrow
shoulders and the narrow chest. The uraeus gleams upon
my brow upraised and ready to strike my enemies. The
enormous Double Crown of the Two Lands sits above. I
am ready to be seen.

I move to my friend and enemy on the wall, I stare at
myself eye to eye while behind me the slaves and nobles
fall away, and in the doorway I am conscious that my parents and my uncle Aye, entering once more, have paused,
stock-still.

The tableau freezes: there I am, gaunt, ungainly, monstrous, grotesque. But I am God and Pharaoh, and I am
not as bereft of confidence or resources as they think. I
hope they do not underestimate me, for I am supported by
their love and Nefertiti's and the love of the people; and
perhaps, if the plans that are forming in my mind take
shape as I want them to, I shall open a new way for Kemet
that will make my name live forever in the minds of men.

Such, in any event, is my intention.

I give myself one last, unflinching look from head to
foot. Then I turn and face them and instinctively they all
bow low, even my mother the Great Wife, even Pharaoh,
my father, my about-to-be fellow God.

"Is Nefertiti ready?" I ask, and in spite of my best efforts, my voice becomes a little hoarse with emotion. I find
that I am trembling inside, though apparently I look calm
and dignified enough without.

"She waits, my son," Pharaoh says gently, and suddenly
I find that I am smiling at them all, and they are smiling
back. There are tears in my eyes, tears in theirs.

I have survived: I am ready: we go.

Amonhotep, Son of Hapu

I DO NOT KNOW what we have created here; but as I stand beside the Queen Mother, her tiny, wizened figure bundled against the cold beneath her gorgeous robes, and hear the swelling shout move south along the river from Malkata, I can only pray that it will be for the good of Kemet and this House.

Presently they will arrive and Mutemwiya and I will take our proper places in the procession, she following after her son and the Great Wife, who in turn will be preceded by the Crown Prince and Nefertiti, I to join Aye and his wife Tey in the file just behind. So far have I come in fifteen years: now I am the highest councilor next to Aye, and to me Pharaoh entrusts his architecture and construction work, his records, his planning for monuments and campaigns—although this last is only on papyrus, for it is quite unlikely that he will ever be able to take the field again. There are many officials under me throughout Kemet and the Empire. I oversee all and it is my charge to make sure all records and details are well kept and to move forward all things expeditiously. I am so important that Pharaoh has already decreed a mortuary temple in my honor on the west bank near his own. Thus far have I come.

In addition, I give advice when it is sought, which is frequently; and in these recent years have been entrusted with my greatest responsibility of all, the formal schooling of the two children.

I have been responsible for all the details of their plans, schedules, studies, programs. This has been my particular charge, as it is my particular skill. But I have other skills:

139

I think, I study, I expound, I philosophize. In such subtle
areas does education truly lie, between pupil and teacher.
I think I can say to my credit that I have done my best to
influence these two avid young minds in the ways that will
be best for Kemet.

In this, of course, I have not been alone: everyone in
and around the Family has had a hand in it, all being
aware of how vitally important it is that they be truly
equipped to rule. Each of us, in a sense, has been both co-
operating and contending for these two minds. And yet
sometimes I wonder if any of us has made an impression,
if any of us really holds the key to what goes on inside
these unique youngsters, he unique in intelligence combined with ugliness, she in intelligence combined with
beauty.

They are difficult—difficult. Enigmatic and obscure.
Given to playful moods, she in particular, when she so
dazzles with challenge, assertion, questioning, conjecture,
that one cannot keep up. He is more silent but equally
blunt, disconcerting, elusive—when he chooses to speak.
This he does not always do, leaving to others (principally
to her, who so often speaks for him) the burden of dis-
course, maintaining a silence speculative, skeptical—un-
nerving. He used to be so open: now he is so closed. Such,
sadly, is the legacy of illness. That, and possibly much
more that we do not dream about—dare not dream about.
(They seem above all to be skeptical of the gods, though
with me they express it in a way so jocular, light and spor-
tive that I am unable to divine how sincere they are or
how deep it goes.)

I know Aye in particular is worried, though he will not
tell me why. Kaires is uneasy, I am uneasy, Pharaoh and
the Great Wife are uneasy, even Mutemwiya who hud-
dles beside me in the chill of wind off the Nile is uneasy.
"What does he intend to do?" she asks me plaintively
from time to time, as if I knew. "What are those two up
to?"

How do I know? I guess, but I keep my guesses to myself and pray that I am mistaken; for if I am not, then
somewhere, somehow, among us all we have done some-

thing terribly wrong in our handling of this strange boy and his dazzling love. . . .

Kaires comes up now, removes his helmet, salutes me smartly, bows low to kiss the Queen Mother's hand. She slips it quickly away before he can rise to his full height again and gives him a fond maternal pat on his shaven skull. He responds with his amiable, easy smile before he slips the helmet back on. Then he turns, surveys the scurrying priests and the soldiers lounging at ease, and shivers slightly.

"It is *cold*," he says. "Ra does not smile upon these proceedings."

"He does above the clouds," I say quickly, seeking to lighten what seems his gloomy mood. "He rides the Barque of Millions of Years through the skies as always. He will come out in due course to bless us. You will see."

"Oh, I am not really worried," he says, more confidently. "I believe this will be a great day for Kemet."

"Do you?" Mutemwiya inquires with a sudden moody glance. "Why?"

"Because I believe in the Crown Prince," he says firmly and I perceive that he has finally resolved his doubts in the boy's favor. "And I believe in Nefertiti. I believe they will be good for Kemet, now that Pharaoh is—" He pauses, realizing he is on ground of some delicacy with Pharaoh's mother.

"Ill," she says matter-of-factly. "But is not my grandson ill too?"

"He has *been* ill," Kaires says respectfully but emphatically. "Now he is well again and ready to be a good Co-Regent and Pharaoh for Kemet."

"You call what he is 'well'?" the Queen Mother inquires, and in spite of her tart tone, a sudden profound sadness touches her weathered face, rouged and painted even more heavily than usual for the occasion.

"He is not as other men," Kaires grants, "but I believe in his heart he is well, and able to do great things for us all."

"He is not strong," Mutemwiya reminds him.

"But he is not sickly," Kaires replies, daring as few do to argue with this old lady who has befriended him, as have the rest of us, so long and so well. "He has great strength of will. It compensates for much."

"Strength of will for what purpose?" she inquires, still moodily, as now, up the river, the rolling wave of welcome comes ever nearer and stronger. She places a hand on Kaires' chest and gives him a little poke for emphasis. "Do *you* know? Do *I* know? Does Amonhotep, Son of Hapu, know? Does *anyone* really *know?*"

"Pharaoh and the Great Wife must be satisfied, Majesty," I interject as Kaires looks momentarily at a loss, "else they would not be making the Crown Prince Co-Regent this day. Is that not true?"

"Satisfied to be relieved of burdens and worries—they hope," Mutemwiya agrees. "Satisfied about other things . . ." Her voice trails away and she gives a heavy sigh. "I do not know. . . . We do not know. *They* do not know. . . ."

"Excuse me, Majesty," Kaires says formally, "but I think they come and I must go to command the troops as they take their stations."

"Good boy," she calls after him as he again bows low, smiles and hurries away. "Sometimes I wish . . ." But again her voice trails away and she only looks at me with the sadness once more upon her. I dare to nod with suitable gravity, and although she turns away without comment while her face assumes its ceremonial expression, I know we understand each other.

So do I wish that such a one as Kaires were to be Co-Regent instead of the Crown Prince. It is a fantastic thought, for I believe—though his background is still a mystery and all my diligent spies have been unable to uncover it—that he is illegitimate and not of us. And I do not believe—although there have sometimes been startling surprises in the way he has risen so rapidly in Pharaoh's service—that he carries any royal blood, or is in any remotest way involved in the line of succession. Yet he is a vital lad, of great force, intelligence and ability, already on his way to become one of the great leaders of Kemet. It is only the contrast that makes the Queen Mother and me entertain our fleeting, futile thought. The contrast . . . and the wistful feeling that if only somehow —*somehow*—things could be different than they are on this fateful day.

But they are not. She knows it, I know it, and quickly I follow her lead in making my face suitably formal as we prepare to step from the tent and stand looking up the Nile, over the heads of the enormous crowds along the shore, to see the flotilla come. The gods have given us this strange boy, we have all done our best with him, and now all we can do is await events and pray to the gods who gave him to us that they will keep his feet firmly on the path he must travel if Kemet is to be truly served. This is no time for adventures, either for the land or for his House. We pray that both children fully understand this.

Now the shout is upon us. It grows, expands, explodes: the first golden ship has touched the royal landing at Luxor. From it there descends, with a slowness enforced by his ailment (which mercifully adds only dignity to his progress), an awkward golden figure topped by the ancient, towering Double Crown of the Two Kingdoms. The figure is visible in its awkwardness only a moment. Kaires' honor guard steps forward and surrounds him, clustering priests converge amid the joyous, shattering tumult. A second later he is seated on a canopied golden throne resting on two long poles of cedar. Eight sturdy young soldiers seize the poles and in one swift, disciplined motion hoist him high above the crowd, where he sits triumphant, his expression solemn but not unkindly, his head turning slowly from left to right as he acknowledges the roar of greeting. Mutemwiya and I look at one another with secret glances of relief. The first step has been successfully taken: the greeting is of love.

Now comes the second golden ship, and the tumult, if possible, grows louder. She is wearing the distinctive conelike blue crown which she devised herself two years ago, and she has never looked more beautiful, more serene or more certain of herself. Already on that lovely face there rests the promise of a growing maturity, a deepening wisdom, a sure and unshakable intelligence. The wise and levelheaded ruler is already present in the sweet, excited girl. Her mother Hebmet was right: A Beautiful Woman Has Come, indeed.

She too is hoisted high in her own golden baldachin behind his, and for a moment a gasp of sheer astonishment and adoration replaces the universal shout. She is overwhelming in her beauty.

We can see him lean down to Kaires, who walks on his right hand beside the throne. Kaires shouts an order, the sturdy soldiers slowly turn his baldachin until it faces hers, and as their eyes meet they smile at one another with a look that is like a flame, so intense, so complete, so enveloping—so *enclosed*—does it appear to us who watch. A cry of sheer delight wells up from the crowd as the soldiers again slowly turn his throne facing forward and move it a few paces ahead so that hers may fall in line behind it. On both their faces, now, there shines a great content, which imparts itself to all and quiets, for a little time, the doubts and worries that haunt those of us who know them best.

Now comes the third golden ship, the biggest and the brightest, and again the welcome roars, filled this time with many things, loyalty, adoration, worship, respect— and a certain anxious tenderness. He has ruled over Kemet, now, for almost twenty-seven years, they know he is ailing, they love him, and it worried them. Today he appears to be feeling reasonably well: his face is solemn yet kindly, its formal smile of benediction fixed yet filled with an answering tenderness. Beside him the Great Wife wears the same expression. She cannot refrain, now and then, from a quick, sidelong glance of worry and appraisal, and this is not lost upon the multitude. They love to see felicity in the royal household, they murmur to one another, "The Great Wife is a *good* wife." And so she is, and a great ruler, too.

They are transferred in turn to the twin canopied thrones they share together. This time sixteen soldiers perform the smooth, quick-flowing operation and sud-

denly there they are above us, as in our minds and hearts
they have always been. Power will be divided and shared
from this day forward, but in certain ways Pharaoh and
the Great Wife will always have a hold upon the people
which someday, if the two children are lucky, may be
equaled but can never be surpassed: Kemet has known
them both so long and so well.

Now the Queen Mother leaves me and moves forward,
to be greeted by yet another detachment of Kaires' troops,
who escort her, to the accompaniment of another affectionate shout, to her own small golden throne and lift her
high. Then in quick order come Sitamon, now a lovely
and dignified figure in the fullness of womanhood, and
towering Gilukhipa, aging but still as shrewd as ever.
They too are hoisted quickly to their thrones, and now
begins that part of the procession that will move on foot.
Aye comes, grave and commanding as always, accompanied by Tey. I move in beside them as we bow to one
another and exchange quick, friendly smiles before our
faces assume their ceremonial solemnities. We, too, receive our share of greeting, as do Ramose, Su-rero the
chief steward to Pharaoh, Mahu, the chief of police of
Thebes, Kheru-ef, steward to Queen Tiye, and the rest.

So presently we are all in line, and waiting; and presently we find that we are still waiting. The procession
does not move forward, and for a very simple reason.
The priest Aanen, who jealously guards these portals and
on this occasion has chosen to remain behind them rather
than ride with the Family as he often does, has not yet
come forward to formally welcome us within.

Can this be deliberate, or is it simply some hitch in
ceremony for which someone, probably not in the least
responsible, will be punished later, so that all may save
face?

It is obvious that the crowd, which murmurs now impatiently but amiably, thinks the latter. It is also obvious,
from the suddenly withdrawn look on the face of the
Crown Prince, the little frown that creases Nefertiti's
brow, and the fixed congealment that is beginning to set-

tle on the faces of Pharaoh and the Great Wife, that the
royal party has a different idea.

For several awkward minutes the impasse lasts. The
crowd begins a puzzled, sibilant whispering. Pharaoh appears about to look around for someone to give an order
to, when the matter is abruptly taken from his hands. A
high, shrill voice, filled with imperious anger, rings out
loudly. An instant silence falls on the world, caused more
perhaps by his tone than by his words, which themselves
are harsh enough:

"The Priest Aanen will open the gates and admit the
Good Gods and the Great Wives and all their party or
we shall have his head!"

There is a universal gasp. His father and mother look
shocked, the rest of us exchange horrified glances; he has
gone too far. Only Nefertiti, though she turns a little pale,
gazes steadily and serenely straight ahead.

And in double time, for he is not quite the fool his
fanaticism sometimes makes him out to be, Aanen comes
running, to fling himself prostrate on the ground before
the golden throne of the furious, excited boy.

"Majesty!" he cries, his words half muffled against the
stone pavement. "Majesty, forgive—an error—a mistake
—someone will be punished—someone—forgive, Majesty, forgive! Enter, Majesty, enter!" And then, rising
slowly from the ground and drawing himself to his full
height, he speaks with a dignity that quite belies his
showy show of consternation:

"The Great God Amon-Ra greets the Good Gods and
the Great Wives and all their party and makes them
welcome in his holy house of Luxor for these holy ceremonies that will bless and make even greater the Two
Kingdoms and all the lands of Kemet!"

And instantly, fervently, desperately relieved that the
dangerous moment has passed, the watching crowd bel-
lows its approval. Our expressions settle back into their
ceremonial patterns; trumpets suddenly blare fanfare
from inside the half-finished complex; a covey of priests
flutters forward to surround us; Kaires' voice rings out
the order; and the procession begins to move slowly for-

ward into the half-finished temple complex, led, with a great show of dignity, by Aanen, his high priest's leopard skin whipping rather incongruously around his skinny bones as Ra remains adamantly hidden and Shu the Wind-God sends chill blasts knifing off the water.

Inside the complex, crowds left behind and only participants present, the procession comes to another halt as Aanen raises high his staff of office. This time, however, it is meant to be—not that the other wasn't, we are all convinced, but there has been no harm done save a new and graver bitterness between Amon and the House of Thebes, and what is that to fools like Aanen? He knows his nephew as well as we do, as much as anyone can, and if he chooses to make of him an immediate enemy now that he is coming to power, who can give a fool the wisdom to do any differently?

So we pause; and in the distance we hear the steady chanting of the priests as they bring Amon in his sacred barque down the sacred avenue of rams from his ancient home at Karnak. Soon we see the first ranks approaching and now it is apparent what Aanen has done: for these are not the customary forty from the ranks of Amon. These are hundreds, and from among their number, whipping high and snapping in the sharp, insistent breeze, fly the standards of Ptah of Memphis, Buto, Sekhmet, Nekhebet, Thoth, Ra-Herakhty, Hathor, Isis, Sebek, Horus and the rest. He has massed all the priesthoods for us today and is saying, in effect: "See what *Amon* can do!" And at this point, of course, there is nothing whatsoever that even an angry nephew can do in reply.

So we wait and slowly, slowly, to the sound of chanting, drums, cymbals and finally a series of long, triumphant blasts from the hundred massed trumpeters Aanen has also thoughtfully provided, Amon comes to rest on his new altar at Luxor, and the ceremonies, finally, are going to be permitted to begin.

It does not take great powers of imagination to realize how we in the royal party feel now.

Nonetheless, aided by the necessities of ritual and by Nefertiti, who, from her throne which now rests beside his, gives the Crown Prince frequent calming and encouraging glances, all goes smoothly at last.

The thrones are lowered, the Family dismounts, the party proceeds through the half-finished hypostyle hall and walks up the gentle slope toward the altar where Amon and his fellow gods await. It has been decreed by Pharaoh that the marriage will come first, and for this he himself has decided to preside. Accompanied by Tiye, he takes his place on the raised dais which has been set up, moving with a little difficulty (apparently the arthritis is sharper today) but managing well. They bow to Amon and the massed priests on each side, turn to the two figures, golden like themselves against the gray, scudding sky, who stand just below. Pharaoh says the ancient words, his son and niece respond in low, grave voices. In five minutes it is done. The newlyweds turn to one another and once again the radiant flame ignites between them, anger and impatience with Aanen forgotten in this moment which has been their destiny from birth.

With a happy and triumphant smile, Nefertiti implants a kiss upon those heavy pendulous lips. I believe we all shrink a little, inside, but for her there is no revulsion, no forcing, no holding back: only a perfectly genuine, perfectly happy welcoming in her gesture. He responds with equal joyousness and for a moment we are all relaxed and united in their happiness.

Then Pharaoh and the Great Wife step down to join them, they all turn to Amon and bow low. Aanen mounts the dais, and abruptly tension returns.

"O Great God Amon," he intones in his pompous, stagy, ceremonial voice, "bless these two who are now united in marriage and give them strength and wisdom to rule over Kemet"—he pauses just long enough to make his point, and then concludes the sentence firmly—*"with your help.* Make them true to you and to all things right and good for Kemet. Give them millions and millions of years!"

And gravely from all the hundreds of priests there comes the chanted response:

"Millions and millions of years, O Amon, millions and millions of years!"

"Neb-Ma'at-Ra," Aanen says, using, as is customary on such occasions, the coronation name of Pharaoh, "Amon understands that it is your desire that Nefer-Kheperu-Ra, your son and Son of the Sun, great of wisdom, farseeing of vision, powerful"—again that slightest mocking hesitation, quite deliberate—"of strength, be crowned this day Amonhotep IV—"

"Life, health, prosperity!" chant the priests.

"—to rule beside you and do all things to assist you in guarding the eternal glory of the Two Lands. Neb-Ma'at-Ra, does Amon understand correctly that this is your desire?"

"He does," Pharaoh says firmly.

"Then upon this Good God Amonhotep IV—"

"Life, health, prosperity!" chant the priests.

"—Amon does hereby confer his blessing, and says unto all men throughout the land of Kemet and to all the ends of the earth, in all places, at all times, forever and ever—"

"For millions of years, O Amon," chant the priests. "For millions and millions of years!"

"—that Amonhotep IV is hereby crowned Co-Regent, Pharaoh, King of the Two Lands, Good God and father forever of his people; and that his wife, Nefertiti, is hereby crowned his Chief Wife, to rule wth him, and with you, Neb-Ma'at-Ra and the Great Wife, Her Majesty Queen Tiye, forever and ever, as long as Amon and the gods may give you strength.

"So be it!"

And from the heads of the Crown Prince and Nefertiti he lifts and then replaces, first the Double Crown of the Two Kingdoms and then her blue conoidal crown; lifts and replaces them again; and for a third time, lifts and replaces them.

The trumpeters blast a mighty fanfare, Aanen and all the priests shout, *"It is done!"* And from outside the walls, starting in Luxor and racing along the river as far as the massed throngs stretch, another great shout, of love, of loyalty, of adoration, affirmation and happiness, rises and races and turns and grows and builds upon itself, until all the world seems filled and overflowing with it.

And so it is done, and while Ra still does not deign to part the clouds and smile down upon us, all appears to have gone well: although it will be a while before those of us who heard it can forget that sudden disturbing flash of near-hysterical anger with which the boy demanded entry.

Our procession turns with great solemnity to watch Amon start his return to Karnak along the avenue of rams amid cymbals, drums, blaring trumpets and chanting priests. Then we follow Aanen and still more chanting priests as they lead us out of the temple of Luxor to the royal landing, the golden ships, the slow passage back up the river to Malkata past the adoring thousands who sing, dance and shout their happiness every excited, crowded, jostling inch of the way.

This afternoon to Malkata will come the envoys of Mittani, Naharin, Nubia, Hatti, Retenu, the Isles of the Great Green, Babylon, Assyria, even wretched Kush, to lay at his feet the tributes of their treacherous and obsequious kings. And then tomorrow the two, no longer children now but symbols of state, will travel down the river, receiving hysterical greetings all the way, to repeat the coronation ceremonies in the temples of Amon and of Ptah at Memphis, so that Lower Kemet, too, may confirm with its own eyes that all is properly completed.

So it is done.

Now the strange, horse-faced boy, whom none of us really knows, is God.

Nefertiti

Now we have the power!

Amonhotep IV (Life, health, prosperity!)

NOW WE HAVE THE POWER.

Now, O laughers, mockers, jeerers of Amon and of Kemet, your "strange, horse-faced boy" is Pharaoh, too. Now *he* is *also* God.

What wonders will you see issuing from this hateful, misshapen body, O mocking, hurtful land of Kemet? What revelations will fall from these heavy horse's lips, O Amon and you other gods, when *this* God speaks?

Softly, all.

Softly.

Wait upon me and prepare to learn.

I have surprises for you.

For I am Akh-en-aten, he who has survived and lived long, and I will do great wonders, such things as you cannot imagine, and I will live forever and ever.

BOOK III

Ascent of a God

1372 B.C.

King of   Nefer–Kheperu–Ra   Son of the Sun   AKHENATEN
the North
and South

  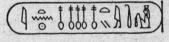

Royal Spouse   Chief Wife   NEFER–NEFERU–ATEN NEFERTITI

Sitamon

THIS EVENING I see a new Nile, though it is the same we
see at Thebes. Perhaps I should say I see a new Kemet,
for I do not see our stark and lovely Peak of the West
turning purple in the dying twilight as Ra-Atum, the sun
in old age, gently leaves the land. The river blazes molten
into gold, then copper, then a last slow shimmering of
bronze, before Nut, goddess of the night, ascends her
throne; and that is as always. But the hills are low and
far away, and not the same.

My brother has brought us here, and none of us, as yet
(except, I am sure, Nefertiti), knows why. I have not had
much chance to talk to him, for as always we traveled in
separate vessels on our way down the river, and when
we have made camp at night I have stayed with our
parents and he has visited us only once. Then, as always,
he remained enigmatic and uncommunicative, even under
our mother's gentle teasing—which conceals, as her children all learn early, a determined and persistent curiosity
that does not rest until it is satisfied.

My brother is the only one of us who never satisfies it;
and this, I think, in some curious way makes her love him
more. He is the one problem the Great Wife has never
really understood or solved; and I can tell from his expression that this is one of the things that pleases him,
and from which he derives enjoyment.

There are others. Already he and our cousin have three
daughters, all named for the Aten: Meryt-aten, Meketaten and Ankh-e-sen-pa-aten. And already he has done
other things for the Aten which have caused much com-

155

ment in the land—and much grumbling in the temples of Amon.

Within a month after Pharaoh had made him Co-Regent he ordered a new sandstone quarry to be opened at Gebel Silsila for the building of a huge temple to the Aten at Karnak. Yet, with the deliberate perversity which he also seems to enjoy, he made all Kemet as confused about his motives as he makes his family. He ordered that there be carved at Gebel Silsila a stela, the inscribed slab, usually of stone, upon which Pharaohs are accustomed to relate their achievements for posterity, and on it he had himself depicted making sacrifice to Amon—in the regalia of High Priest of "Ra-Herakhty, rejoicing on the Horizon in his manifestation of the Light that is in the Sun-Disk"—in other words, the Aten.

Sacrificing the Amon as High Priest of the Aten: such is my brother, the Pharaoh Amonhotep IV (life, health, prosperity!). And this is what not only his mother and his family, but all of Kemet, the Empire and foreign states, are expected to make some sense of.

I must confess that his sister does not, as yet. I, the Queen-Princess Sitamon, am as baffled as any peasant along the Nile. I think there may be a pattern here. I am as curious as Queen Tiye. But he never explains, my brother: he simply does, and the world may make of it what the world will.

So the building of the great temple to the Aten at Karnak proceeds posthaste: I think it may overtake the slow and endless construction of our father's temple to Amon at Luxor. To it, at a formal ceremony when the cornerstone was laid, my brother gave the name "The Aten is found in the House of the Aten"—which many of us took to have the added sense of, *"So do not try to imprison him in your house, Amon!"* Certainly that is what our uncle Aanen chose to make of it, buzzing angrily around the Palace like some bothersome bee: him I hope my brother will squash, in due time, because he is an increasingly annoying man, and I find him not only a bore but an active nuisance. At any rate, his instinct told him this was another of those insults to Amon he is always reading into everything, and he did much fuming on the subject, to the deliberately deaf ears of the Family and the absolute complete disregard of his nephew my brother.

Then just ten days ago, shortly before we all set sail on this unexplained progress down the river, my brother did something even more startling. He ordered placed on the walls of the new temple two cartouches, or name plates, for the Aten exactly like the cartouche of a Pharaoh. And to make it still more pointed, he gave the god the titularies of a Pharaoh celebrating Jubilee, even though theoretically Jubilee, symbol of a Pharaoh's renewal and continuation in office, comes only once in thirty years.

Thus the Aten now is almost a third Pharaoh (at least in my brother's mind—or in my brother's plan, whatever that may be), and his proper form of address are these words which have never before been conferred on a god, even on Amon:

"Ra-Herakhty, rejoicing on the Horizon in his manifestation of the Light that is in the Sun-Disk, Aten, the Living, the Great, Who is in Jubilee, Lord of Heaven and Earth, Giving life forever and ever."

He also caused to be carved on the temple walls a new symbol of the god which he himself, apparently, designed —based on the hieroglyph for sunlight, but enlarged and elaborated so that now it represents a disk encircled by a uraeus, with an ankh hanging from its neck. Radiating out from its edges and more than a dozen long rays, each having at its end a tiny hand, many of those hands offering ankhs and other tributes to my brother, to Nefertiti, and to their daughters.

And he reiterated that he was the High Priest of the Aten and formally appointed Nefertiti the High Priestess. And he also appointed, to universal astonishment, our uncle Aye to be his assistant. And, to universal astonishment, our uncle Aye bowed gravely, seeming not at all surprised, and accepted.

He also has just commissioned the sculptor Bek to carve three colossal statues of himself, one to be placed at the entrance of the Aten's house in Karnak, one halfway along the slope up to the altar, and the third at the altar's entrance.

Where all this puts Amon, I leave to my uncle Aanen and his over-weening priests to figure out. It is a very dangerous game my brother plays, but there are those who deserve it, and Amon, I think, is one.

This sharp sentiment does not sound like Sitamon, who, as I recall her, was a sunny and amiable child who grew into a pleasant and tolerant young girl and then into an apparently happy woman. This I suppose I still am, basically, though testiness has a way of creeping on us all in times like these. I see Kaires with reasonable frequency— as always, he accompanies us now, and is off in camp with his soldiers, half a mile up the river: through the palms I can glimpse the fires burning, hear the distant shouts over the general hum of the Court's encampment. We have a permanent agreement that later we may meet behind some sand dune, but that is hardly the life we should like to have together. I am now twenty-seven, he is thirty-four, and we do not grow younger. Gilukhipa still helps when she can, though lately she has not been feeling well, and is confined for the moment to her own tent, some hundreds of yards away from my parents and me. She cannot help tonight. It will be sand dune or nothing, which has often been the case in our secret romance, begun when I was fifteen and continued without a break ever since.

I should like to marry him, but this of course is impossible. My father pre-empted me to confirm his own claim on the throne, and not even my brother, who would normally have married me to secure his own claim, could ever do anything about that.

Nor, as a matter of fact, has my father; although there was an occasion, just after Kaires and I suddenly realized that we were in love and must find our own secret channels for expressing it, when I thought he might try.

It was late, in the Palace of Malkata. The Great Wife had gone to bed. Pharaoh, presumably suffering one of his periodic bouts of illness, was confined to his room. I was practicing the harp, pretending to gossip with my ladies in waiting and inwardly planning desperately how I might next see Kaires. Suddenly there came a summons: Pharaoh desired wine, and I was to bring it to him.

Instantly everyone in the room made an assumption. I also made the assumption and, strengthened by my new-found love for Kaires, followed it with an iron determination that, for this royal daughter, it was not to be. A citizen of Kemet is taught from infancy that whatever Pharaoh desires Pharaoh must have, automatically and without question; and I suspect, had I not just fallen in love with Kaires, that I should not have objected. It is the customary thing in the royal House: I should probably, though it might at first have seemed a little strange, have welcomed the chance to bear a possible heir to the throne. I had no particular antipathy to the prospect, which I had long expected and to which, except for Kaires, I would have willingly agreed. But—there was Kaires, fair to me then, and fairer even to me now. So I took the wine, gave my ladies one sharp look that silenced their softly smiling titters, and walked alone, save for the guard who customarily accompanies me, to Pharaoh's door.

There I nodded dismissal to the guard, who also gave me a secret, knowing glance which only served to strengthen my determination; called out clearly, "Father, I have your wine," and was bade to enter.

As I suspected, the room was darkened and Pharaoh was naked on the bed, bearing a close resemblance at that moment to the god Min, the only god in Kemet who is ever portrayed sexually. Min is always a very vigorous and obvious figure in this respect, and so was Pharaoh; and something—a combination, possibly, of my determination, my nervousness, my fright, and a sudden sense of the ridiculous that Hathor, Sekhmet or someone equally friendly sent winging to my rescue—prompted me to make the comparison aloud.

"You look just like Min, Father," I said, "only I think possibly he is a little bigger."

And abruptly I began to giggle—quite hysterically at first, I must admit, but in a moment with a sure, deep, genuine amusement that presently had me clutching my side and, I am afraid, sloshing the wine about a bit, spattering the floor and the single flimsy thickness of cotton which at that moment was all that stood between me and a possible heir of the throne of Kemet.

For a very long moment Pharaoh simply stared at me as if he could not believe his ears. Anger, shock, bafflement, uncertainty crossed the face that was already turning a little soft, a little heavy. First he flushed, then he paled, then he flushed again. Meanwhile, I was pleased to note, the resemblance to Min could not maintain itself, the shock was too great for it, too: it crumpled away and slunk between his legs. And then suddenly, mercifully, he also began to laugh, as genuinely and completely as I. In a moment we were crowing together like two fools, and I knew Kaires and I had won, though it was many years before I told Kaires of the battle.

"Daughter," he said finally, wiping his eyes on the bed sheet that he had pulled over himself in the midst of our hilarity, "you are one worthy of your mother. Return to your ladies, sleep well. And as you go, send in one of the house servants. I really *do* want some wine!"

And he opened his arms to me with an entirely honest affection, I leaned down and kissed him on the forehead, he patted me smartly but impersonally on the rump, gave me a shove and a heartily amused "Be off with you!"

And that was how the Queen-Princess Sitamon saved herself for her true love and did not bear a possible heir to the throne of Kemet.

He never attempted it again, of course; but for years after that I felt every time Kaires and I were together that we were very probably risking death should Pharaoh find out. However, I think in recent years he and my mother have come to suspect, and have even co-operated. It has become much easier, I have noted, particularly since my brother became Co-Regent, for me to slip away from the Palace to meet Kaires in Gilukhipa's rooms, in the rushes along the Nile, among the sand dunes, or wherever else the gods have seen fit to permit our happiness. Our love has not been easy, neither has it been really difficult; and as such things go, I suppose we have known a reasonable content, even though we should have liked to marry and give a happy life to the two sons and a daughter I have been forced to dispose of while they were yet unborn.

My parents, as I say, have silently co-operated; yet I think the co-operation has been greater since my brother ascended the joint throne. The young Pharaoh believes as firmly as the old that people should lead lives of happiness and pleasure, but he extends it beyond the Palace or his own bedroom. He seems to regard almost all men with a certain generosity, possibly because he survived his illness as he did. He wants them to be happy. If, sometimes, this seems to mean happy *on his terms,* that is just something one must learn to live with when dealing with a Pharaoh— certainly when dealing with this one, who is a most imperious and determined man.

I think, in fact, that even my parents are becoming a little alarmed, now, about my brother. They have perhaps instructed him too well in his defiance of Amon: he has perhaps truly slipped out of their fingers and into the multiple hands of the Aten. Our mother, who has secretly prided herself for years that she really governs the country behind the façade offered by our father with his erratically declining health, is not so sure, now. Temporarily, at least, she seems to have lost even her usual close communion with my uncle Aye, who appears to have joined my brother in worship of the Aten. She was not consulted about Gebel Silsila, she was not notified that a huge new temple to the Aten was to be built at Karnak, she was not told of the startling changes in the Aten's titles that he announced ten days ago before we left Thebes. Nor does she know, any more than I or anyone—saving, always, Nefertiti—the purpose of this progress down the river, or why we have encamped on the edge of this great empty plain in a bend of the low-lying eastern cliffs.

She stood at the rail as we approached it and said only, "I recognize this place." And although of course she has passed it many times over the years on their journeys up and down to our northern capital at Memphis, I realized she meant "recognize" in a deeper sense. For this is the place where he had his greatest welcome when he first resumed his appearances before the people after his illness. Her tone sounded troubled and sad, for she does not know what he proposes to do here tomorrow—and secretly, I think, she fears it.

Because he does propose to do something here tomorrow: he has announced nothing, but there is too much of a pattern. The announcements and ceremonies of the recent days—the apparently abrupt but, I suspect, long-planned decision to bring the entire Court north down the river to this desolate emptiness forsaken by gods and men alike—the carefully suppressed but palpable excitement which neither he nor Nefertiti can quite conceal, for all their determination to appear impassive . . . something is to happen.

Another temple to the Aten, in this desolate place? The entire Court forced to perform rituals to his new god, on this barren ground? Some new assault upon Amon, already horrified, affronted and angry enough?

He will not tell us and indeed none of us, including the Great Wife, has quite had the audacity to press for the reason. But it is in the air, we all feel it: tomorrow, something momentous happens.

When he and Nefertiti came to us for the second time, earlier this evening, we were eating. They arrived virtually without ceremony, accompanied only by Kaires, who bowed low to my parents, smiled quickly at me and withdrew discreetly to the corner from which he never hesitates to speak up, respectfully but firmly, whenever his opinion is sought, which is often. He is virtually a part of our family after all these years: that we two should be forced to be clandestine is so ridiculous and frustrating that it is sometimes almost impossible not to cry out in disgust and anger and demand that it be rectified. But of course this can never be as long as Pharaoh lives; and even then I do not know whether it could be. My brother might wish to marry me were I still of childbearing age. So far he has only daughters, and these are not enough to secure the throne for his own line, though Smenkhkara, beautiful and somewhat fragile-appearing but basically healthy, stands ready to carry on the direct descent if anything should happen to both our father and brother.

Tonight, in fact, it was Smenkhkara who spoke up first, as boys of ten are sometimes wont to do.

"Why have you brought us here, Nefer-Kheperu-Ra?" he demanded, suspending his attack on a roast duck's leg long enough to stare up at the Co-Regent with his customary adoring but insistent look. "It seems a most dismal place to me."

"Does it indeed, monkey?" our brother said, tugging Smenkhkara's sidelock of youth with the special patient affection he has always shown him. "Perhaps that is a secret only the gods will reveal."

"Which god?" Smenkhkara inquired, laying aside the duck's leg and beginning to look really interested, as were we all. "Amon, or your friend Spider-Legs?"

So swiftly that we could hardly see the motion, our brother struck him across the face with the back of his hand, toppling him from his seat not so much by the force of the blow as by the sheer surprise of it. But even as Smenkhkara stared up ludicrously from the floor, his face contorted with amazement and the beginnings of tears, the Co-Regent fell awkwardly to his knees, his grotesque, ungainly body enveloping the boy's, holding him tenderly, rocking him gently and protectively as though he were one of his own daughters.

"I am sorry, little brother," he said, his voice croaking with emotion. "But you must never speak of the Aten in such a fashion again."

"No, Majesty," Smenkhkara said, his voice shaking on the edge of tears. "Oh, no, Majesty, I will never— never—"

And then he did begin to cry, more than anything else with fright and disbelief that the older brother he so obviously adores, and who so obviously adores him, should, under some strange compulsion not understood by any of us, have reacted so sharply to what had begun as an innocent child's jest about the new god.

I doubt if anyone in his life had ever struck my little

brother—certainly never the Pharaoh Amonhotep IV (life, health, prosperity!).

Never.

For some moments we were all silent while he hoisted himself awkwardly to his feet again, our faces showing varying degrees of consternation, puzzlement and fear. Only Nefertiti, though paler, remained as calm and composed as ever. I had a glimpse into that marriage for a second: she has obviously become used to such storms. But she never wavers in her love and support for him.

Never.

Presently Pharaoh, our father, broke the silence.

"Here," he said heavily, thrusting the forgotten duck's leg toward Smenkhkara. "Take this, stop crying, be a man. Your brother has apologized, you have apologized, he will not do it again, you will not do it again. It is settled. I must say, however"—and he turned to stare full face at our brother—"that your conduct puzzles all of us, my son. Why are you so tense? What are we doing here? Why have we come? What is it you propose? Why are we, your family, not worthy to be taken into your confidence?"

"Tomorrow," my brother said.

"Why not tonight?" Pharaoh demanded.

"Tomorrow!" my brother repeated sharply, his high voice again acquiring the heavy thickness it always succumbs to under stress.

Again there was silence while we all stared at him. Quietly and naturally, a gesture apparently so accustomed that it was accomplished with such ease and dignity that we were almost unaware of it, Nefertiti glided to his side and placed a hand on his arm.

"Son of the Sun," she said softly, addressing our father, "you must forgive Nefer-Kheperu-Ra. It has been a long journey, he is tired—"

"We are all tired," the Great Wife interrupted bluntly. "That does not excuse an exhibition as unbecoming as this. I think you are in danger of becoming besotted with the Aten, my son. A Pharaoh must have stronger nerves and broader vision than that."

Again there was silence while some inner struggle apparently went on within my brother. Finally he responded, his voice still threatened with emotion, but calmer as Nefertiti's tiny hand maintained its steady grip upon his arm.

"Do not underestimate my nerves, Mother," he said. "And do not underestimate my vision. And above all, do not underestimate my devotion to the Aten. It is not besotted: it is real. Have I not proved this already in several ways?"

"Too many, I sometimes think," Queen Tiye replied, and for a moment it seemed he would again explode into anger. But Nefertiti, never relaxing her grip, added to it a gentle but firm stroking motion of her fingers that seemed to recall him to himself.

"I am sorry," he said presently, in a tone that told us the storm was probably over. "I am tired, tomorrow will be a most important day, and we must all have our rest. Kaires, I would like you to be sure all the soldiers are ready, for I have sent out many messengers"—we all exchanged startled glances, for we had not known this—"and I expect many, many thousands here to witness us as we perform our ceremonies. Order must be maintained, though I think they love us and would not willingly do harm except in the exuberance of the moment."

"Yes, Son of the Sun," Kaires said soberly, his own tone revealing how disturbed he had been made by the scene we had just witnessed. "All shall be done as you wish."

"Good," my brother said. He turned formally to our parents.

"Son of the Sun and Great Wife," he said, "I cannot command you to attend me tomorrow, but it would please me greatly if I had you by my side. Will you do so?"

"We have always been by your side," our mother said in a voice filled suddenly with a sadness she made no attempt to hide. "But why will you not *tell* us, so that we may know what to expect?"

"Because I do not wish it!" he said, sharpness abruptly returning, Nefertiti's firm little hand once more busy on his arm. More quietly he concluded. "All will be clear tomorrow—you will see. It will not harm Kemet or hurt our

House. It will be wonderful for everyone. You will see. Trust me."

"Evidently we must," Pharaoh said, his voice, too, sounding sad and tired.

"And happily, Father," my brother said. "Happily, for it will be a happy day for the whole world, forever and ever."

"I pray so, my son," Pharaoh said, unmoved. "By your god and all the gods, I pray so."

"Pray to my god only," my brother suggested with a sudden smile that for once was completely open and genuine, full of a serenity that in some curious fashion both reassured and frightened us, "for he knows, is, and will be, all things."

"We do not understand you, Nefer-Kheperu-Ra," our mother said, "but we will be there."

"Good!" he said. Nefertiti relaxed her grip, his face softened, he reached down to Smenkhkara, seated again on his stool, his lithe young body still trembling a little, his duck leg cold and forgotten in his hand.

"Little brother," he said, "forgive me. Tomorrow after the ceremonies you and Sitamon will join your cousin Nefertiti and me in our chariot and we will ride the length and breadth of this great plain. We will ride and ride and ride!"

"Like the wind?" Smenkhkara asked, his voice still uncertain, but beginning to smile a little in excitement and anticipation.

"Like the wind!" the Co-Regent promised, once again giving Smenkhkara's sidelock an affectionate tug. "And all our people will cheer and cheer and cheer us with their love and their devotion, and they, and we, and our House, and Kemet, and the Aten will all be happy forever and ever, for millions and millions of years!"

"May I hold the reins sometimes?" Smenkhkara asked eagerly. And finally we all did relax and join in the laughter as our brother repeated, with a fond amusement in his eyes, "Forever and ever, for millions and millions of years!"

And so it ended, the strange little episode, and so I won-

der, as do we all in this troubled night, what it all meant
and what it portends for tomorrow.

The last purple light has faded from the hills, the last
trace of bronze has melted from the river. Ra has begun
his journey through the underworld. Nut now commands
the night.

Somewhere in the rushes the god Thoth's surrogate, the
graceful ibis, calls once, sharply, to its mate. But the call
does not fool me.

It is not Thoth but Kaires who comes; and presently, after we have had our happiness, we will discuss the strange
doings of my strange brother, for I know my love is as puzzled, and as disturbed, as I.

Bek

I AM THE APPRENTICE of His Majesty, I have been taught
by the King: sculptor am I to Amonhotep IV (life, health,
prosperity!), as my father, Men, is sculptor to his father,
Amonhotep III (life, health, prosperity!). Here in Kemet,
court offices have a way of passing from father to son. But
I think my father has not been called upon to do such
things as I.

Such wonders as this One demands, and such wonders
have I created for him! Fifteen temples to the Aten in five
years, the greatest of them in Karnak, where we have almost completed the huge structure, far ahead of the lei-
surely pace with which my father is completing the Good
God's temple to Amon. In both cases we move at the pace
ordained by our masters: the young Pharaoh is more im-

patient to pay tribute to his new god than the old Pharaoh is to pay tribute to his old one. There may be reasons here which I, a mere servant of my lord, do not understand. But I do know this: great haste attends most things upon which Amonhotep IV (life, health, prosperity!) embarks. And most hasty of all, and most secret, have been the projects undertaken on the boundaries of this barren plain.

Tonight I stand in carefully hooded torchlight, before the second of them, watching closely as my little band of workmen—three only, pledged to utmost secrecy, promised the greatest rewards if they maintain it, threatened with certain death if they should violate it—put the final touches to the polished stone. They have kept the trust: no word has escaped. Very shortly now all will be in readiness for the ceremonies tomorrow. Once more the concealing cloths will be put back in place, the hiding sand will be shoveled over, we shall depart as silently and secretly as we have come. There will be just one difference this time: when the cloths are replaced, we will attach draw-ropes to them, their other ends cleverly hidden in the sand in the exact places the young Pharaoh has commanded. Thus will he be able to pull them away at the exact moment he wishes, revealing all to the multitudes who are expected tomorrow to fill this empty place.

And so will begin the greatest of all the projects with which he has entrusted me. It will be the greatest wonder, as it will be, for him and perhaps for all of Kemet, the most challenging and the most dangerous.

Yet even without this, he has done great wonders, such things as no other Pharaoh in history has done. Early in his reign, indeed at the moment he took me with him to open the new quarries and inscribe the commemorative stone at Gebel Silsila, he attached to his titles the words "Living in Truth"; and in this spirit he has commanded me to show him and his family ever since.

At first I was hesitant to do such things as no other sculptor in our history has done. Was I indeed to portray that grotesque, exaggerated, potbellied body as it actually is? Was I to show the Chief Wife swollen with child-bearing? Was I to portray them naked, with all the de-

tails of their sacred bodies bare to public view, as few if
any Good Gods and Chief Wives have ever been portrayed in all of recorded time?

But, "Yes!" he said: "*Yes!* I command you, Bek, and
you are not to be afraid. After all"—and into his eyes there
came that hurt, hidden look that I soon came to know so
well, and which I am going to try to capture in the new
colossi he has just commanded me to sculpt at Karnak—
"after all, it is not the artist they will marvel at when they
see your work. It is the man they know has ordered you to
portray him in this fashion. They see me as I am when I
go among them, and their eyes tell them I am different.
You must put it in stone so that it will last forever and
ever. You must put it in stone so that they will never
forget it, so that it will confront them in every place and
be with them night and day. When they think of me
they must think: *He is different.* And before them they
must always have the proof, because then they will marvel, they will respect, they will be proud of, and adore,
my difference. They will fear"—his voice dropped suddenly to a thoughtful low and he concluded very quietly
but with tremendous force—*"and they will obey."*

So I have done as my lord commanded, though at first it
was not easy. Tentatively I began to elongate the body, to
broaden the hips, to flab out the belly, to lengthen the
neck and the long horse-like head, to slim down the arms
and shoulders to their true skinniness, to make the lips as
heavy and pendulous as they are.

I am his to command in all things, to lift up or cast down
as he can any citizen of Kemet, but I am also a talented
man: I have my own self-respect as an artist. I did as he
wanted, but it has not been easy.

My first such sketch I took to him with a fear and trembling of my own. I knew as an artist that it was good,
that it was a long reach on the road he had laid out for
me; but I still feared a change of heart, I still thought it
might be a whim that could dissolve in terrible anger that
would lay me and all my family waste. We have learned
in Kemet over many centuries that the will of kings is a
capricious thing, working mostly for our good but capable

sometimes of frightful transformation. I expected such. And what happened?

He took the sketch. He studied it. He held it at arm's length. He drew it close. He held it away again. He put that oddly misshapen but, from my artist's viewpoint, strangely beautiful head first on this side, then on that. His expression remained solemn and thoughtful, no sound emerging from the heavy lips save an occasional, "Hmmm . . . Hmmm . . . *Hmmm*." I died several thousand deaths but somehow managed to remain as expressionless as he. Finally he shook his head abruptly and said the one thing I could not possibly have imagined:

"It is not enough . . . Here!"—and a joshing, almost playful note came into his voice as he took from my hand (suddenly, I am ashamed to say, quivering with relief) the rush pen, the pot of red ink, the papyrus, and shuffled toward a table at the side of the room. "Hold this steady for me . . . Now: *this* should be more exaggerated here . . . *that* should have a broader stroke there. . . . You have been too timid *here*. . . . Let us live in truth, Bek, my belly looks like *that,* not like that. . . . My chest is thus. . . . My private parts are thus. . . . Take this back and do it as I command you, Bek. And stop trembling: I *am* different, *make* me different. You are a great enough artist to do it. I assure you, you would not be Chief Sculptor to the King, else."

I am the apprentice of His Majesty, I have been taught by the King. What would you have done, I ask you? Exactly what I did: I did what he said, and I have done so ever since.

So he and the Chief Wife and their daughters live in truth in a hundred statues, a thousand sculptings, on temple walls and pylons, in bas-relief and paintings the length of Kemet. It has been done as he ordered, and he was right: it *has* made men marvel, it has made them respect, it has made them fear. And in some curious way that I do not possess the words to define, though I can make it happen with my chisel and my drawing pen, it has made them proud that they have as Pharaoh and Co-Regent one who is unique, and so startlingly different from other men.

And now come the final challenges: the one here on this great plain, and the three colossal statues he has just commanded me to sculpt for him in the House of the Aten at Karnak. In this place I shall guide, direct, plan, supervise, now and again put my own chisel to the stone when the final niceties are called for, though there will not be too much opportunity for that. Supervisory duties will command much of my time: it is fortunate I have my apprentice Tuthmose and several other excellent aides to assist me, for both these projects are very dear to his heart. The project here is dearest, but he does not wish me to slight the statues, nor do I want to slight them, for in them, perhaps even more than here, I hope to capture for all time Nefer-Kheperu-Ra, Son of the Sun, Amonhotep IV, Prince of Thebes (life, health, prosperity!), that very strange youth who nonetheless commands from me, as he does from many in his court, an awed but quite genuine affection—springing from I know not what exactly, unless it be a combination of fear and respect for his great position . . . admiration for his great intelligence . . . and pity and compassion for the terrible vulnerability, springing from his terrible tragedy, that only I as an artist, his family, and perhaps a very few others, see and understand.

So, the statues. Two are to be complete with crown, uraeus, staff and flail, pectorals, bracelets, jewels, pleated golden kilt, golden sandals—the full imperial regalia. One will stand at the entrance to the temple of the Aten, on a pedestal on which will be carved his own cartouche, the cartouche of the Aten and the words *He Who Has Lived Long*. The second will stand halfway up the gentle slope that leads, through open pillars filled with sunlight and air (not the dark, hooded, ominous, covered hypostyle halls of Amon), toward the altar. Its pedestal also will bear his cartouche and the Aten's, equal and side by side, and the words *He Who Opens the World for Aten*.

And the third, which I am beginning first, and which does not surprise me, for little he does can surprise me any more, will stand at the entrance to the inner sanctum containing the Aten's plain and unadorned altar. It will be stark naked, missing no detail even down to the genitals, reasonably large but, when at rest, almost hidden in the folds of fat from his sagging belly. I shall make them a little more prominent, for I know that he, as the father of three daughters and, please Aten, soon of many sons, will wish it so. And on this pedestal, again with the two cartouches side by side, but in letters half again as large as those of the other two, will be inscribed: *He Who Lives in Truth With Aten.*

It is as though he wished to say something with this third colossus, and I am sure he does. He wishes to say:

I am Pharaoh. I am the protector of my god as my god is the protector of me. I wish you to see me as I am BECAUSE I WILL BE HEARD.

And he *will* be heard there—and here, too, on this vast plain where our little group now completes its work and retires to await tomorrow. We hide the rope ends as he has instructed me, we toss on the last concealing shovelfuls of sand, we douse our carefully shielded torches and prepare to return to our tents through the ghostly moonlight that shines down upon us from Khons' silver boat.

In the far distance to the west, all along the Nile, can be seen the flickering campfires of the royal party and the Court, of the nobles, and of all those thousands and thousands of common folk who are gathered here to witness what he has planned for tomorrow.

Around us as we trudge slowly back toward the thin edge of humanity along the river lies the vast and empty plain. It is utterly silent. Only we four and two others, His Majesty and the Chief Wife Nefertiti, know that, beginning tomorrow, it will never be silent again.

Tiye

HE BAFFLES ME: but then he always has. I do not remember a time since his illness when I have fully understood him, and I am getting beyond the point, and the time in my life and his, when I think it will be possible. We have drifted far apart, particularly in these five years of his coregency. It saddens me, but I do not know what to do. I am his mother, the Great Wife, Queen Tiye who has been for many years Pharaoh in all but name of the Two Kingdoms —and I do not know what to do. Thus far have we traveled on our separate roads.

I still say "Pharaoh in all but name of the Two Kingdoms," but in my heart I know it has become increasingly an empty boast. My husband continues his erratic decline in health, sometimes lapsing, sometimes becoming almost fully himself again—but each time, it seems to me, he falls a little further behind, regains not quite the ground he has relinquished. He still consults me in all things, still takes my advice on most of them, still comes to my bed with loving regularity: it is quite possible I may yet bear another god for the House of Thebes. But what will that matter when, of the three I have borne already, one is murdered and long dead, one is a tenderhearted child who may never live to rule and the third is a malformed giant who has become so obstinate and headstrong that even I, the Great Wife, his mother, have long since ceased to exercise any real control over what he does?

I think now that the co-regency was a mistake. I think Pharaoh could have continued to rule with my help and guidance until our son succeeded in the natural course of things. I do not think it was necessary for us to give him such power so precipitously and so soon. We were moved by pity and by what seemed to be my husband's need.

But that is hindsight, of course, and neither Amon, whom he is pressing so hard, nor the Aten, with whom he is so besotted, can give even the Great Wife the gift to go back and erase the mistakes of the past.

So our son has the power, and when I attempt to caution him in the uses of it he turns upon me only that bland and enigmatic smile and says, with a shrug of those sadly emaciated shoulders, "Mother, I thank you for your kindness. No one is less deserving of it than I or appreciates it more."

And goes his own way.

And where does that way lead us? To new temples to the Aten, to greater godhood for the Aten, to greater deification of himself as the spokesman and sole intervener with the Aten—and to an indirect but inescapable challenge to his father's power, and mine. It seems to me that in these past five years, even though they have included his father's first Jubilee and the building of the great temple to Amon at Luxor, it has been the young Pharaoh, not the old, who has made things happen in Kemet. And they have not always been good things, in the judgment of his mother.

There has come, with his increasing absorption in the Aten, what I can only describe as a general loosening throughout Kemet and the Empire. It has been hard enough for me to rule the land with an ailing husband, let alone a willful and wayward son.

In a sense, my husband has always played at being Pharaoh. He came to the throne at the height of our Dynasty, he had nothing left to conquer, he had nothing to do but enjoy his wealth and magnificence—*providing he would do the necessary things to hold it all together.*

These were not, to begin with, very great. When we took power over the Two Lands the administration of the government was in the hands of wise and good men. We are fortunate that many of them surround us still: Ramose—Amonhotep, Son of Hapu—my brother Aye (though him, of late, I am beginning to question, something I never dreamed could be possible)—and many more. The machinery of ruling functioned smoothly throughout Kemet, in all our vassal states, and with those on our distant borders who were dutiful and anxious to be our friends. Pharaoh did not have to do very much to maintain what the gods and the blood of our House had given him. Presently I found that he was forgetful of even that.

So the glamor passed and the worrisome times, for me, began. "Amonhotep the Magnificent" became enthralled with his own magnificence. He began the great building projects which continue today and will continue to his death, and far beyond, until they are all completed. He acquired two harims, which were his right as Pharaoh and which I accepted without protest, for such is our custom, and I knew he loved me best and would always give me equal power. He contracted various state marriages, most notably with our somber Gilukhipa, who has never liked it here and never will, even though as the symbol of our alliance with Mittani she has received, the gods know, every possible luxury of her own. And in a casual way, he paid some attention to government and the Empire.

But not enough, I fear: not enough. So it fell upon me to do all for him, in which he acquiesced with unfailing good humor—while he, too, went his own way. I did what I could, but there have been limits to how openly I could order things done. The forms of Pharaoh's rule are often as important as the rule itself: sometimes the necessity for observing them got in my way. Thus the loosening began, and continues today. And it, too, will continue long after his death, with who knows what consequences for Kemet . . . unless the Co-Regent changes his ways most drastically and does the task which I appointed him to do.

And this he will not, of course, as long as he pursues his dream of the Aten, and as long as he keeps the priests of Amon constantly stirred up. My brother Aanen is a tiresome man, increasingly so as we all grow older, but his disaffection has spread throughout the priesthood and everywhere in Kemet. So far, in my judgment, he has been alarmed without much cause. It is true that my son has built fifteen temples to the Aten since he came to power, but aside from the labor involved there has been little competition with Amon. We always have more than enough workmen, particularly at the time of the Nile's inundation, when our people are idle from July through September while Hapi replenishes the land. In very ancient times it is said that the people were enslaved and forced to work for Pharaoh, but that passed many, many generations ago. Now every ambitious herdsman, felucca pilot or peasant who wishes can find gainful work on Pharaoh's payroll building temples or tombs or monuments. Labor is no problem for Ramose, or Amonhotep, Son of Hapu, or any of the others who oversee the work for us. Their problem, indeed, is often too many applicants for the work available. When this happens, both Pharaoh and Amon provide food from their granaries, and so the land comes safely through another season.

Thus the Co-Regent's temples to the Aten have provided to Amon so far only competition for workers, not for priests, because it is his concept of the god that, as his temples are light, airy and open, so should his priesthood be kept to the absolute minimum. Thirteen of his temples, in fact, have four priests each: they do the minimal housekeeping, sweep the courtyards and accept the daily sacrifices of food on the bare stone altar. My son has no statue like Amon to represent his good, only the many-armed hieroglyph on the walls, and the rays of Ra descending benignly through the open roof. His priests also do very little proselytizing. It seems to be my son's belief that only those who wish should come to the Aten. Very few have, and that is another reason why Amon, with his swollen temples and millions of worshipers, really need not fear too much.

Nonetheless, of course, Aanen fumes and fusses and professes to see great threats to Amon everywhere. In Memphis, where my son has built a major temple to the Aten covering many cubits of ground and employing more than a hundred priests, and at Karnak, where his temple is even larger, there is some visible ostentation that Aanen can cite when he makes his complaints to us and to his priesthood. But even in those two temples my son still does not direct his god to gather converts actively. He seems to be quite content that he himself should be the principal worshiper—and the only one through whom the blessings of Aten are to flow to the land.

For this reason I am as puzzled by my brother Aye as I am tired of my brother Aanen. I can understand my son naming his wife High Priestess of the Aten as he names himself High Priest, but I cannot understand my brother accepting the position of his assistant. It does not make sense to me, and since he has refused to confide in me about it, I am apparently going to remain mystified. I do not like this, but here, too, I am beginning to feel powerless. I am beginning to feel that many things are slipping from my hands. This is not a pleasant sensation for the Great Wife.

Now we are come down the river on this scatterbrained expedition whose purpose even Aye, I am happy to say, does not know. My son asked us to come, and since he made it very clear that he considered it an affair of such great importance that our absence would be regarded by him as an act almost of personal betrayal, we felt we must comply. But he refused to tell us why, and he refuses still. It is only apparent, most notably in such things as his startling overreaction to his brother's mild little joke, that he is under very great tension about it. And one thing I have learned about my elder son, which I suppose is one more of those endless ramifications and result of his illness: when he is under very great tension, something drastic is going to happen.

I can only hope that it will not be something we will all regret, and he most of all; not some foolishness to end all foolishness, some tribute to the Aten which will really turn Kemet upside down, or some further outrageous example of his hectic determination to justify his favorite designation, "Living in Truth."

If this were so, then Pharaoh—snoring loudly at my side while I lie awake staring up at the golden tent top and worrying, as always, about my family, my country and my son —might be forced to take very drastic action.

Would he do so? Could I force him to do so, if it became necessary to save the land? Would he want to do so? Would

I want to do so, against my son who has already suffered so much in his short twenty years?

My son—my son . . . The Great Wife fears tomorrow and grieves for you thereby. Would that she were not your mother, for then she could be snoring happily too. But, alas, she is.

Amonhotep III (Life, health, prosperity!)

I SNORE LOUDLY so that she will think I am asleep: but I am not asleep. I am thinking of our son, and given such thoughts, how can Pharaoh sleep?

How could any Pharaoh sleep, given such a son as no Pharaoh before has ever had?

I think back upon my life and I see no cause for this. It cannot be Amon's further punishment for his mother and me, because we have appeased Amon in many things, and we have given our son every strengthening of love and support that a child could possibly receive. We have made the expressions of our love even deeper and stronger because of his illness. Never have we failed him. Why, then, is he failing us?

Many years ago, on the day he was born and his brother murdered, I decided I would dedicate him to the Aten: but it has gotten out of hand. The counterweight to Amon, the balance of gods which I thought would restore to the House of Thebes its rightful powers without having to worry about the constant inroads of Amon, has not come about. Instead he has pushed far beyond what I contemplated, and tomorrow, apparently, intends to push even further, toward —what? We do not know. As with everything that goes on behind that secretive face, he does not tell us. Only my niece Nefertiti knows what he really thinks, and I suspect that even she is frequently in the dark. But her strength, of course, is that she believes—still believes, as devoutly as she ever did.

Tiye and I no longer do. Now we worry, though it is rare that we express it to one another candidly. If we did I should probably stop this pretense of sleep and we would discuss it now. But it has been one of my bad days, and I do not feel like endless discussion of the riddle we have produced. My teeth hurt, my limbs ache. Three draughts of wine for relief have proved more skull-splitting than medicinal. Min did come to my aid sufficiently an hour ago for me to render dutiful tribute to the Great Wife and all her many remarkable qualities, but that is enough. I am exhausted now, and who knows: perhaps the result will be another such as keeps us awake tonight—though I cannot really believe that Amon would take such further revenge. The Co-Regent has given him enough to think about: he would not want two of the same kind after him!

Not, of course, that there could ever be two of the same kind. The older he grows and the more he does, the more I believe Nefer-Kheperu-Ra to be unique among men, perhaps unique in history. Certainly he is unique among Pharaohs, for never has there been one who so openly and determinedly challenged *ma'at* and the accustomed order of things. He is very stubborn, our son. We see him on a certain course, thinking maturity would mellow and moderate it into a smooth and diplomatic approach that would enable him to accomplish what we wished without creating antagonisms that could ultimately bring him down if he goes too far. We reckoned without his illness, which changed all things. It brought him, I think, great visions; but it also, I fear, removed in him some balance that is necessary if a Pharaoh is not to place himself beyond the area in which ordinary men can understand him. For on that understanding, though we be gods, rests the acceptance of our divinity. Without it, even we must fail.

With almost no exceptions, we Pharaohs have been, though divine, what one might almost call "ordinary men." We have in our ranks no great madmen, no great fanatics, no great monsters killing and murdering. It is on the whole a gentle record, a record of averages, a record of decent and kindly things in which most of us have taken seriously, and worked hard at, our task of ruling the Two Lands with fairness and with justice. The Double Crown is ours by divine right, but we have taken it as a sacred trust. Witnessing the constant chaos on our borders, I do not think any other nation has been equally blessed.

So in my time have I also ruled, though I know there have been occasions when this dear little head beside me has not thought so. It is true I have not led great conquests to win new lands: I did not need to, all the land Kemet requires Kemet has. It is true I have not promulgated many new laws: it has not been necessary, the laws handed down have for centuries proved sufficient to govern the Two Kingdoms peaceably. It is true I have not shown myself along the borders, made expeditions to frighten allies constantly quarreling among themselves: but why should I? Babylon, Mittani, Gebal, Syria, Megiddo, the Hebrews— let them squabble, it only makes Kemet stronger. Or so I see it, though I know that Tiye, Aye and many others, including Amonhotep, Son of Hapu, and Kaires, have often urged that I take such journeys. I have always refused: I like it here.

But I have built. How I have built! At Medinet Habu and Malkata I have built an enormous complex of palaces, temples, granaries, court offices, nobles' houses, army barracks, servants' quarters. At Sakkara I have built the Serapeum for the burial of the Serapis bulls sacred to the Sun. At Karnak I have added the first row of pillars for what may someday be an even greater hypostyle hall leading to the altar, and I have erected the massive Third Pylon in tribute to the god. I have also built a temple at Karnak to Mont, the original god of Thebes. I have built a viewing-temple for Amon on the west bank of the river at Thebes, and have built a temple to him at Sulb just north of the Third Cataract. I am building the Southern Sanctuary of Amon at Luxor, the greatest single temple ever erected to the god, to his wife Mut and to their son Khons.

For myself, I have built a palace at Memphis and a hunting lodge in the Faiyum, the great oasis southwest of the Delta where many Pharaohs before me have relaxed to hunt ducks, geese, lion and other game. And connected with the Palace of Malkata by a causeway across the Nile marshes, I have built a mortuary temple to myself which exceeds in size and beauty any mortuary temple ever built by any Pharaoh, even Hatshepsut (Life, health, prosperity!). This beautiful temple to myself (where I go frequently, attended by the Court, to worship myself) is made of the best white sandstone, inlaid with gold. Its floor is silver, its pillars and portals are painted with electrum. It has a great stela inside, covered with gold and precious stones, which proclaims my glory. Along its mammoth hallway stand many beautiful statues of myself, some carved from the fine granite of the Elephantine Islands at Aswan, others of hard red quartzite and many other fine stones and jewels. It has a sacred lake which is filled by the Nile, and many priests and officers care for it. It is guarded by two colossi of myself which stand side by side at the gates, so that the visitor must pass between them as he enters. Thus may he pause as he does so and marvel at my greatness.

And my wife, my brother-in-law and my most trusted lieutenants say of me that I have done nothing for Kemet! I believe there must be jealousy there, for the gods know I have done more than any other king.

And furthermore: at my first Jubilee three years ago, I made a deliberate attempt to restore the balance with Amon which my son by then had already done so much to overturn. He had already started eight temples to the Aten, including the enormous ones at Karnak and Memphis; he had named his first two daughters for the Aten as he was subsequently to name his third; and he had begun to abandon the daily rituals that all Pharaohs have always performed for Amon at the dawn of each day. It is true that last year he named a senile old man, Maya, to be High Priest of Amon, but this was regarded by everyone as simply a gesture, and an insulting one at that. It did not please Amon and it only blunted the nose of my brother-in-law Aanen, who remained the still all-powerful Second Prophet of Amon and became even more embittered and subversive toward his nephew. So I felt I should do something.

Therefore when the time came for my First Jubilee—and what a magnificent ceremony I caused that to be!—I formally changed the name of Medinet Habu and the Malkata complex from "The-House-of-Neb-Ma'at-Ra-Shines-Like-Aten" to "The-House-of-Rejoicing."

My first intention was to rename it "The-House-of-Rejoicing-Which-Is-Pleasing-to-Amon," but that was not to be. The idea brought the first open argument between the Co-Regent and me, and it proved to me beyond all doubt how headstrong he had become. Because, I regret to say, he won.

The Great Wife and I had returned from our northern capital at Memphis, where the Jubilee was celebrated in conjunction with the festival of the falcon death-god Sokar. These secret rites, which only Pharaoh is permitted to attend, are a reminder to Pharaoh of his mortality and also a reminder of the very ancient time when the thirty-year Jubilee was held for the purpose of killing and dismembering the King, presumably by then a fairly old man, so that a new and vigorous ruler might assume the crown. If this ever really happened it is lost in the mists of time, but the priests of Sokar over the centuries have taken it upon themselves to act as what they like to call "the conscience of the King" by re-enacting it in mime for each of us who reaches Jubilee. They deem it good, and the people seem to agree, that Pharaoh be reminded of this presumed grisly fate of his probably mythical forebears. It is the custom of ages. So one attends, solemnly—all participants knowing full well that if anyone nowadays dared so much as touch the hem of Pharaoh's garment without permission he would be instantly struck down.

That pleasant duty performed, and suitable time having been spent in Memphis to satisfy our loyal subjects of Lower Kemet, we embarked upon the river and sailed south through our adoring people to come again to Thebes. There the Great Wife and I were towed in a barque along a canal in western Thebes, our passage an imitation of Ra's as he moves through the final hours of night to emerge once more in the east for glorious rebirth. So did we emerge at the end of the canal, which terminated at the foot of my two colossi, and there were once more formally recrowned by Aanen and his priests of Amon.

I announced, amid wild rejoicing (led noisily by Aanen), that I intended to rename Medinet Habu in Amon's honor and would presently issue a scarab containing the new designation. Tiye, Aye and I had just returned to Malkata, congratulating ourselves that we had done much to make Aanen happy and pull the sting of his anger, when word came by flustered messenger that the Co-Regent, instead of recrossing the river to the small palace he has chosen to build for himself and his family in southern Thebes, was on his way to Malkata to see me.

"I came to warn you, Son of the Sun," the messenger said humbly from his position face down, prostrate at my feet. "His young Majesty is angry."

I reached down, touched his shoulder in a kindly way, and said:

"Thank you, good friend. I think I know why, but it need not trouble you. Take this jewel, and go."

And I detached a small carnelian from my ceremonial belt and gave it to him. He backed out, bowing low and uttering many grateful sounds, arriving at the doorway just as my son started to enter. Bowing to me, he did not, of course, see my son, and, in fact, bumped into him. When he turned around and saw who it was, he turned so completely white that we all thought he would faint.

"Here!" the Co-Regent said, grabbing his arm to steady him, though the sudden movement almost upset his own somewhat precarious balance. "You are all right, my good man. You are all right! There is no harm. Go, now!"

And for a moment, as he watched the poor devil flee in relieved confusion down the corridor, he could not suppress a smile. It did not last as he turned to face us.

"Father," he said evenly, "what is the name you intend to give to this place?"

For a second I contemplated some evasion; but he has an instinct, sharpened no doubt by adversity—one more of the damnable consequences of his damnable ailment—

which very often permits him to see through evasions. And I am, after all, his father and Pharaoh, and hardly afraid to speak.

"The-House-of-Rejoicing-Which-Is-Pleasing-to-Amon," I said with a calm indifference I did not entirely feel, for I did not know what explosion this might produce.

"I forbid it," he said, very quietly but with unmistakable force.

"*Forbid* it?" I cried in astonishment, and at my side Tiye cried also, "*Forbid* it? How dare you address Pharaoh like that?"

"I, too, am Pharaoh," he said, still quietly, still evenly, still with the same soft but adamantine force. . . . "Would you uncrown me, Son of the Sun?"

There have been times, I must admit, when I have thought this might not be such a bad idea; but he knows as well as I that it is impossible. Once done, it is done, forever and ever. He also knows that his mother and I love him too much to do him the violence which has disposed of some other obstreperous heirs to the Double Crown over the centuries. So it was not with gratitude but with something close to mockery in his voice that he repeated calmly:

"Would you uncrown me, Father?"

"I may not do that," I said, keeping my own voice steady with great difficulty, "but I could send you on an expedition to Punt or Kush or Mittani or Naharin and keep you away for as long as it pleases me."

I was aware of a small warning movement from the Great Wife, which of course instantly weakened my authority; followed by a discreet but insistent clearing of the throat by my brother-in-law Aye, which did not help either. My son, who for a split second had looked shaken, took these signs to mean exactly what they did.

"I should refuse to go," he said.

"I should *order* you!" I shouted, aware as I did so that the shout in itself was an abandonment of authority: I should somehow have managed to keep as calm as he, but for the life of me I was unable.

"Then you would have to kill me," he said with perfect control, "for I still should refuse to go."

"You would *have* to go!" I cried.

"Son of the Sun," he said, "I would *not* go."

For several moments I am afraid I glared at him, simply too frustrated and angry to speak. He returned me gaze for gaze from those long, narrow eyes that reveal so little he does not wish them to. And presently, once again, my brother-in-law Aye gently but insistently cleared his throat.

"Yes?" I snapped, turning on him sharply, relieved to be able to vent my anger on someone who at least thinks and acts like a normal human being. "What is it, Brother?"

"Majesty," Aye said quietly, "we are all aware that there is no purpose to be gained by threatening Nefer-Kheperu-Ra. We all know that he lives in truth and speaks the truth. When he says he would die rather than go, we know he would die rather than go. Therefore I think there must be some other way to resolve this impasse."

"And who has created this 'impasse'?" I demanded with an anger made greater by the fact that my teeth, as always when I am under stress, seemed to be choosing this partic-ular moment to hurt worse than ever. "*He* has, by his ri-diculous attempt to interfere with *my* desire to rename *my* palace as *I* wish in whatever way is pleasing to *me,* who am Pharaoh and King of the Two Lands."

"But as he truly says, Neb-Ma'at-Ra," Aye pointed out, respectfully but firmly, "so is he. And therefore he perhaps has some small voice, though I will agree a junior one, in a decision bearing so directly upon the relations of your House with the priests of Amon."

"Does he consult me when he idolizes the Aten and thereby offends the priests of Amon?" I demanded bitterly; and my son, of course, turned it upon me, which I suppose I had invited.

"Who first urged me to worship the Aten, Father," he asked quietly, "if it was not you, O Son of the Sun?"

For a moment I was at a loss to reply, and it was the moment Aye had been waiting for, because, as always, he had a compromise to offer. Aye is full of compromises, which is why he will probably survive us all. But he is a good and shrewd man and has helped our House times be-yond measure. I cannot be too harsh with him—even though now, with this new move of accepting the assistant priesthood of the Aten, he has me somewhat puzzled, though I think I see his reasoning.

"Perhaps the solution is a simple one, Majesty," he said to me. "And perhaps if your father agrees, you will be considerate enough to agree also, Majesty," he said to my son.

Neither of us gave ground at that moment: we simply stared at him and waited.

"Neb-Ma'at-Ra," he said, "why do you not be content to rename Medinet Habu simply 'The-House-of-Rejoicing'?—but tell my brother Aanen at the same time," he added quickly as I started to protest, "that of course this means rejoicing for Amon—for it were not so, why, then, have you built such great works for Amon? On every hand he sees them rise. The sounds of the hammer, the adze, the chisel and the shovel are everywhere in Thebes, ringing from Karnak, ringing from Luxor, to the greater glory of the god. Surely if there is rejoicing in Medinet Habu it is rejoicing for Amon. Aanen and his priests can see this with their eyes and hear it with their ears. Why, then, is it necessary to spell it out?"

"Because I wish to spell it out," I said, but less certainly.

"It is not necessary, Son of the Sun," Aye said. "It is apparent in everything you do."

There was a pause while I thought. My son, as always, remained absolutely silent, absolutely still. No expression, of interest, triumph or concern, appeared upon that long, unsmiling face. Only the eyes were alive behind their narrowed lids; and them I have long since stopped trying to analyze.

It was his mother who finally spoke, siding, as I expected, with her brother and her son.

"Son of the Sun," she said, "my brother speaks much wisdom, as always. It is not necessary to emphasize to Amon what Amon already knows. And it is not necessary to insult our son and the Aten, which such a complete renaming as you propose would do. In fact, if you insult the Aten you will not only please Amon but you will seriously weaken the Aten as well. And I do not think you wish to please Amon *that* much."

"Of course you do not, Majesty," my son said then, so calmly that one would never have guessed the triumph he must have been feeling. "Why do you not simply announce that you have decided to add the name 'The-House-of-Rejoicing' to the name 'The-House-of-Neb-Ma'at-Ra Shines-Like-Aten'? Those who choose may use either. Thereby both gods will be appeased, the balance will be kept, all will be happy. Is is not so?"

Confronted by their massed opposition, and by what Tiye has since succeeded in convincing me was a quite logical argument (my son's compromise, ironically—not Aye's, after all), I presently yielded. I told them I had secretly arrived at these conclusions myself, and had only wished to test them with my seeming obduracy. I congratulated them upon their shrewdness in correctly perceiving my own ideas. I said I would proceed as I had always intended to proceed: the old name would stand, but to it would be added a new designation which those who so desired might freely use; namely (I told them) the name I had always secretly contemplated—"The-House-of-Rejoicing."

I then dismissed them, telling them my teeth made further conversation too painful at the moment. Aye went to his house in the compound, Tiye retired to her chambers, the Co-Regent, face impassive, bowed low, kissed my hand, and departed for his boat and the short sail across the Nile to his palace in the south of Thebes.

I sent immediately for my brother-in-law Aanen and told him flatly and without embellishment what I intended to do.

"But—" he stammered in anger and amazement. "But you told me—"

"I did not tell you everything," I snapped, "nor do I need to. You will go now and tell your priests that they may rejoice at the new name of my House, for it honors Amon as many, many other things I have done have honored Amon."

"But—" he sputtered.

"*Go!*" I shouted, rising from my throne; and while Aanen does not often look terrified of me, for I am basically an easygoing man who does not often try to terrify people, this time he did.

Even so, after he had backed humbly and silently to the door, his head suddenly shot up, his eyes glared and he snarled, "That monstrous boy has bested you, Neb-Ma'at-Ra! Who is it who *truly* rejoices when he comes to 'The-House-of-Rejoicing'?"

Then he turned and stalked hurriedly away, fleeing the sound of my enraged shouts that followed him down the long corridor past the startled soldiers, who watched in amazement a sight that is almost never seen in Kemet: the open anger of the Good God.

But he was right, of course; and although none of us ever mentioned the matter again, it marked the beginning of the decline of my power and the increasing dominance of the young Pharaoh. Now it is all Amonhotep IV (life, health, prosperity!) and the Aten. Amon believes himself to be, and is, hard pressed, though as yet it does not extend to any actual physical attacks upon him or his power. And perhaps I should not concern myself if it does: perhaps I should simply enjoy in luxury whatever years remain to me. It would be easier that way, and I am not in sufficient health to fight the battles with my son that would be necessary to reverse his policies. Nor am I sure I want to. The Aten is a happy god, unlike dark Amon. Perhaps it may be for the best. . . .

Though still, of course, I worry. He is young, he is impulsive, he is determined, he is adamant. He is not flexible. He does not bend as a good ruler sometimes must.

Tomorrow he will reveal to us, he says, new wonders that will be good for our House, for Kemet and for everyone. Tiye has started snoring now and I believe I may dare cease my own pretense and think about this quietly for a time until Nut lets me sleep—if she does. She is aided by my son in keeping me awake: and my son is a powerful force.

I do not know quite what his mother and I have given Kemet. I marvel at it every day and only pray—to both Amon and Aten and, I assure you, with equal fervor—that it will not be the ruination of the land and of our House.

Aanen

WHY MUST MY FOOLISH brother-in-law always attempt to place me in the position of being the villain? He is losing his grip on Kemet, on the Empire, on his son, on his throne —and he prefers to turn on me when I dare to tell him the somber truth of it, which is that Nefer-Kheperu-Ra is running away with the country. Running away with the country and running away with the very *ma'at* and order of things, which the gods will not forgive. Certainly Amon will not forgive it if I have anything to say about it. And in spite of doddering old Maya, that joke of a High Priest foisted on us by the Co-Regent, I do.

My nephew is beyond belief. I will admit that he has not yet attacked us openly, he has not yet invaded our granaries, our temples and our stores: but he will, he will. I have sensed it coming for many years, ever since Pharaoh began to direct the thoughts of his misshapen son to the Aten. He unloosed a force he did not reckon with, that day; and now he cannot control it. Tomorrow something awful is going to happen: I feel it. Tomorrow Amon is going to have to fight: I know it.

Do not ask me how or why.

Amon tells me, and I believe.

We camp on the edge of this empty plain under the enormous desert stars, all of us waiting on one headstrong, willful, unpredictable youth of twenty obsessed and possessed by his dream of the Aten. There are some among my priests who say: "Do not worry, Amon is supreme and all-powerful. Nothing can injure Amon. He will live forever and ever, for millions and millions of years. No youth, even a Pharaoh, can destroy Amon. Amon lives forever."

But they do not know my nephew, and they do not know the hesitant way his parents and the Court react when they are warned of the perils of his course. They do not know Neb-Ma'at-Ra, who is fat, self-indulgent, ill and weak. They do not know my sister Tiye, who thinks she rules the Two Lands in her husband's shadow but has never, since his illness, been able to rule her strange, impatient son. They do not know our slippery brother Aye, who will do anything, even lend his name to the Aten, if it will prevent an explosion and preserve a compromise. They do not know the Queen Mother, whose body is now but a frail fragment of herself but whose will in some things is still as strong as Tiye's and who fears yet coddles her grandson. They do not know our niece Nefertiti, who has been trained from childhood to adore him, and whose faith, while it is shaken from time to time, remains basically serene in the conviction that all things her husband does are right and correct. They do not know Amonhotep, Son of Hapu, and Kaires, who I know must also have misgivings, but who so far have decided them in favor of the Co-Regent. And they do not know how I am mocked and despised and made fun of when I persist in reminding of the dangers that are implicit in the policies of Amonhotep IV (Life, health, prosperity!).

For, look you, I do not speak without warrant and I do not speak without example. It is true his temples to the Aten elsewhere in Kemet do not represent any great threat to Amon, because for one thing very few of the people pay attention to them and, for another, they do not take away from Amon any great number of priests. Even in Memphis and Karnak, while the temples are huge, he has not assigned to them many priests. Even these we could live with.

Even, I suppose, could we live with the virtual crowning of the Aten in Jubilee, even with the show of Pharaoh's pomp with which my nephew has surrounded his god, even with the way in which my nephew increasingly makes himself the sole intermediary between the people and the Aten. The problem is more subtle than that; and I submit that I am not foolish, or stupid, or overly concerned, or too insistent, when I worry about it.

The matter is basically psychological—so far. The young Pharaoh is gathering things unto himself, slowly but surely, in preparation for—what? This I do not know, but all logic points to some form of direct challenge to Amon, sooner or later. The others prefer not to see this, for if they saw it and admitted it they might be forced to intervene. And they do not wish to intervene, because if they did they would face a battle with my nephew. And secretly, though they are too cowardly to admit it to anyone, particularly to themselves, they do not wish such a battle. Secretly they are afraid of him, and they are no longer sure they could win.

Therefore I am not wrong to be concerned for Amon. Nor am I exceeding my authority or my rights in attempting to protect him. Amon has helped the Eighteenth Dynasty to govern Kemet for three hundred years, and there have been many times when Amon has saved the House of Thebes from disaster. Amon has blessed its Pharaohs, supported its conquests, collected its tribute, confirmed its hold on the people, strengthened it in all things. Amon has been its partner in every way for generations. Amon has *a right* to his power and influence, *because he has earned them.* And now Amon is to be pushed about, diminished, made mock of and given second place by a malformed, headstrong boy?

Not while Aanen lives!

Pray Amon I may live long enough to muster the forces of Amon if what I fear comes true! Pray Amon I may live long enough to see my arrogant nephew humbled and restored to the true faith of Amon where he belongs! The others may be cowards, but I am not. I fear only Amon, not my nephew. And Amon will strengthen *me* in all things, too, for I am righteous in his eyes, and with his blessing for works well done I will live forever and ever, for millions and millions of years.

Nonetheless, I am uneasy tonight as the cook fires one by one go out and silence settles finally over the great encampment and the empty plain that stretches away behind us eastward toward the hills. It is a strange place. I do not believe there have ever been any temples or habitation here. It is quite typical of the Co-Regent that he should bring us to this place, quite typical that he should keep his reasons a mystery. We rarely speak these days, but last time we did, he said only, "Uncle, I am visiting another place. I wish you to accompany me." And gave me such a long and disconcerting stare from those narrow, hooded eyes that I suddenly felt a positive shiver go up and down my spine.

"Yes, Majesty," I said, for it was all I could say: and here I am.

But I am not here to take idly whatever he has dreamed up in that odd, misshapen head. He does not frighten *me*.

Amon! Give me strength to meet his challenges, for I am your servant in all things, and you I will not fail!

Aye

IT NEARS MIDNIGHT. Ra is halfway gone on his journey from west to east beneath the earth. It will only be a short while before his barque will come in sight of its resting place and the first faint hint of dawn will awaken this hushed encampment again to life. Already I think I can hear in the distance along the riverbank a faint rustling, the beginnings of movement toward the plain: the multitudes will presently stream blindly toward its center, thinking instinctively that somehow at the center they will find the mystery my nephew has prepared for them.

Whether it will be there or elsewhere on the vast expanse, I do not know, for he has, as usual, preferred to remain secretive and obscure. But in one sense I do not think it will be at the center: Amonhotep IV (Life, health, prosperity!) has moved far from the center in the five years of his co-regency. He is taking Kemet in new directions, far from the balance and the center which have for many hundreds of years kept the Two Lands relatively stable, peaceable and free.

On this journey I have gone much of the way with him, and I know my sister, my brother-in-law, my brother and many in Kemet wonder why. Partly, I suppose, it has been a matter of uneasy conscience: I was perhaps the principal encourager of the young Pharaoh and my daughter Nefertiti in their questionings of the gods: or at least I was their principal friendly ear . . . I did not say no. If the result is to be dangerous to Kemet, then it is I who must help bring it back within bounds. It is I who must offer the principal moderating force, which I believe they will accept from me, as their preceptor, more easily than they will from anyone else.

In this I may be mistaken, but nonetheless it is the path I must pursue. Conscience will permit no other; and Aye, who has been the conscience of the House of Thebes in so many things, cannot fail it now or he should never be able to face himself again.

So when he asked me if I would join him and my daughter in the hierarchy of the Aten, I said I would; not knowing what it would portend, but knowing that so far, at least, his devotion to the new god has not seriously harmed the old. It may, as my tiresome brother Aanen fears: there may yet come a direct assault upon Amon. But so far it has not appeared. So far our nephew seems to be more concerned with moving in his own direction than in challenging Amon. The only thing he has actually done to Amon is to neglect him: and this, of course, infuriates my brother and all his busy priesthood. They love power and during the Eighteenth Dynasty they have acquired far more than their safe share of it. It is very annoying to be ignored by the One who will presently be the sole ruler of the Two Kingdoms. Annoying and, I suspect, frightening in its potential.

But as yet, even so, nothing that Amon can really complain about. My brother-in-law still maintains the forms

of daily worship, continues to build his vast temple to
Amon at Luxor, honors the god with other favors in other
places. He, too, tries to play the tricky game of walking
the rolling palm log over the flooding Nile. Having encouraged his son to embrace the Aten, he has steadily
backed away and tried to balance it by appeasing Amon.
It has not worked very well, but at least it has kept
things from coming to crisis; and him, too, I have encouraged, for only by keeping the two opposing forces in
equal tension with one another can Kemet be spared the
devastation that might ensue were conflict to come and
bring one or the other completely unchallenged power.

It is my hope that my nephew realizes this also, though
there are many times when I wonder what goes on in that
enigmatic head. He is fond of elliptical phrases, oblique
meanings, mysterious hints. "Uncle," he said on the day he
asked me to serve as Assistant High Priest of the Aten,
"you will assist in wonders."

"What wonders are those?" I asked in a voice as close
to scorn as I dared, for I wish to discourage these mental
adventurings he seems to be on all the time. "Surely there
are no wonders left that Kemet has not seen in her two
thousand years of history."

"Kemet has not seen *me*," he said, with a certain rising
emphasis in his high voice that made me realize he was
in full earnest. "I am such a wonder as Kemet still does
not know what to make of, and I shall do such wonders
as Kemet will not know what to make of, also. You will
be with me, Uncle. It is a great honor."

"Oh, I know that," I assured him, though I had my own
thoughts about it. "It is your purpose, then, to make the
Aten equal with Amon, I take it."

For a moment he simply gave me a bland stare. Then
an ironic little smile touched the heavy lips.

"Uncle," he said, and at his side Nefertiti, too, permitted a small, ironic amusement to cross that lovely face
as he replied, "that *would* be a wonder, and it *may* be the
one I contemplate. Again, it may not. Who knows? Perhaps we should await events as Amon and the Aten bring
them to us, and see."

"Do you really *know* what you intend to do, Majesty?" I pressed in dead earnest myself, now.

"Oh, I know," he said, and at his side Nefertiti said earnestly, "Yes, he *knows,* Father. Be assured of that."

"And you support him in it, you are sure it is for the good of Kemet, and of this House?" I asked, giving her the steady look that once, long ago before she became so completely devoted to her cousin, used to produce the truth. And of course it produced the truth now, as she sees it.

"I am convinced that it is for the good of Kemet and of this House," she said solemnly, and I perceived that she meant it absolutely.

"But neither of you will tell the Assistant High Priest of the Aten what it is," I said in a musing tone and deliberately looked out the window, apparently studying the hurrying river busy with boats. "How very strange. . . ."

"High Priest, High Priestess, Assistant High Priest," my nephew said airily. "All must await the wisdom of the Aten, which I shall presently reveal."

"I thought you said Amon and the Aten would reveal it together," I said quickly, and as quickly he replied:

"*I* shall reveal it when the Aten tells me, for I am the Aten's son and only I can understand him. Amon," he added, and again the ironic little smile touched both their faces, "will receive the revelation too—when the Aten gives it to *me*. Amon may then join in revealing it to the people, if he chooses—in fact," he added slowly, "I think I shall command your brother to attend me when I reveal it. That will be the height of the jest."

"What jest, Majesty?" I demanded sharply, too alarmed by his tone and the general drift of the conversation to be diplomatic. "You speak of 'jests' as though this were a game you are playing with Kemet and the gods. Pharaoh does not play games with Kemet and the gods. Pharaoh takes his trust seriously in all things."

"So I have observed," he said with a sudden devastating dryness, "in my father."

And Nefertiti laughed aloud (as she rarely does nowadays), an almost girlish, completely amused and com-

pletely disrespectful sound that instantly magnified my
concern a hundredfold.

"Daughter," I said sharply, "be more respectful of the
Good God!"

"But he is so *funny*," she said and then he joined her
in laughter, their private laughter which seems to spring
from some secret known only to them—and presumably,
I suppose, to the Aten, for now *he* seems to be their
principal confidant in everything.

"I do not wish to discuss it further, Majesty," I said
stiffly. "I beg leave to go now." And I started to bow low
and back out of his presence. But he stopped me by raising a hand like long talons on a long, thin arm.

"You are too serious, Uncle," he said. "No one can
serve the Aten in such a mood. He is a happy god. Smile,
Uncle. Smile!"

"I hope you know what you are doing, Son of the Sun,"
I said gravely; and suddenly grave himself, he replied
slowly:

"I do, Uncle. And it will be best for all. I, who am living in truth, promise it!"

He makes much of this living in truth, I thought as I left
them then; but what is the truth in which he lives? Is it
the ancient truth of Kemet, or is it some new truth he has
devised for himself? Is it a truth by which the land can
live, or is it a truth that will bring death?

Now we are here at this nameless bend in the river,
waiting for Ra to return so that the young Pharaoh may
perform whatever ceremonies he has in mind. My sister
and brother-in-law are here, Aanen is here, we are all
here. Some have come willingly, like myself, some reluctantly, like Aanen, some with many misgivings, like Pharaoh and the Great Wife; but all have come. The thoughts
of all Kemet are concentrated here at the river bend, because my nephew has sent out many messengers to
announce that he plans a great event for the Two Kingdoms. And many wonder, I am sure, why Aye will be at
his side.

Well, it is as I say: I helped to bring him here, I helped

to prepare whatever it is that is coming—inadvertently, not deliberately, but nonetheless I played my part. It may mean great good for Kemet, in which case I shall rejoice with all; but if, as to his elders seem more likely, it is something of danger or even disaster which impends, then it is Aye whose conscience says he must stand by and help to set it right. My nephew trusts me, I think, more than he does his parents, perhaps more than anyone; and Nefertiti is still my daughter. They will, perhaps, listen to me if I must speak in defense of Kemet. I must be with them when the hour comes, for their sake and for the Two Lands.

He has instructed me to join them in procession beginning two hours after dawn. The ceremony is to be at noon when Ra stands directly overhead. Presumably the hours between will be filled with driving across the plain to greet the people. Then will come the revelation, and his purpose will be known.

I should like to sleep, but I do not think I will. A moment ago I lifted the tent flap and stared out across the huge, mysterious plain which stretches away to the east. The boat of Khons had almost disappeared. Its silvery light was dimmed. The full movement of the multitudes had not yet begun. Empty, mysterious, haunting and dark, the ageless sands stretched far away.

What does he see out there, my strange, unhappy, touching nephew? What "wonders" will he conjure up from those eternal dunes and gullies, so utterly barren of life? Who speaks to him, out there in that eternal silence?

He hears a Voice we do not hear, sees a Vision we cannot see. And he believes. This I know. He sincerely and completely believes.

I look out upon that empty plain and I say to Whoever or Whatever it is that has brought him here: "Be good to him. Be good to us. He believes he is doing what is right, he believes he is living in truth. Help him, and help us."

No answer comes. I shiver and drop the tent flap, turn back to my pallet and cushions on the ground.

I should like to sleep.

But I do not think I will.

Nefertiti

AN HOUR AGO he slipped away, his unmistakable form disguised in a loose-flowing, simple white linen gown such as minor officials sometimes wear. I think he would have gone naked, as we all do sometimes in Kemet, in the Palace and even in the streets, in the dreadful heat of summer, were it not that his body is too familiar, now, to any who might surprise him. I do not think any will, out on the plain where soon he will perform his wonders. It is a brave man who would venture upon that desolate expanse at this time of night; and no man, not even the young Pharaoh, would go alone.

He did not take me with him. For the first time since our marriage that I can remember, we are apart. Only Kaires attends him, and this, as he explained to me, solely for protection if they should be surprised. Yet of course he is his own protection: no man would dare touch Pharaoh. I think he fears—what? I do not know. I do not think he knows. But he does not want me exposed to it, if it should be there. He wanted a man beside him, and Kaires, brave and solid—and still, as we call him sentimentally, our "big brother"—was the logical choice.

So after the Court was asleep, they slipped away. Kaires had arranged earlier that two horses be tethered perhaps a half mile out upon the plain. I do not know his excuse, but he is now Chief Scribe and Commander of the Horse of Amonhotep IV (life, health, prosperity!), and no one questions. Sometime shortly before 3 A.M., when all the camp was silent and sleeping at last, there came the tiniest scratching on the golden tent where its folds loop low above our heads. Instantly my husband turned to me, kissed me, rose from our golden bed and began to struggle to pull the linen garment over his head. His arms became caught, he thrashed about awkwardly: I do not believe he had ever worn such a thing in his life. I got up immediately and helped him; together, after some further tugging and pulling, we managed. He looked at me and we almost laughed aloud for a moment at the spectacle he made: the god enfolded in the commoner's garb. Then amusement fled, a somber, almost frightening expression came into his eyes.

"Wish me well, beloved wife," he whispered.

"In all things, beloved husband," I whispered back.

Again we kissed, a strange desperation in it now; he lifted the tent fold from its peg beside our bed, ducked awkwardly under and disappeared. I heard one quick sibilant whisper of greeting; then all was still again; and now they are somewhere on the desolate plain.

Desolate now: but at noon when Ra stands straight above it will be desolate no longer. Then all our dreaming and planning will come true. And desolation will be gone from the plain, from Kemet, and from the hearts of men, forever and ever, for millions and millions of years.

This do I believe. This does he believe. Together we will make it come to pass.

Then all who oppose and question us now will realize that from the beginning we have been concerned only with their welfare and happiness. And all doubts will vanish and they will see that the Pharaoh Amonhotep IV (life, health, prosperity!) is the greatest god who ever lived.

So do I see him, I, Nefertiti, who have been his Chief Wife for five years, his friend, companion and principal supporter for twenty. And I do not say this to detract from such other great gods as Menes, My-cer-i-nus, Amose I, Tuthmose III, Hatshepsut or any of them (life, health, prosperity to them all!). It is simply that my husband is greater than them all. His name will lead all others. This do I believe.

I am aware that there is much whispering in the Court about our marriage, as there is much opposition in the country to our policies. My cousin Sitamon is convinced, I am sure, that the Co-Regent probably has fits of temper in which he beats me. Pharaoh and the Great Wife wonder how I maintain my serenity in the face of what is, I must admit, a very stubborn nature. My father, Kaires, Giluk-hipa, Queen Mutemwiya, Amonhotep, Son of Hapu—I know they all have questions and conjectures. But I give them nothing. They will never have from my expression, my words or my actions any answers to their questions, any food for their conjectures.

For I, too, am stubborn, if they know it not; and I, too, have pride. And my life is dedicated to my husband's, which should not surprise them, for it was their idea.

Knowing him so well, and having lived through his illness with him as intimately as I did, I was aware after it passed that it had left him with great tensions inside that now and again must find release. But never has he struck me, never has he raised his voice in anger against me—never. His angers and impatience have always been directed against others. They should be thankful to me, not critical or gossiping, because far more often than they know it has been I who have soothed his anger, diverted his impatience, directed the tension toward harmless things upon which it could expend itself without doing hurt to anyone or anything. It is I who have made it possible for him to maintain his public calm many times when without me he would have given way to fury.

I look in my mirror when my faithful Anser-Wossett, still my principal lady in waiting though I know she does not approve of the Aten, brings it to me in the morning. I no longer see the girl I used to see: the youthful plumpness of face has thinned away, the cheekbones are finer and more pronounced, the mouth is mature and thought-ful, the eyes gaze forth upon the world with a steady, un-derstanding and compassionate glance. The girl is gone: a beautiful woman has truly come, at last.

Life has made me ever more striking than I was: and
life, as it does, has exacted its own price therefor.

I find, now, that I rarely laugh any more. I find that I
am given more to moods, that I am apt to fall into thoughtful silences, that I move less quickly and erratically, at a
slower and more stately pace. I find that I no longer
have to work at being Queen of the Two Lands: I *am*
Queen of the Two Lands—and I am even more. For
the Aten has placed in my hands responsibility for my
husband's life and stability, as it has placed in his hands
responsibility for the life and stability of the Two Lands;
and in such a circumstance Kemet is most fortunate that
I have matured as rapidly as I have.

At first it was almost play, with us. We would build
temples to the Aten, we would shock Amon and particularly our tiresome uncle Aanen, we would break with the
old traditions of lifeless art that have always surrounded
Pharaoh and his family, we would launch a new naturalism, we would go naked about the Palace and even in the
streets, we would show ourselves to the people exactly as
we are, we would live in truth. But living in truth is not
an easy thing, and for it we have had to pay in gossip,
criticism and concern.

And for each of our tributes to the Aten we have had to
pay in growing animosity from Amon. And within the
Family we have had to meet and overcome a usually suppressed but steadily growing resistance that has not quite
dared challenge us openly but has nonetheless been a silent—and sometimes not so silent—reproach.

All this has dragged upon us: it has clouded the joy
with which we have embraced the Aten and embarked
upon our course of living in truth. Things that should have
been happy have not been happy. Exciting new adventures begun in joy and hopefulness have turned into con-
tests of will and stubborn tenacity. It has, I am afraid,
made us harsher; and this, too, life has drawn upon my
face, in lines too subtle, perhaps, for most to see, but unmistakable to the one who has studied it in closest detail
every day for the better part of her twenty years.

We have come now, we feel, to something of a crisis.

Fifteen temples have been built to the Aten. Our three daughters, Meryt-aten, Meket-aten and Ankh-e-sen-pa-aten have been named for him. The fourth child I am presently carrying (we pray constantly to him that it will be the son we desperately hope for) will be named for him. For him we have entirely abandoned the rituals of Amon.

Nonetheless, we have done no real harm to Amon with our attentions to the Aten. We have not suborned his priests or robbed his granaries or sacked his temples. And although we live in truth, we have not required it of anyone else, though my husband might easily have done so by simple edict and all of Kemet would have been forced to obey.

We have harmed no one, we have simply gone our own way: hoping that those of our people who wished to do as we do would find themselves, after many centuries of being bound by tradition and fear, free at last to live as they please and to worship the Aten, who is light and gentle and happy, not dark and heavy and threatening like Amon.

It has not come about.

But still we have had to take the criticism for it, and fight battles nonetheless real for being mostly in the hearts of our family and our people.

And so we have decided on the course that my husband will announce at noon when Ra stands overhead.

For me, this is the only logical and practical thing to do. For my husband, it is something more—something which even I, perhaps, cannot understand entirely. I support it because I am logical, because I see its inevitability—and because I love him and believe in him.

He has deeper reasons, I think, which he has tried to explain to me but which I do not really grasp. He moves, I think, on a higher, more mystical level, though I follow him as best I can. Sometimes even I do not know what goes on behind that closed, defensive face. But I love, I believe and I follow.

Now he is far off somewhere on the plain with Kaires

—sound, steady, solid Kaires, who understands no dreams or mystical things, only practical realities.

I wonder if my husband is even now explaining to him, as he has to me, what he has in mind and how he thinks? If so, I know Kaires, and he will never understand, though my husband talk for hours.

Or are they standing in silence while my husband dreams of what tomorrow will bring and Kaires waits, patiently—as he is always patient (and careful)—until his master decides to come home?

Rather more likely the latter, I think: honest Kaires, who has always loved and supported us so well!

Together my husband and I have made great plans and dreamed great dreams. Some of them we have already made come true. Now the greatest of them all is about to unfold.

I am happy for him, though he travels, sometimes, into regions where even I, who have worshiped him from a child, cannot completely understand or truly follow.

Kaires

HE HAS LEFT ME here in the middle of the plain and gone on east into the shadows of the night. He has left his horse and his garment. Stark naked and utterly alone, he is shuffling slowly and painfully, but with a terrible determination, through the clutching sand toward the eastern hills. Only Nut knows where he is now. In an hour I am to light a torch to guide him back.

Where does he go, strange Nefer-Kheperu-Ra? What is he after? What does he seek?

I do not know.

I am afraid of what will happen at noon when he performs his "wonders."

I am afraid for him, for Kemet and for all of us.

I have come with him thus far upon his strange life's journey, but I do not know how much farther I can go.

Amonhotep IV (Life, health, prosperity!)

BEHIND ME I have left beloved Nefertiti, faithful Kaires, my parents, my people, the world and all. I am as I entered the world and utterly alone upon my plain. Only the Aten, though he still travels beneath the earth and has not yet appeared in the eastern sky, knows where I am. He always knows, he always talks to me and guides me. He tells me what to do so that I may grow strong and enduring in his eyes and the eyes of all men for all time, forever and ever, for millions and millions of years.

I must have walked, now, in that painful shuffle which I permit very few of my people to see any more, almost a mile from where Kaires patiently waits. It is enough. He cannot see me or hear me and I cannot see or hear him. No sound breaks the hush of this vast expanse I first saw crowded with hundreds of thousands, seven years ago. Now that Khons in his silver boat has vanished down the western sky, no light touches it. Darkness and silence enfold me, unbroken and complete.

Thus have I desired it, for I must be alone for a little time to think of the god, to worship him, to contemplate what has been and what will be. In this lonely hour I must open my heart to him completely, receive him utterly, so that when he stands high above in the form of Ra at noontime, I may proceed firmly and unafraid to do what I know is right: so that I may live in truth this day as I have never lived in truth before, openly and completely and forever, in all things.

I have borne with great patience in the years of my co-regency, it seems to me, the things that have been done to me. I have suffered patiently the continuing overbearing presence of Amon; the sometimes rather ridiculous attempts of my father to first weaken, then appease him; the steady erosions of the power of Pharaoh and my House at Amon's hands; the attempts that have been made to thwart and mock my worship of the Aten, which has not harmed anyone but has only been intended to free my people and return them to what should be their only true worship, the worship of the Aten and of the Good God, myself, who is the Aten's only emissary and sole prophet upon earth.

Always the Aten has told me to be patient, to be gentle, to be tolerant—and to be *firm*. He had told me to build my temples to him, to pursue my plans for his enthronement, to live in truth and to proceed with my own anointing as the intermediary between himself and my people. And he has told me what my parents told me when they told me of Amon's murder of my brother Tuthmose V: if you find yourself forced to act against someone or something who is obstructing the truth in which you live, wait—prepare—choose your moment—and then, if you must, strike.

This, with the Aten's help, I plan to do; yet even now, though it will cause much consternation, I do not think I shall do Amon any really dreadful harm. Certainly it will not be half so dreadful as the wails of my bothersome uncle Aanen and his swarming white-robes will have the world believe.

I think, however, that he and they would do well to accept and not complain too much.

It will be better so.

In the Aten, and in living in truth, I have found such happiness as I expect to find while I, a god, live among men. Much of the happiness of ordinary men—above all, the simple happiness of *being left alone*—has been denied me by my station; even more has it been denied me by the effects of my illness, which used to make me a thing of wonder and mockery but now make me a thing of wonder and awe. For that I thank the Aten, who has taught me that life should not be dark and threatening, as it is with Amon, but should be free, open and happy; who has taught me that only by living in truth can one— even such a One as I, born to godhood—be truly free; that only by living in truth can one—even such a One as I, whom the gods have wantonly abused—rise above fear, rise above hurt, rise above *caring* . . . or, at least, caring quite so much. . . .

No longer, since I have come to believe so completely in the Aten, do I find that I shrink inwardly from public view in spite of my brave outward appearance. No longer do I cringe from some of the thoughts I know must be in the minds of those who see me. No longer do I hesitate to make my wishes known as emphatically and naturally as any normal Pharaoh would . . . or at least, no longer all of these—quite so much. . . .

Long ago I told Nefertiti, as I have since told others, that I would deliberately make of my malformation an instrument of awe, of superstition, of fear and of power —and I have done so. But for quite a long time, until the Aten came to my aid and shared his strength with me, I did it with an inner defiance and hurt so terrible that many times I did not think I could continue. I began to live in truth, openly—and often, quite literally, nakedly —to make of my monstrosity a fact of life in Kemet so overwhelming as to be completely inescapable. But I did these things without ever being quite convinced in my heart that what I was doing was right.

Then I began to understand the Aten and believe in him. He comforted and confirmed me in all things. He told me I was right. He drove fear and pain from my heart . . . as much as it can be driven.

Do you wonder that I glorify him?

Yet I have not attacked Amon. I have preferred to live in truth in a more positive way in my adoration of the Aten. I have built his temples to be light, open, airy—and small, with the exception of the two large ones at Mem-

phis and Karnak, sites that demand enormity. I have
named our daughters, as I shall name our sons, for him.
I have lived in truth and have hoped by my example to
encourage my people to do the same. And Amon has
continued to thrive.

But he has not been content. Pushed on by my uncle
and by many others high in Amon's hierarchy, restlessness
has spread through the temples and the land. Other gods
have been enlisted, hostility against me has been roused
by Amon with Ptah at Memphis, with Hathor at Den-
dera, with Bast at Bubastis, with Horus, Hapi, Isis, Thoth
and the rest. In the necropolis of Thebes beneath the Peak
of the West the priests of Osiris stir and grumble because
I have not yet begun my tomb there; and even they are
inflamed by Amon.

Unlike my father, I have decided that Amon cannot be
appeased, ever. He will always want more wealth and
power. He will never rest in his attempts to undercut and
weaken Pharaoh. He will never be content. The arrogance
that has caused his priest to refer to him as "the king of
the gods" during our Dynasty will never permit him to
live in harmony with the greater god whom I have proclaimed.

And I have decided: so be it.

But the gentle Aten still tells me that I should not attack Amon directly. He tells me I should continue to be
patient and forbearing. He says to me, simply: "Withdraw. Go your own way, which is the way of right. Live
in truth and fear not. And the people will come to believe, and all will be done in good time as you desire."

And I have decided: so be it.

Very far, very faint, just starting to touch the low
ridges of the distant hills, I see his light beginning to spread
across the world. I turn my face to the east, I lower myself with clumsy awkwardness to kneel upon the sand,
and I say to him:

O Aten, Great Father, Great God, in you I believe!
I shall not be afraid.
I shall do as you direct me in all things.

I shall proclaim your glories throughout the Two Lands and to all the ends of the world.

I shall live in truth with you and together we will rule forever and ever for millions and millions of years.

I face you naked as I entered the world and I say to you: Only you and I understand, O Aten, Great God, Great Father! Only you and I know.

I will never betray you, though I live through all eternity.

I, your son Akh-en-aten, so pledge myself!

A little wind is rising. Soon the day will come. I must return to camp and get ready for my wonders.

I turn to the west. Kaires' torch flares up, beckoning me back to the world of men.

I do not go alone into that harsh territory.

I go armored with the love of my god—*the one God*, who loves me as I love him.

Kaires

HE RETURNS TO ME out of the east as the first thin edge of Ra begins to rise above the jagged hills. His figure is tall and misshapen against the light as he shuffles forward. Hurriedly I help him struggle into his concealing garment. We mount and flog our horses back to camp as fast as they can cross the sand.

From time to time in the growing light I give his face a quick, surreptitious glance as we hurry on.

It is transfigured, unearthly. He has gone out of himself somewhere.

My fear increases.

tells me, Na-phu-ria's Chief Wife, Nefertiti. But already he has done a lot, I would say! He and Nefertiti have been out since two hours after their sun-god Ra rose in the east, and together with two of their three daughters and my new sister-in-law and brother-in-law, the Queen-Princess Sitamon and the Prince Smenkhkara, they have been riding back and forth across the plain in a great electrum-plated chariot to greet the thousands who have gathered to witness his "wonders."

And how many thousands there are! Thousands and thousands and thousands! I heard Na-phu-ria's uncle the Councilor Aye (he is *very* dignified and *really* forbidding) tell the old Pharaoh (whom we call Nib-mua-ria) that he estimated there were probably more than two hundred thousand. Now we of the royal procession, which includes other members of the Court—the old Queen Mother Mutemwiya; a funny, dried-up, wise-looking little old man with the curious name of Amonhotep, Son of Hapu; the Chief Scribe and Commander of the young Pharaoh's troops, Kaires (small and sharp-featured but kind and also, I think, very wise); and many other court dignitaries—have come to the center of the plain where a big empty block of stone has been dragged into place just this morning. And there seems to be a solid sea of faces dwindling off into the distance as far as one can see.

They are restless but happy, at this moment. They shout greetings to us constantly, great waves of sound keep coming from them. In my birthplace in Mesopotamia we do not have such thousands; a few hundreds only, at the most, attend upon my father when he rides out. But here—my goodness, how many people Kemet has! Five *millions*, so Kaires tells me. And how they love the House of Thebes! Every royal progress draws thousands and thousands; my own trip up the river when I came here, and now our trip down again, have been examples. Everywhere, people, people, people! And all happy, cheering, welcoming, adoring—at least of the old Pharaoh and the Great Wife, though it seems to me perhaps not quite so much of the young Pharaoh and Nefertiti.

In this, I expect I am probably imagining things, but it has seemed to me as we all came down the river, and this morning as we rode in our chariots (so much gold, so many jewels, so many beautiful things I now have, to own and wear! It is *wonderful!*) onto the plain, that there was a note of hesitation, almost of puzzlement, when my new husband (it still seems strange to me to say that. I think I shall just call him Naphuria as we always have) —when Naphuria and Nefertiti appeared. There seemed to be almost a coolness.

Everyone in the party pretended this was not so, and they acknowledged the greetings with the rest. In fact, they were much more open about it as our procession approached the great altar stone. Nib-mua-ria and Queen Tiye remained solemn and stately, but Naphuria and Nefertiti suddenly began smiling and waving very informally—almost in an undignified way, I thought, it was so open and natural and not at all like the style of the others. I am not sure the people liked it. It was then, it seemed to me, that I noticed the little hesitation, the puzzlement—almost, one might have said, the doubt. It was as though the people thought their young Pharaoh and his Chief Wife were *too* friendly—as though they wanted them to remain remote and not come down, so to speak, to the people's level.

But everyone in our party pretended this was not so, and everyone continued as they were, Nib-mua-ria and Tiye and Aye and the rest being very solemn (I did my best to be solemn, too. It is not easy at fourteen, but now I am a Queen of the Two Lands and I must learn. I think I did very well, really), while Naphuria and Nefertiti grinned and went on like two peasants on the banks of the River Nile. It was odd, in a way, and rather disturbing. I suppose their motives were all right, but I must admit it puzzled *me* somewhat, too. It seemed to me that they carried it so far that at moments it became almost hysterical. It didn't feel right, somehow. It was as though they felt differently inside, maybe tense, and were going too far the other way, as a result.

Anyway, we have arrived now at the big stone, which

Sitamon whispered to me was intended to be an altar to her brother's new god, the Aten. It is not at all like the altars of the king of the gods, whose name is Amon-Ra. His altars are hidden away at the end of long, dark corridors. Altars to the Aten—which is a funny-looking sun disk with a lot of thin arms—are out in the open where their sun-god Ra can shine down upon them. I like the Aten's altars better, though I already sense there is some big argument going on, in the Family and in Kemet itself, between the two gods. I probably should not offend the priests of Amon, who I can tell are pretty powerful, by showing my favoritism. I expect I had better just watch and keep my mouth shut, at least for a while.

Now we are all taking our places in a big space in front of the altar that has been cleared by the troops of Kaires. Kaires looks somber and tense as he goes about giving orders, and now that we are nearing the moment for the ceremonies to begin, the young Pharaoh and Nefertiti look somber and tense too. In fact, all the Family and all the court officials look the same way. Everybody seems afraid of something, and suddenly I feel afraid too, though I am a stranger here still and do not yet understand Kemet and its many mysterious ways.

I wonder why I should feel afraid?

Because I do.

I really do.

Now their sun-god Ra is reaching his peak, he is standing almost directly overhead. The shadow of the altar stone has almost disappeared upon the sand. It is very hot today; we are all very thinly clad.

Naphuria, who with Nefertiti and their two little daughters, has not stepped down from their chariot, but has waited while we all disposed ourselves to listen, gives his horses a sudden thrash with the thong tied to his wrist. They start and leap forward to the center of the space before the altar. He yanks them roughly to a halt, then yanks them to the right. They turn and spin about, Nefertiti clinging tightly to her girls to steady them, until he and his family are facing directly out upon the enormous throng.

Suddenly and deliberately, he and Nefertiti raise their hands to their shoulders, unhook their golden garments, and let them fall.

Naked, she in her beauty and he in his strange ugliness, they stand before us.

A great silence falls.

Suddenly I am dreadfully excited. Nothing yet in all of Kemet has been as exciting to me as *this!*

In his high, thin voice, which now is descending almost to a croak under the great emotion he obviously feels, he begins to speak. At my side Amonhotep, Son of Hapu, who is wise in all things including languages, kindly translates.

Amonhotep IV (Life, health, prosperity!)

Now, THEY SEE ME, O Aten, as I truly am, naked before them and living in truth. They are absolutely silent, absolutely still. All the great plain, no longer desolate but crowded from edge to edge with my people who will soon grow to worship you and me as we worship one another, waits upon my words.

I take a step forward so that I stand at the chariot rail with my family behind me, and I begin to speak, slowly and carefully so that those in front may hear my words clearly and be able to pass them on back to those beyond who cannot hear. Ra is directly above, there is no more shadow on the sand. And thanks to you, O Aten, there is no shadow on my heart, nor will there be shadows anywhere if my people will but believe in you and me and the wonders we will bring to them together.

"Good people!" I cry, and my voice, in spite of my angriest inner efforts to prevent it, turns to its croaking note under the stress of my emotion—but no matter, Aten, that you cannot help, no one can help, I shall do my best anyway. "Good friends of Kemet, draw near and listen as your Pharaoh speaks!

"Great wonders have I prepared for you this day, and great will they be forever and ever, for millions and millions of years!"

I pause, for I seem to be losing my breath, and in front of me I see the solemn faces of my parents, my sister, my brother, the new child Kia, Aye, Kaires, Amonhotep, Son of Hapu, Aanen, and all. All, all are tense and somber. Momentarily I feel a great panic, but suddenly on my arm is Nefertiti's tiny reassuring hand, and in my heart I hear your loving, protective voice, O Aten. And I continue:

"People of Kemet, you all are aware how almost five years ago I became Co-Regent with the Good God Neb-Ma'at-Ra. You know that in that time I have labored long and hard to serve you and to be a Good God worthy to sit beside him.

"You are also aware that from the beginning it has been my purpose to befriend all the gods, but to keep to myself the privilege and the right to worship as I please the god that to me seems best.

"You all know that this is the Aten."

Again I pause, and become aware that to my right, standing just a little apart from the line of the Family, my uncle Aanen for a second has cracked his somber mask and is looking at me with a savage anger in his eyes. My eyes narrow to the cold slits I can make of them when I too am angry and he drops his head and looks hastily away. I go on, satisfied and feeling much stronger inside.

"It is the Aten!

"Yet, people of Kemet, you know that I have not attacked Amon or any other god. I have not desecrated their temples, or robbed their granaries, or struck down their priesthoods, or done them any bad thing, anywhere, at any time.

"And yet do they hate me."

There was a gasp from someone in my family, taken up and echoed on back through the crowd.

"Yes!" I cry. "*Hate* me, for such is the only word that describes their constant interference with my will. But what have I done to cause their hate? Nothing, I say to you, and you know it—nothing!

"I have only worshiped in my own way. The Chief Wife and our daughters have joined me.

"I have built temples to Aten, yes. I have glorified his name, yes. I have offered him to you to be your god, too —yes.

"But have I ever asked you to do what you would not do of your own free will? Have I ever forced you to come to the Aten's temples? Have I ever required you to worship him? Have I ever ordered you to live in truth with him as I do?

"Never have I done these things, never! And Amon and all the gods know it well, as you know it, my people of Kemet.

"But Amon and the gods are not content with my worship of the Aten. They are not pleased that I offer him to you. They do not like his temples, which are open and bright and full of happiness. They do not like the joy he offers you if you will but worship him, and me, who am his Son.

"They are jealous. They defy me and they seek to drive you from the Aten, and from me, who am his Son.

"So I have drawn you here this day to hear what I intend. It is this."

I pause, and abruptly there is silence while the sibilant whisper, "It is this! It is this! It is this! . . ." runs back and dies out in the crowd. Below me I see my family and the Court grow yet more tense. On my arm Nefertiti's firm little hand gives me strength and in my heart you, O Aten, comfort and encourage me.

"From this day forward," I say, and my voice, which has steadied into its shriller register, again grows low and choked with emotion, "I shall no longer be known as Nefer-Kheperu-Ra, Amonhotep IV.

"From this day forth I shall be known, and all my

cartouches, monuments, sculptures, paintings and titularies shall bear it, and all men and all women everywhere, be they great or small, shall address me as:

"Nefer-Kheperu-Ra Akhenaten, 'The Incarnation of the Aten.'"

At this there is a great gasp from everywhere, a murmuring that rolls back through the crowd in a giant wave.

"And also," I cry over it, so that it abruptly ceases and gives way to my words, "the Chief Wife Nefertiti shall no longer be known as Nefertiti, but as:

"Nefer-Neferu-Aten Nefertiti, 'Fair Is the Goodness of the Aten.'

"And so shall she be styled in all things, and by all shall she be so addressed."

Again there is the great gasp, another wave of murmuring, louder and more troubled. But you are with me, O Aten, and I must do as you direct. I must live in truth and so must they. I am determined that *I* will. And by my example, *so will they*.

"My father the Aten," I resume (but this time the silence does not quite return as it was, there is still a sibilant murmuring and whispering, an uneasiness that might upset and distract me did I not have Nefertiti and you, O Aten), "has brought me to this place. He has said unto me, 'It belongs to no god, goddess, prince or princess, and no man has any right to act as its owner.'

"And to him I have replied: 'Only you, O Aten, Great Father, Great God. To you it belongs, and in it I will make for you a Place of Origin, a Horizon and a Seat to have your Being.'

"Thus on this day do I dedicate this place, to be known forever and ever, for millions and millions of years, as Akhet-Aten, 'The Horizon of the Aten.' I decree that all men shall so receive it, and here do worship of the great god Aten."

I come to full stop, turn to Nefertiti. Together we take from the hands of our wide-eyed, solemn little daughters, Meryt-aten and Meket-aten, two baskets of fruit and other gifts. Together we descend from the chariot and, clothed only in your love, O Aten, approach your altar. Now

there is absolute silence again as we place the baskets on
the huge, bare stone. Only our voices ring out loud and
clear together as we bow low to the altar and chant:

"So do we honor you, Great God, Great Father, Aten,
who speaks only to his son Akhenaten and through him
to all peoples! So do we bring offerings to mark this sacred
day and the founding of your Horizon! So do we call on
all men to join us in your worship, O Happy, O Beneficent! So do we honor you, O Aten, forever and ever, for
millions and millions of years, founder, creator and protector of all things on this earth!"

Then we turn with quiet dignity and remount the
chariot. Again I step forward. I can sense a relaxation in
my family and in my people. I sense that they are saying
to themselves, "Oh, this is all it is. He wishes an altar
here. We do not mind that. So be it."

But I have other wonders for them, O Aten, and you
know what they are.

And when I begin to speak again, my damnable voice
begins to choke once more with emotion, and they know,
instantly, that they have not yet heard it all. And again
the tension returns and grows in all who listen, here on
my enormous plain, drenched in Ra's fierce light.

"O Aten, Great Father, Great God," I cry, "I ask of
all those witnesses, is it not true what we have said, and
do not these witnesses agree?"

I stop and look out upon them with an air of challenge
and demand that I deliberately exaggerate, so that it becomes at once an issue between you and me on the one
hand, O Aten, and the Court and my people on the other.

Very silently and tensely, now, the members of my
family regard me, for they are closest to me and it is, of
course, their duty to reply for the people. For a second I
think perhaps it will be my father who replies, though I
know this to be impossible for him, in the face of Amon:
he would not be so brave. Instead, after a few seconds of
almost unbearable tension, it is my uncle Aye who steps
a little forward and bows low. Then he raises himself to
his full height and his voice fills the silence:

"We hear your words, O Son of the Sun! We attend

you! We witness for you this day that Aten will disclose his wishes only to you, and that all nations will come to this place to give tribute to the Aten, by whom all things live on this earth, forever and ever, for millions and millions of years!"

He steps back and again a long, low sigh of release moves through my family and my people. Again they think: "This is all." But my next words swiftly disabuse them.

"O Aten, Great Father, Great God," I cry, "hear and bear witness, with all these other witnesses, to these further things which I decree for you this day:

"I decree that here on your Horizon there shall be built a great city, and I shall not hearken to the Queen Nefer-Neferu-Aten Nefertiti nor to anyone who seeks to persuade me to build it anywhere else. Here it shall be, O Aten, your city Akhet-Aten. Its boundaries to the east, north, south and west shall be marked for you, and thus do I mark the first of them!"

And quickly I reach for the ends of the ropes which Bek and his men have cleverly hidden in the sand. I tug on them, and slowly, helped by many eager hands along the way, whose owners do not know my purpose but spring automatically to assist Pharaoh, they begin to emerge from the earth. To the north and to the south the great throng parts like a sea as the ropes emerge. They appear slowly for hundreds and hundreds of feet, thousands and thousands. Every night for two months Bek and his men have worked secretly on these wonders for me, no man seeing them under cover of Nut, no man passing on Hapi's swift-flowing waters ever guessing that wonderful things were being readied on the plain.

Presently, four miles to the north and four miles to the south, the pre-arranged signals come. There flash from mirrors held by Bek's man to the north and his man to the south, catching Ra's rays to send the message, the news that the purpose has been accomplished. The cloths have fallen from the North Boundary Stela and the South Boundary Stela. These two limits of the city are now eternal.

"People of Kemet!" I shout as the winking mirrors repeat their message. "Go you when you have heard me speak, go you when all these wonders have been done, to the north and to the south. And do you witness there the stelae which I have caused to be inscribed to mark the Aten's city. And know you all that soon there will be others to mark the boundaries of this place. And do you know that on them I have related these things:

"That in this great city there will be many temples, many altars and many houses. There will be a Mansion of the Aten, which shall be called 'the Smaller Temple,' a house of the Aten, which shall be called, 'the Great Temple,' a Sunshade of the Queen where she may go to worship the Aten, and a House of Rejoicing for the Aten. All these shall be here in this central spot which shall be called the Island 'Aten-Distinguished-in-Jubilees.' There will be also the apartments of Pharaoh and the apartments of the Chief Wife, and their children, and of all Pharaoh's wives and all his children. There will be houses for the Good God and the Great Wife, and for my Court and for nobles and for people and helpers of all kinds.

"And I shall not leave this place to seek lands for the Aten beyond its boundaries. Only this shall be his city, and here he shall stay, forever and ever. Here will I be buried—"

All had been watching me with tense attention: this statement brings a sudden renewal of the gasps, the whispers and the murmurings. I think now, O Aten, that they begin to perceive at last the full extent of my wonders.

"—and here shall the Chief Wife, our children, and all who attend me, be they of high or low degree, be buried, so that in the afterlife they may worship the Aten and worship me, who am his Son, through all eternity. Here, too, shall be buried the Mnevis Bull, sacred to the Sun.

"From this day"—and my voice chokes once more with emotion, and suddenly they are utterly silent, utterly tense—beginning to be terrified, at last, I think, of what may be coming next. So I emphasize ¯it, in the hateful, croaking voice which I despise but cannot help:

"From this day forward shall I make my principal residence here with the Aten. From this day forward I remove from our cities of Thebes and of Memphis all authority, power and status as the capitals of Kemet, and all such authority, power and status do I give to Akhet-Aten as the capital of Kemet. And from this day the name of Thebes shall be changed from No-Amon, 'City of Amon,' to No-Aten, 'City of the Aten'—"

But here I am interrupted by an animal wail of such anguish and anger that it is barely recognizable as human. I see my uncle Aanen start forward, forgetful of Pharaoh's station, forgetful of his own station, forgetful of time, place, everything, forgetful of the Aten—and *forgetful of me.*

It is then that I hear you speak, O Aten, and tell me what to do. It is then that my murdered brother Tuthmose joins you, crying, "Yes! *Yes!*" It is then that I raise my voice and shout an order to Kaires. And it is then, after a fearful moment in which our eyes lock as his meet mine in challenge, defiance and dismay, and mine meet his with a towering anger and a furious determination, that he surrenders his will to me and moves with a sure and terrible swiftness to do what my god and I command.

Amonhotep III (Life, health, prosperity!)

No. No. No! *But it is happening! Oh, by the gods, it is happening! How awful, how awful! Oh no, no,* NO!

Tiye

My son, my son! Oh! My son!

Aye

Ah, you must not—must not—ah, Son of the Sun, what madness are you—

Mutemwiya

Child, child! Oh, awful, awful! The horrors you will bring upon this House! Oh, Majesty, Majesty, please—

Nefertiti

Kill him! KILL HIM!

Aanen

——*Ahhh* . . .

Amonhotep, Son of Hapu

IT IS VERY STILL. The campfires are out. No sound comes
from the crowded riverbank, the silent river, the once
more empty plain. Khons rides above in his silver boat,
carrying the souls of the dead through the night sky. It as
though the mad dream had never happened, but indeed
it has. Khons carries one more, passenger tonight, and the
world of Kemet is no more the same.

I could not believe my eyes. I could not believe my
eyes. Around me the Family and the Court stood
thunderstruck, across the vast crowded expanse a moan
of horror swept from end to end. Aanen died as he had
lived, still screaming imprecations against his nephew.
But this time there will be no amends made to Amon, no
apologies to the world. Nefer-Kheperu-Ra rules supreme
in this hour and no man, not even his father, his fellow
god, dares raise his voice to challenge him.

I am growing old in the service of this House. Already
I am fifty-four, and I have seen too much already. What
more shall I see? What more do I *want* to see? Nothing
again such as I have seen today, believe me. Yet I think
I may, before the rule of this Good God, and *his* god, is
done.

Somewhere down the years we have lost Nefer-
Kheperu-Ra: "Akhen-aten." (I wonder how long it will
be before that name comes naturally to the tongue? Probably not too long: men adapt to the vagaries of gods,
and this one is determined that they will adapt to his.)
Whether the murder of his uncle was the wild decision of
the moment or a deliberately planned act of policy we
will never know, for he will never tell us. But in two
awful minutes it has taken Kemet far, very far, in the direction he wants it to go. It has implanted great fear in the
land. Whether in time he can translate that fear into
love and the basis of a lasting rule, we shall have to see.
In time the people, shocked, may change and come willingly his way. But the shock is presently so great that
this may never be.

He professes peace: he takes the sword—Kaires'
sword. And that one, poor shattered friend, must somehow find within himself the strength to put it all aside,
perform his duties, and go on. He will do so, I think, for
Kaires has strength—great strength, which this Pharaoh
can appreciate when he bends it to his own purposes.
May he appreciate it also should it turn against him, for
that, too, may come to pass. If it does, will he bend in
turn, and adapt and be wise? If not, I fear for him, for
Kaires' strength is very great.

I wonder, now, if Akhenaten *is* wise. It has been customary in the Family and in the land to refer to him
as a youth of great intelligence. So, basically, he is. But
with it, maturity, judgment, soundness? Increasingly in
recent years I have not been so sure. I am not sure at all,
now. The Aten has claimed him, and he may already be
so far lost in dream that he can never return again to
the ways of men—or even of gods, as Kemet has known
them.

One thing is certain: he can never return again to the
ways of Amon, for Amon will never forgive what has
been done this day. He may not, as he says, directly attack Amon again, but in this one act he has done enough
to guarantee that someday, when the chance comes right,
Amon will attack him. It may be long in coming, but it
will come, for Amon does not forget. From this day Akhenaten must be on guard. As one who still manages to
find in my heart a continuing affection for him, I hope
for his sake this may always be so. For now there is war,
though he may choose to pretend it does not exist, and
may wish to fight no further battles in it.

He has his "wonders," and he has his city. At dawn
when Ra, whom we of the Court must now call Aten,
first begins to spread his light in the east, the work begins.
Bek—his helper Tuthmose—myself, who will be in
charge of much of the work—have given the orders,
we have mastered the men. Six hours from now we venture out upon the plain, and starting from the great altar
at the center (the sands in front of it long since drawn
carefully over to conceal the blood), we will build outward in all directions until such time as the city is completed. He wants it in two years or less: if we are lucky
we may have it for him in three. All is ready. We will
proceed. Akhet-Aten will become reality and occupy
the plain.

With it will come many problems, and already my half
brother Ramose, still Vizier of Upper Kemet and still
worrying endlessly in his conscientious fashion, has begun
to fret about them. He, too, has responsibilities: housing
and feeding the many thousands of workmen who will

build this place, bringing here from Thebes the craftsmen and artisans who will work at our direction to beautify and embellish the city, establishing the quarters where the priests of the Aten—for here, surely, there will be many —will live. Stores, supplies, granaries—foodshops, workshops, wineshops—all the small necessary accompaniments of daily life—Ramose and his scribes with their never ending records will have much to do to keep track of them all. It is no small project to change the capital of a country from its old, established place to another as yet unbuilt. It is, in fact, revolution.

Thus have we wrought with Nefer-Kheperu-Ra "Akhenaten," we who have always prided ourselves that we were teaching him to be a good Pharaoh worthy of the House of Thebes and a Good God worthy of the land he was born to rule. It is not what we intended, but though we thought we knew him, of course we did not. No one does, save perhaps Nefertiti—or, I suppose, I should say "Nefer-Neferu-Aten." And I doubt that she does, though she must convince herself of it to be able to stay by his side.

And still I cannot find it in my heart to abandon him, any more than she can. Not only because he has asked me to stay with him here in the new capital, but because I find myself bound to him by strong ties of concern, affection and, yes, love.

In spite of what he has done this day, he is very vulnerable, our Akhenaten. To those of us who have been close to him in the past twenty years he is not the fearsome Pharaoh Kemet now believes him, although of course he could, if he wished, have our heads in a moment, too, just as he had Aanen's. He is a god, and no power on earth could stop him should he turn against us. But although it now appears more dangerous to be subject to his will, actually, for myself, and I think for the others, it is not. There is a certain element of playing with fire, of lying down with lions, but we feel, perhaps mistakenly, that he likes us too well for us to be afraid. He did not like Aanen, and with good cause: none of us did. Aanen invited disaster and he got it. Akhenaten does not feel that way about us. And even if he did, we would still pity him and, perhaps with a curiously willing compliance, accept whatever fate he might decree for us.

"We would still pity him." That, I think, is the key to it. He has been through so much in his twenty years. He began his life so beautifully, he was such a handsome, well-favored lad, everything was moving so smoothly and perfectly for him toward a great and happy reign—and then came the dreadful illness, and with it disfigurement, grotesquerie, disaster, pain—an outward and inner hurt from which he has never recovered, and from which, I think, he never will recover. It is not surprising, perhaps, that he should have turned away from the gods who did this to him and turned to a new god he could not consider responsible. It is not surprising that he should wish for all his people the comfort and apparent peace of mind that worship of the bright and open Aten seems to have given him.

No, I shall not abandon Akhenaten. I look back upon him across the distance of thirty-four years between our ages, and I think: he needs me. He is still, inside, the lonely, frightened boy who sat at my knee to learn the arts of the scribe and bombarded me with questions about Kemet and the gods. In some way apart from ceremony, he is not Pharaoh to me: he is almost one of my sons.

He confronts us, and the Two Lands, with a great challenge: we must keep his revolution within bounds. We cannot do it by abandoning him. We must stay close, and soften and gentle where we can.

I stand here in the silent night staring out across the haunted plain where in six hours' time a great city will begin to rise, and I am not so sure that he is wrong in his worship of the Aten. Amon is old and dark, threatening and fearsome. Perhaps it is time for a gust of fresh air to blow through Kemet. Perhaps it is time for a new light to shine upon the world.

I shall not abandon Akhenaten, though there may be some who will. I shall accept his revolution, observe it, try to understand it—and direct it, where and if I have the opportunity, into safe channels. The death of Aanen was a shocking spectacle, but it was caused by the fierce and much-provoked anger of the moment. It does not change him inside. And though, like all, I never expect to know all that is inside, what I do know leads me to decide in his favor.

I pray for him and for Kemet that all will go well for him. Aye is beside him; I am; Kaires, I think, will be, once he has recovered from this day's deed. Nefertiti (I shall probably never be able to use the new construction of her name: that is too bizarre) will be beside him; his daughters; even, I think, though with many misgivings, Pharaoh and the Great Wife. And perhaps, in time, his people, too, though for the moment they tremble with fear of him from one end of Kemet to the other.

We must go with him. There is no choice.

Now all is still: at dawn his city rises.

His "wonders" are just beginning.

We must welcome them willingly if we would not lose him altogether and drive him irretrievably down pathways most awful for the Two Kingdoms and for him.

Ramesses

HE SITS BESIDE ME in the tent and shivers. Waves of shivers pass across his body. Sweat drips from his forehead. His hands are clenched, his eyes staring. From time to time he mumbles something incoherent, and now and again, with an almost animal groan, he drives the fist of one hand against the fist of the other. Terrible grimaces come and go. He rocks with anguish. I try to comfort him but I do not know what to do. I do not know what to say. Never have I seen my friend Kaires in such a state.

Kaires

A<small>H</small>, I <small>WISH</small> that I were dead, *dead like Aanen!* I deserve it, I deserve it!

I am in some other world, not this. Gray mists swirl through my head. Red haze—red, red, red, like blood! —covers my eyes. I see it—I see it! His face, contorted, hangs before me in the air. I raise my sword!—I strike! —his skull splits asunder!—he collapses on the sand! Red haze—red haze. I wish that I were dead. *Dead like Aanen!* I deserve it. Ah, I deserve it!

Poor Ramesses does not know what to make of me. Is this his old friend, veteran of so many years in the army together? Is this he who has fought in Kush and against the Hittites on the borders of Hatti, who has killed men before at his Pharaoh's bidding and in his Pharaoh's cause?

Yes, it is he.

But never before such a Pharaoh.

Never before such a cause . . .

It repeats itself incessantly in my mind, I cannot stop it. Not just the death but what went before. Not just my sword slashing the sweltering air until it collides with brains and flesh and a mass of resistance suddenly sagging and fireless, but the eyes of Akhenaten—our terrible look, binding up together in blood and brotherhood, trust and mistrust, love and hatred, forever and ever, for millions and millions of years . . . until one of us breaks permanently the will of the other, as he broke mine this day, and as someday I will break his.

What is he, this strange boy? He is twenty, I am thirty-five. For fifteen years I have been "big brother" to him and his wife. I have played with them as babies, been their companion in childhood's adventures, served them loyally since they became Co-Regent and Chief Wife. And in gratitude for all this, it is me he turns to when it comes time to murder his uncle—and mine. What is he? Who is he? Who will ever know?

In one way, I suppose, I should be flattered and pleased that instinctively, in his blind rage and desperate anger, he should have turned to me to do his deed for him. At least it shows that I am so much a part of him that even in his blindest and most unthinking moment he automatically calls on me as the one he can trust to do his bidding. I suppose I should be flattered at such terrible proof of confidence. I think I should have been happy could I have been relieved of such trust before it became too late!

Yet must I be honest here, though my head grows dizzy with the effort: I wanted his trust. I have deliberately sought it out, all his life. I have made it my constant and undeviating purpose to rise to stand at his right hand. I have done so. Would I have not made the bargain had I known from the beginning the price it would exact? The answer springs from my *ba* and *ka*, the very soul and essence of my being: of course I would, for I have ever been determined to rise.

But even so: *this* price? This I had not bargained for. . . .

He knew, however, that I would do it. I think even in that wild, blazing moment when he was blind with rage and scarcely thinking at all, I am sure he knew that I would do it. Our eyes locked and for a moment made even more terrible by our joint knowledge that I might just—just—*not* do his bidding, our *kas* intermingled and became almost one in a furious battle of wills that no one else in all the world could see. And I gave in and killed the screaming fool who presumed to threaten Pharaoh, as all who threaten Pharaoh must be killed . . . if they are such fools as to do it openly. And thus did I join him in bringing horror and fear to Kemet, which has been free of them for many years.

The gray mists swirl, the red haze comes: there are moments when I cannot think at all. I see it! I cannot think at all. . . .

But these moments pass, though I continue to rock from side to side and Ramesses does not know that my mind is working again. It is best he should not know, dull, lovable, faithful Ramesses whom I have brought with me in my rise and whom I shall take with me even higher someday, perhaps. He is a contented soul, with his placid wife Sitra and their bright little son Seti, whose obvious brilliance must be some mysterious joke of the gods, his parents are so decent and so dull. But Ramesses would kill for me as I have killed for Akhenaten, I know that. The only difference between us is that he would not even pause to think about it. He would shrug and smile and wipe his sword and go on. My curse—as it is my blessing, of course—is that I think. Therefore I need a Ramesses. Does Akhenaten need a Kaires?

And does *that* matter?

Kaires needs an Akhenaten.

That is more to the point.

I think, now, that I must begin to follow my own purposes more. My old friend Amonhotep, Son of Hapu, told me that I have them, on that long-ago day in Thebes when a death and two births shook the Eighteenth Dynasty. New come to the City of Amon, an innocent in the Two Lands, I did not know then what he already shrewdly suspected: that my love for Kemet would make me increasingly impatient, over the years; that it would make me more and more desirous that I move into positions from which I could have something to say about that rule; that I should seek power in the land that I may do good in the land. He knew then, wise Amonhotep, Son of Hapu, and he has helped and encouraged me ever since. "I am old," he has said, very often. "You are young, Kaires. Kemet needs you and you must work always for Kemet. You are young, and there is time."

But I am not young any longer, and time may no longer be my friend. Now I must begin to take advantage of what I have gained. For I have sought trust, and this day I have fulfilled it in a way that he who has placed me here can never forget. From this day forward I will truly be one of those who stand at the right hand of Akhenaten.

There are others, but I think secretly we all have the same purpose. I know Amonhotep, Son of Hapu, does, and I know my father does, though we have never discussed it directly. Sometime soon I must talk to him: I am thirty-five now, the time for pretense is long past, new responsibilities require new dignities. It is time for Kaires to become someone else, a figure in his own right when he stands below the throne at the right hand of the King. When the moment is right I shall move: such is my rule in all things, and it is only because today I have not been the mover but the moved, because today I have been forced against my will to do a deed that can only damage Kemet, that I am shaken and not myself.

Nefer-Kheperu-Ra shall have me a while longer. I shall go with him as he desires me, on this strange life's journey. In my heart are many misgivings, but I shall conceal them yet awhile. I shall do his bidding. I shall be his servant, I shall serve his purposes—until much time as I can serve Kemet's and my own. When that time comes, I shall not hesitate.

I perceive that Ramesses is studying me thoughtfully. I have been silent too long. Even that plodding mind will begin to wonder if I calm myself too soon.

I moan, I groan; fists thud, face contorts, sweat pours, body rocks. He looks concerned again, dear stupid, faithful Ramesses. How much I love his simple love for me, his unshakable, unbreakable, undeflectable loyalty and faith. His only purpose is to love me and serve me. My purposes build on his, as they build on those of many others. Together we will rise.

For the time being those of us who stand at the right hand of the King will continue to serve him loyally as he wishes. But in due course, if we decide we must, we will do what Kemet's good requires.

It rests with Nefer-Kheperu-Ra to determine when, or

BOOK IV

Dream of a God

1367 B.C.

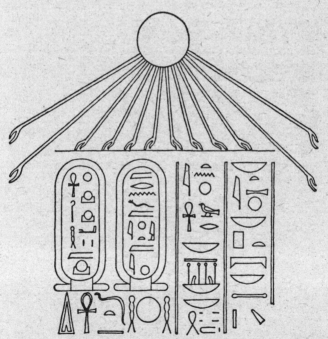

Live, Ra, ruler of the Horizon, rejoicing in the Horizon, in his role of light coming from the Sun's Disk, giving life forever and to all eternity, Aten the living, the Great, Lord of Jubilees, Master of all that encompasses the Sun's Disk, Lord of the Heavens, Lord of the Earth,

THE ATEN

Burnaburiash of Babylon

To NIBMUARIA, the Great King, the King of Kemet, Son of the Sun, my brother who loves me and whom I love, at his seat in the city Akhet-Aten of his son Naphuria: Burnaburiash, the Great King, King of Babylon, who loves thee and is thy brother.

It is well with me: may it be well with thee, with thy house, with the Great Wife and all who love thee and whom thou loveth.

Burnaburiash, thy brother, knoweth not the truth of the rumors he hears, but he tells his brother Nibmuaria thus: Be it known that it is common knowledge among thy friends, thy vassals and thine enemies as well, that not Nibmuaria, not Naphuria, nor anyone in thy land of Kemet sends gold, or arms, or any precious thing to those who love them. Nay, it is said Nibmuaria and Naphuria turn their backs upon those who love them. It is said they no longer send envoys, they no longer send gifts, they no longer send armies to strengthen their friends and punish their enemies. It is said they care not what happens to the land of Kemet, they care not what happens to the friends of the land of Kemet, they care not what the enemies of Kemet do. It is said they spend their time in idle pursuits and care not for statesmanship or empire. It is said they care not if their enemies go unpunished or if their friends who love them do not receive gold and other precious things.

Burnaburiash, thy brother, says to Nibmuaria, his brother whom he loves: it is said all things fall away in the land of Kemet while Naphuria worships the Sun-God Aten and cares not for the things of government. It is said

Nibmuaria pays no attention also, that he does not correct Naphuria. It is said the hand of Nibmuaria the Great King, Son of the Sun, lies light and uncaring upon the land of Kemet, not strong and sturdy as it did when Nibmuaria, like thy brother Burnaburiash who loves thee, was young and vigorous. It is said Naphuria does all things as he pleases, and that it does not please him to care for the land of Kemet, only for the worship of his Sun-God, Aten.

Burnaburiash, thy brother who loves thee, says to his brother Nibmuaria: Babylon my kingdom doth not want. It doth not tremble. Burnaburiash, thy brother, governs all things well in Babylon, and mine enemies are defeated and dare not plunder Babylon. But this is not so in the land of Kemet. Burnaburiash, thy brother, says that Babylon sends arms to punish her enemies and gifts to her friends who love her, and whom she loves. This is not so in the land of Kemet.

Therefore thy brother Burnaburiash, who loves thee, says to his brother Nibmuaria: awake thyself from slumber! Attend to thine armies! Attend to thy friends! Attend to thy son! Control thy bothersome vassals who on all sides squabble and fight and ignore the wishes of Kemet. Love thy friends, as thou once did when we were young together!

Burnaburiash, thy brother who loves thee, says to his brother Nibmuaria: send gold, so that I may know my brother Nibmuaria still loves me! And tell thy son Naphuria also, whom I love: send gold! Send gold!

Tushratta of Mittani

To NIBMUARIA the Great King, the King of Kemet, Son of the Sun, my brother-in-law, who loves me and whom I love, at his residence in the city Akhet-Aten of his son Naphuria: Tushratta, the great king, thy brother-in-law, who loves thee and is thy brother, King of Mittani.

It is well with me: may it be well with thee, with thy house, with the Great Wife and thy many other wives, with thy son Naphuria and thy other sons, with thy chariots, thy horses, thy nobles, thy land, and all that is thine, may it be well with them indeed!

So says Tushratta, thy brother-in-law, thy brother, who loves thee.

Grievous news hath come to thy brother, Tushratta who loves thee! It is brought to him that his sister Gilukhipa, whom he loved, Queen of the Two Lands, wife of Nibmuaria for twenty years, hath died in Nibmuaria's Palace of Malkata at Thebes. Tushratta weeps for his sister and grieves for thee, Nibmuaria!

Grievous also to the ears of Tushratta are the reports he hears of his brother's land. It is said thy vassals defy thee, thy friends fall away, thine enemies advance. It is said all is chaos on thy borders and dismay within them. It is said Naphuria forgets his duties and spends his time in worship of the Sun-God Aten. It is said Nibmuaria does not control this. It is said Nibmuaria grows old and tired and cares not what happens to Kemet.

Tushratta, thy brother who loves thee, grieves for Nibmuaria and thy land of Kemet as he grieves for his sister Gilukhipa, thy wife and Queen of the Two Lands for twenty years.

Therefore be it known to Nibmuaria, Great King, great brother whom I love, that Tushratta, thy brother who loves thee, hath thought in his grief how he might ease the grief of Nibmuaria, his brother whom he loves. And Tushratta says to Nibmuaria:

There lives in my palace my daughter Tad-u-khi-pa, niece to Gilukhipa. She is surpassing fair, I assure my brother Nibmuaria. Though she is presently but ten years, she hath much learning, great knowledge, much intelligence besides her beauty. And she is beautiful, Nibmuaria! I, thy brother Tushratta who loves thee, tell thee truly: she is beautiful, thy Tad-u-khi-pa who loves thee.

Why doth not my brother Nibmuaria take my daughter Tad-u-khi-pa unto him as wife and Queen of the Two Lands? Though she be but ten, the years speed fast and it will not be long before she will enter thy bed and be thy loving companion. She will be loving and faithful to thee until death, Nibmuaria! I, thy brother Tushratta who loves thee, father to Tadukhipa who loves thee, promise it!

Further do I say to thee, Nibmuaria, my brother: if thou doth take my daughter Tadukhipa into thy bed, young and beautiful as she is, all will go well with Nibmuaria, who will be young again! All will go well with the land of Kemet, which her beauty will bless! All will be strong again between us, and thy alliance with the land of Mittani will be renewed and preserved by this marriage. Grieve for my sister Gilukhipa, Nibmuaria! And marry my daughter Tadukhipa, that our friendship may remain strong and unchanging forever!

I say this frankly to my brother Nibmuaria, whom I love, for this reason:

Whereas thy fathers in their time kept fast friendship with my fathers, thou hast increased the friendship. Now, therefore, that thou and I are friends thou hast made it ten times closer than with my father Shuttarna, whom I have succeeded. May the gods cause our friendship to prosper! May Teshup, the lord, and Amon ordain it eternally as it now is!

I write this to my brother that he may show me even

more love than he showed my father. Now I ask gold from my brother, and it behooves me to ask this gold for two causes: in the first place for war equipment and secondly for the dowry of Tadukhipa.

So then, let my brother send me much gold, without measure, more than to my father. For in my brother's land gold is as the dust of the earth.

May the gods grant that in the land of my brother, where already so much gold is, there may be ten times more gold to come! Certainly the gold that I require will not trouble my brother's heart, but let him also not grieve my heart. Therefore let my brother send gold without measure, in great quantity. And I also will grant all the gifts that my brother asks. For this land is my brother's land, and this my house is his house.

And may Nibmuaria find that all goes well again in the land of Kemet when he marries my daughter Tadukhipa and sends me much gold! And may Naphuria whom I also love, send me much gold as well! For gold is as the dust of the earth in the land of Nibmuaria and Naphuria.

Send gold! And all shall be well there!

Amonhotep III (Life, health, prosperity!)

LITTLE SNIVELING GREEDY MEN, off on the edge of Kemet, off on the edge of my life! What do they know of the troubles we suffer in this land? What do they know of the sufferings of his mother, and of me?

More miracles, more "wonders"! Now the Court and the people are to gather this afternoon under the archway that runs between his apartments and hers, beneath the "Window of Appearances" where they will show themselves (probably, as usual, naked) and announce his latest wildness. Have we not had enough of it? Must we go through another play-acting? It is too much: too much. And to think I am old and ailing as always, unable to stop him, unable to influence. There are days when I believe I am going to die, and there are days when I believe I should. Certainly I contribute nothing—except, of course, one thing:

As long as I live he cannot have complete authority and complete control.

It is worth pushing this fat old body on a while longer to keep that from happening. For when it does, Kemet, the gods, the House of Thebes, and all, may go into the darkness of the afterworld and nevermore return.

It is five years almost to the day since he brought us all to this place to announce the founding of Akhet-Aten. Five years almost to the day since he changed their names, proclaimed the Aten, and called on the people of the Two Lands to follow his lead. And what has he got from it all, except his city, which indeed he has? He has not got the following of the people. He has not got their loyalty. And he has not got their love. And starting a year ago, after four years of comparative quiet, he has begun again to arouse their uneasiness. For he has begun to make real inroads upon Amon at last, and all the fears that had arisen with Aanen's murder but had gradually subsided, as they lived quietly in their city and ventured seldom forth, are grown again.

My brethren Burnaburiash and Tushratta are arch in their knowledge of what goes wrong here; arch and, I fear me, accurate. I shall send them a little gold, if it will keep them happy, and I shall probably marry Tadukhipa, out of respect for Gilukhipa's memory if nothing else. She never liked it here, but she bore her burden well and was a good friend to my House in her own odd, glowering way. But for her, I suspect my darling Sitamon and sturdy Kaires would have had far fewer happy nights, and for that I thank her. None has had exactly the happy lives they would have wished, but together they have given one another solace, the young people valuing her secret assistance, she basking in their love and gratitude in return.

She was ill for a year before she died, a sad, unhappy thing. She lies now in the Valley of the Queens, where she will lie forever and ever, far from Mittani. At Tiye's suggestion I gave her a full royal burial, and I do not regret it. She was a good woman. I hope Tadukhipa may be the same, though I may not be able to wait for the years to run on much longer before I take her to my bed. I wish to do it while I am still able.

And in that, thanks to Min and various potions prepared for me by his priests, I am. Akhenaten and Smenkhkara were much surprised three years ago when their mother suddenly starting bearing again. First came the boy and then, a year later, the girl. I think this will probably be all, but their coming was a great delight to us. Smenkhkara, who has become a beautiful youth, sleek and golden, almost like a woman in the soft perfection of his looks and the gentle grace of his manner, welcomed them with an innocent glee and happiness. The Co-Regent, in what I see now was really the beginning of his new attack upon Amon, took a more direct approach.

"What do you intend to name the child, Father?" he inquired in each instance, actually making the trip all the way to Thebes both times for no other purpose, apparently, than to ask the question.

"I like the name," he said slowly each time when I told him. Then his eyes narrowed and his face assumed its usual basilisk look. "But I would like it better if it were Tut-ankh-*aten* instead of Tut-ankh-*amon*." And for the girl, the same: "I like the name. But—I would like it better if it were Beket-*aten* instead of Beket-*amon*."

And such was his manner, and such was his look, which chills the Great Wife and me as much as it does anyone else when he turns it upon us, that after some fumbling and mumbling we gave in both times and announced to the world that the new god and his sister were indeed to be known as Tut-ankh-aten and Beket-aten. This did not please Amon, but we have gradually learned that it is better that we please our son.

And of course, I will say for him, he is consistent. Six little princesses now fill his own household. Three more

have joined Merytaten, Meketaten and Ankhesenpaaten.
Of the six, four bear the name of the Aten. The names
of the last two end in "Ra"; he refuses ever again to use
the name "Amon."

Six little princesses, and no little son. It is I, the old
Pharaoh, who produces the sons. Neb-Ma'at-Ra is not
dead yet, by the gods!

Secretly I know this worries them very much: they
wish a son who would succeed to the Double Crown and
carry on the work of the Aten. It appears more and
more likely that this will never be. Beautiful Smenkhkara
stands next in line, and now my little Tut-ankh-*aten* after
him. What will they make of their brother's heritage, such
as it is? Tut is too young to know, as yet, and Smenkhkara
is too gentle and diplomatic—and at heart, I think, too
much in awe of his older brother, and too adoring—to
express opposition, but I wonder if he really believes. I
watch him closely for signs, but so far the only signs I see
are that he prefers his brother's company to that of any
woman, which may or may not be a good thing. No doubt
it will change: he is very young yet, in many ways much
younger at his age than Akhenaten, who, it sometimes
seems now, was never young.

My brethren Tushratta and Burnaburiash say true
when they describe the state of Kemet, yet they are unfair when they blame me for it. I am ill, I have been ill
for many years; I never had much enthusiasm for whipping my vassals, though I did make expeditions to
Nubia and Sidon when I was much younger, and there
punished bands of rebels, as you may see on my monuments. Mostly I have preferred to hold them to me, as I
have held my people, by beneficence, though I know this
has often worried Tiye and Aye, Amonhotep, Son of
Hapu, and Kaires. They have felt, and often said, with
varying degrees of politeness and temerity, that I should
take a firmer line, send my forces far afield, perhaps
every two or three years go myself, just to prove that I
am here and that Pharaoh's power is still supreme. I do
not worry as they do about our vassals: let them squabble
with one another, as I said before. It only makes Kemet

stronger, and leaves her in peace to enjoy the calmness of my rule. And it permits me to enjoy it, too, which has not always been the case with some of my hard-working ancestors!

"Enjoy," I put it. I wonder how long it has been since I have really *enjoyed* wearing the Double Crown. Quite some years now, I am afraid. Ever since my oldest son began his erratic reign. Ever since he gave himself, his family, and—if he could do it, which I thank all the gods he cannot—Kemet away to the Aten.

More temples dot the land, more priests wear the crimson robe of Aten. And still there are no great throngs flocking to his altars, no great streams of tribute coming to his coffers. My people leave the Aten as severely alone as my son, up to now, has left Amon. Now my son is beginning to change his indifference; and this, to me, suggests unhappily that my people may before long begin to change their indifference to him and to the Aten—and not in a way that my son will like.

In the two years that the major part of this city was abuilding, he and Nefertiti (I cannot bring myself to say "Nefer-Neferu-Aten"—"Akhenaten" is hard enough) had much to occupy them. They were into everything, consulting with Bek and Tuthmose, with Amonhotep, Son of Hapu, and Ramose, with all who were concerned with the great task. I doubt if there is a single temple he has not personally supervised, a single garden or pathway that she has not designed. Ten thousand peasants have worked here steadily night and day for two years to create Akhet-Aten out of desert and a ridge of hills; and although the number has now dropped to about two thousand, they still work incessantly, putting the finishing touches to the paintings, the sculptures and the hieroglyphs on the walls that all hymn the praises of the Aten. Bek and his colleagues, like all of Kemet's sculptors and artists, abhor a blank wall. As has been the custom throughout our long and ancient history, there is scarcely a square inch uncovered anywhere. In this new city as in all the older ones, the mind is bedazzled by so much.

It is not, I think, impressed, as it is in the cities of Amon.

Again, as so many times before, I wonder: what would have happened if I had been content to fight alone my battle with Amon? If I had not dedicated my son to another god? If I had not underestimated both the son and the god? If I had let well enough alone?

It is perhaps the only instance in my rule when I have not left well enough alone. It is also, of course, the most disastrous.

Even so, it has not ever been quite so disturbing as it is now, because now he is showing some signs that the toy of Akhet-Aten is beginning to bore him. He is finally beginning to show some impatience that the Aten has not made the advances in the people's hearts that he wishes it to do. He is finally beginning to show an increasingly open anger with Amon—not the searing flash of rage that finally brought my brother-in-law Aanen the death he deserved, but a steady, smoldering, unyielding, implacable dislike, which appears to be husbanding its fire and awaiting its opportunities. This, I think, bodes ill for Amon, for Kemet, and for him. I pray to both Amon and Aten that it will not be so, but my worries grow the more as my ability to influence my son grows less.

Of course, the Great Wife and I cannot complain that he is not a thoughtful and considerate son. He has built us small palaces here, he has built a sunshade like Nefertiti's for Tiye, where she may sit and meditate, he hopes, about the Aten. Personally, I think she sits and broods about him, though we rarely discuss it nowadays, and when we do she sounds harried and sharp. She is looking much older, now. These years of uncertainty with him, now perhaps to become even more uncertain, have taken their toll of her as they have of Nefertiti. Nefertiti remains as always outwardly serene, composed, assured, every beauty line and shadow of kohl in place, every inch of make-up perfect as though glued to her face: but I think she too has tensions.

Their days pass in prayers and sacrifices to the Aten;

in frequent ceremonies at the Window of Appearances, where they disburse gold trinkets to those whose work on the city has particularly pleased them; and in frequent wild dashes with their daughters in an open chariot about the confines of the city, while all the workmen down their tools and join the people to cheer them with the good nature of those who know where their next meal is coming from. Now and again they have made state progresses to Memphis, sudden journeys to Thebes; now and again, I believe, he consults on the public business with Aye's son Nakht-Min, who at twenty-three is already a Commander of Horse and an assistant to faithful old Vizier Ramose—so rapidly do we rise, in this new world of his. And of course he consults faithfully with Aye himself, and with Kaires, who is always there, always thoughtful, always patient—and, I have the feeling, always ready: for what I do not exactly know, but if I were my son, I would pay more attention.

But I am not my son, and thank the gods for that. I am only dull, sick old Amonhotep III (life, health, prosperity to me!), who is capable only of making little princes and princesses, and of being loved by his people. For I *am* loved. Recently Tiye and I traveled the length of Kemet for my Second Jubilee, and everywhere in their millions my people turned out to greet me with their love. They worship me, both formally as a god—they have done this for many years (and indeed I frequently worship myself, particularly at my big mortuary temple near Medinet Habu)—and, with a deeper instinct, as their beloved King and Pharaoh.

Akhenaten, as he cannot match me in princes, also cannot match me in the love of our people. I think he still fascinates them with his ugliness. They watch him and they fear him. But they do not love him. I doubt if he even realizes, so absorbed is he with the Aten. He and the Aten love each other, and that for him is apparently enough.

I must send for Amonhotep, Son of Hapu, who is still my favorite scribe and confidant. There is time before we must gather at the Window of Appearances. Together we will draft replies to my brethren of Babylon and Mittani.

I may be ill, old, fat, bald and waddling, but I can still turn a phrase or two.

They will hear from Nibmuaria, though it will please me to give them considerably less gold than they wish to have.

Then listen to them squeak!

Tiye

HE IS IN BETTER SPIRITS than he has been for some time, now that he has been given renewed proof that the people love him more than they love our son. This has done mighty wonders for his ego, as has the arrival of our happy little Tutankhaten and our sweet little Beket-aten. You would think *I* had nothing to do with these two, only Neb-Ma'at-Ra. Such are *men,* even when they are gods.

I, too, have been pleased by these events. Now, as always with our people, I, the Great Wife, have received my equal share of love and adoration. In our tri-umphal progress the length of Kemet for our Second Jubilee, I sat as always beside the King, full and equal in dignity and power. Up to us from the endless throngs came such a wave of greeting as we had never received be-fore. It was as though the world split open for us every-where we went. There was a hunger in it, too, a yearning, a wistfulness which I, at least—being, as always, more sensitive than he—could sense. I knew the sad rea-son, too: because we represent something that is going, great days that are no more; a stability, a peace, an order and a joy in Kemet that no longer exist. Ever closer comes the day when we will not be here: ever closer the day when something they mistrust and instinctively fear assumes full control of the land. Ever closer comes the full and unrestricted kingship of Akhenaten. No wonder the desperate wistfulness in the people's greetings to his mother and father.

On all sides, the land falls apart. Abroad our vassals squabble, our allies fulminate, our false friends such as Babylon and Mittani utter their puling cries for gold even as they busily spin webs against us. False, false, false! There is not one we can rely upon: there is not one we can trust. And, carefree and happy as he dashes about his city playing god, my son pays no attention.

At home the Two Kingdoms deteriorate under his lackadaisical rule. Corruption creeps in at many levels. The central government remains relatively free of it, but in the twenty-two nomes of Upper Kemet and the twenty nomes of Lower Kemet, the political subdivisions of our land, local governors, overseers, petty officials, grow fat on their secret exactions from the people. Thievery and venality advance hand in hand, and no one says them nay. Constant complaints come in to Akhet-Aten (no longer to Thebes or Memphis, of course: now Thebes and Memphis sleep beside the Nile) and in their faithful way Ramose and the others do their best to respond. But they are only men; they are not the One whose diligent care and just commands could right all this. The central force that drives the wheel is not there.

Carefree and happy as he dashes about his city playing god, my son pays no attention.

True, you will say, it all began with his father and he is only reaping the harvest of what Neb-Ma'at-Ra has sown over the years. But say this not to *me,* the Great Wife, Queen Tiye! It is not *I* who have been slovenly and uncaring. It is not *I* who have permitted our alliances to deteriorate, our local governments to become corrupt. I, the Great Wife, Queen Tiye, *I* have done *my* best all these years to carry the burden the Good God has been too self-indulgent and too lazy to carry. It is only thanks to *me* that *some* order has been preserved. The wonder is not that we have so little now but that we still have as much as we do. It is not all gone, though it is going. Such as remains is a tribute to me. I, Queen Tiye, for many years Pharaoh in all but name of the Two Lands, have done this.

And, like so many, I have been bitterly disappointed that my son does not have the devotion to duty and the integrity of purpose that his mother has. For if he did, the Two Lands would be in much better condition than they now are.

Life is a round of worship, family frolics and happy gambols now. He and Nefertiti, who grows if anything more chillingly composed and more glacially beautiful as she ages, spend hours every day making offerings at the great altar stone of the Aten. Usually they take my granddaughters, so the people are treated constantly to the spectacle of his grotesque, ungainly figure, hers, trimmer but sagging a good bit from childbirth, and those of six little girls like six little steps descending in height from Merytaten to the youngest, Set-e-pen-ra, who can barely walk—all naked, of course—making their way by chariot through the streets to the House of Aten. There such few as gather to watch—they are not many, for it has long since become a sight too usual and too accustomed (my son has never grasped the royal mystique of not doing too much too often)—watch in a silence respectful but almost sullen, as his family performs its rituals. They sing, they chant, they solemnly beseech the Aten, and from him, apparently, receive some message that satisfies them. Meanwhile the people stare, sometimes with an air so close to boredom that it becomes virtually treason—or would be, were he a Pharaoh who cared more about his position. Then, ceremonies over, they remount the chariot and are off and away.

Sometimes in this second phase of it they will spend another couple of hours simply dashing through the city. He loves the plain that gave him his first great welcome after his illness, and it may be in pursuit of those lost echoes that he so frequently roams from end to end of it. He has never found them, nor, I predict, will he: for he baffles the people now. They do not understand him and I am very much afraid that they no longer care whether they do or not. And this is very sad and very rending to me, who am still his mother, for all that I criticize him, and who still remember him as a happy little boy, and who often cry in the night because it has all gone so wrong for him.

So they dash about. Sometimes when the Good God and I come down from Thebes to spend a month or two, as we do from time to time each year, he will invite us to go with them. Usually my husband pleads some excuse of tiredness or necessary work. (I hardly consider it so: he usually brings four or five girls from his harim with him, and I know the kind of "work" it is. Our late-arriving children have inspired him anew. But no matter.) It is mostly I join them in the chariot, thinking that courtesy and the necessity to put a good public face on it require my presence, at least occasionally.

After we have worshiped—and again it is for reasons of public policy that I do this, not any great devotion to the Aten, though he is easier to follow than gloomy Amon—there is usually a picnic.

We go far across the plain, leaving the center "island" of temples and palaces, passing the residences of the Court and the nobility, the humble homes of the servants and slaves, finally going past the barracks where the workmen of the city live and so come at last to open desert. We drive on at his command until we reach the low ridge of the eastern hills. Sometimes he directs us to what we have come to know as the Southern Tombs—where he has already ordered a magnificent resting place for my brother Aye, now his Private Secretary as well as Councilor—sometimes to the Northern Tombs, where work is already under way for lesser dignitaries. On occasion it is even to what we know as the "Royal Wady," the cleft midway along the ridge that runs back about four miles into the barren hills.

This is where he is preparing his own tomb and that of his family, and where he is also preparing tombs for his father and me. Personally my inclination is to lie beneath the Western Peak at Thebes as Kings and Queens of

Kemet have done for hundreds of years, but I am not arguing it with him now. Magnificent tombs for the Good God and myself are already excavated, decorated and waiting in the old necropolis. But if it makes our son happy to dream of us lying here, let him. We shall see who outlives whom, for he is frail beneath his fanaticism, and may not live as long as he thinks he will. There is no point to argument over that, when there are so many more serious things to argue about.

So we come to whichever resting place he has determined upon for the given day, and there the servants spread an elaborate feast and we dismount and eat. In the Royal Wady he used to love to talk of his plans for the new necropolis, and how he was going to create a new style of tomb as he had created a new style of art. (Actually it only exaggerates the old, but as with everything to do with the Aten, he prefers to call it "new.") Instead of being buried hundreds of feet beneath ground, covered over with tons of rock to hide us and protect us so that we may live forever without the kindly ministrations of the grave robbers of Qurna who persist in desecrating the tombs of our ancestors at Thebes, we would all be buried in small, open, free-standing temples, each confaining the sarcophagi of one royal individual.

"But," I once objected, "you will simply make it easy for the grave robbers, my son."

"There will be no grave robbers here," he replied serenely, "for all who come will come in the love of Aten, and they will think no evil thoughts or do any evil thing. We will rest safe in their love."

"Then you had best guarantee their love with good, strong guards," I said, I am afraid somewhat tartly. But it did not disturb his serenity, particularly when Nefertiti gave me a cool, amused look and agreed calmly:

"Do not be concerned for your safety, Majesty. The Aten loves you and will permit no harm to any who loves him."

I did not respond to this obvious bait but only gave her cool look for cool look and asked Merytaten, the oldest, to pour me a little more wine. The subject dropped, but it

was typical. And typical, too, perhaps, that after offering
this idea he should later have commanded Bek to begin
excavation of a royal necropolis dug back into the rock
like all the rest.

It is the commanding elevation over the plain provided
by the row of Northern Tombs that he most enjoys
visiting, and it is there that we have had most of our picnics following worship. I have always been surprised, in
fact, that he did not select this site for his palace, so spec-
tacularly does it afford one an overview of the city—and,
indeed, of Kemet itself, for from here one can see all
of the narrow strip of green, no more than three or four
miles wide on each side of the Nile, which, breaking
sharply and decisively into desert at its eastern and western edges, contains all that there is of our long snakelike
land. So it goes for more than six hundred miles along
Hapi's meandering route. Here would have been the ideal
spot, to my own eye. But of course I have always supposed that he preferred to be nearer to the temples of his
god, and so it was done.

There is something about that site, however, that seems
to encourage the brooder and dreamer in him: not, the
gods know, that it takes much to encourage that side.
But in that place it always comes out.

He talks then about all his plans for Akhet-Aten and
Kemet, while I come close to drowsing from too much
good food and good wine, and while Nefertiti interrupts
from time to time to call sharply, "Girls! Girls!" when the
princesses, bored by their father's monologue, stray too
far down the steep side of the cliff. (Their mother prides
herself on being a good disciplinarian, but she is not. They
are all hopelessly spoiled.) It is then that I, who begin
by feeling drowsy, come slowly awake again to the
gnawing fear that haunts me always, the fear of what will
happen to this strange son whom I have loved, and still
love, so much: he who seems determined to defy all the
history, traditions, customs and *ma'at* of Kemet and yet
manage to escape the retribution which all the ancient
past can bring to bear upon rebels, even royal ones.

Sometimes I cannot resist a taunt, in an attempt to bring him to reality.

"My son," I say, while, below, the crowded jumble of Akhet-Aten's whitewashed mud roofs and gold-tipped temples dances and shimmers away into the distance, "what good are these plans of yours? What have they availed you? You have been Co-Regent for ten years, now, and I do not perceive that you have done much to change the ways of Kemet. You have your temples and your priests, you have your city, you and your family worship as you please—but what of our people? They have not changed. Amon still reigns in their hearts, and reigns too much in the land. The High Priest Maya may be senile, but he has assistants who have not been frightened by the death of your uncle. And they still have the people's love—or least their fear, which suffices."

"*I* have their fear!" he says with a dry acerbity that persuades Nefertiti to reverse herself and say sharply, "Run along and play, girls!" to Meketaten and Ankhesenpaaten, who have strayed too close to this conversation of their elders. "I have their fear," he repeats, more softly; and then, alarmingly, his face begins to contort and I think he may be about to cry as he adds, softer yet, "though, I will grant you, I do not have their love."

"But, my son," I say, and I start to lean forward and touch his arm, only to draw back instinctively even as he too draws quickly away, like some hurt animal—my own son, and I can no longer comfort him, as a mother's heart cries out to do!—"my son, you could have their love, too, did you but seek it out."

"Pharaoh should not have to 'seek it out'!" he says with a sudden anger that obliterates the threat of tears. "It is Pharaoh's *right*. It is the Aten's *right*. We do not have to 'seek out' love from anybody!"

"Perhaps if you did not seek it together," I suggest, feeling his anger but determined to make my point, for Kemet's sake and for his. "Perhaps if you let the people come to love *you*, and only then, if they so desire, request of them that they love the Aten—"

"I *have* 'let them come to love me,' if they but would,"

he says harshly. "And I have not *requested* of them—
though I could have—I have *suggested* to them, far
more by example than by word—that they come to
love the Aten. I have not forced either myself or my god
upon them, for my Father Aten tells me that only if men
make free choice will they make lasting choice. And they
have ignored me. Thanks to Amon's constant appeals to
the superstitious and the ignorant, they have ignored me.
But I think"—and his eyes narrow in the way they
have, long slits of contemplation, resolve and pain—
"I think Amon may not succeed forever in alienating the
people from me. I think they may soon ignore me no
longer."

"What do you propose, O Son of the Sun?" I ask in
sudden alarm, a panicky concern striking my heart at his
somberly determined tone.

"More wonders, Mother," he says dryly. "What do you
expect? I have not performed many lately. Do you not
think it about time?"

"My son," I say gravely, "do not jest with the Two
Lands. You have caused enough concern with your name,
your city and your abandoning of the old gods for the new.
Is that not enough to satisfy you? Do not push it further,
I beseech you."

" 'Satisfy' me?" he demands, his voice a mixture of
irony, anger and pain. "Do you think I worship the Aten
just to 'satisfy' myself?"

"You satisfy no one else," I cannot resist saying, instantly shocked at my own temerity, but after all I am the
Great Wife, for many years Pharaoh in all but name of
the Two Lands, and he is still my son. I expect an explosion and decide with a sudden recklessness that I am
ready for it. It is time someone talked to him like this,
and since his father does not dare, it must fall to me.

But, amazingly, the explosion does not come.

For a long moment he too stares across the plain, over
the enormous, bustling city he has created, shimmering
away, like the dream it is, toward the southern hills. When
he speaks it is with a curious gentleness, as though from
a far distance, in realms where I cannot follow.

"Mother," he says, "you must understand me: it is not for my own satisfaction, though I have it and in great measure, that I worship the Aten. It is not for her satisfaction or theirs that my wife and our daughters join me in worshiping the Aten. It is, rather, that we would bear witness to what he is: that we would say to our people:

" 'Look you at this Great God, Father Aten, and see how kind he is! Look you how he is fresh like the morning and sweet like the dew! See how he is the Great God, the Sole God, the Universal God! See how he gives life to all things on earth! See how he makes the grass grow, the birds fly, the animals leap, the waters move! See how all men and all women spring from his serene brow to gleam like jewels of glory in his crown! See how he loves his Son, Akhenaten, who brings you his message and reveals how he will comfort you in all things and all places! Great is the glory of Aten the Father and Great is Akhenaten his Son!' . . . *This* is what we say to the people, Mother: this, and no else."

"But if your god is the greatest god—"

He interrupts instantly.

"The *Only* God! Amon and the rest are but profanations now!"

"If he is, then, the only god," I persist, "why is it that the people must worship anyone besides him? Why must they worship you, my son? Why cannot they worship the Aten directly without your intervention?"

"Do the people worship Amon directly without the intervention of my father?" he asks sharply; and there, of course, he has me. "They worship Father Amon and they worship my father who is his son—Father and Son, indivisible. They would not dare worship Amon did they not also worship my father. He speaks for them to Amon; he speaks for Amon to them. So they are worshiped jointly. Is it not so? Has it not been immemorially so? Therefore do I ask them to worship me, who am the Son of Aten, that I may speak for them to the Aten, and for the Aten to them. It is no different . . . except," he adds softly, "that it is *my* god who will ultimately prevail."

"I wonder, my son—" I begin, and fall silent for a moment while I consider whether to say what I wish to say next. Over the cliff's edge we can hear Merytaten screaming furiously at Ankhesenpaaten: there is already bad blood between the two little girls, both already prideful of position and apparently destined to become jealous women as they are now jealous children. Nefertiti, who has been listening to us with close attention, springs up and strides toward them as one of the royal nursemaids comes puffing up the hill from the servants' resting place below.

"I wonder, my son," I resume when we are alone, "whether in your heart, in your *ka* and *ba,* the very essence and soul of your being, you wish the people to worship the Aten to glorify the Aten—or whether you wish them to worship the Aten because it will glorify *you?*"

For a split second his eyes narrow dangerously and again I expect an outburst of rage. It does not come. He controls himself. A bland, ironic smile comes to the heavy lips.

"Mother," he says, "I have witnessed my father's way with Amon: I have witnessed what the lack of a firm hand with priests can do to the power and might of Pharaoh. I have seen the inroads of Amon upon this House. Surely you, the realist, the practical one, surely you who have been for many years Pharaoh in all but name of the Two Lands"—I have never told him I feel this, and secretly I am thrilled to learn that he recognizes it, too—"can understand. When I became Co-Regent the pattern was too firm, the direction too set. As a young Pharaoh of fifteen I should have been even less able than Neb-Ma'at-Ra to control the priests of Amon. But now I have created a new god, a new priesthood. Who is to say me nay with them? I created *them.*

"Thus shall *I* be Pharaoh again as Pharaoh was always meant to be—truly supreme in Kemet. Thus will the House of Thebes regain its full powers in the Two Kingdoms, and over all the Universal God will spread his unifying rays. . . .

"You should approve of me, Mother, for I work toward

the same goal that you always have, only to be prevented by the Good God's weakness."

"Do not speak thus disrespectfully of Pharaoh!" I say automatically, but he recognizes its ritual quality, for he openly smiles.

"I do not speak disrespectfully of *this* Pharaoh," he says, touching his narrow chest with a long, bony finger. "Never of *this* Pharaoh!"

And so, somewhat (if not entirely) relieved, I laugh. And he laughs. And thus Nefertiti finds us when she comes back up the ledge leading a chastened and obviously punished Merytaten.

She smiles in open relief that we should be agreeing thus amicably. I smile back in a rare moment of unity with my daughter-in-law. It is only later, after we have completed our meal and dashed back across the sands into the city, after I have been deposited at my own small but beautiful palace in the southern section that they have dashed on away to their own beautifully painted apartments on the "Island" that the doubts return to me.

He spoke most fervently as priest when he discussed his faith, but he spoke most calculatingly as Pharaoh when he discussed his power and the power of this House. Was the blind faith what he really feels, and was the emphasis on practical considerations something he offered deliberately to appease and divert me from his true intentions?

When he admitted that the people have for the most part ignored him and the Aten up to now, why did he say with such chilling certainty, "I think they may soon ignore me no longer"?

I do not trust my son, though it breaks my mother's heart to say so. Many things move beneath the strange surface of him the world now knows as Akhenaten. This afternoon he wishes the Court and the city to gather at the Window of Appearances for another of his "wonders." He indicates this will not be the usual awarding of gold to faithful servants. Something more portentous impends.

We have learned to mistrust Akhenaten's "wonders," in Kemet. Which of his two sides will he show us this afternoon—the mystic follower of the Aten, or the jealous

Good God who lately is becoming more and more impatient with Amon and more and more determined to challenge him openly at last?

He has been slow to provoke, enwrapped as he has been in building his city, extending his temples and extolling his god. Meanwhile Amon has not rested, though since Aanen's death—a fitting murder-for-murder, though I could wish it had taken place more discreetly and out of public view—the white-robes have been more secretive and more circumspect.

During Neb-Ma'at-Ra's reign (I already speak as though it were over, though he lives; we plan his Third Jubilee for next year, but I wonder) there was continued grumbling, a steady pushing to gain more power and influence, a hundred thousand little gnats nibbling away at us and our throne. In recent years this has increased, encouraged by the general breakdown in civic control and general morality. Aanen's death has only driven them underground. They have become more circumspect on the surface, more treacherous beneath.

I do not blame my son for the gradual end of what has been a monumental patience, re-established at great cost to himself, with Nefertiti's help, after the wild spasm of my brother's murder. But I fear the result.

I shall go with the rest to the Window of Appearances at three o'clock. He has just sent word that he wants his father and me to stand with them in the opening as he speaks: he wants us to sanction with our presence what he does.

He does not do us the courtesy to tell us what it is.

He does not tell us whether it will be safe or dangerous.

He simply asks us to attend and expects us to comply.

And because, unlike the people, we do truly love him, we will be there.

Aye

HE CALLS US AGAIN to the Window of Appearances. So
many times to that place, so many lavish distributions of
gold, so many showings of himself and his family, usually
naked and "living in truth"! So much pomp, so many
ceremonies! And not only here but throughout the land,
for they have traveled far in their attempts to spread the
faith of the Aten.

And what has it availed? For ten years he has been Co-
Regent, built his temples, called on the people to worship
his Universal God . . . and still the temples are mostly
silent and deserted save for a handful of red-robed priests,
a few furtive worshipers inclined his way but frightened of
Amon, and the sycophants of the Court who model themselves upon Pharaoh, since they must.

I watch them come to the great temples of Aten here,
the great temple of Aten at Karnak, dutifully bowing and
scraping and bringing their offerings: Pa-ra-nefer, butler
and chief craftsman to the Co-Regent; Bek the sculptor
and his assistant Tuthmose; Ipy, chief steward of Memphis; Penthu, High Priest of the Aten and chief physician
to the King; devious young Tutu, the Foreign Minister;
my own son Nakht-Min, assistant to Vizier Ramose;
faithful old Ramose himself, face in perpetual grimace with
his worries about the increasingly erratic course of the
Two Kingdoms; pompous, self-important Mahu, chief of
police of Akhet-Aten; Kheruef and Huya, stewards of
Queen Tiye; Pin-hasy and Mery-Ra, also high priests of the
Aten; Surero, chief steward of Amonhotep III (life,
health, prosperity!); Menna, overseer of crown lands;
Kha-em-het, overseer of the granaries of Upper and

Lower Kemet; Amonhotep, Son of Hapu, Kaires and the members of the Family, more out of personal loyalty to him than anything else; and, of course, last but certainly not least, the Councilor and Private Secretary Aye, doing his duty as always for the House of Thebes, whom men must call the biggest sycophant of them all. . . .

Well: am I? He has ordered dug for me in the southern ridge the most elaborate of all the Southern Tombs, indeed of all the tombs of Akhet-Aten save the royal mausoleum itself. I have already had it inscribed: "My lord taught me and I carry out his instructions." Thus may all men see—for these tombs, unlike those in the necropolis at Thebes, are not secret places but open to public view, and indeed private parties of the people go there all the time to marvel at the way the work progresses—how loyal I am to Pharaoh. Behind the dutifully humble words, of course, a man of fifty-five does not yield his views, his personality or his character—particularly if it is as tenacious as mine—to those of a youth of twenty-five. If that youth is Good God, King and Pharaoh, his elder defers in public and most times in private. But he does not cease to press his ideas when the moments are ripe.

And there still are such moments. He still trusts me, he still depends upon me. Occasionally (though not as often as before) he will fall into contemplative mood in my presence and we will talk philosophically of the future of the Two Lands, of the Aten and of himself. And rather more often than she did before, I estimate, my daughter comes to me with a troubled air and we talk alone. For all is no longer well in that marriage.

And all is no longer well in the Two Lands. The gradual erosions that began under the slothful hand of my luxury-loving brother-in-law have spread like an insidious growth through Kemet. My sister has tried valiantly to hold him to duty, to strengthen his resolve, to bring him back to the onerous demands of worthy kingship: he laughs (if he is feeling well), groans (if he is feeling ill) and, in either event, turns her aside with a ruthless gentleness and continues as he pleases. Every-

where the land suffers, and abroad the Empire, always a
fragile thing at best, crumbles away.

Weekly, almost daily, it sometimes seems, the dis-
patches come in, written in the Babylonian cuneiform that
serves the world as diplomatic language. Tutu translates
them and, at Akhenaten's orders, sees to it that I receive
copies. Their plaint is unanimous and universal, whether
they come from Burnaburiash, Tushratta, Rib-Addi of
Gebal or the sly and sneaking Aziru of the Amorites who
constantly foments trouble north of Damascus. They beg,
of course, for gold, since as Tushratta so delicately stated
it to my brother-in-law ". . . in my brother's land gold is
as the dust of the earth." This may or may not be—some
of the mines in Nubia are beginning to assay increasing
impurities, and the endless glittering stream that winds
through our history may conceivably be receding—but
they all think so, and demand it. They also fight constantly among themselves, ignore the attempts of our generals and viceroys to maintain calm along our borders, and
generally flaunt the authority of Pharaoh. The reason for
this, in my judgment and that of my sister, is very simple:
Pharaoh—neither Pharaoh—ever appears among them.
The great days and great campaigns of Amose and
Tuthmose III (life, health, prosperity to them both!) are
long gone. Two weak successors, one old, one young, permit the precious fabric to fray away.

I say two weak successors, yet in truth I think I can
only apply the adjective to my brother-in-law. For my
nephew is not weak. He is many things, but he is not
weak. His powerful personality, though it seems to lie
dormant, is no less powerful for that. Lately there are
signs it may awaken—but in what direction, no one can
predict. Probably not, it seems likely, in the direction of
restoring empire, or of restoring the ancient *ma'at* and
order of Kemet which have also become sadly frayed in
recent years.

The Two Lands drift ever more rapidly as the years
speed by. Again, it began under my brother-in-law: it
continues under my nephew. He cares no more for administration than his father, as long as the inhabitants of

Akhet-Aten remain suitably respectful and he can worship the Aten and ride about his plain, with an occasional visit to Thebes or Memphis to break what he pretends is not the monotony. But I know it is, and I know from his own remarks at unguarded moments, and from my daughter's increasing unhappiness, that monotony is causing things to happen in the King's House that may yet become open scandal.

Six daughters are in that house, no sons. The eldest daughter, Merytaten, is ten. In his desperate search for sons, apparently, my nephew took her to bed at nine. A sickly daughter who lived six months resulted. He has not tried again in that fashion and indeed I believe Merytaten was injured in the delivery to the extent that he will not be able to. But next comes Meketaten, now nine; and although all of this is entirely unknown to Kemet at the moment, my daughter tells me my nephew awaits only the first show of blood to try with her. How long can such things be concealed when he who prides himself on "living in truth" may at any moment abandon the secrecy that so far shrouds the effort?

Meanwhile, he and my daughter continue to appear always together in public, and to maintain the outward show of a warm and united family. And, as much as many families, I suppose they are. What he has done is presumed to be not shocking to our people when it is done by a god, and in our ancient history this is far from the first time such things have happened. But I say with calculation that what he has done "is *presumed to be* not shocking to our people." I have gone among the people in disguise many, many times over the years as the eyes and ears of Pharaoh, and I know what the people think. The people do not say anything. We in the palaces take them for granted as a vast, anonymous, obedient mass, and that, amazingly, is what they seem to have been through all our history—never complaining, never questioning, never protesting, never rebelling. But they think. And they watch. And they feel. And whether we admit it to ourselves or not, they pass judgments upon us which never surface, but are always there.

Basically they are extremely conservative. They accept the idea of the Good God bringing forth a child upon the body of his daughter because they have been told from infancy that this is what Good Gods sometimes have to do to preserve the purity of the blood of Ra. But I know them. I have sounded them out, I have tested their peasant prejudices. Far down in their hearts where they really judge us, it makes them uneasy, it strikes them as unnatural to the eternal *ma'at* of things, and they do not like it.

So when he comes forth, as I suspect he will someday, to announce that he has been "living in truth" with his own daughters, it will not be accepted. It will be held against him, secretly but profoundly. It would not be if he were his father and had his father's amiable, easygoing, fervently loved popularity. But he is not his father. He is not loved, my poor Akhenaten; and that is one of his many problems.

And now of late, Nefertiti tells me, he is seeking a "son" —or something it is not yet clear exactly what—somewhere else. Smenkhkara, too beautiful and too graceful in his lithe golden sleekness for his own good, is becoming the intimate of the King. He is only fifteen, but he is surpassingly fair; and he is not averse to it, so my daughter says. He has always worshiped his older brother. Now they are very often together, not in public view, but secretly, in hidden places. So far, she believes, they only talk, about the Aten and about Kemet, much as he talks to me. But she believes, as I do too, that something else may not be far behind.

Why can he not find a soldier, if that is his desire? They are available by the hundreds and even that, though much less common in our history, is not unknown to Pharaohs. Kaires (it will be awhile before I get over calling him that) has told me frankly that when he is absent on campaigns and far from Sitamon he and Ramesses have not hesitated. It comes and goes, is over in an hour, matters nothing. But when Pharaoh turns to his own House, when god lies with god and the destiny of the

House of Thebes and the weal of the Two Kingdoms is involved, then it matters much.

We pray, my daughter and I, that the infatuation, which probably at the moment rests more with Smenkhkara than with him, will pass before it can do harm. Soon Smenkhkara will be married to one of the daughters, probably Merytaten, to secure his own succession to the Double Crown if Akhenaten never produces a son. We hope it will be soon, though marriage does not always prove a preventative in such matters.

She worries about these things, my strikingly beautiful, icily composed, iron-willed daughter, and she worries about others as well. Because, for good or ill, she still adores her husband as she has all her life. She worries, as I do too, about the endless drift he seems to live in, and what will happen when, we both think inevitably, it ends.

Lately to both of us he has given indication that this may not be far off. Three weeks ago he called me to his apartments and suggested that we take a chariot ride (another chariot ride!) to his favorite thinking-place, the high ridge that fronts the Northern Tombs and commands the majestic prospect of the city and the plain. I accepted with alacrity, for it had been some time since we had found opportunity to talk, and I thought I might gain some clue to his attitude and purposes. I was not entirely disappointed, though at moments, as usual, he was cryptic and oblique. But I think I gained a little better understanding of his present mood.

"Uncle," he said when we were seated in the shade of the row of palms he has ordered planted there, "what would you say I have accomplished, as King of the Two Lands?"

I hesitated, which with his customary sensitivity he instantly perceived: one does not say, "Not much," to the Good God when he asks such a question. But in his case, of course, the unexpected, as usual, happened. It was the Good God himself who answered his own question:

"Not much. . . ."

I made some sort of protesting No-No sound, but he ignored it and stared out for a long brooding moment upon his domain, which I really believe is more truly his kingdom to him than the whole length of Kemet. Then he repeated with a heavy sigh:

"Not much. . . . But I have tried, Uncle—I have tried. You know that, do you not?"

"Yes, Son of the Sun," I said gravely, "I do know that. I believe your heart has been good and your purposes sincere."

"Then why have I accomplished so little?" he asked, the long eyes narrowing in pain as they so often do, but not hooded and defensive as they are with most—open and candid with me, whom he trusts. "Why have the people not understood my purposes? Why have they not followed the urgings of my heart? Do they not see that all I want is to make them happy, that all I wish is for their good? My Father Aten and I have only their welfare in our hearts. Why will they not worship us and let us lead them to the wonderful happiness and peace that belief in us can bring to them?"

Again I hesitated, choosing my words with great care, and again he of course perceived it.

"Tell me frankly, Uncle," he urged; and then added with his customary dryness, "It has been five years since I cut off a head. Yours is safe."

"You had cause," I observed tersely; and went on to speak what was in my heart.

"Nefer-Kheperu-Ra," I said, "no one, I think, can deny to the King the worship of whatever gods or god he may desire. It is impossible to deny him that, as it is impossible to deny him anything. And I think—and I say it honestly to you, Majesty—that you have not been harsh or cruel in your worship, neither have you imposed it upon the people, neither have you demanded that any follow your lead. You have simply offered the Aten as your Father and yourself as his Son, and have invited all who wished to draw near and worship. And some have."

"But not many," he said with sudden bitterness. "Not many, Uncle. Only those who depend upon my favor, only those who want my tolerance and my gold. Only those"— and the heavy lips twisted in a savage scorn—"who trem-

ble at Pharaoh's frown and seek the crumbs of preference
at his feet. Not the people, Uncle: *not the people.* You
say it is impossible to deny the King anything. There is a
thing, the one thing they *can* deny me: they have denied
me their love, and they have denied it to my Father Aten
. . . and I am wondering, Uncle," he said, and abruptly,
quite chillingly, his voice dropped to a softer and more
thoughtful register, "if it is not time for me to require it
of them. What say you to that?"

"Son of the Sun," I said, and though I am twenty-five
years older than I was on the day I similarly defied his
father, I spoke unhesitatingly and with a conviction that
overrode, if it did not eliminate, fear, "I say to that, that
such a course would be insanity. Yes!" I repeated sharply
as he swung and stared at me with eyes suddenly widened
in fury. "Insanity! That would truly destroy the Aten—
and yourself. They would hate you for it. They would
never forgive you. They would never love you. You cannot win love for yourself and your god in that fashion.
Do not do it, Son of the Sun! *Do not do it!*"

Had Kaires been there then, I think I might have suffered the fate of my brother. But presently, as it had with
my brother-in-law on that day so long ago, sanity re-
asserted itself in the being of my nephew. A terrible
struggle obviously went on inside for a few seconds; then
the anger faded from his eyes, the glare departed from his
face. As simply and directly as he used to ask me questions as a little boy, he asked quietly:

"Then what should I do, Uncle? They do not worship
the Aten who is my Father, they do not worship me who
am his Son. And throughout the land Amon works everywhere and always to subvert us." He gave me a long, level
glance, a certain irony came into his tone: he was no
longer the little boy. "Perhaps you will let me do something to Amon, Uncle? *He* deserves it."

For a moment I looked out upon his city and his plain,
looked farther to the narrow breadth of Kemet itself, hugging the Nile who gives it life. I thought of the Two
Lands, and again I said frankly what was in my heart.

"Majesty, I said before that no one can deny the King

the worship of whatever god or gods he may desire. I said no one can deny him anything. And quite correctly you replied that they could deny him love. But what does love rest upon, Son of the Sun? It rests upon good administration, upon a good husbanding of the land, upon the hard work of ruling, upon close attention to the good of the people—upon *good kingship*. We are utterly alone and you may kill me for saying it if you like, but you know as well as I that Neb-Ma'at-Ra has not done his duty along these lines. You know Kemet suffers. If you would be loved and worshiped, if you would have your god worshiped, *first be a good King*. The love, and the worship, will follow."

"You are saying to me that I have not been a good King," he said bleakly; and once again, not knowing what the results would be, I answered honestly:

"Yes."

There was a long silence, very long, while I did not dare look at him for fear of the awful anger I might see. But when he spoke at last, it was again to amaze me.

"And that is why," he said gently, "there is a Private Secretary and King's Councilor Aye, who stands at his right hand and gives him good advice in all things. . . . So tell me what to do about the priests of Amon, Uncle. It may be I need your gift for compromise."

I did so: and after he had thought about it gravely for a while without ever indicating his reaction, he heaved himself awkwardly to his feet (accepting my hand, which he does with me, Nefertiti, Smenkhkara, Kaires, Amonhotep, Son of Hapu, and absolutely no one else) and we walked slowly toward the waiting chariot and its horses soaked with sweat in Ra's suffocating rays.

Just before we left the ledge he turned for a last sweeping look over his plain, his city and his kingdom, shading his eyes with a long, thin hand against the blinding reflection of white roofs and gilded temples stretching far away to the southern hills.

"But we still do not know, do we, Uncle," he remarked softly, "what we are to do about the people's love and their need to worship me and my Father Aten. For I, unlike you, think that I have been a good and loving King, and I think it time, now, that I devise some way to have them love me in return."

And I, who had thought I had gotten through to him, was left speechless and said nothing further as he shuffled slowly on to the chariot and I followed dutifully after.

Next morning my daughter came to me, much troubled as she usually is of late. It seemed he had returned moodily to the Palace, summoned her and the girls, taken them to the Great Temple for worship (watched as usual by small groups of respectful but undemonstrative subjects) and then had returned, close to the supper hour, to summon Smenkhkara from his quarters and disappear with him for the rest of the night. By the humiliating but (she seemed to feel) necessary expedient of going herself to the stables and talking to the overseer, she learned that he had again ordered the chariot and had gone again, apparently, to the Northern Tombs.

What he and his brother did there, we of course will never know, but we must assume that he was doing exactly what he told my daughter when he departed, using much the same words he had used with me—"I must go and decide how to make the people love me and Father Aten." Presumably he wanted company in this, but significantly—as she confessed sobbing to me when her perfect composure finally cracked and she flung herself desperately into my comforting arms—it was the first time he had sought company other than hers to assist him in something so intimately involved with their god.

Since then he has gone about abstracted, brushing aside even the meager details of necessary administration that Ramose, Amonhotep, Son of Hapu, Kaires and I have dared place before him. And about Smenkhkara there has seemed to hover a golden aura even brighter than he usually carries. I do not think—I do not think—it is for the reason Nefertiti imagines, though of course I cannot know. I think it is rather that a boy of fifteen has been entrusted by his worshiped older brother with that brother's innermost thoughts and most secret plans. In-

deed, he told me as much when I took occasion to query
him, with a careful innocence, only yesterday.

"What are you so happy about, Smenkhkara?" I inquired with the fond familiarity we always use with him,
he is such a sunny and outgoing lad with everyone.

Quite uncharacteristically his open expression changed
to one of an innocence as careful as mine.

"Am I happy, Uncle?" he asked. Then suddenly he
could contain himself no longer and laughed in sheer exuberance, a boisterous, charming sound. He leaned toward me, placed an excited hand on my arm and lowered
his voice to a whisper.

"Uncle, *I know what Nefer-Kheperu-Ra is going to do.*
He has told me *everything!* It is marvelous, Uncle. *Marvelous!*"

"Then you will keep the secret and not reveal it to anyone, even me," I said sternly, "for Nefer-Kheperu-Ra
trusts you, and a god must not be betrayed by a god."

For a second he looked positively stricken at the
thought, his face almost drained of color, the finely chis-
eled bone structure suddenly standing out, the golden aura
dimmed, so earnest and intent was he.

"I shall never betray Nefer-Kheperu-Ra, Uncle," he said
solemnly. *"I shall never betray him!"*

"That is good," I said in a kindlier tone. "Run along,
then, and enjoy your games. I believe your little brother
is waiting for you to play ball with him."

"Oh yes!" he said eagerly, at once distracted so that I
realized that he is really just barely out of childhood himself. "Tut thinks he gives me good competition, though the
little devil"—and his tone became loving, for he is very
fond of the chubby three-year-old, as are we all—
"can still barely toddle. I always let him win, Uncle. He
thinks he is great, that one, beating me!"

"Good for you," I said. "You have a kind heart,
Nephew. Don't let it"—I had not meant to become serious again, but something impelled me to say it—"do not
let it betray you into doing things you should not do."

Again for a split second something, some shadow,
some secretiveness—or did I imagine it? I hope so—flick-

ered in his eyes. Then he laughed again, all happiness, all innocence . . . I think.

"I have it under control, Uncle," he assured me lightly. "It obeys"—and he struck a sudden dramatic pose and thumped himself sturdily on the chest—"it *obeys* the God Smenkhkara! It would not *dare* do otherwise!"

"Be off with you," I said, joining him in his delighted laughter, for there was after all nothing else to do. "Be careful or your brother will beat you again!"

"He had better," he said with another delighted laugh. "I would never forgive him did he not!"

And he raced away—happy and golden and, in his own outwardly sunny way, as elusive as ever his older brother can be.

So I do not know what portends at the Window of Appearances this afternoon. It may be peaceable, it may be violent, it may be a combination of the two—one does not know, with Nefer-Kheperu-Ra Akhenaten. Always up to now, with the single harsh explosion of my brother Aanen's death, his ways have been gentle, his methods peaceable. I believe he still wishes to pursue his purpose in this fashion. But in this, of course, I may be letting my wishes run away with me.

In any event, Private Secretary and King's Councilor Aye will be there with the rest: prepared, as always, to serve the House of Thebes and help it where he can.

I see, perhaps too gloomily, several areas in which this may presently be more necessary than it has ever been.

Bek

I AM THE APPRENTICE of His Majesty, I have been taught by the King: many are the wonders we have created here and throughout the land of Kemet, and to all its borders and boundaries—yea, even to the endless bleakness of the

Red Land near the Fourth Cataract in the south, even to the lands of Palestine and Syria and Mesopotamia to the north.

He lives in truth as he wishes, wherever men know the name of Kemet, and that is everywhere. So, too, do the nobles and courtiers who live, not "in truth," but by his favor, and pattern themselves upon him because they must. So even do I, for lately I have begun to make clay models for a quartzite stela of myself and my wife Ta-heret, and I find that, with the ease which has now become habit, I am giving myself the same bulbous breasts, the same protruding stomach, the same spreading hips and spindly legs that he has. I am giving Ta-heret the same characteristics. And I ask myself, even as I know the answer: why? Why make her, who has always been, if not the world's most beautiful woman, at least very satisfying to me, such a grotesque figure? Why am I making myself, who has always been, if not the world's handsomest man, at least a sturdy and respectable figure, as odd and, yes—though I almost dare not breathe the word even to myself—as laughable, as he?

I do it because here at Akhet-Aten we of the Court have no choice if we wish to remain in his good graces: and great could be the evil consequences did we not. Not, mind you, that he has ever killed anyone—save his uncle Aanen—for disobeying him. Not that he has ever removed anyone from power or laid waste his estates or proscribed him and his family or banished them. But he is Pharaoh *and he might*. Therefore we all do our best to stay in favor, even though he seems in most ways the mildest of men. It does not pay to take chances with a Good God, particularly one so strange and unknowable as this.

I do it, also, for another reason: because in our years of close association, from the time I first began to sculpt his statues for him on through the building of his city to the present day, I have come to hold in my heart a deep respect for his mind, his artistic beliefs, the "new art" as he calls it, which he has caused to be created in the Two Kingdoms.

Actually, of course, it is "new" only in the sense of its exaggerations. The things I was taught as a child by my father Men, chief sculptor to Amonhotep III (life, health, prosperity!), in general still hold true. There is simply a greater naturalism, an easier play of light and life across our scenes, a kindly humanism (although such has always been present in some degree throughout our history, in tomb-scenes depicting daily life) which illumines our efforts.

In two things only has he broken completely with the past: the depiction of himself and his family which, as I say, many of us find ourselves forced by our own fears of him, no doubt exaggerated, to imitate; and the decoration of tombs and temples, where he has abandoned the old customs and turned us, by his example and in some cases on his orders, to new.

In the old tomb, and temples—you can see them by the hundreds wherever you travel in Kemet, from Sakkara to Thebes—you find the emphasis on Osiris and the afterlife which has been characteristic of our civilization for two millennia. There you find the brilliantly colored paintings of the afterlife, the voyage of the deceased down the underground Nile, past the forty-two Judges of the Dead, to their reward in the Fields of Rushes and Offerings. And you see the offerings themselves piled high around all the artifacts of living that the dead will need when they revive to life forever in the celestial fields. All of these, from time immemorial, have come out of ancient pattern books that we artists have for many hundreds of years simply copied into each new tomb.

For the monuments and temples of the Kings, we have followed similar traditional designs. Some slightest changes of visage may distinguish one Pharaoh from another, but very little else has changed through the centuries.

The King is shown being invested, usually accompanied by falcon-headed Horus and ibis-headed Thoth, their hands resting protectively on his shoulders. He is shown bringing offerings to them, to Ptah, to Amon, to Hathor, Nut or whomever. He is shown in triumph, trampling "the Nine Bows," the nine nations that have always been our traditional enemies (whether or not—usually not— he has ever actually fought them). He is shown sometimes with his wife, their arms about one another in friendly connubiality. He is shown at the hunt, slaying vast quantities of game, of lions or cattle or whatever happens to have pleased his fancy when he ordered the fresco made. He is presently shown dying, as even gods must do, and, like the rest, going through the stages to become Osiris and revive in the afterlife.

In a sort of eternal sunlit serenity, he is always shown full body with profiled face, staring off into some impossibly peaceful and perfect prospect that he alone can see.

So it has always been.

In sculpture, he is shown in the round, but again, always heroically so. He is usually colossal, ten, twelve, twenty, sixty feet high, dwarfing us mortal men who worship at his feet. He strides forever down the centuries, following himself as through a hall of mirrors, unchanged and unchanging, whoever he may be . . . until now.

Yet even with Akhenaten we have our traditional scenes. He, too, has ordered us to show him standing atop the Nine Bows. He, too, has ordered himself depicted smashing an enemy with a club. In the same fashion he has even had us depict Queen Nefertiti raising a club like a Pharaoh to strike down an evil one. He still wants us to present them both in the traditional warlike style of the Pharaoh, even though in actual life he has never taken arms, never gone on expedition, never expressed any interest in conquest or the military art. It is but another of his puzzles which such as I have long since ceased trying to unravel. We do his bidding and leave the understanding to others whose personal happiness depends upon it more nearly.

In the temples of the Aten, and in the small forest of altars that has grown up south of the House of Rejoicing, there is no holy trinity such as there is in the case of the other gods, since he believes the Aten to be alone, the Only God. Amon has his wife Mut, his son Khons; Ptah has Sekhmet to wife and Nefertum as son; and so on. But the Aten stands alone—except that he does not stand alone. The Co-Regent has provided him with a human family. It is Akhenaten, Nefertiti and their daughters who appear on the stelae. It is they who have become the Holy Family. It is they who receive the tribute of those who worship Aten. Thus does the King make himself indivisible with his god, in all his depictions and paintings.

Sometimes when the day's work is over and desert and Nile are lying exhausted from the heat, in that swift hour when Nut rushes to take over the world, I pause to study these things and to wonder if in them I can find the secret of the King. I do not think I or my workmen have captured it, though physically we have the outlines as he desired, and indeed as they are: the bloated figures, the odd elongated heads of the girls, the pendulous breasts and protruding stomachs, the divine ugliness. I think it is more at Karnak that I find him; and even though I am the one who did it, I can stand there for hours and study his colossi and still not know exactly what I have captured in the stone . . . though I know what I intended.

I intended to capture arrogance and humility—gentleness and strength—assertion and self-defensiveness—confidence and terrible inner pain . . . for I think he is all these things. Have I done it?

In the harsh light when Ra stands high above in bleak clarity, or casts his shadows slantwise on the stone, the harshness comes out and I think I have failed, I think he has eluded me. At dawn or in the twilight hour when the light is gentler, the gentler things come out, and I think I have captured him as I wished. But I do not know, nor do I know what he thinks himself, for he has never told me. He simply lets them stand, as if to say, as he always says, by his actions and often by his words: "See me. Here I am, living in truth. Make of it what you will!"

There, and in his city, most truly speaks Akhenaten. And what a city it is! What a wonder have we created for him, here on the Aten's once barren plain! What a city has *he* created, for let there be no mistake: this is indeed his doing and no one else may take the credit.

In the center, on "the Island of the Aten," rise such

structures as the Great Palace, stretching for almost half a mile along the main thoroughfare, running west to the royal landing stage on the river. To the east is the Great Temple or House of the Aten, enclosed in a rectangular wall half a mile long by approximately eight hundred feet wide. Within this enclosure are also the sanctuary and the "House of Rejoicing," which leads on to the Gem-Aten, or "Aten Is Found," which is the central place of worship. To the south rises a smaller temple, the Mansion of the Aten, similar to the sanctuary of the Great Temple. (He has provided ample places to worship his god, I must say!) In addition, as I have noted, many hundreds of smaller altars have been built south of the House of Rejoicing. Most contain icons of himself and the Queen, or of themselves and some of the daughters, all worshiping the Aten; some few others are bare stone only. Offerings—sometimes very modest, baskets of fruit and flowers or the like, sometimes very lavish, rich with gold and jewels—are placed daily before all these altars. They are collected at sundown by the red-robed priests of the Aten, who by now number almost a thousand here in this city.

Between the two temples lie other structures such as the King's House, connected to the Great Palace by the archway over the street in which he has placed the Window of Appearances. Nearby are the Office of Works (where I have my office), directing the building that still goes on in many sections of the city, particularly to the north; the House of the Correspondence of Pharaoh, where hundreds of clerks under the direction of the Foreign Secretary Tutu copy, file and index the letters from allies, tributaries and vassal states; and the Police Headquarters where pompous old Mahu shuffles his papers and pretends to keep order in Akhet-Aten, which fortunately is a relatively orderly city anyway.

Here also are the houses of the wealthy attached to the Court in some capacity or other, such as those of the stewards Huya and Meryra, the major-domo Pa-ra-nefer, and the like; the more modest dwellings of lesser servitors; and finally the mud-brick huts of the necessary poor, who do the menial tasks that must be done with characteristic cheerfulness and good will.

Physically much of the city is beautiful, but over much of it hangs a stink, for we have no sewage system save the canals we have brought in from the Nile, which are sluggish and do not sweep away the effluent dumped into them quite as rapidly as delicacy would enjoy. Nor do we have domestic water on the plain; it, too, comes in by canal from the Nile. Sometimes the purposes of the two sets of canals become confused in the minds of those who use them: the incidence of infection, at times, is rather high.

To the south lie the houses and offices of some of the greater officials, such as Aye, Ramose, Amonhotep, Son of Hapu, Kaires and the rising young Nakht-Min. (Who would *not* rise, with Aye for a father?) There also is a Maru-Aten, a pleasure palace with a lake and running streams, brightly painted walls and pavements, and frescoes of the Aten and the Holy (human) Family in various intimate poses, inlaid with colored stones, glass and faïence from the King's Glass Works. Here also are the sunshades or kiosks of Queen Nefertiti and the princesses.

Building materials in most of the city are mud brick—glazed and painted in the homes of the wealthy and the great officials, simple and unadorned in the hovels of the poor. In the wealthier homes thresholds, window grilles, column bases and doorjambs are usually stone. Bathrooms have stone splash guards, stone squatting places, and stone tables for washing and anointing the body. The Great Palace is the only structure built of limestone, which is quarried in the western hills across the river near Hermopolis. Its state apartments are decorated with granite, alabaster and quartzite, covered with many beautiful paintings and hieroglyphics of the Aten and the Sacred (human) Family.

To the north are the homes of the merchants and tradesmen, the quays where the produce cultivated in the western portion of the city across the Nile, and from elsewhere in Kemet, is brought to us by the busy boats that come into Akhet-Aten as they used to come into now slumbering Thebes.

Farther north still is what we call the North City, site of the palaces of the old King and Queen Tiye, the small, newly completed palace shared jointly by the Princes Smenkhkara and Tutankhaten, and the just-laid foundations of the new palace of Queen Nefertiti. (We do not know why she desires one of her own, but he has ordered it without comment, and so we will build it without comment at his command—or, at least, any comment that can be overheard in the Great Palace.)

Such, in essence, is his city, sprung from the empty plain in two short years. Its roofs are whitewashed, its temples gleam with gold, gorgeous streamers of all colors fly from every possible peak and cornice. We have not solved the sewage problem and we do have the slums of the poor, which no city seemingly can exist without (and which he prefers to ignore as he ignores the poor themselves). But all else is as he wishes.

To the eye that looks down upon it, as his so often does from the ledge along the Northern Tombs, it appears to be, like the Aten, light and airy and gleaming with the hopes of men. Certainly I believe it still gleams with his, though all may not have gone as swiftly or as happily as he perhaps orginally wished.

A week ago he asked me how I was progressing with work on the tomb of his uncle Aye, largest and most impressive of the Southern Tombs. When I told him we had been able so far to sculpt only the entrance pillars and do the preliminary chiseling for the cutting of the inner chambers, he said:

"Good. I would have you leave on one wall a blank space suitable for many words."

"You do not wish, then," I began respectfully, "the Councilor's family to be depicted—"

"Oh yes," he said impatiently, "yes, yes, yes! There will be ample place for that. But I want you to reserve a space for me."

"We already plan to show Your Majesty and the Family—" I said, but again he interrupted.

"Bek, Bek! Do not anticipate! 'Words,' I said: I want space for *words*. You will receive them in due course. Do you intend to come to the Window of Appearances next week when I reveal my latest wonder?"

"As you have directed me, O Son of the Sun," I responded humbly.

"Good!" he said. "Then you will understand. In the meantime, do as I say and leave space. Will you do that, Bek?"

"Majesty!" I exclaimed, shocked. "How could I do otherwise than what Your Majesty commands?"

"There are some who do," he said, and a momentary grimness came into his eyes. Then his face lightened and he smiled as he sometimes does, a smile of amazing charm on that angular face, when he wishes to employ it. "But that does not apply to you, my faithful Bek. Together we live in truth, is it not so? Always and forever, in truth!"

"As you command me, Son of the Sun," I said.

"As you *wish*, I hope, Bek," he responded, still smiling; and of course I smiled too and bowed, for though I find his religion strange, I have always believed in the genius of His Majesty.

"As I *wish*," I echoed, and went off speedily thereafter to the Southern Tombs and instructed the workmen to leave the space he wants.

He did not tell me exactly how large he wants it, so I have made it very large. Whatever it is supposed to contain, there will be room for it. I am prepared to believe it may indeed be wonderful, for such has been, in general, my experience of His Majesty.

Sitamon

AND NOW WHAT, from my strange brother? The latest buzz going about the Court concerns the new palace he has commanded for Nefertiti. It is to be at the far northern edge of the city. It is to contain apartments for her, apartments for the Lady Anser-Wossett and her other ladies in waiting, servants' quarters, a large temple to the Aten—and, possibly, apartments for him. At least there will be adjoining apartments for someone, though there was nothing in his order to indicate that he intends to move there—or, indeed, that she does, for that matter.

Apparently she has requested that it be built—just in case. And he has agreed—just in case. And "Just in case of what?" is the question that whispers through the corridors of the Great Palace and our other palaces and, no doubt, through all the streets and temples and houses and hovels of Akhet-Aten as well.

Some of us, of course, think we know, but as yet no word of this has trickled to the streets. The gossip of Kemet, which travels like lightning up and down the river, and will soon have the Delta, Memphis, Thebes, Heliopolis—and no doubt even Nepata at the Fourth Cataract—flapping away as busily as this ingrown city, will continue, I trust, to speculate without substance. In common with all the Family, I hope and pray that what could be will never be.

But: my cousin Nefertiti prepares herself for it, if it should come. I think, myself, that she jumps too quickly to conclusions, sees too many things where none exist, is putting herself in position to make too much of something which, if intelligently handled by her, could be nothing more than a fleeting episode that will pass without ever leaving a trace anywhere—except, perhaps, in her heart.

It has taken me many years to understand that my cousin has a heart, beneath the icy perfection of her beauty and her seemingly unshakable composure at all times in all situations; but I have come to realize that underneath she is as sensitive and as easily hurt as he— though, the gods know, without his reason. Now in the mature fullness of her beauty, even I, the Queen-Princess Sitamon, have to admit that there is no woman anywhere lovelier than my cousin Nefertiti. Should she not, then, possess the serenity of knowing that she is favored above all beings? Should it not be enough?

Being woman, I know that it is not enough. I, too, have given devotion as absolute as hers—even greater, perhaps, for mine has had to undergo long absences, periods of deprivation, the frequent strain of having Kaires (the name which will be announced this afternoon at the Window of Appearances still rings strange: he will always be Kaires to me) at my side on innumerable occasions during ceremonial duties, yet being unable to touch, to smile or even to glance at one another. In recent years, of course, this has become much more relaxed: I am sure they know now, even in Nepata, that Sitamon and Kaires are lovers and have been for many years. But even so, it has not been easy.

Nor has it been easy to face the ghosts and specters of what he was doing when away from me, which Nefertiti has never, until now, had to face. Since we could never marry, he has not been under formal compulsion to remain completely faithful to me, and since he is a vigorous man, I knew very early that he was not. I was prepared for temple girls, prostitutes, noble ladies, peasant girls; I was even, with some instinctive knowledge I dreaded yet forced myself to accept, prepared for soldiers. But I never queried, I never pressed; and eventually of his own accord he told me, and I think truly, that while at one time or another he had, when far from me, found himself driven in sheer desperation into other arms of many kinds, none of them meant a thing to him other than simple physical release.

Nor, he assured me, had they ever been as numerous as I, in my jealous imaginings, had supposed—a fact which I believed, of course, but which I nonetheless took pains to confirm with Ramesses, who is good and dull and honest, and also easily cowed by threats of banishment. When sufficiently frightened he told me all I wanted to know: after which we again became firm and lasting friends. And I stopped worrying about Kaires, who gave me three children we could not keep and would have married me in an instant had I not, of course, been married to my father.

So I can understand my cousin Nefertiti, though I must admit I find myself a little contemptuous of her, now. I think she makes a pyramid of an anthill. Smenkhkara is fifteen and a hero-worshiper. She ought to understand that, for she has always worshiped the same "hero." It will pass. I doubt if anything has happened, or will. It will pass.

Much more to the point, it seems to me, is the condition of my brother's "doctrine," and there, I suspect, lie tensions even deeper between them—tensions which conceivably have much more to do with the building of her new palace than anything she fancies about my brothers. Certainly it is something which concerns me, for I fear that an impatience grows in him at last that could find its outlet in some action wild and completely out of control. I suspect that much more than Kaires' new name will be announced at the Window of Appearances this afternoon. I pray it may not do unchangeable harm to Kemet and to our House.

I think impatience grows in him and I think boredom grows in her. She has been completely faithful to him and to the doctrine: she has performed her functions as High Priestess of the Aten without ever once complaining or ever once failing to do as he desired. Yet days have lengthened into weeks, weeks into months, months into years—ten of them!—and nothing has changed the unvarying routine. The offerings in the temples, the visits to various parts of the city to watch the building, the frequent picnics and broodings at the Northern Tombs (I have been included often enough in these so that I now find some polite excuse not to be there to listen to his endless dreamings), the mad dashes through the streets with the banners flying, the people gaping and the girls hanging on for dear life—and on it goes.

And *it never gets anywhere.*

Two or three times a year, of course, they go up the river to Thebes or down the river to Memphis: he makes his duty calls, and they stay for a while at Malkata or at the Great Palace in Memphis, and along the Nile the people come out dutifully to see them pass. But they are not the triumphal progressions they were when he had just become Co-Regent and the two were newly married. Now the people come out because they are curious, not because they are loving; and of late, even *they* seem to have become bored. The crowds are not, so Kaires tells me (for I usually take the opportunity during these events to stay at Thebes, which is still home to me), as large as they used to be. Nor are they filled with excitement, or with the sort of adoration our parents can still command after almost forty years on the throne. Not even we who see him so intimately and so often (and are frequently moved by pity) can ever quite get used to that strange, ungainly figure. Many of our people still come out to see it in awe and wonderment: but even the novelty of that, for many, is evidently beginning to pass.

And he feels it: he feels it. He has asked me sometimes, in a tone almost despairing:

"Sister, where have I failed?"

And I have only been able to reply soothingly, my heart wrenched by his troubled and unhappy sincerity:

"Son of the Sun, you have not failed. It is simply that you have not yet made yourself *understood.*"

"Under*stood?*" he cried sharply the last time we had such an exchange, which was only a few days ago. "And 'not *yet*'? But I have been on the throne ten years! And I have been a good King! A *good* King! Why have they not 'understood' me?"

"They will, Brother," I said, still soothingly. "Give them time: they will."

"They have *had* time!" he snapped with a sudden savagery that quite took me aback and frightened me, it was so unlike his normal placid mien. "They have *had* time!"

"Give them a little more," I said, almost pleading in an attempt to change his mood.

"I do not know how much more *I* may have," he said somberly, which also startled me and took me aback; for while he has never been noticeably strong, neither, since his ailment ended, has he been particularly sickly.

"You have lived long, Son of the Sun," I said stoutly. "You will live longer. All will be well. You will see."

"*They* will see," he said darkly; and repeated as if to himself, "*They* will *see*."

"Yes, Majesty," I said with a deliberately exaggerated humility—for after all, I am "Majesty," too, and need not defer too deeply—bowed low and withdrew. I have learned it is best to leave him in such moods. They used to be very rare but they are becoming more frequent. They worry me.

Boredom—boredom and impatience. They are becoming the twin curses of his city. They explain why, I think, my uncle Aye is moving gradually, making certain plans, looking far ahead as he has always done. They explain why Kaires is making plans, and Amonhotep, Son of Hapu, who confides his worries to me from time to time when we can find occasion, usually at Thebes, to talk unobserved. They explain why, perhaps even more than, or at least equally with, her troubled thoughts about Smenkhkara, my cousin Nefertiti has asked for her own palace. They explain why my parents consult one another in frequent long and worried talks, and draw together more closely, as if in preparation.

My father may not live too much longer. Akhenaten may soon be the only Son of the Sun, Living Horus, Great Bull, King of the Two Lands, Pharaoh . . . What then?

I think then I shall marry Kaires, for I shall be released from my life-long bondage to the Good God Amonhotep III (life, health, prosperity!) and it will no longer matter that I bear the blood of direct descent that carries with it the right to the Double Crown. Akhenaten will not need me, his succession will be confirmed. Merytaten will then carry the blood and will be married to Smenkhkara to guarantee his succession.

I shall not be too old. I am only thirty-three, still possessed of a good figure, a pleasing face, the great wealth of palaces, jewels and cultivated lands that my father long ago settled upon me that I might own them forever. Kaires is already established beyond dislodgment in the new reign. He will be greatly strengthened if I am openly beside him.

I rather look forward to the change, as a matter of fact, though I shall miss my father. And I worry, of course, as one must, about what will happen to the Two Lands.

I wonder if I worry enough? . . .

Perhaps someday I, too, could become a real Queen instead of just my father's figurehead.

I must talk to Kaires about that. . . .

Kaires

WE DRIFT, DRIFT, DRIFT. Today, perhaps, at the Window of Appearances, we drift no longer. Yet if we move, where will it be?

I know where it will be for me: to a new recognition, a new dignity, a new power. This will be symbolized by the announcement of the new name I have chosen for myself. It will be made forever unchallengeable by the fact that my father will at last acknowledge me, that the Co-Regent will thereupon grant me legitimacy and that I will henceforth take my place openly as a member of the Family, which I am and have always been.

Then we shall see how things proceed with those "pur-

poses" which Amonhotep, Son of Hapu, told me he dis-
cerned in me, so many years ago. . . .

I believe at first my father was reluctant to do this; yet
when I laid before him facts he could not deny, it did not
take him long to agree. He is a practical man, after all,
despite his years of power. And I believe that he also feels
the time is near when those of us who are truly concerned
for the future of the Two Kingdoms must gather closer together in preparation for whatever may shortly come.

I discussed it with him in the Palace at Malkata a month
ago during our most recent visit to Thebes. At first he pretended he did not know what I was talking about but I
soon dispensed with that.

"Father—" I began as soon as I had kissed his hand,
and at once he interrupted sharply.

"Do not call me that!"

"Why not?" I demanded, no longer impressed as I used
to be by his shows of anger: the time has passed, for that.
"Such is your name, to me."

"I warned you years ago—"

It was my turn to interrupt.

"Years ago I was a youth of fifteen. I have honored for
twenty-five years the pledge I gave you then. It is enough,
with the country in the condition it is. It is time for me to
take my rightful place."

"What is it you wish to discuss with me?" he asked
coldly.

"A long-dead girl you met on an expedition in your
youth," I said. "And the need to stop a game that was
never necessary."

"Indeed it was," he said, more reasonably. "You are not
aware of all the intrigues that have swirled about this
House."

"Most of them," I said. "I am not a fool, Father. Most
importantly am I aware of the stewardship of Nefer-
Kheperu-Ra and how it has diminished the Two Lands, at
home and abroad. I am in his confidence and I intend to
continue to aid him where I can—"

"You must aid him in all things, as he wishes," he said
flatly.

"Even if I believe them to be destructive of the King-dom?" I demanded. "How can you counsel me so?"

"Because if you are at his side you can modify, you can soften, you can see that things are done not quite so harshly as he might, perhaps, command. And in time you can perhaps bring them back to the condition that will be best for Kemet."

"Not unless I have my own recognition and my own power in my own right, Father," I said firmly. "And that can only come with your recognition and its formal con-firmation by Akhenaten so that no one dare challenge it. He trusts you, Father. He will listen if you persuade him."

"May be," he said with a sudden moodiness that is un-like him—or perhaps it is, but I had never before been al-lowed to see it. "May be, my son, though of late he seems bent upon having his own way, and it may not be so easy."

"It is to his advantage, Father," I said. "I sense that he intends to do something soon—something forceful. He has been slumbering, in a sense, ever since the building of Akhet-Aten. Now there will be a change. He has said nothing to me, but I sense it: he will move."

"You are shrewd," my father said. "He *has* said some-thing to me. You are right: he will move."

"How?"

He sighed.

"I do not know, Kaires. He asked, I suggested, but—I do not know. I too sense his mood. He is finally becoming impatient, with Amon and with the people. I do not know how he intends to treat them—I am not sure he knows. But he is coming to feel that he must do something."

"All the better, then," I said crisply, "that I have my rightful place and be in a position, as you say, to modify, to soften, and to see that things are less harsh. Is it not so, Father? And must not all of us who feel the same stand together against whatever madness he may devise?"

"Do not speak so of your Pharaoh!" my father said, but it was half-hearted and automatic; and, emboldened, I said:

"I speak so of my kinsman. I know it will go no further than your ears."

"No," he agreed, suddenly somber. "It will go no further. Nor will what I say now. . . . You are right: he may be mad, though I have never really believed it, perhaps because I have pitied him and loved him. Yes"—for I had made a slight gesture—"I know that you have loved and pitied him too. If he is indeed mad, then it is right that you stand beside him, for the sake of Kemet and this House . . . What name do you wish to take?"

When I told him, he said, rather wryly, "It is unusual, but perhaps it will grip men's minds better so. It will take me a time to get used to it, but I will, Kaires. I will. And how soon would you like me to acknowledge you?"

"As soon as possible, do you not think?" I suggested. "Perhaps it can all be done together."

He nodded.

"He said something to me the other day about holding another ceremony soon at the Window of Appearances. I gathered he intends some announcement, some action—this may be the occasion we fear. Perhaps I can persuade him to make the announcement for you then. It may distract him from the other. I return to Akhet-Aten tomorrow. Will you be coming with me? He may wish to talk to you about it."

"Thank you," I said, "but I must remain in Thebes for several days to attend to matters of the garrison here. I shall be back Friday week if he wishes to see me. Convey him my love and respects."

"I shall," he said; and paused; and for the first time smiled; and extended his hand. "And do I have them too?"

And suddenly I was overcome with emotion at the infinite kindness and astuteness of this great figure, and gripped his hand in return, momentarily without words as my eyes, like his, filled with tears.

"Always, Father," I managed finally to blurt out. "Always."

"Good," he said. "I shall meet you next in Akhet-Aten and we shall see what can be done for this beloved land, and how we can best help your—kinsman—to find the

happiness he has never known but is determined to have
. . . and yet not destroy the Two Kingdoms in the process."

"It will not be easy, Father," I said soberly.

He gave me a look equally grave.

"No. But somehow it must be done. I count on you to
help, my son."

"Always, Father," I said again, fervently. "Always."

Next day he sailed downriver to Akhet-Aten. Four days
later I followed, taking horse down the highway that par-
allels the river, instead of boat, to facilitate my speed. On
my arrival I went at once to Sitamon and spent the night
in the charming little palace her brother has given her
along the river. She was moody and preoccupied, worried
about him as we all are, but glad to see me. Promptly next
morning I received summons from the Great Palace: the
Co-Regent wished to see me, at my convenience. He received me alone, seated on his throne. His generosity overwhelmed me. Always, out of Nefer-Kheperu-Ra, there
came surprises.

"Your father has spoken to me," he said, without preliminary.

"Yes, Son of the Sun," I said quietly.

"I am not surprised," he said with a smile. "I always
knew—or at least always hoped—that so sturdy a servant
of Kemet and our House might be related to me. I have
always loved my 'big brother.' Now there is added reason
for it."

"Thank you, Majesty," I said, genuinely moved. "And
I, as you know, have always loved you."

"Yes," he said quietly. "I shall never forget our many,
many happy times together when you were so kind to my
wife and me."

This was the first time in my memory that he had not
called her either "Nefer-Neferu-Aten" or simply "Nerfer-
titi" to me. I took no notice, but filed it away.

"I like your new name," he said. "It has an interesting
ring to it. Men will not forget it. How did you happen to
come upon it?"

"I do not know, exactly," I said. "One night a few
months ago, bivouacking under the stars."

"With whom?" he asked quickly, and then laughed. "But I must not press you on that, 'big brother.' We must not press one another, eh?"

"No, Son of the Sun," I said with a smile, again making a mental note. "Better not. I am glad you like it."

"It has a good sound," he said. "I shall be pleased to announce it, together with your formal recognition as a member of the Family, at the Window of Appearances next week. You will be there?"

"Yes, Majesty," I said cautiously. "Will you announce wonders?"

"Kaires!" he said. "Won't you be wonder enough?" Then he laughed again. "You will be, when you hear all that I have in mind for you."

And he proceeded to unfold wonders indeed; so much so that I could only exclaim, "Son of the Sun! *Son of the Sun!*" when he was through.

"I hope *that* will satisfy you, Kaires," he said. And added with complete sincerity: "For I trust you with my kingdom as I trust you with my life."

"I shall never betray your trust, Nefer-Kheperu-Ra," I said solemnly, going back for a moment to the old familiarity. "Never."

"Never," he said, "is a long, long time." And repeated with a sudden somber emphasis that brought a momentary shiver to my spine for the abysses it appeared to open at the feet of both of us: "Never is a long, *long* time. . . ."

To this there was really no adequate answer, so I attempted none, only standing quietly until it pleased him to bring back his glance from the faraway place where it seemed to have gone. Then I spoke with a seemingly innocent interest that of course did not fool him for an instant.

"Will you announce *other* wonders, Majesty?"

"And will I tell them to you, 'big brother'?" he responded with a light but not unfriendly mockery. "Yes, I shall announce them, and no, I will not tell you what they are. Does that satisfy you?"

"Not exactly, Majesty," I said with a lightness to match his own, "but I suppose I must be content to wait, like the rest of Kemet, until I hear them formally from your lips."

" 'The rest of Kemet,' " he repeated, again sounding far away. " 'The rest of Kemet.' . . . Yes, the rest of Kemet! *That* is the problem, the rest of Kemet! But I think—I think"—and he paused, his eyes widened in thought—"I think the rest of Kemet will come to understand and love me, yet."

"You are understood and loved, Son of the Sun," I began, but he cut me off with a sharp gesture and a sudden angry look.

"I am not about to give you such authority in order that you may treat me like a fool!" he said harshly. "Do not talk to me like an imbecile! We both know how I am 'understood' and 'loved'! Is it not so, 'big brother'?"

"Majesty—" I began; and then began to flounder, cursing myself inwardly, knowing it was hopeless. "Majesty—"

"It is so," he said decisively, "so we will speak no more about it . . . except to say this, Kaires—except to say this: the wonders I announce at the Window of Appearances will do much to bring them my way, I believe. They will not be overly harsh, but they will be emphatic. They will, in fact, follow a suggestion made by Aye, whose wisdom is unending. That will be part of it. Then will come a further wonder which I myself have devised. And this will be wonder indeed, and one forever lasting."

"Forever, Majesty," I ventured, not knowing later how I dared, "is a long, long time."

But one can usually count on Akhenaten not to react as violently as one expects (except for the one awful time which lives always unspoken between us, when he made me kill our uncle), and so I was not surprised when he agreed quietly:

"You are usually right, 'big brother,' but this time I think you may be mistaken. This time I think my wonder may indeed live forever. And it will show them—it will *show* them what I mean and what my Father Aten means. And they will know. They will *know*. . . ."

And he seemed to retreat again into his faraway place, looking rather like Nekhebet, the vulture goddess of Upper Kemet—the long intelligent eyes narrowed in some inward contemplation, the bony hands lying loosely on the knobby knees, the skinny shoulders fallen forward around the narrow chest, the long, narrow, yet not unattractive head pulled back and staring upward into some distance where I could not follow but only shiver again, to see him go.

"Yes, Son of the Sun," I said finally, very quietly. "I thank you for all your many favors to me, those past and those to come. I shall serve you faithfully always. I go now, if you will permit, for I must tend to Your Majesty's business in the barracks of the army."

"Yes, go," he said, coming back from wherever he had been, once again alert and attentive, giving me the smile that can be so warm and all-embracing when he chooses. "Thank you for coming, Kaires. It pleases me to honor you, for you are one of the few things in my life that has always been consistently good."

"Nefer-Kheperu-Ra—" I began in a voice protesting, frustrated and deeply moved—for who could not be touched by such a man? But he waved me away as the smile turned sad but still gallant.

"Go, now. And if you see Smenkhkara running about the place anywhere, send him in. He amuses me, that golden boy."

"Yes, Majesty" I said, thinking: *It is probably true;* bowed low; and departed.

In the courtyard I did indeed see Smenkhkara, playing ball as usual with tiny Tutankhaten, toddling about like a little crowing butterball, perfectly happy and excited with his adored elder brother. It occurred to me wryly that elder brothers *are* adored, in this House, though Tut has years to go before he knows what I believe Smenkhkara may know.

"Smenkhkara!" I said. "Nefer-Kheperu-Ra wishes to see you."

"Then," he said, flinging me the ball with his flashing smile, so quickly that I instinctively grabbed for it and caught it, "I must go to him. I wish you luck with the little scoundrel here. Play ball!"

And this, perceiving that Tut was looking after him with his mouth working and his eyes beginning to fill with tears, a great wail obviously building as his favorite playmate vanished, I hastily did, bouncing the ball quickly with a loud cry to catch the child's attention and then rolling it toward him. Diverted, he gurgled with laughter, caught it and rolled it back. This went on for quite some time and was, I am sure, very good exercise for me, until Nefertiti came out presently, scooped him up, still gurgling, gave me a fond if somewhat absent-minded smile, and took him off to lunch.

So now I await Akhenaten at the Window of Appearances with excitement and anticipation for myself, fear and uncertainty for Kemet. Thus it has been always. Always, he keeps us guessing; always, we never know. But at least from this day I shall have more authority. Perhaps with me at his side things will begin to *move*— and in a good direction. I am determined that it shall be so, and I know that my father—Amonhotep, Son of Hapu —good Ramesses—and many another—will be with me in the effort.

Nefertiti

I AM DRESSING NOW for the Window of Appearances. The ladies have bathed me in oils and unguents, perfumed my body (which will be clothed, this time, in sheath of gold; it will *not* be naked, whatever he says), dressed my hair, placed my blue crown carefully upon my head. Now it is time for gentle Anser-Wossett, still my faithful friend and helper though she has never understood or really approved of what we are trying to do in Kemet, to rouge and paint the skin, to shadow the eyes with malachite, to

pencil in the eyebrows and the long lines above and below the eyes that elongate them almost to the temples, to
touch the lips with ochre and highlight perfect cheekbones—to make me, in short, what I am, the most beautiful woman in Kemet and in all the world.

Even on the days when I do not show myself in public, I devote two hours to this: it has always been, in a
sense, my principal weapon. I am fearful now that it
may become my only one. . . .

"Window of Appearances!"

Appearances are what we mostly maintain, nowadays.

I accompany him here, I accompany him there: we
worship with the girls at the Aten's temples, we show ourselves to the people, we hold our picnics, we make our
occasional visits to Memphis and Thebes, we have earnest
old Bek and rising young Tuthmose portray us in informal domesticity as no Pharaoh and his family have ever
been portrayed. We live in truth . . . and my heart cries
for him, even as I feel him turning against me.

Two things cause it, I think. One is this damnable boredom, which seems to be both effect and cause, as it seems
to drain his energies and hinder him from advancing more
rapidly and decisively toward his objective of establishing the Aten as Sole God over all the other gods of
Kemet. The other is my cousin Smenkhkara, who, quite
innocently at first, but now I fear not so innocently, plays
upon boredom to achieve—what?

I do not know, really, for he already has everything. He
is as near physical perfection in his way as I am in mine.
He is a prince of the blood and thereby automatically a
god himself. He is presently heir apparent and unless we
have sons will remain so and—if he lives—will in due
time succeed my husband on the throne. He will soon—
very soon, if I have anything to say about it—be married
to Merytaten, that jealous and ambitious girl, and that
will confirm his succession beyond all challenge. Why
cannot he not be content with all this? Why must he do
me the ultimate insult of trying to take my husband from
me?

But let me, of course, be honest also: let *me,* too, live in truth. No one is ever taken from anyone who does not want to be taken. Smenkhkara is, I think, both thrilled and delighted with his new role; but he would not have it were it not the will of Akhenaten to give it to him.

Why this is I do not know. I have been his love and he mine since childhood, I have supported him unflinchingly through his illness, I have given him six daughters, I have been his faithful and unflagging companion in all his adventures of the mind and of the spirit. I have been at his side without a moment's rest or hesitation in ten years of attempting to raise the Aten to its rightful place as Supreme Ruler of the universe. I have adored him always and I have felt that he always adored me. I would like to think that he still does. I *do* think that he still does. But there is a withdrawing, a retreating, a subtle but growing reserve in our relationship. Behind it I see the gleaming smile and laughing eyes of my glittering cousin, who goes about the world attracting the adoration of all as naturally as he breathes.

So, once, did I. So, still, do I. But I begin to fear it is not enough to hold the one heart beside which all others are as dust to me.

In truth, you might ask, why should I care about it so much? See him as the people see him, see him as even faithful Bek and Tuthmose and gentle Anser-Wossett see him: see him as the grotesque about whom all Kemet secretly jokes, even as they come out in dutiful thousands to watch him pass. See him as the evil jest that Anser-Wossett, with fear and trembling but with the courage of her love for me, placed before me just a day ago: a child's toy she had purchased from a vendor in the street, the man of course all unknowing her connection with the Palace, else he would have fled in terror. . . . A tiny chariot, drawn by tiny horses; a tiny woman and six tiny girlish figures at her side; and holding the reins, the figure of—a monkey.

See him as he is, the grotesque, the malformed, the monstrous, the awkward One who shuffles as he walks, who can barely rise without assistance, whose belly is fat, whose breasts are pendulous, whose hips are as broad as though he had borne ten children himself, whose shanks and arms are spindly, whose face and head are narrow and elongated—"Horse Face," my spies tell me they call him in the bazaars—whose voice is either near falsetto in normal conversation or near croaking when filled with emotion. And see how such a One misgoverns Kemet, letting all drift while he pursues his crazy dream of the Aten!

Grotesque, malformed, incompetent dreamer! Why should I love such a One or care what happens to him or be worried if he removes his ungainly presence from my side and foists it on someone else? Why should I care, I Nefer-Neferu-Aten Nefertiti, Chief Wife, Queen of the Two Lands, most favored, most lovely, most serene, most beautiful woman in all the world?

Why should I love to joke? *Why, by the Aten, should I care what happens to him?*

... But I do.

I do: I do. And it does not ease the pain in my heart one bit to realize that the emotions that motivate my cousin Smenkhkara are undoubtedly very close to mine: an adoration complete from childhood, an implicit belief in what his brother is trying to do for his god, a very fond and genuine love—and pity, the final ingredient which in the end crushes at last all resistance and leads on to whatever the beloved desires. ...

Were Smenkhkara a street boy or a soldier, I could deal with him better. But he is not: he is my own blood, and him, too, I have loved, in a different way, since he was a baby. And about him, too, I care, for I understand, and I respect the impulses that are driving him—may already, I fear, have driven him—into his brother's arms. For his brother's need for love and affection is desperately great, and if I have somehow failed him, then in one part of my heart, though it kills me, I can say: if there does exist someone who can satisfy that need where I have not, then for his sake I wish them happiness. ...

But it is hard: it is very hard. I must pretend, I must go about the cares of family and affairs of state as though all were before. I must never permit the mask to crack,

I must always be calm, composed, serene, unchanging ... and so I am. I have only broken down once, and that in secret and with my father, who knows all and tells no one. He comforted me as best he could, but I know he too is very worried: for once, his enormous strength of character was not enough to quiet my heart. If anything, I only disturbed the balance of his, which is not good for the Two Lands or our House, since so much depends upon his steadiness.

Anser-Wossett adds an extra touch of kohl beneath my eyes and gives me her sweet and gentle smile, as understanding as she dares permit it to be: there are dark circles she wishes to hide, and I think she begins to suspect the reason. All Kemet must be wondering, now that I have asked for my own palace. It indicates something, certainly. I am sure the speculation runs through the nobility's houses, the peasant huts, and all the bazaars and market squares from the Delta to the Fourth Cataract.

I shall probably have to give some public reason soon, if only in order to quiet all this; it will be no help to the Co-Regent or to me to have it rumored that we are on the verge of an open break—if indeed we are. I do not feel that way: I feel curiously lightheaded, remote, almost detached. I cannot believe the situation to be as serious as my request for a separate palace would seem to indicate. Therefore the public reason will be of help to me too: perhaps I can partially believe in myself, and thereby negotiate more easily my passage through the days.

I think I shall let it be known that I have decided that the upbringing of the older girls now requires some separation from their younger sisters. It can also be publicly put about that Merytaten and Smenkhkara will soon be married, and that I wish to instruct Merytaten—as if anyone can instruct that cold little fish!—in the duties of wifehood. I must also separate, if possible, Meketaten from her father, before he attempts to do with her what he did with Merytaten—one more pathetic and no doubt equally foredoomed attempt to beget the son I have not so far been able to give him. (I believe his plan would be to declare the child, if a boy and if it lived, *my* son.)

Also, I need to supervise Merytaten and Ankhesen-paaten more closely, because already there is a fierce rivalry between the two girls, not only competition for their father's affection and mine, but looking forward to the time when they may be vying for the throne itself. Meketaten we will marry to Tutankhaten in due course, if she lives—but she is a sickly girl, and it may be, particularly if she is forced by Akhenaten to bear his child, that she will not survive. Ankhesenpaaten is as tough and strong-willed a child as Merytaten (though she conceals it better under a smiling manner), and I rather suspect that both sense that it is they who will be the survivors. They seem to fight over everything, and the battles which are so bitter now, when Merytaten is only ten and Ankhesenpaaten only eight, are not going to decrease, I am afraid, as they grow older.

Also there is Tut himself, that tiny chunk of happiness, a little Ra all his own, always beaming upon us with inexhaustible good will. The God Tutankhaten is three, and we all adore him. His mother the Great Wife Tiye gives him such time and affection as she can, but her involvement with the government and her growing cares with the old Pharaoh as he slips ever more steadily into decline mean that she looks to me increasingly to supervise the care of both Tut and Beketaten. Tut in particular is my favorite, as he indeed is everyone's. I find it almost impossible to refrain from hugging him too often and too much; I have to fight myself to keep from spoiling him even more than he is already . . . because, while my husband and the world may not give me credit for it, it is true, you know: I too hunger for sons.

But though I bewail in secret many hours the fact that neither the Aten nor any other god will answer my prayers for one, I do not want them by Akhenaten's method.

I want them *of my own flesh*, not that of my daughters, even though such unions are sanctioned by divinity

and the blood of Ra and traditions in the royal House going back many, many generations.

They are not sufficient for me.

I am the Chief Wife, *I* am she whom Akhenaten has
loved from a child, and who has loved him. I did not deliver cold-blooded Merytaten or sickly Meketaten or
sweetly smiling, determined Ankhesenpaaten to step into
my place and so be able to flaunt in my face forever the
fact that they could give their father a son where I,
Nefertiti, could not. I was not sorry when Merytaten's
child—a daughter, so what good did it do him anyway!—
died soon. I shall not be sorry if the same fate awaits
any child of Meketaten by him, or any child of Akhesen-
paaten.

I have, in fact, already given some thought to this. I
have had several serious discussions with my stepmother
Tey, whom Akhenaten and I honored some years ago
with the formal titles "Stepmother, Nurse and Tutor to
the Queen." We have never expressed the ultimate
thought openly to one another, but if need be, I believe
she will help me. It is simply a matter of bribing the
midwife, after all, and then making sure that she is either transported far away or killed, so that she will never
talk. It would not be difficult to arrange.

The girls may yet realize where their steel comes
from. There will be no sons from the loins of the King
unless they are borne by the Chief Wife. Laughing
Smenkhkara may have the throne and the King as well
before any son of Akhenaten who is not also the son of
Nefertiti wears the Double Crown!

But of course I never wanted it to be so, when our life
together began. How far do the gods take us from our
first idealistic intentions! All should have been happiness,
peace and achievement for beautiful Nefertiti and handsome Amonhotep IV! Then came illness, transformation,
new religion, new hopes, daughters, frustration, boredom,
the stagnation of the new god, the erosion of the new
hopes, the collapse of harmony, the withering of love . . .
perhaps the end of love, though that I still will not accept.

My cousin is my enemy, my own daughters are my enemies: the Chief Wife has fewer friends than she did have, fewer hearts she can depend upon. I have not followed my mother-in-law's policy, I have not made myself a co-equal on the throne, a Queen so loved by the people in her own right that it has armored her against those who would diminish her and pull her down. I have subordinated myself always to him, I have submerged myself and my life always in his. Now, if he rejects me, where will I go? What will I do?

Well: I will tell you.

I am a daughter of Aye, a Queen of the Two Lands, Nefer-Nerferu-Aten Nefertiti, "A Beautiful Woman Has Come," and I shall not wither and die. I shall fight back. I have requested my own palace, he is going to give it to me: if I am forced to go there, I will do so. But I will not give up. I will not yield my dignities. I will not yield my crown, I will not surrender to the sadness in his heart which I know is only temporary. I will defy him if I must, for the sake of the love I bear him, though I hope he does not make me do so. . . .

I must have stirred. My eyes, which have been far away, have apparently reflected something of my pain. I realize that Anser-Wossett is looking at me with loving alarm. I must conceal my feelings even from her. I manage a laugh, which she does not for an instant believe, and begin to chat of gorgeous jewels and golden gowns and similar unimportant things.

Soon they will summon me to join him in the chariot. Soon we will stand together once more at the Window of Appearances.

For the first time that I can ever remember, I am as ignorant as anyone else (save possibly one) of what he plans to do.

It is a strange experience for Nefertiti, loveliest and—of course!—most serene of women. But I dare say I shall manage to carry it off, as I have all else.

Smenkhkara

SOON, NOW, WE GO; and it is me he has asked to assist him in the final stages of his dressing. All others have been sent from the room. We are alone.

About the swollen hips I have fastened the pleated golden kilt, on the swollen feet I have strapped the outside golden sandals, around the thin neck I have gently clasped the glittering jeweled pectorals. I have attached the false beard, held by hidden threads to the enormous wig that covers the bulging, elongated skull (which all the girls have inherited). I have carefully draped the striped cloth of gold over the wig and adjusted its folds to frame his face and rest neatly on his chest. He awaits now, to be added at the last moment before the departure, only the heavy golden crook and flail and the enormous, ungainly Double Crown of the Two Kingdoms, which today he will wear.

Today he goes, not living in the truth of being naked as all have seen him so often, but living in the truth of what he is, was born to be, and ever will be: the Living Horus, Son of the Sun, Great Bull, Lord of the Two Lands, King and Pharaoh.

My brother appears in all his splendor today, for he has wonders indeed to announce to Kemet.

An hour ago he sent me to the chambers of the Queen with instructions.

"Tell her we will dress in full regalia. Tell her she need not go naked. The occasion will demand more dignity."

"I did not know," my cousin said dryly, "that he had ever considered dignity an obstacle to living in truth.

299

However, tell him I had already determined that I should dress in full regalia, regardless of what he did. So the request is unnecessary."

Some devil, which I instantly inwardly cursed, prompted me to murmur:

"I took it to be an order, Majesty, not a request."

For a moment she looked at me sharply. Then her expression softened.

"Smenkhkara," she said quietly, "you are a nice boy. Don't spoil it. Don't let him make you insolent. It will not hurt him, but it could hurt you in the eyes of all who love you."

"Nefer-Neferu-Aten," I said with a contrition that suddenly, and to my complete surprise, brought me close to tears, "I did not mean to be insolent, particularly to you. I, too, was surprised when Akhenaten decided to wear his regalia. It has not been like him in these recent years. It is a change."

"Many things are changing," she said, giving me a level glance from those serenely beautiful eyes. "He is. I am. Perhaps, Smenkhkara, even you are changing. Is it not so?"

"Cousin—" I began, "Majesty—" And then I fell back on my first, and almost always most successful, line of defense: I laughed, sounding, I think, happy and quite genuinely amused. "I never change! I am always the same, just as you see me, wishing all well and doing harm to no one!"

"I think you think you do not do harm," she said; and added quietly, almost as if to herself, with a sudden deep sigh, "and perhaps you do not. Perhaps you do good, in your own way: perhaps you do good to him. I do not know." She swung toward me, on her bench before the polished granite table covered with a hundred tiny cosmetic jars, and looked me full in the face. "Do *you* know, Cousin?"

For a moment our eyes held, hers lovely, calm and searching, my own, I hope, open, candid and steady. But it was, of course, mine that looked away first.

"No, Cousin," I replied, voice low, but honest, "I

know only that he thinks I do. And I love him, as you do. And so I help him, if I can, as he wants me to do."

I glanced back furtively then. Still those lovely eyes held mine in steady command, but now I could see that they had filled with tears.

"We do both love him," she agreed, also very low. "As I think, in a different way, we love each other. That is what makes it—not so easy."

"I am sorry, Majesty—" I began, a conventional and inadequate sentiment for which I hated myself, but what else was there to say? But her head came up proudly then and she even managed a smile. In spite of the conflicting emotions that tore me, I was still able to marvel, as we all do always, at her self-control.

"Do not be sorry, Cousin," she said more firmly. "Your heart is kind and good, and there is nothing to be sorry about in that. It is rare enough, in this world. . . . You may tell Anser-Wossett she can come back in, now. I have almost"—and marvelously she managed a little laugh that sounded quite natural and relaxed—"almost ruined the kohl. And all because of you, you naughty boy! Now run on back and tell His Majesty I shall be ready when he is. And may the Aten keep you."

"And you, Cousin," I said, and bowed low and backed out of her presence; finding to my amazement my own eyes filled again with tears, my voice again choked with emotion, so that I was unable to speak but could only gesture to the Lady Anser-Wossett. She bowed gravely, her face expressionless but, I felt, understanding more than she ever acknowledges, and went out. The door closed and I was alone—suddenly, I felt terribly, terribly alone. She is so good . . . and I am—what?

Standing in the empty corridor, I leaned my arm against the wall, my head against my arm, and gave way to a sudden grief that swept my body and completely astounded me. This weeping thing Smenkhkara the always confident and laughing? This shaken, weakling boy the God Smenkhkara? Oh no, oh no! . . . but, as I knew with a cold and certain anguish beneath my desperately strangled sobs, Oh yes . . . *oh yes.*

Mercifully no dignitary of the Court passed by, no servant blundered in, during the five minutes or so that it took me to regain control of myself. Presently I was able to brush the tears from my eyes, open them very wide, dash them with water from a drinking jug that stood nearby against the wall. Then I took a deep breath and went back, by side corridors and devious pathways, to the dressing room of my brother, who gave me a single sharp and penetrating look, stopped readjusting his kilt in front of the full-length mirror he has kept with him ever since his illness, and came toward me, arms outstretched.

Again I collapsed and sobbed, hating myself but helpless, this time against the thin but iron-hard chest, until at last the storm was over. Gently he released me, put a hand under my chin, raised my face until we stared at one another eye to eye.

"Smenkhkara," he said softly, "if you do not wish—"

"Oh *no!*" I cried, and again dissolved to tears, which I despised but could not stop. "Oh no, my brother—" and I fell to the floor, I hated that, too, but I could not help myself, I clasped his legs with my arms. "I wish! *I wish!*"

"Then," he said, his voice kindly but matter-of-fact, "I suggest you remember all the vast dignity of our ancient and royal House and rise like the god you are and beam upon me with your usual sunny likeness to Ra the Aten who smiles upon all things. Come now, get up! I need help with this accursed outfit which looks so impressive but takes so much bother. Today I must look every inch the god, because today"—his voice lost its jesting note and dropped abruptly to a somber and serious level, for the moment I might as well not have been there at all—"today I bring to *my* god a gift which will make all men marvel and make them realize at last that they must worship him, who is my Father, and me, who am his Son. Today we shall be truly worshiped and adored. Today we shall be *recognized*. From this time forward Akhenaten and his Father Aten will at last take their rightful places over the earth, over the water, and in the sky. I, Akhenaten, decree it!"

"Yes, Brother," I said, my face still stained with tears,

my voice still shaking with emotion. "It will be a wondrous thing."

"It will," he said with a conviction so calm that I did
not realize until later that for the first time, ever, he had
used the words *I decree it*. . . . "Now, help me. And
later, after the day is ended, we will talk together quietly
of your laughter and your tears." He smiled and again
placed his hand under my chin and raised my eyes to his.
"Perhaps," he added softly, "I may be able to banish the
tears, which disturb me, and restore the laughter . . .
which delights . . . my weary days."

And for a moment, on these last words, which he said
with such a sad and heavy emphasis—*"my weary days"*
—he looked so gorgeous in his regalia and so lost and
desolate in his eyes that a great wave of love and pity
swept my heart and my body: and I knew then that from
now on I would do, always, whatever he desires.

"Yes, Son of the Sun," I said humbly. "It will be as
you say."

Akhenaten (Life, health, prosperity!)

THERE IS A SMALL WINDOW, concealed by golden draperies, just at the beginning of the arch that leads from my
private apartments to the Window of Appearances. Here
I often stand for a few moments before we go out, so
that I may estimate the size of the crowd and gauge its
mood.

Normally it is not as numerous as I would like, though
I have long ago grown used to that: for one thing, the
street is narrow and cannot accommodate too many, and
for another, they just don't come. And usually the mood,
which the Family and the Court assure me (I do not

know why they still pretend to me: I do not pretend to
myself) is wildly welcoming, is far more often one of
dutiful boredom, laced now and again with a sly and almost evil curiosity. It is as though they were saying to
one another, as indeed I expect they are, "What is Horse
Face up to now? What crazy 'wonder' will he offer us today?"

These are, of course, my subjects among the common
folk. The members of the Court have a much more spe-
cific curiosity.

"Whom will he honor today? Who gets the gold pectorals and bracelets this time? What lucky soul will go
home luckier still, his hands burdened down with the
jewels our odd King flings down so carelessly from his
window? Will it be you? Me? Or that completely unworthy and worthless one over there?"

It draws them like flies. I can always be assured of a
basic audience. The hopefuls are always here.

Today I am at my secret aperture a little early, for
Smenkhkara, overcoming his tearful spell—which disturbed me, for I do not know the reason and he would not
tell me—has dressed me quickly and efficiently and gone
to his palace to change to his own ceremonial garb. It
gives me a little time to read over what I intend to say
(the heart of it in my own hand, as I have written and
rewritten it to perfection over many days and weeks) and
to prepare myself for the ordeal of appearing in public.

For it is an ordeal still, though they know it not.

I still do not like to be watched, to be studied, to be
made fun of; and all of these, of course, occur. I suppose
I shall never get used to it, though I have ruled for a decade, had six daughters—seven—and been on almost constant public display all my life, saving the dark period of
my ailment. I am King, Pharaoh, Good God, Living
Horus—and I am also an object. I will never really enjoy it, Father Aten, even with your help. Never.

Yet, of course, it must be done; and today it must be
done, as I am doing it, with an extra pomp and splendor.

Today they must take notice.

And they will, for today I have much for them.

There is firstly the news of Kaires, which will give him new stature and raise him to new power and dignity at my right hand. I believe this to be best for me and best for Kemet. It is also best for him. I am trusting that he will be grateful and will not betray me. My "big brother" has always been a constant in my life and I expect him to continue. My mother, I know, considers it something of a gamble. But Nefertiti agrees with me, and although we are not quite the single heart and single breath we have been all our lives, I still trust her judgment in many things.

I try to reflect at times—you know, Father Aten, how often I have discussed this with you—upon the reasons for the subtly growing rift that has come between us, but I usually wind up baffled. I thought at first it might be my union with Merytaten, though to me—and I think to my daughter, though she never said and I am not sure—it was a perfectly natural attempt to secure for myself a son and so pass on the blood of Ra in direct line from myself to the Double Crown. That the child was born sickly and soon died did not disturb me unduly, for it was simply the failure of a purpose that can be duplicated easily, though not, I am afraid, with Merytaten, who appears to have been injured in some way. Now, if it had been a son I had lost, I should have been seriously upset. And it was, it was forgotten in a day—by me, at least, though not, perhaps, by either my wife or my daughter.

Merytaten is a fierce and ambitious little girl. I feel she resents me now, yet in some curious way I think she resents her mother even more. I once overheard her cry out bitterly, "Why did you let him—" But then they heard me shuffling along the corridor. Voices were abruptly hushed. When I entered the room they were placidly knitting and chatting of innocuous things.

It was, in any event, a stupid question.

It was not a matter of anyone "letting" me.

How could anyone stop me?

Nor, when it comes to that, as presently it will, can

anyone stop me with Meketaten, or if that fails with
Ankhesenpaaten, or with Nefer-Neferu-Aten Junior, or
with Nefer-Neferu-Ra or with Set-e-pen-ra, if it comes to
that. They are all my daughters, I am their father; I do
it only with love in my heart, for them, for our House and
for Kemet—and above all, for you, Father Aten—and I
know they understand this.

So I do not worry.

Nonetheless, I think it may have had some effect upon
Nefertiti. I sense a withdrawal, slight but inescapable.
Now she wants her own palace and I have ordered it for
her. Yet surely she has no just cause for complaint. I have
tried six times to have a son with her and six times she
has failed me. I am not going to banish her, as some of
my fellow monarchs in other less progressive and en-
lightened lands might do in such a circumstance. She will
always be my Chief Wife, Queen of the Two Lands, my
first and still . . . I think . . . my only love. What excuse
does she have to be upset?

I have, as I say, puzzled over it many times. The only
thing I have been able to conclude is that she did not like
the secrecy of it. She must have felt that this was in some
way degrading, that if whispers of it got about the people
would consider that I had done it against her will and
over her protest—that for the first time we were not in
agreement on an act of major policy—that for the first
time, we were not living in truth.

She should be pleased, then, with what I have to say on
that subject today.

Not today, but in due course, I shall also live in truth
about the other matter which I suspect upsets her; though
that I shall discuss privately but directly with her first, as
befits her dignity as Chief Wife and Queen of the Two
Lands. I believe she will understand, knowing that she is
still first in my heart and that the one who has come to
dwell there now holds a place that may perhaps sometime
equal, but can never surpass, her own. I do not think she
will begrudge me that. I do not see logically how she can.

It is not as though my younger brother were a stranger
to me or to this House. It is not as though he were an ig-

norant peasant or a bored soldier or a dirty street boy. He, too, is of the blood of Ra; and his is a disposition so carefree and outgoing, a nature so decent and kind, and a physical presence so perfect, that it seems to me only fitting that he should become the beloved of the Good God—for in him the Good God sees himself, not as he is now but as he once was. And so in him I love myself.

Thus was I, before my illness struck. Thus was I, before horror came and my world turned upside down. Thus was I, before I became monster, grotesque, "Horse Face" and all the other bitter things my people call me—and which, in moments of darkest despair, I call myself.

Smenkhkara is myself as I was and as I would have been, had the gods who chose to betray me permitted. He laughs for me, he runs for me, he leaps for me, he is beautiful for me. He *is* me. I *am* he. In him I see myself, youthful and perfect and golden and beloved by all, as I might have been—as I *should* have been, but for the gods. I hunger for that perfection, which now I shall never have, as I hunger for sons, which also I may never have. And so I intend to take him to myself, hoping that in such a union Akhenaten may find what he has never found but always seeks: happiness, at last, and peace of mind.

Is this too much for a god to ask? It is not denied the simplest peasant in my realm. There is scarcely a one who is not happy in his simple life, who does not sing and joke as he goes cheerfully about his work in the fields. There is scarcely a slave in my household, or in any noble house, who does not have, if not perfect happiness, at least far more than I. There is not an artisan, laboring over his scarabs or his sculptures or his paintings, who does not exceed me in contentment. From the Delta to the Fourth Cataract, I am surrounded by happy people. It is only their King who is denied this. In the youth who is myself as I was meant to be, I intend to find it, if I can.

In this I mean no slight or hurt to Nefertiti, though I am afraid that already, even before the fact, she is choosing to take it so. It is no reflection on her that she is not the mirror image of what I should have been. This is something aside from, and beyond, the love she and I have always had for one another from our earliest days. She has been my constant companion, my beloved wife, my faithful supporter in my worship of you, Father Aten. She has not given me sons, though she has tried; it is not her fault that the gods, vindictive toward me still, should have remained adamant on that. Even you, Father Aten, have not been strong enough to overcome the other gods —yet. But you will.

You will.

And so I must discuss this with Nefertiti very soon, for very soon—probably tonight—I intend that it will happen. I know she will understand. She loves me. I love her. And we both love and trust in you, Father Aten. How, therefore, can there be friction?

Bless my union with Smenkhkara, Father Aten. Keep strong my union with Nefertiti. Make fruitful with sons my unions with my daughters. Permit Akhenaten, your son, to find his happiness, which he has never had in twenty-five years upon this earth. Help him in this, Father Aten, and he will continue to glorify and strengthen you in all things. On this he gives the word of your fellow god, a King and Pharaoh of the Two Lands, living in truth forever and ever, for millions and millions of years. . . .

Now the murmur and bustle of the crowd are growing very loud outside. I peek through the draperies, as behind me in the room I hear Nefertiti, our daughters, my parents, Smenkhkara, Aye, Kaires and Sitamon enter. It is time for us to appear. I turn and gesture to them all with a welcoming smile which they all return, somewhat uncertainly—they, too, are not sure what wonders "Horse Face" has in store for them today. I adjust the Double Crown more firmly on my head, take a deep breath, give a sign. The servants pull back the draperies, I shuffle slowly forward to face the multitude, the others follow and group themselves around me, Nefertiti at my side, my parents flanking us, the rest in line behind them.

A dutiful shout goes up, to be followed instantly by an abrupt and rustling silence. I step forward to the balcony's edge, again take a deep breath, and begin to speak, not too fast, not too choked with emotion: clearly, I think, and in a lucid voice which I must maintain, Father Aten, most particularly when I come to you.

But first there is Kaires.

"Good people of Kemet!" I cry, and even the rustling ceases as their massed faces, hundreds and hundreds of little brown dots, turn up to me as to the Sun—which for them indeed I am. "I have called you here this day to hear pronouncements concerning the Court and concerning the God Aten. I shall tell you of my Court first."

I can sense the sharp increase in their interest, especially among those who actually work in the Court. Who will get the baubles? They will be surprised and disappointed. The greedy will not be rewarded today: only the truly faithful.

"You all know," I go on, almost conversationally as I have their rapt attention, "how long and well my dear servant Kaires has assisted me. As a man, yea, even as a child, has he assisted Akhenaten. In all things has he assisted Akhenaten. For this we bear him great love.

"As you all know, Kaires came to join our royal House and serve Akhenaten from a secret place, many years ago. He is the son of a great figure of our Court, who has never revealed this fact. Today he has decided to do so. I present to you the Private Secretary and King's Councilor Aye."

And as they gasp and murmur and exclaim, I turn to my uncle Aye and gesture him forward beside me. He comes and stands, stares out upon the multitude with all his great and unassailable calm and dignity. Silence and rapt attention return.

"Good people of Kemet," he says, and his strong voice carries to the farthest reaches of the street and all the nearby buildings, where even on the roofs the curious stand tightly packed to hear our proceedings, "it gives me infinite happiness to recognize before you all, at last, my dear son Kaires, older brother to the Queen Nefer-Neferu-Aten"—the crowd gasps, and behind me I hear the Family gasp, too, Sitamon and Nefertiti louder than the rest—"to the General Nakht-Min and to the Lady Mut-nedj-met. Come, my son—" and for once my unshakable uncle shows some public sign of emotion as he turns and gestures Kaires forward. Tears roll down his cheeks as he embraces his son, and tears are in the eyes of Kaires, too, and of all of us.

A great, happy, approving shout goes up. Quietly my uncle steps back. Kaires, his face working with emotion, remains beside me.

"Thus do we welcome you to our House," I say gravely, and leaning forward, give him the kiss of ceremony on both cheeks. "Thus do we declare you a legitimate and ever valued member of our royal Family. And further do I say to you this, my faithful servant and cousin, and to all these good people of Kemet assembled here:

"From this day forward you shall be known as, and shall have all the rights and duties of, the King's Scribe, the King's Steward, Master of Works and Commander of the Troops of the King. And to honor your now fully recognized position as Cousin and Member of our House, and to symbolize your new duties and authorities and the new era of your life upon which you now enter in our House and in our service, I am pleased to confer upon you forever and ever the new name you have chosen for yourself:

"Hail to you, Horemheb!"

And I gesture commandingly to the crowd, and as one great voice it follows me as I chant solemnly:

"Hail to you, Horemheb!

"Hail to you, Horemheb, King's Scribe, Steward, Master of Works, Commander of the King's Troops! Hail, Horemheb, for millions and millions of years!"

My cousin—my "big brother" as I shall still always consider him—bows low to me and to the crowd, his eyes still filled with tears, his face still contorted with many emotions. Again he bows to them, again to me, and then steps quietly back to stand beside his father; seeming somehow to have acquired a new dignity and stature, which of course he has, and to have almost grown physically in our eyes. I am very pleased: he has always served me well and he will continue to do so. My rule rests on several solid rocks. Kaires—Horemheb, as I must come to remember—is approaching his father as the most solid of them all.

"People of Kemet," I resume presently when they have again become quiet, "I wish now to tell you of my plans to give to you a son who may someday succeed me on the throne of the Two Lands when eventually I return to my Father Aten."

Behind me I can sense a stirring among the Family. I turn and smile at Nefertiti and am amazed to find that her eyes look suddenly stricken. This is unfair and unjust to me. My face, I am afraid, hardens as I turn back. Strongly I speak:

"As you know, the Chief Wife Nefer-Neferu-Aten and I have no sons, though we have six daughters who bear the blood of Ra. It is to them I must look for sons."

For a moment there is silence, broken then by a rising swell of murmurs and exclamations as they realize my meaning. Yet why should they exclaim? It is not unusual in our history (witness most recently my father and my sister Sitamon—though there, true, the purpose was not sons, which he has, but legitimacy to the throne).

I do not look at Nefertiti now: there would be no point. I proceed, living in truth in their eyes and in yours, Father Aten, as you wish me to do.

"With the Princess Merytaten I have already had a child. This child was a daughter. Unfortunately it died young. I am told the Princess Merytaten will be unable to bear further children. Accordingly on this day I declare my marriage to my second daughter, the Princess Meketaten, whom I dearly love, and who I hope will bear me sons."

And I turn, again avoiding Nefertiti's eyes, and beckon to Meketaten. Shyly the nine-year-old comes forward, looking a little frightened but also pleased (as who would not, to be a Queen of the Two Lands?). I take her hand, raise our hands together before the crowd and say:

"I so decree it!"

There is a curious sound, part applause, part hesitation, part—I do not know. It cannot be disapproval, for I hope to give them a son. And it is in our history.

Again I raise our linked hands, while Meketaten shyly smiles. And now there is a burst of shouts and applause, although in it I still think I detect something hesitant, reserved, withheld. But I cannot worry about that, Father Aten. It is done, as it must be done, in truth in the eyes of the world and in your eyes.

Gravely I lean down and kiss my daughter full on the mouth. A curious little sigh escapes the crowd. I gesture her tenderly back to stand with her mother and sisters. This time my eyes and those of Nefertiti meet. She is looking at me as at a complete stranger. Momentarily I regret this: but it must be done.

And now, Father Aten, I come at last to you, and to our glorious moment together, in which all things will be made clear and all things made right.

"People of Kemet!" I say once more, and now there is an absolutely intent, enrapt silence. Now they *really* do not know what to expect, I have given them such wonders already. This is one both practical and lovely. And it, too, is something that must be done.

"People of Kemet," I repeat, and my voice at last threatens to croak with emotion, though I fight it as best I can, "for ten years I have been your King and for ten years I have commended to you the worship of my Father Aten. For ten years my family and I have worshiped him, and have been joined by some of you. But always we have been opposed by the priesthood of Amon. Always there have been resentment and whispering and secret attempts to thwart us.

"We have done nothing to Amon, but Amon has not rested in his attempts to weaken us. I have been infinitely patient with his betrayal. But now—now"—and here my voice grows thicker with excitement and emotion and their attention, if possible, becomes more intense—"*now this must stop!*"

I pause, and off to one side of the crowd where stands

doddering old Maya, High Priest of Amon, propped up by a small group of his white-robed fellows, there is a stirring and a quivering as they fear, and rightly, what may come.

Through the crowd runs a murmuring and a wonderment: Horse Face the Ever-Patient is angry at last!

"Therefore I, Akhenaten, Living Horus, Son of the Sun, King of the Two Lands, do decree and establish:

"That from this day all the wealth of Amon shall be divided in equal portions, half and half, with my Father Aten."

There is a gasping and groaning from Maya and his sycophants, an agitation and a stirring—and, finally, a shout of approval, begun by Nakht-Min and Ramose, standing just below the balcony, which is taken up and carried back through the crowd until it overwhelms all other sound. I expect it may be only duty, but at least it is there—public approval, public affirmation. It is what I need. I go on, my voice steadying and becoming clearer.

"I do decree and establish further that from this day forward one half the priests of Amon shall be separated from the temples of Amon and shall be assigned to the temples of the Aten, so that my Father Aten may be suitably worshiped and glorified throughout the length and breadth of my kingdom.

"To my dear cousin the General Horemheb, King's Scribe, King's Steward, Master of the Works and Commander of the Troops of the King, I give the duty of seeing that these things are done as I decree, through all the length and breadth of Kemet, throughout the Two Lands, from the Delta to the Fourth Cataract and wherever on this earth the writ of the Living Horus runs.

"I so decree it!"

I pause to give them time to digest this, turning to glance at Kaires—Horemheb, rather—whose face has turned pale with the shock of these sudden new responsibilities, but whose eyes meet mine unflinching as he bows low with impassive and impressive dignity. Beside him my uncle Aye, whose compromise this is, meets my eyes with equally impassive air and, imperceptibly to all save me,

nods, ever so slightly, approval. I turn back to look for
Maya and his priests, but they have already slunk away.

And so now, Father Aten, I come finally to the secret we
have known together in these recent months. I come finally
to your Hymn, which I have conceived with my own mind
and written with my own hand, and which all men hereafter shall recite in your temples and to your glory, forever and ever, for millions and millions of years.

"People of Kemet!" I cry, and now my damnable voice
is really choked and cracking with emotion. But I force
myself to go on, as I have had to force myself to do almost everything in my life, it seems to me. "I call upon
you now to hear the Hymn which I have devised to my
Father Aten, which all his priests in all his temples, and all
of the people of Kemet everywhere, will from this day
forward address to him. Listen to me well, for it shall be
the framework and the charter of your days, now and
for all times hereafter."

I pause, take a deep breath, sip deeply of water from
the golden cup that Smenkhkara steps forward to hand
to me, as I have instructed him. I feel suddenly that I
can trust my voice, that you are with me, and slowly and
clearly I say these beautiful words to you, my Father
Aten:

"To Aten, the Living, the Great, Lord of Jubilees, Master of all that the Sun-Disk encircles, Lord of Heaven and
Earth, Giving Life Forever and Ever!

"*Thou arisest fair in the horizon of Heaven, O Living
Aten, Beginner of Life. When thou dawnest in the East,
thou fillest every land with thy beauty. Thou art indeed
comely, great, radiant and high over every land. Thy rays
embrace the lands to the full extent of all that thou hast
made, for thou art Ra and thou attainest their limits and
subdueth them for thy beloved son, Akhenaten. Thou
art remote yet thy rays are upon the earth. Thou art in
the sight of men, yet thy ways are not known.*

"*When thou settest in the Western horizon, the earth is
in darkness after the manner of death. Men spend the
night indoors with the head covered, the eye not seeing its
fellow. Their possessions might be stolen, even when un-*

der their heads, and they would be unaware of it. Every lion comes forth from its lair and all snakes bite. Darkness is the only light, and the earth is silent when their Creator rests in his habitation.

"The earth brightens when thou arisest in the Eastern horizon and shinest forth as the Aten in day-time. Thou drivest away the night when thou givest forth thy beams. The Two Lands are in festival. They awake and stand upon their feet for thou hast raised them up. They wash their limbs, they put on raiment and raise their arms in adoration at thy appearance. The entire earth performs its labors. All cattle are at peace in their pastures. The trees and herbage grow green. The birds fly from their nests, their wings raised in praise of thy spirit. All animals gambol on their feet, all the winged creation live when thou hast risen for them. The boats sail upstream, and likewise downstream. All ways open at thy dawning. The fish in the river leap in thy presence. Thy rays are in the midst of the sea.

"Thou it is who causest women to conceive and maketh seed into man, who giveth life to the child in the womb of its mother, who comforteth him so that he cries not therein, nurse that thou art, even in the womb, who giveth breath to quicken all that he hath made. When the child comes forth from the body on the day of his birth, then thou openest his mouth completely and thou furnisheth his sustenance. When the chick in the egg chirps within the shell, thou givest him the breath within it to sustain him. Thou createst for him his proper term within the egg, so that he shall break it and come forth from it to testify to his completion when he runs about on his two feet when he emerges.

"How manifold are thy works! They are hidden from the sight of men, O Sole God, like unto whom there is no other! Thou didst fashion the earth according to thy desire when thou wast alone—all men, all cattle great and small, all that are upon the earth that run upon their feet or rise up on high flying with their wings. And the lands of Syria and Kush and Kemet—thou appointest every man to his place and satisfieth his needs. Everyone receives his sustenance and his days are numbered. Their tongues are diverse in speech and their qualities likewise, and their color is differentiated for thou hast distinguished the nations.

"Thou makest the waters under the earth and thou bringest them forth as the Nile at thy pleasure to sustain the people of Kemet even as thou hast made them live for thee, O Divine Lord of them all, toiling for them, the Lord of every land, shining forth for them, the Aten Disk of the day-time, great in majesty!

"All distant foreign lands, also, thou createst their life. Thou hast placed a Nile in heaven to come forth for them and make a flood upon the mountains like the sea in order to water the fields of their villages. How excellent are thy plans, O Lord of Eternity!—a Nile in the sky is thy gift to the foreigners and to the beasts of their lands; but the true Nile fiows from under the earth for Kemet.

"Thy beams nourish every field and when thou shinest they live and grow for thee. Thou makest the seasons in order to sustain all that thou hast made, the winter to cool them, the summer heat that they may taste of thy quality. Thou hast made heaven afar off that thou mayest behold all that thou hast made when thou wast alone, appearing in thy aspect of the Living Aten, rising and shining forth. Thou makest millions of forms out of thyself, towns, villages, fields, roads, the river. All eyes behold thee before them, for thou art the Aten of the day-time, above all that thou hast created.

"Thou art in my heart, but there is none other who knoweth thee save thy son Akhenaten. Thou hast made me wise in thy plans and thy power!"

So do I conclude my prayer to thee, my Father Aten; and over all is a great hush, for they have been following my words with great intentness; and nothing stirs.

"From this day forward," I say quietly, and so still is it that I need raise my voice hardly at all to carry to the farthest limits, and blessed art thou, O Aten, for my voice is steady and sure:

"From this day forward, all men shall worship Aten the Father and Akhenaten his Son, in all their temples and in

all their highways and byways, and on the river, and
on the earth, and in the sky, and wherever men shall live,
forever and ever hereafter, for millions and millions of
years.

"The Living Horus so decrees it!"

And I bow gravely to them as they remain absolutely
silent and wide-eyed before me. I turn and gesture to the
Family, they turn and precede me. We disappear within.

And behind me as I go there begins, at first faint but
then gathering force like the coming of a storm, a sibilant whispering and exclamation that grows and swells
and rises at my back until I reach my apartments, and the
great gilded doors are closed, and I hear it no more.

And it is done.

Kia

I SIT BESIDE THE OLD LADY, who is dying, and I wonder
what has happened at the Window of Appearances. We
are quite far from the Great Palace, here in the small
palace built by my husband for his parents, and no one
has come to tell me. I was not invited to attend—indeed,
I am seldom invited to anything, and I really wonder often
why he ever bothered to marry me, so little does he see of
me and so rarely does he deign to correspond with my father, who sent me here with such high, naïve hopes that I
would somehow procure for him the friendship and the
gold of strange Naphuria.

Strange Naphuria has other things on his mind, and I
am least of all his concerns, of that I am quite sure. The
days have stretched on into years, five of them, now,
and each is more empty and more boring than the last. I
cling, because I must do so to keep my sanity, to the advice

good Gilukhipa gave me before she also died, two years ago.

"Life has little here for a Queen who is not a Princess of Kemet. These people think themselves superior to all beings who walk the earth, they despise anyone who is not of Kemet, they look down upon us all. Particularly is this true of the young Pharaoh and Nefertiti. So pay them no attention. Make your own life. Concern yourself with the Family as much as you can—be helpful and kind to its other members, most of whom are also kind when they are not involved in ceremony. Involve yourself with the children, be a friend to his brothers who may someday rule—above all, be a friend to Kaires and to Sitamon, whose friend I have been, and whose friendship has done much to keep *me* sane. And do not worry if Akhenaten never comes near you. In fact, be thankful, for he is very strange and not as other men—stranger even than a god should be strange, for if gods are to be understood and worshiped they must be at least a little like men. And Akhenaten is like no other man. He is unique, and it is well to stay far from him . . . even though," she added thoughtfully, a surprising sadness coming into her voice, "it is impossible sometimes not to feel pity for him. He has not had an easy life."

I have tried to follow her advice, and I have even come in time to understand her final comment; for I, too, sense the deep underlying sadness of Naphuria's life, which he carefully conceals on most occasions but which now and again breaks through in unexpected ways. I believe the sculptor Bek has caught it best of all in the colossi that stand at Karnak. I am surprised, in fact, that Naphuria has let them stand, for deep in their brooding expression much of his inner pain is apparent to to those who are sensitive enough to see it. I believe he must be aware of this, for he is very sensitive himself—at least where he himself is concerned—and he must know how revealing these stone portraits are. It is as though once again he were saying, "Here I am, living in truth. Take me or leave me: thus am I."

I concluded long ago that he was too complex for me

to understand. I decided that was Nefertiti's task, and I have been happy that it has been a very long time since he expected me to share in it. He visited me a few times in my bedchamber, a process I did my best to assist him with—because, of course, if *I* were to bear him a son, I should suddenly be something very much more important than just a minor forgotten Queen from Mesopotamia —but I was unable to conceal my distaste, not having been trained and schooled for it all my life as the Chief Wife was. I tried very, very hard, but as I say: he is very sensitive where he himself is concerned, particularly where his physical deformities are concerned; and he knew. He knew. I never conceived, and the last time, which is now almost three years ago, he actually apologized to me, after. There was something so abject in this that I could not help but burst into tears: I knew then very well what Gilukhipa meant. He cried too, and for a few fleeting moments we clung to one another in a genuine love and sympathy. But then he arose awkwardly, refusing my assistance; the usual mask came down over his face; his eyes again became hooded; the moment passed. He never came near me again, nor have I made any attempt to seek a private audience with him. Sometimes he asks me to be present at the Window of Appearances, once in a great while he invites me to join him and Nefertiti and the girls on one of their picnics or on a furious chariot dash around the city to observe the builders' progress. But most of the time we leave one another strictly alone, only a moment's melancholy touching us both when we happen to meet accidentally in the corridors of the palace and exchange brief, formal greetings as we pass.

So I have, as good Gilukhipa suggested, busied myself with the rest of the Family, and have not been too alone or too unhappy. Sitamon and Kaires are very kind, the Councilor Aye is also kind if somewhat remote, the old Pharaoh and the Great Wife, in their rather absentminded fashion these days, have sometimes gone out of their way to include me in things, and of course to always laughing Smenkhkara and gurgling little Tutankhaten I am, I think, a genuinely loved "big sister" whom they often include in their games. And I have my ladies in waiting with whom I gossip, and my knitting and spinning, and my jewels and my musical instruments and my comfortable quarters, and good food and good wine—the years pass. Now and again I receive a letter from my father asking anxiously if I am all right. I always answer cheerfully that I am; and this, I suppose, is as near the truth as it is when anyone on this earth says it to anyone else. And actually I should be thankful, I am much better off than most: I shall never want, I shall live all my days in luxury, and be buried with these gods-on-earth. I cannot complain.

The old lady stirs and groans, and instantly I am at her side inquiring gently, "May I get you something, Majesty?"

Queen Mother Mutemwiya is sixty-seven and dying of some wasting disease our superstitious quacks can neither diagnose nor treat; and in the past few months, as the illness has attacked her frail body with ever increasing savagery, she and I have become very close. No one else in the Family has had the time—or, perhaps, the courage—to sit with her day in and day out and watch her shrink away. I think it has been just too painful for them, because I know they genuinely love her. Yet aside from an occasional dutiful visit at intervals several weeks apart, her son and the Great Wife have almost never appeared in her room, and the others have been similarly preoccupied. Only Kaires makes it a point to visit her on every possible occasion. He and I together are the concluding solace of this tiny little bag of bones that once was a very great Queen who ruled with her husband over a very great empire.

Now she awakens at the sound of my voice. Her eyes, shrewd and intelligent still in the sunken face, light with a little smile as, after a moment, she recognizes me.

"Just a little wine, dear," she whispers, and carefully I pour it into a cup, place my hand under her head and lift it gently so that she can sip a few drops before she signals with her eyes that she has had enough, and I let her gently down again.

"Have you heard what he said today at the Window of Appearances?" she whispers. I shake my head.

"No, Majesty."

"You did not go?" she inquires, forgetting that I told her this before she dropped off into her increasingly deep sleep a couple of hours ago.

"No, Majesty. He did not invite me."

"My grandson is—" She pauses and searches for the word, cannot find it, and with a faint but visible annoyance with the mind that no longer responds, abandons the attempt.

"Yes," I agree with a smile, "he is."

This amuses her, and together we laugh, I aloud and she with a very faint, very fragile humor that momentarily crinkles the paper-thin skin stretched so tightly across the tired old bones. She starts to say something else, hesitates, and in the interval is distracted as the door swings open without announcement and on the threshold Kaires stands. Now she smiles again, a deep and genuine fondness in her eyes. I start to rise, but he gestures me down again with a kindly firmness.

"Majesty," he says, bowing to Mutemwiya and gently kissing her tiny hand. "Majesty," he says to me, bowing and kissing mine. "You must both hear what has happened this day at the Window of Appearances. His Majesty has provided us with several wonders, and I thought you both should know."

And he sits down, still holding the Queen Mother's hand gently in his strong, brown-skinned one, and generously and patiently tells us of the day.

When he has concluded neither of us speaks for several moments. Then with that faintest of smiles, the Queen Mother whispers:

"I shall not be here long enough to learn to call you Horemheb. You must not mind if I still use Kaires."

"Majesty," he says, in that little game we all play with the dying and which the dying so gallantly play with us, "you must not say such things! You will be about

again, and you will learn to call me Horemheb with the
best of them! But in the meantime," he adds with a gentle
smile, "I shall not feel at all hurt if you continue to call
me Kaires."

"Good," she whispers. "It would be hard to break the
habit of twenty-five years. . . ." A frown, faint like all her
expressions now, but still unmistakable, creases the
ghostly-gray forehead. "You must serve my grandson well,
but if—if—"

She pauses and we both lean closer to the bed.

"Yes?" he asks, suddenly intent.

"If you find that he is destroying Kemet, then"—her
eyes open full and she returns his stare with the terrible
intensity of those who wish to impart final instructions before they go—"then . . . you must not hesitate."

He gives me a quick sharp look which says, as if in so
many words:

I trust you with this confidence forever—I nod gravely
—and he turns back to the tiny figure on the bed.

"Majesty," he says, "I shall not hesitate. On that I give
you the pledge of Kaires and the word of Horemheb."

Her eyes open wide again, she clutches his hand with a
sudden surprising strength, half raises herself in a fashion
we thought we would never see again, cries with a startling loudness, *"You must not hesitate!"*—clings for a
second to his hand—suddenly relinquishes it and falls back
—utters a long, rattling sigh—and is gone.

For many minutes we remain silent beside the bed,
heads bowed, weeping. Finally he rises, gently draws the
sheet over her face, holds out his hand, takes mine and
raises me slowly to my feet.

"In your presence, Majesty," he says somberly, "and
in hers, I pledge once more: *I will not hesitate.* . . . And
now, come. We must call the servants, spread the news,
begin the preparation of all things suitable for the safe
passage into the afterworld of this very great Queen and
very dear lady, our friend Mutemwiya."

Amonhotep, Son of Hapu

ACROSS THE MOLTEN RIVER the light lies soft and purple on the distant hills of the West. Soon it will be gone altogether and Nut will assume her dominion of the world. The silver boat of Khons, a narrow sliver in these early phases of his passage, rides low in the sky. It carries tonight Mutemwiya and no doubt many another who has departed Kemet for the afterworld this day. And it looks down, as always in these recent years, upon a troubled city and a troubled House.

He has offered us further wonders and with them, as always, further cause for concern and worry about his course and the future of the Two Lands. His appointment of Kaires—Horemheb, as we will learn to call him now —confirms my own judgment of the bright lad who came to us mysteriously so long ago. I am happy I have been able to assist his rise and I regard his new authority as perhaps the single most hopeful thing that has happened to Kemet in a decade. It does not surprise me that he has the parentage he has: like father, like son. Greater strengthening—and, if need be, greater discipline—for the House of Thebes and its reigning King there could not possibly be. Akhenaten will do well to trust him, to support him, and to be guided by his wisdom and the wisdom of Aye. To this, in my modest way, I also hope to contribute.

Leaving aside Kaires, what else is one to say of the Co-Regent's performance this day? It has left many mixed emotions in the Court, in the city and, no doubt, when word of it is carried up and down the river, in all of Kemet and the world beyond.

He has finally, after all these years of patience and

forbearance, moved against Amon. Yet it is, in a way, a
curiously halfhearted attack. He has gone halfway, to
take half of Amon's goods and half of Amon's priests, but
in doing so he has stirred up far more than half of Amon's
wrath. Has he thought beyond this curious compromise,
which Horemheb tells me was first suggested by Aye? Perhaps in this instance Aye's advice was not as wise as it
usually is. Or perhaps Aye, who sees far ahead in many
things, has some purpose in mind that is not apparent to
us now. In any event, it leaves neither Amon satisfied nor
the Aten fully in command. If I had been asked, I would
have said: strike completely or not at all, for time is not
in the habit of granting second chances. I think he would
have been better advised to do nothing or to do it all.
But even now, apparently, his peace-loving nature will
not permit him the unchecked anger, the necessary violence, to achieve his will. And so he finally declares a war
but then hesitates to fight it to the full. He may in time
pay bitterly for this.

And his marriages to his daughters? The desire for sons
is understandable: it is also, I am afraid, rather pathetic
and unnecessarily public. He antagonizes Nefertiti, who
has given him complete devotion all her life, and to what
purpose? Why was it necessary to announce it, if this is
what he wishes to do? Why could he not simply do what
he wishes in the privacy of the Palace and then declare
the sons, if sons there be, the children of Nefertiti? I suppose he would not consider this "living in truth"; and I
suppose, since she has always followed him faithfully in
this very risky human pursuit, that she should not justly
complain. But it is one thing to live in truth in an ab-
stract sense and quite another to have one's pride and
dignity as wife and mother affronted before the whole
world. This, too, he may live to regret, however proud he
is of himself at the moment for his "living in truth."

And his "Hymn to the Aten"? It is lovely and moving,
and perhaps it may be that the gods will yet decide that
this is what Akhentaten will be remembered for when all
our present questioning has been forgotten. But whether
the words are enough to persuade the people to abandon

Amon and the other gods and willingly worship what he chooses to call the "Sole God" seems doubtful to me. The Hymn is the noble conception of a mind undeniably brilliant, for all its strange quirks; but no matter how omnipresent he may make it—and already, I understand, riders carrying hundreds of papyrus scrolls are taking the river highway north and south to post them in the market squares of every village and town—it takes more than reiteration to create faith. It may in time create a dulled acceptance, but whether it will create the living faith that he himself has in his "Father Aten" is at best, it seems to me, a tenuous hope.

And there is one other matter, whispered in the Palace, but as yet, I believe, unknown in the streets: and that is the matter of the golden brother. If this comes about, which many little signs seem to indicate, will he eventually try to "live in truth" about that, too? If so, I would really fear for him, because I know the common folk from whom I come: they are deeply conservative, and some things they will never accept. That, though he might try to impose it upon them, they would in truth never accept. Yet, as I say, the signs are there and he seems determined to do it; which, I think, Smenkhkara expects and does not—alas for them both, and perhaps for the Two Lands as well—reject.

Even now they are alone together on the ledge that runs along the front of the Northern Tombs: I can see in the far distance the brightly lighted place where they stand, and I can visualize it well as twilight hurries on into night and stillness begins to fall on the heat-exhausted land.

I was there myself scarcely an hour ago: so were Amonhotep III (life, health, prosperity!), the Great Wife Tiye, Nefertiti, the Princesses, Sitamon, Aye, Horemheb, Smenkhkara, even little Tut, crowing and gurgling in the excitement of it all.

Great flares burned on either side. Below, the servants waited in humble curiosity. What would happen now?

There sounded the booming of a great drum and the blare of trumpets; and then in a loud voice he cried:

"Let us now give praise to Father Aten!"

And each of us obediently opened the roll of papyrus we had been handed as we stepped at his command upon the ledge; and facing the city, we all began to chant in unison as he led us in his high, shrill voice:

"Thou arisest fair in the horizon of Heaven, O Living Aten, Beginner of Life. When thou dawnest in the East, thou fillest every land with thy beauty. Thou art indeed comely, great, radiant and high over every land. Thy rays embrace the lands to the full extent of all that thou hast made, for thou art Ra and thou attainest their limits and subdueth them for thy beloved son, Akhenaten. Thou art remote yet thy rays are upon the earth. Thou art in the sight of men, yet thy ways are not known.

"When thou settest in the Western horizon————"

Three times he had us repeat the Hymn in unison, following him. Then he directed me, Aye, Horemheb, Sitamon and the servants to leave; and as we left, he began the chant again. As our chariots moved slowly down the hill the voices grew fainter but we could see them still: his parents, his brothers, Nefertiti and the Princesses standing on either side of his ungainly, unmistakable body.

Still farther down we turned and looked again, and this time he had reduced the number again: other chariots were coming slowly down. In the brightly lighted space only he, Nefertiti, their daughters and Smenkhkara remained.

And farther down yet, we turned again, and this time yet another chariot was descending, and on the ledge only two tiny figures remained, their voices carrying very faintly on the soft wind rising out of the Red Land to the east: the young Pharaoh and his brother.

And so we all came back to the city, and far in the distance the lighted space still glows and apparently the chanting still goes on.

It is a strange and somehow frightening spectacle, both impressive and saddening: as if he thought by sheer insistence to invoke his Sole God and have him work his magic upon the city, the plain, the Two Lands and the world.

It is all very typical of this strange Son of the Sun.

He lies with his own daughters, he seduces his own brother, he lets the Two Lands and the Empire slide to a point which will soon mean actual disaster—and he produces something as powerful, as reverent and as moving as his Hymn to the Aten.

What is one to make of him, Nefer-Kheperu-Ra Akhenaten, Living Horus, Son of the Sun, Great Bull, Lord of the Two Lands, tenth King and Pharaoh of the Eighteenth Dynasty of the land of Kemet?

I do not know . . . I do not know. I am an old man and getting older, and the more I know the less I know, particularly about this One.

I am beginning to suspect, now, that none of us will ever know, that there is no consistency, there is no answer—at least visible to us, his contemporaries. We can only follow, while he lives: however long his god—and all the gods—may permit that to be.

I look once more to the north, though I know already in my heart, with a sad, unhappy protest, what I will see.

The city lies dark and hushed.

Khons rides above in his silver boat.

Nothing stirs.

On the ledge along the Northern Tombs, the lights have been put out.

BOOK V

A God Against the Gods
1364 B.C.

AKHENATEN

Pani

HE LIES NOW in his bath of natron, where he has been for seventy days. This afternoon he will be taken out and placed upon a mat of reeds, which will absorb the excess moisture from his body. This will be done—like all things preceding and all that will come after until he goes beneath the ground—to the chanting of priests, court officials and professional women mourners, who have appeared in the streets twice each day since his death to extol his virtues and offer appropriate tributes in the temples for his safe passage into the afterworld.

Tonight his body will be smeared with heavy oils and unguents. With great care my corps of expert embalmers will take long linen strips, about three inches wide, dip them in water to moisten the gum with which they have been impregnated, and will bandage individually his hands, fingers, arms, legs, penis and toes. Then they will begin to bandage his entire body, working upward from the feet. After they have swathed his body to the armpits, with many thicknesses of linen, extra linen strips will be knotted across to keep all in place. Then beneath his shoulders one end of a thick bandage of twenty-five folds of linen will be placed. The other end will be drawn over his head and down upon his shoulders to rest evenly upon his chest. Further strips of linen around the neck will hold this head-wrapping in place.

Thick pads of linen will be placed around his ankles so that his feet will not be damaged should his sarcophagi be placed upright in the tomb. (In his case, of course, he will rest recumbent, but the wrapping has always been

331

done in this fashion, and so it will always be done, according to the eternal ways of Kemet.)

A heart-scarab of lapis lazuli, inscribed with a chapter from "The Book of the Dead," will be placed above his heart, and within the linen folds will be tucked jewels, items of gold and the blue faïence and steatite *ushabti*, small figurines representing those who will serve him in the afterworld. Upon his mummified head the wig and gold uraeus will be placed for the last time. Heavy jeweled pectorals will be placed around his neck. His tightly wrapped arms will be drawn into place across his chest and in them, in their proper position, will be placed the crook and flail.

Then still more bandages will be wrapped about the whole. These final bandages will be painted with special prayers for his safety and further chapters from "The Book of the Dead." And finally his mummy will be placed in the sarcophagus of gold that bears the image of his face, youthful and handsome as he was, and as he will be when he is returned to life in the afterworld.

Over the inner sarcophagus three more, made of wood gilded with gold, will be tightly fitted and sealed.

Further prayers and incantations will be said.

And finally, about the time that Ra's first faint flush appears in the east to begin the day of entombment, Amonhotep III (life, health, prosperity!), Son of the Sun, Living Horus, Great Bull, Good God, ninth King and Pharaoh of the Eighteenth Dynasty to rule over the land of Kemet, will at last be ready to make his final journey through his capital of Thebes to lie beside his ancestors in the Valley of the Kings beneath the Western Peak.

I, Pani, overseer of the Theban necropolis as my father Maya was before me and as my son Maya will be after me, have given to the preparation of this great King my deepest care and devotion, for he deserves it. He was much beloved in the Two Kingdoms, wise, generous, far-seeing, ever alert to protect his people and to guard Kemet against all her enemies. He was a good servant and father to us all. He was a *good* man. It appears unlikely that we shall soon see his like again.

Great fear stalks the Two Lands because of this.

During these prescribed seventy days of mummification, I have not been tied exclusively to my duties here. I
have excellent assistants, including my son who will succeed me: in deference to my advancing years, they have
begun to assume much of the burden. There is, in addition, a long period of waiting while the natron does its
work.

So for the first time in many years I have not been captive here. I have been able to go to Memphis and Sakkara, I have been to Akhet-Aten and Heliopolis and
many other cities, making arrangements for the ceremonies that will accompany and suitably honor the interment
of the Good God at the precise moment he goes beneath
the ground tomorrow. And what I have found has greatly
disturbed me.

We live, in the necropolis, in a world of our own—the
world of the dead, in which we are constantly preparing
new bodies for mummification as they come to us daily
from the nobility, the court officials and all the higher
ranks of Kemet. It is only because my son has recently become old enough to relieve me of some of the burden that
I have finally gotten out. It must be twenty years, literally,
since I left the necropolis. Reports and rumors have of
course reached us over the years, even in our special
hushed world. But I had no idea of the actual state into
which the Two Lands had fallen.

Everywhere I have found dismay and disarray, the
spread of internal corruption, the intimations of distant
chaos and disaster along the outer reaches of the Empire.
And universally I have found that the people blame, not
the Good God, whom they have come to love ever more
deeply as he has slipped inexorably away from them, but
his son, whose rule—if rule it can be called—has become
ever more erratic and unsettling in these past two years
as his father has grown weaker and less able to exercise
the care that has for so many years guided and protected
our beloved land.

Everywhere I went I was told that the King Akhenaten
—whom many refer to secretly as "Horse Face," but many

more are coming to call (in whispers, but they are increasing whispers) either "the Heretic of Akhet-Aten"
or "the Criminal of Akhet-Aten"—has embarked upon
strange courses and followed strange paths, both in the
pursuit of his god the Aten and in pursuit of other
things.

He has reduced the temples of Amon substantially, but
the only result apparently has been to make the people
love Amon and the other gods more. He has built further
temples to the Aten and has caused his "Hymn to the
Aten" to be inscribed on stelae, in tombs and on walls in
many public places throughout the land. But it has not
increased his converts outside the Court, where those who
seek preferment and riches must necessarily do as
Pharaoh wishes.

He has sought sons from his daughters, but so far has
achieved only two dead daughters, of the Princess Merytaten, who survived the experience, and the Princess
Meketaten, who died only two months ago as a result of
it, and was followed within two weeks by her child. (They
were buried at Akhet-Aten in the new necropolis there that
I know nothing about.) Now it is rumored that his daughter Ankhesenpaaten is pregnant by him.

He has become openly enamored, apparently—or so
goes the crude gossip in the bazaars—of his younger
brother the Prince Smenkhkara, and openly neglects the
Chief Wife Nefertiti, whose loveliness and goodness all
people everywhere admire. He pays little attention to
civil administration, ignores or deliberately flaunts the
overtures of Kemet's friends and allies abroad. His days
pass in prayers and dreaming, so it is said; and *ma'at* and
the safe protected life of centuries falls away into confusion, uncertainty and fear.

And now he is sole King and Pharaoh, supreme in
power over all Kemet. And the Two Lands lie helpless
beneath his hand, because Amon, who might choose a
successor to displace him, no longer has that power, and
there is no unity in the people that could rise against
him. Insurrection, indeed, would be unthinkable, because
after all: is he not the Good God, King and Pharaoh?

Only the gods could displace him; and he has weakened them so that they cannot. The people themselves never have done such a revolutionary thing, and never would.

So I have returned to the necropolis as to a special refuge, which indeed, for me, it is. Here I have spent my life, here before too long I also will lie for seventy days in natron, and go in my turn to the Valley of the Nobles to join my ancestors in the beautiful life of the afterworld.

I stare down into the tub wherein lies all that remains of a great King. His once heavy body is thin and shrunken now, the face that smiled so often and so pleasantly upon us is tight and leathery, drawn in death.

Tomorrow when the procession is over and he lies in the enormous tomb that awaits him beneath the Western Peak, the King Akhenaten, who rests this night in the Palace of Malkata, will stand before him and, using the sharp-pointed iron instrument that tradition prescribes, will perform the Ceremony-of-The-Opening-of-The-Mouth, so that his father may speak when restored to life hereafter.

I wonder what he would say at that moment, could he actually speak? Would he call down imprecations on Pharaoh for all his strange, unsettling ways? Or would he, as we hear he did in life, still love, still try to understand, still forgive?

The speculation is pointless, of course, but I think it might be the latter. Because everywhere I have gone in these recent weeks I have heard that the Good God whose mortal shell lies here before me did indeed love and grieve over his son, and tried to understand and help him.

I think perhaps that is what we, his people, must still try to do, though it is not easy, and our time of tolerance, I sense, is running out.

Tushratta of Mittani

To TIYE, Queen of Kemet, Tushratta, King of Mittani.

May it be well with thee, may it be well with thy son, may it be well with Tadukhipa, my daughter, thy young companion in widowhood scarce two years wed.

Thou knowest that I was in friendship with Nibmuaria, thy husband, and that Nibmuaria was in friendship with me. What I wrote to him and negotiated with him, and likewise what Nibmuaria wrote to me and negotiated with me, thou and Gilia and Mani, my messengers, ye know it. But thou knowest it better than all others. And none other knows it as well.

Now thou hast said to Gilia, "Say to thy lord: 'Nibmuaria was in friendship with thy father and sent him the military standards, which he kept. The embassies between them were never interrupted. But now, forget not thou thine old friendship with thy brother Nibmuaria and extend it to his son Naphuria. Send joyful embassies; let them not be omitted.' "

Lo, I will not forget the friendship with Nibmuaria! More, tenfold more, words of friendship will I exchange with Naphuria thy son and keep up right good friendship.

But the promise of Nibmuaria, the gift that thy husband ordered to be brought to me, thou hast not sent. I asked for golden statuettes. But now Naphuria thy son has had them made of wood, though gold is as dust in thy land.

Why does this happen just now? Should not Naphuria deliver that to me which his father gave me: And he wishes to increase our friendship tenfold!

Let thy messengers to Yuni my wife depart with Naphuria's ambassador, and Yuni's messenger shall come to thee. Lo, I send gifts for thee, boxes filled with perfume and many good things.

Let Naphuria send gold as Nibmuaria thy husband promised, so that our friendship may increase tenfold as he says. Tell thy son Naphuria to send gold! Send gold!

Tiye

MY WORLD ENDS, and this little man cries gold! Had I the troops, the weapons, the means to transport them instantly to his land, I should strike him dead where he stands, this sniveling piss-pot of a grasping king! How can he bother me with things so petty at such a time! I wish the gods might do the work for me, and strike him dead this instant, this very moment! Aiee, I wish him dead! . . .

But—no. Of course—no. I, Queen Tiye, the Great Wife, for many years Pharaoh in all but name of the Two Lands, must be more responsible than that. Anger is no good right now, it only blinds and confuses. Tushratta and all the rest must be kept at my side, and if possible bound closer. I shall indeed speak to "Naphuria," though if I know my son the cause is lost already.

Yet I cannot admit that the cause is lost already. I cannot admit that any cause, of the myriad I fear, is lost already. That would be to concede all things to Akhenaten. And that, for the sake of Kemet, our House and his own life, I cannot do.

My husband goes to lie beneath the Peak of the West, and I am left alone to save the Two Kingdoms if I can. To help me I have allies, but in the face of all the traditional power of Pharaoh we cannot be open about it: we must be close and we must be clever. My brother Aye—my nephew Horemheb—my daughter Sitamon—Amonhotep, Son of Hapu—and yes, my niece Nefertiti—stand with me. All the rest belong to Akhenaten now, some by virtue of his power and some by virtue of their own willing subservience. We must move subtly if we are to save the land from him, and him from himself.

Both of these I wish to do. I believe that—for the present, at least—the others agree. How much longer I can hold them to the gentler course I do not know. Aye is ever subtle but capable of reaching irrevocable decision in time. Horemheb has inherited the subtlety and the patience, but he too can eventually become adamant. Sitamon, as always, will do as he says. Amonhotep, Son of Hapu, is a philosopher, but his greatest love is Kemet and we have never tested the limits of his tolerance where its ultimate good is concerned. And my niece the Chief Wife? (No one, even now, gives her my title. I shall always be "the Great Wife," to the day I die. And rightly so: I have earned it.) Her motivations are mixed and many, but in the final reckoning I do not care, as long as she stands with me. And I think she will.

In these final two years of my husband's decline (he barely roused for his Third Jubilee—it was held at Thebes and was over in a day), my niece and I have become much closer than we have ever been. That perfect mask, always calm, always cool, always serene and never shattered in public, has shattered for me on one or two occasions of late. An anguished woman has looked out, turning to me for sympathy, not as niece to aunt or daughter-in-law to mother-in-law, but as woman to woman. I know her concerns and she knows mine. If the time is coming when we must all make a final choice, I believe we will be together—though she loves him still. As, may the gods have mercy on me, so do I.

She is spending increasing time, now, in her North Palace at Akhet-Aten (though she has not yet formally moved there), taking with her the two older girls. The three younger, too immature to be objects as yet of their father's desperate desire for sons, remain with the royal nursemaids in the King's House. Merytaten, married last year to Smenkhkara, is twelve, consumed by ambition for the throne: it is well her mother has her where she can keep her under constant watch, for if Merytaten can increase the alienation between her father and her mother and thereby assume her mother's power, she is certainly going to do so. Ankhesenpaaten, ten, is pregnant by her father but has secretly asked both her mother and me if we cannot find a midwife who can arrange a miscarriage —"accidental," as her father's wrath might be great and unpredictable if the child were a son, and he ever discovered our plotting. We hope to do so. Ankhesenpaaten's ambitions are as fierce as her sister's—their rivalry has increased to the point where they barely speak—but she has prudently decided to remain her mother's friend, at least for now.

At the North Palace there also reside my own sweet little Tutankhaten, now five years old, and my daughter Beketaten, now three. I have been too preoccupied with their father's slow dying (as prolonged and sad, in its way, as his mother Mutemwiya's) to give them the attention I should. Nefertiti volunteered to take them for me, and I was glad to accept. I have seen them when I could, but the care of their father and the crushing burdens of government, devolving increasingly upon my shoulders, have often kept me from them. Nefertiti loves them both and is a fine and gentle "substitute mother" to them, aided by her odd little sister Mut-nedj-met, always traipsing about with her two dwarfs in attendance. I am very grateful to my daughter-in-law for that.

I am also grateful to her for not having parted openly and finally with my son, even though she has been given much cause. As it became increasingly apparent that my husband was finally dying and that our son would soon be sole Pharaoh, it became increasingly important that the appearance of a united Family be preserved. The moment of Akhenaten's accession would certainly not be the moment for a separation from his wife. Nefertiti has an earnest care for the fitness of things, and it is to her great credit that she is concealing her unhappiness from the people and doing all she can to make the transition smooth and acceptable.

I pray constantly that my son will be equally responsible. But I have great fears. Tomorrow my husband will be entombed at noon when Ra stands high above. We will then all travel by state barge downriver to Akhet-Aten, where ten days from now my son's coronation durbar will be held. It is an occasion that cries out for more of his "wonders." Knowing him, I do not think he will be able to restrain himself. I shudder at the possibilities.

I weep over them, too, more than the world, or anyone save Nefertiti, will ever know. There was one time recently, the time when we finally opened our hearts completely to one another and spoke candidly of our mutual fears, when we wept together.

But it happened only once. And there is a difference.

She weeps for one of my sons.

I weep for two.

Ever since the night of the day when Akhenaten revealed his Hymn to the Aten, he and Smenkhkara have been more than brothers: of that their mother is certain. There has been about my elder son too much of an air of secret satisfaction, about my younger too much of a glow. He is seventeen, now, married to Merytaten, but I do not think he goes near her: his feeling for his brother enthralls him too much. This suits Merytaten, who cannot have further children anyway, and of course it suits Akhenaten, who has no rival. So the two gods consume one another, having moved far beyond the innocent idealism with which both, I believe, began. And Kemet gossips, sniggers and stands appalled; and my elder son continues headlong down the path he has set for himself, which can only lead to disaster for his marriage, for our House, for the Two Lands, for his brother—and for him.

He comes to me tonight, very late, at the hour when Pani tells us all will be ready in the embalming house. There, too, will come Nefertiti, Smenkhkara, Aye, Horemheb, Sitamon and Amonhotep, Son of Hapu. Together we senior members of the Family and our most faithful servant will pay our last private respects before we go before the people tomorrow morning in the long procession that will move through Thebes from Luxor to Karnak and thence across the river to the Western Bank and the final resting place.

Before we watch my husband's mummy being sealed away forever in his sarcophagi, I have arranged that we will have a time to talk. I have mentioned my purpose to my niece, to my brother, and to all save the two lovers. They will be surprised and no doubt furious with us. It does not matter. There are things that must be said. I, Queen Tiye, the Great Wife, for many years Pharaoh in all but name of the Two Lands, have decided it must be done. I am prepared for the consequences and so are the others. It will not be pleasant. But it must be done.

Sitamon

MY MOTHER has summoned us to her apartments tonight before we go to the embalming house. It promises to be an interesting conversation.

I wish it might touch, though I know it will not, on the future of the Queen-Princess Sitamon and her plans to marry her cousin the General Horemheb. These plans appeared to be quite feasible seventy days ago when my father died. Now they are not so clear. I wonder why this is?

I think perhaps it is my fault. I should not have approached Horemheb so soon. I should have waited several days. I should not have gone to him immediately upon leaving my father's deathbed, still in tears (increased by the ridiculous ritual wailing we women must always do on such occasions), to throw myself upon his compassion and, I thought, his love.

Now I am not so sure of either. Now I begin to see my lifelong companion in a new light. Is Horemheb capable of compassion? Is it possible for him to love? Or does he have purposes that preclude both?

I cannot believe it of one who has been so kind and tender with me for so many years, the father of my three lost children. It is simply that he is distracted by events, absorbed in affairs of state, deeply enwrapt in the problems of transition which now confront all Kemet. Great responsibilities fall to him and his father in this difficult time. Indeed, they fall to us all, who must somehow bring a control and balance to my brother's rule that he may wish and may violently resist.

Akhenaten is twenty-seven and embarked upon strange courses. His marriages with his daughters have caused uneasiness in the Two Lands, particularly since they have not produced the sons that have been their ostensible purpose. Unfairly, perhaps, but nonetheless inevitably, a harsher interpretation gains ground, so Horemheb tells me. Simple lust is easier for the people to understand, particularly when at heart they do not approve. I do not believe this. I think his purpose, while pathetic, has been genuine. But not everyone is so tolerant. The ugly gossip grows.

With my younger brother Smenkhkara he has become as besotted as he is with the Aten, and alas, almost as openly. Again, there may have been some more innocent original purpose there, some pathetic grasping, perhaps, after a physical perfection taken from him by the dreadful illness that changed so many things in him, and thus so many things in Kemet. But here, too, the gossip has it that the end result is the same. And here even I, who like all the Family have always loved and tried to protect him from himself, find that I am wavering. Much can be forgiven a Good God, Son of the Sun and supreme ruler of us all. But there are areas where, in time, forgiveness ends and sniggering speculation begins. And sadness comes, in the hearts of those who love him.

With Amon he exists in a half truce so tense that it affects everything in the Two Lands. Doddering old Maya

and his white-robed underlings had no choice but to bend
to my brother's will when he halved their wealth and their
priesthood with the Aten. But a deep and vengeful hatred
has resulted in their ranks. Those who were assigned to
the Aten have of course subverted him as much as they
dared, and the rest have kept the people constantly
stirred up with their agitations against what they whisper
to be an unnatural order of things. And so, of course, in
the context of our ancient history, it is. Aten is the new-
comer here, not Amon. Ancient tradition, sympathy, loyalty, power, aid Amon. To this day, Hymn to the Aten
and my brother's orders notwithstanding, the people as a
whole still belong to Amon.

And now, without challenge, and without my father's
easygoing influence to soften the fact, the people also belong to Akhenaten. And in the Palace we are constantly
informed, by those whose business it is to find out for us,
that they are terrified of what he may see fit to do to
them.

I myself do not think it will be so severe—and yet, I
must confess, this rises more from hope than knowledge.
I see him very rarely now, not being one who has to fawn
upon him in Akhet-Aten, but one who spends most of her
time here in familiar, comfortable old Malkata. Half-
deserted Thebes dozes beside the Nile and for the most
part I doze with her, since Horemheb, knowing my aver-
sion to the new city, visits me often here. He is very diligent on my brother's business, but he still manages to
come to Thebes every few days . . . which leaves me even
more puzzled by his evasiveness concerning our wedding
plans.

For these, I have already obtained Akhenaten's consent, which I do not necessarily have to have, but which
makes it easier—or would make it easier, were Horemheb
so inclined. There was a moment—apparently wry for
him, more than a little tense for me—when I suddenly
thought that my brother had other ideas. It turned out to
be but one more of those ironic games he plays increasingly with the Family. It is, I think, part of his grow-

ing isolation from us: he jests to hurt now, not, as he once did, as a form of self-defense.

"Sister," he said slowly when I asked my question, "are you very sure this is what you want to do?"

"But, yes, Majesty," I said, unable to keep the surprise from my voice. "You know how it has been with Horemheb and me for many years. What else would I desire, now that our father has returned to the Aten?"

"I am glad you do not say 'returned to Amon,' " he said dryly. "Many of my people still do."

This was the first time, I think, when I really realized, with a chilling inescapability, that they are indeed, now *his* people. I tried to turn aside what I feared to be his anger with them.

"But many do not, Son of the Sun. Many say, as you and I do, 'returned to the Aten.' "

"He wished to be buried at Thebes in the old faith," he said moodily, his eyes getting their faraway, brooding look. "After all these years, he still wished to be buried by Amon."

"Will you permit it?" I asked. He gave me a sharp glance, eyes abruptly direct and angry.

"I loved our father," he said flatly. "I shall do as he wished, even though it galls me to give Amon the satisfaction."

"I am glad," I ventured to say, "for I think a little satisfaction for Amon once in a while will not do harm."

"Any satisfaction, now, for Amon will do harm," he said. "But it cannot be helped. After— . . ." His voice trailed away and the enigmatic eyes grew clouded and distant again. He repeated softly: "After— . . . we shall see . . . But," he resumed abruptly before I could question, which I would have done—we all have grown more challenging lately in our attempts to divert him from his course—"you have a different problem, Sister. Are you sure what you propose would be best for our House? Might there not be another plan that would better serve the Dynasty and the Two Lands?"

"What is that?" I demanded, unable to keep the alarm from my voice, for we have always, even in these recent months, been very close, and I thought I could perceive his meaning; which I did, right enough.

"I need sons," he said, almost dreamily, eyes narrowed and watching me carefully. "You are a 'widow' now, you have the blood of Ra. You are my sister. Why should not—"

"Brother," I said sharply, and I am afraid my voice grew a little shrill with tension, but I did not flinch before him: *"We will not."*

"Oh?" he said sharply. "Do you defy Pharaoh?"

"I live in truth," I said with an angry sarcasm that might have cost me my head but I no longer feared, I became the daughter of my mother and her iron was in my heart, "and I do not care if you kill me for it. Yes, I defy Pharoah! There are enough—" I almost finished, *"affronts to nature going on in this land!"* but very fortunately restrained myself and repeated only, "I defy Pharaoh! Will Pharaoh take vengeance on his defenseless sister for this?"

He stared at me from the eyes which can so quickly grow so blank and cold and for several moments said nothing. I returned him stare for stare, for, as I say, there are times when I am the daughter of Queen Tiye, and I no longer cared. Then abruptly his face relaxed. He smiled—but not, as he used to do, in a kindly way. Instead it was mocking, almost harsh, contemptuous.

"Sister, I would not steal you from your love. Marry Horemheb, if he will have you, with my blessing."

"He will have me!" I said with an assurance strengthened by the anger of relief. "You may be very sure, he will have me!"

"I hope so," he said, turning away, dismissing me with a discourtesy that also was unlike him—or at least, unlike him as he used to be. "I should hate to see such eternal devotion gone for nothing."

"Do not mock, Brother," I said, not bothering with "Majesty," or "Son of the Sun," or other courtesies, for I was too angry. "The day may come when you will need the support of those who love you. Do not drive us away with mockery."

He turned back abruptly and his eyes filled with a

naked unhappiness that still could touch my heart, even
then.

"I have always had it," he said, very low, "and what
good has it done me?"

"Much good, Brother," I said, suddenly filled with a
desperate pity and a desperate need to reassure him.
"Surely you realize that!"

"Yes," he said with a heavy sigh. "I do realize, even
though— . . ." But he did not finish, and this time when
he turned away, I knew I really was dismissed and he
would not speak longer with me.

So I left him, frustrated and saddened as we all are
these days when we try to talk to Akhenaten, and went
to find Horemheb. And there received, as I have re-
counted, excuses and evasions and half promises and uncertainties. At first this crushed me: then my anger grew.
Now I do not know whether I love him or hate him. But
he is much too strong in the land for me to take any
vengeance, even were I so inclined. I must be patient
and approach him more softly. He is, as I say, distracted
by events. Tomorrow my father will be buried. All will be
changed. Perhaps when we meet at the Great Wife's
apartments tonight he will have a friendlier sign for me.

Certainly we will all need to stand together then, for I
do not think my mother intends anything gentle with my
brothers.

Nefertiti

MY MOTHER-IN-LAW SPOKE to me briefly in the corridors
of Malkata this morning. Guards and soldiers stood about,
ladies in waiting hovered, priests of Amon, restored to a
brief moment of importance in Thebes as they supervise

the burial of my uncle, lingered as close as they dared and strained their eyes and ears.

She placed a hand on my arm, leaned close and whispered:

"The Family will gather in my chambers one hour before the viewing. We must talk while his presence still lingers. It may be the last chance to control the King."

"Majesty," I said, and I am afraid my eyes showed the sadness I felt, "I do not think there is any longer any chance to control the King."

"There must be!" she said, her voice fierce but still held tightly to a whisper. "The madness must stop!"

"He does not consider it madness," I said sadly, "and so it will not stop. However, I shall be there, of course, as you wish."

"Will you help me argue with him?" she demanded, and I thought suddenly how drawn and worn that once smooth, complacent face has become in these recent years. It is not easy being the mother of sons evidently —anyway, such as these.

"Majesty," I said, "do you think I have not argued?"

"Tonight we will all join you. Surely he must listen to us all!"

"I will join *you*," I said. "I will not take the lead again, for I have done it already too often."

We parted and returned to our respective apartments while the watchers stirred and buzzed. I have no faith in what the Great Wife proposes. But she is determined to make one last assault upon the citadel. I expect those who live and love within will ignore it, as they have all else.

Yet perhaps she may be right. Perhaps if we all unite in our protests, he and Smenkhkara will listen. Perhaps if we all reason quietly but firmly—

But what nonsense am I talking to myself! It is long past that. All, all is gone, beyond sense and beyond caring.

"Fair of Face, Mistress of Happiness, Endowed with Favors, Great of Love—" so he called me once, and so commanded that my statues be inscribed. Now it is rare

that we even speak, and then it is always to quarrel—
always to quarrel. It has been two weeks since we have
been able to discuss matters calmly, and then it only
ended, as it always does of late, in bitterness and uncertainty and more confused unhappiness for me. My
control never breaks any more, even with my father: I
am past that point. But my heart is eaten out as if by
lions. And the lions are merciless. Pride alone sustains
me: pride, and a love which will not ever die, no matter how he slaughters it.

"I have called you here," he said abruptly on that
last occasion, when I dutifully appeared in the throne
room in response to the always shining, always laughing
messenger he sent, "so that we might discuss certain matters that concern us."

"Must our cousin remain?" I inquired coldly, while
Smenkhkara looked at me with that look I have come to
know so well, no longer loving and respectful as it used
to be, but appraising, now, a little mocking, somewhat
pitying, even smug.

"I should like him to," Akhenaten said.

"I should prefer that he leave," I replied, still in the
same cold, level voice; and decided to add, for his
anger no longer concerns me overly much, "else I shall
go myself, and that would defeat your purpose, would it
not, O Son of the Sun?"

"What is my purpose?" he inquired with a sudden sharpness.

I shrugged.

"To hurt me. What other purpose does my lord have,
these days?"

At this his face suddenly contorted with pain, his eyes
actually filled with tears. I perceived that *I* had hurt
him, which gave me an agonized and unhappy pleasure:
I had not intended it, but since it had occurred, I both
enjoyed it and despised myself for the enjoyment.

"Go, then," he said quietly to Smenkhkara.

"But, Son of the Sun—" the golden one protested.

"Go!" he ordered harshly; and then added more gen-

tly, "I shall see you later, I would talk now with my wife."

"Yes, Son of the Sun," Smenkhkara said, suddenly sounding more humble than I think he feels of late. Yet he turned to me with a sudden fleeting resurgence of the old feeling, bowed low, kissed my hand, started to say, "Cousin I—" and then stopped, his face also strained for a second with pain and bafflement. For what was there to say?

Our eyes held for a long moment, which I broke by saying matter-of-factly:

"Go, Cousin, and be happy in your fashion. I shall no doubt see you about the Palace from time to time. Be of good cheer."

"Cousin—" he tried again, and then abandoned the attempt. The defensive expression returned. "You, too, Majesty," he said as he swung on his heel and left the room, not bothering even to say respectful farewell to Pharaoh, so confident and so insolent has he become in the certainty of his love.

This was here in Malkata, where we came some fifty days after my uncle returned to the Aten. It had been obvious for some weeks that his death could not be long delayed, but both of us hate Thebes—in that we are still united—and Thebes, I am afraid, because this is still the seat of what remains of Amon's power, hates us. So we put off returning here as long as we decently could. We sent dutiful messages to the Great Wife, of course, and my father Aye, Amonhotep, Son of Hapu, and other court officials soon came up the river to take residence until the ceremonies are over. Horemheb, though busy on my husband's affairs in Akhet-Aten, has also taken occasion to visit every few days. My aunt has had good company during the period of mummification, and I understand that she has shown herself to the people twice a day, dutifully weeping as ritual demands.

We have done the same at the Window of Appearances at Akhet-Aten, and have curtailed somewhat our drives about the city—on which, in any event, Akhenaten has in recent months requested his brother, far more often than his wife and children, to accompany him. He has ordered memorial services to be held without ceasing in all the temples of the Aten, and for seventy days and nights relays of priests have performed them constantly the length of Kemet. He issued no orders to Amon—he has simply ignored Amon in the last two years, after making sure that Horemheb carried out his orders for the transfer of half of Amon's goods and priests to Aten. But Maya, growing ever more ancient and senile, but supported by an active group headed by an apparently brilliant young acolyte from Memphis named Hat-sur-et, has made sure that Amon has also been much noticed. Similar unceasing services have taken place in his temples, and of course my uncle's decision to return to the old faith for his burial has brought a brief revival of Amon's pomp and circumstance here in Thebes. But it is only a flickering light which will soon be damped down again after the funeral. Amon whispers and conspires all the time, but it is all he can do. His priests do not dare attack my husband openly, particularly now that he has inherited the full power of the Double Crown.

It was this full power, of course, that I challenged in our last unhappy talk. But it was not I who desired the challenge. It grew out of his summons to me, made more insulting by his choice of messenger. I could not escape challenge, were I to retain my self-respect and my place beside him as the Chief Wife. I am not Nefer-Neferu-Aten Nefertiti, daughter of Aye and Queen of the Two Lands, for nothing. I may be desperately unhappy, but I have my pride and self-respect—and, as I said, and may the Aten pity and help me for it, love him in spite of all.

After Smenkhkara left there was silence for a while. Akhenaten did not look at me, simply staring off without expression at the Nile, not so busy as it was in the days when we grew up here, but beginning to fill up with the anchored boats and feluccas of the thousands who are gathering for the Good God's interment.

When he finally spoke it was abruptly, still not looking at me, with a hurried and embarrassed harshness.

"I think it might be best if you were to move fully to the North Palace when we return to Akhet-Aten."

For what seemed a very long time I was unable to answer anything at all. I felt that my heart had stopped, my breath was gone. The world whirled about and I felt for an awful second that I might faint away and so lose whatever advantage I might still retain.

But I am of tougher stuff than that. Presently the world settled down, my heart resumed, my breath returned. An icy and unshakable calm took possession of my *ba* and *ka,* my soul and being. I spoke in a level and unimpressed voice.

"Why is that, husband? I am happy where I am."

"But you spend much time in the North Palace," he said, turning about now so that he faced me, his expression somber but his eyes, as always, alert and watchful.

"Only because you and your"—I hesitated deliberately and changed the word he knew I was about to say— "your brother are too often in the Great Palace where I prefer to live. I go only to gain a little peace for myself, and to keep an eye on the children."

"How are the children?" he inquired, not choosing for the moment to pick up the challenge of my reference to Smenkhkara.

"All in good health," I said. "Ankhesenpaaten carries your child in the second month, of course, and you know how she is. Merytaten does not seem to mind being a wife without a husband—"

He made a protesting movement of his hand, but I ignored it.

"—Tut is well and Beketaten flourishes. The rest of the girls are well, as you know when you occasionally permit us to accompany you to worship the Aten. We all survive, though we do not see you so often now. I am not surprised you had to inquire after your own family, for it has indeed been weeks since you have deigned to have us with you. And how," I added with a deliberate cruelty in my voice, "is Smenkhkara? He appears to be well and flourishing also."

"Smenkhkara, as you have seen, is well," he said, more mildly than I expected. "Why do you not sit down?"

I realized suddenly that I had indeed been standing all this time; but then, he had not asked me to sit, and I had been too absorbed in my anger to notice, and insist upon it.

"Thank you," I said, still coldly, "but I think I prefer to remain standing."

"As you like," he said, still mildly. He gave me a sudden sharp glance, then looked away again to the river. "Well then, what of the North Palace?"

"What of it, husband?" I inquired crisply.

"I should like you to go," he said, and again for a second the world threatened to spin away. But I reached for it and held it firmly in place.

"And if I prefer not to go?"

He sighed deeply, a sudden sad sound that might even now have overwhelmed me with sympathy, as it has so many, many times, for poor Akhenaten, child of unhappiness all his life. But things had gone beyond that now. I remained rigidly silent and politely attentive.

"Then I may have to order you," he said at last.

"I will not go," I said, remembering a conversation many years ago in this same room between himself and his father, and taking inspiration and strength therefrom. "I live in truth, and I would rather you kill me than that I go."

"I *want* you to go," he said, his voice rising slightly but his face remaining its usual impassive mask.

"Then you must kill me," I said quietly, and although his eyes widened suddenly with anger I did not flinch, any more than he had on that long-ago day when his father threatened him.

For several moments, while we stared at one another in open hostility—for I was past caring now, I was not afraid to let my feelings show, rage consumed me—he said nothing. Then he took me off balance with an entirely unexpected remark.

"You have not given me sons. Therefore you will go."

"It is not that!" I exclaimed, and I am afraid my voice rose. "It is not that! It is not sons you want in the Great Palace, it is—"

"Be careful!" he cried with a sudden terrible harshness that fortunately returned me to my senses. *"Be careful!"*

With a great effort I managed to control myself. I said only four words. I said them calmly, coldly, and with an iron steadiness as great as any he has ever been capable of displaying, and then I turned and left, to the sound of his angry shouts behind me.

"I will not go."

"You will! *You will!"*

But I did not reply, I did not look back. His shouts died in the distance as I hurried away past startled guards. And since that day we have not seen one another or spoken.

But tonight we will speak, in the Great Wife's room. Tonight we will all speak. And then, fine husband and glittering cousin, I shall tell you what I think before them all.

I pray that love will not betray me, and that I may say what should be said as calmly yet as firmly as Nefer-Neferu-Aten Nefertiti, Queen of the Two Lands, should.

Smenkhkara

MY MOTHER WANTS US to meet with her before we go to watch my father being placed in his sarcophagi. Something in her tone warns me that she wishes to say something critical of someone. There are only two possibilities, because all else still moves as the Great Wife desires.

I wonder if we are afraid?

I know that I am not, for Akhenaten is not; and I am Akhenaten as he is Smenkhkara, and together we will defy our mother, if defiance is what she wants.

I am quite prepared for it and so is he. We have often discussed the possibility. We are not concerned. How can we be? He is now the only King, and all things everywhere, on earth and in the sky, bow down to him. Our mother will do the same or he will have her head.

She will not dare attack us too harshly.

She knows it would not be safe. . . .

Do I feel regret for this? I do not know, entirely. Sometimes I think I still do. Strange moods of melancholy and weeping sometimes still overtake me, when I hide from him because they hurt him and he does not understand them or know how to handle them. But they seem to come seldom now, increasingly far apart as the years pass and we move deeper and with more accustomed ease into the union that gives him happiness and me . . . what?

Again, I do not know, entirely. At first it was strange and almost repellent to me, but pity and love swiftly overcame that. The first time, on the ledge along the Northern tombs, after the excitement and the celebration and the long hypnotic chanting of the Hymn, it was inevitable, overwhelming, marvelous. Next day came reaction, revulsion, contrition, dismay. These lasted until he called me again to his apartments that night. I moved in various ways down fantastic pathways, entered the vortex, drowned, revived, emerged—never, I think, knew such happiness—and never looked back again. . . .

Except, as I say, that now and again I am swept by melancholy, which really has no place between us, and so I do not believe it can be caused by what we have. It must be that I still feel responsibility toward my mother and my cousin Nefertiti, for they are the ones I know have been hurt the most by what, to us, has become the most comforting and most natural of things.

So perhaps at heart I am not so defiant of the Great Wife as I like to think I am—as I hope I can appear to be in her rooms two hours from now. I do not like to hurt people deliberately, it goes against my nature, which has always been sunny and open and loving of the world. The God Smenkhkara has always been a good boy. Not once in all my seventeen years, I think, have I ever been deliberately cruel to anyone. I do not mean to be now, but I feel they may interpret it so. This hurts *me* and so, I suppose, I defend myself with flippancy and arrogance, and that hurts *them*.

It is a tangle. But it is not one that they can persuade me out of with either endearments or harshness, for it has become my life. And I now know, and would have, no other.

The Good God needs me—more, he makes me feel, than he has ever needed anyone, even Nefertiti. How can I abandon him, who is not only my King and Pharaoh but my brother, my being, my heart, my world? How can I betray such love as he gives me, when it obviously brings him more happiness than he has ever known in all his sad and lonely life? And besides: he tells me that the Aten considers it right and holy. And what the Aten considers right and holy, we who believe in his son Akhenaten also consider right and holy . . . except, of course, the Great Wife and my cousin. And just possibly my niece and wife, Merytaten, though I do not really think she cares very much.

We have been married now two years, and we have never spent the night together sexually, though many in Kemet no doubt think so, seeing us pass behind properly closed doors into properly shuttered rooms. Invariably this ends in a game of senet, at which my wife is quite good, actually: she moves the pieces with great good fortune, her black ones conquer my white ones with steady regularity on the checkered board. Between throws we sometimes talk, quite philosophically, about our situation. She explained on the very first night that she had been injured bearing her father's child, and that she had no desire to risk having another.

"In any event," she said, with something of the dry manner she has inherited from him, "this does not

greatly distress you, Smenkhkara. You have other interests. Not so?"

"I would be willing to father your child, nonetheless,"
I said evenly, "if it were a son and heir to the Double
Crown."

"But suppose I only had daughters," she said lightly.
"My mother is cursed with daughters, my father is cursed
with daughters—perhaps our House is fated to go
down in a welter of women."

"Not for a while yet," I said, I am afraid rather
sharply. "I stand ready to succeed Akhenaten. Tut will
succeed me. Among us we have the possibility of many
sons. After all"—I could not resist a small dig, since
Merytaten is always so superior and smug—"you may not
be the only wife I take. The next may not be handi-
capped as you are. She may be able to bear me sons."

"You say you would father sons, Uncle," she said,
knowing the term annoys me since we are only five years
apart, "but I doubt you would go near any woman."

"We will not know, will we," I inquired with something
of her own dryness, "since you say you do not wish
me to touch you?"

"Even so," she said calmly, studying the board. "Even
so— . . . There! I have you on that move!"

"Perhaps," I conceded, examining her play in the hopes
it might yield some way out of the fiasco; but, as usual,
it did not. I scooped the pieces off the board and we began rearranging them. "What do you think your mother
will do, now that your father has got Meketaten with
child?"

"I do not give a fig for sniveling Meketaten, that sickly
girl!" she said with a sniff. (This was before that poor
unfortunate died.) "Or"—her eyes narrowed—"for my
mother, either, she has always been so beautiful and
perfect. I am tired of her. Tired of her! I can hardly
wait until I can take her place."

"How can you do that?" I asked; rather blankly, I
am afraid, for this was the first glimpse I had been given
of Merytaten's ambition—which is, I have learned, quite
boundless.

"She will leave him in time," she said calmly, "because of us girls, and because of you. And then I will take her place, and all the world will bow down and honor me."

"As his wife?" I asked, startled. "How could that be? You are *my* wife!"

"*You* are *his* wife," she said with an acrid humor. "*I* am his wife's wife. As such, if my mother leaves, I will receive her privileges, her palaces and her power. He will need a woman about for spectacle, whatever he may do elsewhere. As the oldest daughter, it will be I. Then if you all die or are killed," she added, still with that acrid, oddly embittered humor of hers, "I may emerge as the second Hatshepsut, who knows? It would not be such a bad fate for a Queen of the Eighteenth Dynasty."

"You will be my Queen when I take the throne," I observed mildly. "Will that not satisfy you enough?"

"If you live," she said indifferently, lifting her hand and, in her accursed fashion, making a move that swept three of my men off the board. "That remains to be seen, dear Uncle."

I did not attempt to answer this, because it was beneath my dignity. Merytaten is an unlovable girl, and even if I were not—even if I did not love Akhenaten— I doubt if I should touch her anyway. She is too sharp and prickly for me—and unkind about it, too. "*You* are *his* wife," indeed! "*I* am his wife's wife."

There is no need to be so crude.

She does not know—no one knows—the wonderful world in which we live. It is a happy world, a world filled with love, with harmony, and with constant prayers and hymns to the Aten, who simultaneously creates, knows, understands and forgives all that exists on earth and in the heavens. We do other things together, of course, but above all else, I can truly say, we devote our days to the Aten in perfect love and understanding of one another, and of him.

But only slowly—still so slowly—the doctrine spreads. We talk constantly about this. My brother keeps himself in constant turmoil over it, he considers and rejects many things he might do to speed the process. Always he meets opposition, from within the Family, from the lingering priests of Amon (who appear to have gained a new lease on life under young, ambitious Hat-sur-et), and above all, as he acknowledges, the people.

"They still do not see," he told me sadly a month ago. "They still do not understand. They go through the rituals I decree, they worship me and the Aten because I tell them they must, but in their hearts they do not really understand that it is all for their good. They do not see that the Aten means freedom for them, from old tradition and superstitious awe and the crushing weight of overweening priests. They do not realize that they must believe in the Aten, for the Aten will set them free. . . . Sometimes," he added bitterly, his voice low, "I think they do not *want* to be free. I think they are content to remain just where they are, the slaves of the centuries. . . ."

"Now you are the sole King, Brother," I said soothingly. "Now you can truly order them to do as you desire and no one in all the world can say you nay."

"I could," he agreed gloomily, his eyes acquiring their faraway look, "but it would still be gesture only. They would give me lip service because I am Pharaoh, but they still would not believe in their hearts. And until they do that . . ." His voice trailed away; and then suddenly he spoke with a renewed vigor, his eyes became animated, his voice excited. "But perhaps they will, now that I am sole Pharaoh! Perhaps now they will see that the Aten has preserved me all these years, and has let me live long and finally brought me total power, for some purpose. They will see what the purpose is: that I may preach to them the true doctrine, and thus lead them in my Father Aten's footsteps so that all the world may be happy and free in the light of his glorious beneficence. They must see this," he concluded, very quietly. "They *must*."

Then we came up the river to Thebes, where we have been these past twenty days awaiting the final mummification of our father, and since then we have not had much chance to talk, as we have been engaged daily in the rituals for the dead that have required us to go among the people at regular intervals to display our mourning. We have made sure that we could be together often, but he has said nothing further about what is in his mind, and I have not pressed. We all have too many things to attend to, until our father goes beneath the ground. Then will come new excitements—the coronation durbar at Akhet-Aten when all our allies and dependencies (we still have some, though there has been a considerable falling away, I understand, in the past few years) come to pay tribute—and perhaps even changes in the Family.

But in our love for one another there will be no change, for I am Akhenaten and he is Smenkhkara; and no matter what anyone says, we shall continue to live in our own world, the world of gods no mortals dare challenge—blessed and comforted by our Father Aten, who creates, knows, understands and forgives, all things.

I hope our mother and the Family realize this, else they may truly risk the wrath of Pharaoh. And that would be a sad thing, for them.

Horemheb

My cousins dream away the days like two enamored fools, in some fantasy world where they apparently feel no one notices or cares.

But the real world notices and cares.

Kemet and all notice and care.

Word comes that even in far Naharin, even in wretched Kush, they notice and care.

Everywhere gossip, sniggers and outrage erode the throne.

It is not enough that Nefer-Kheperu-Ra has done all
the rest that he has done: now he must do this.

It is madness.

He actually believes, I think, that divinity makes him
immune to the restraints of ordinary men. True, it makes
him immune to the punishments reserved for ordinary
men. But there are punishments reserved for kings, even
kings who are gods, and he is not immune to them.

It is madness.

I think the time grows closer when I must keep my
pledge to our grandmother. But all must be ready, all
must be done in due time. Mystical protections surround
Pharaoh, even such a One as this, in the minds of the
people: it takes much to make them ready for his removal.

So awesome is his place in the Two Lands that even
I, who feel increasingly that the gods may have placed
me on earth to help save Kemet, flinch inwardly when I
think the word "removal." But I do think it, and the day
will come when I say it. I feel this in my *ba* and *ka*,
the very soul and essence of my being.

Akhenaten and I have an appointment with the gods.
Everything he does hurries me to the day. I pray constantly that I may never have to do what the gods
seem to hint they want me to do: but the time grows
closer.

Perhaps the Great Wife can yet save her son, yet turn
him back, yet bring them both to their senses before it
is too late. We shall see tonight. But I am not hopeful.
Nor is my cousin Nefertiti, nor my father Aye, nor dull,
faithful Ramesses, nor Amonhotep, Son of Hapu, nor all
the rest, great and small, who grieve for Kemet under
such a One.

I do not want to do what we may all have to do. I
shudder away from it as I know the others do.

But every day the time grows closer.

Now he has supreme power. Those who would remove
him from it must be very careful, very clever, very discreet—and very strong.

All of these I am and have ever been. And daily, as
he grows more profligate, irresponsible and uncaring,

I grow calmer, more certain, more careful and more determined.

We shall see which of us has the final say.

I have done his bidding for twelve years, first in little things, then in great. He gave me high honors, raised me to his right hand, used me to kill our uncle Aanen, used me to enforce his decree stripping Amon of half his wealth and priesthood, gave me great administrative powers over the Two Lands, has depended upon me many times for the running of the kingdom and such fragments of empire as his uncaring ways still allow us. But aside from those instances where I have managed to act first and report to him later, he has been an erratic mentor, a dragging weight upon my arm, a wavering and uncertain force that now encourages, now holds back. He would rather hymn the Aten and lie with Smenkhkara than be consistent in his kingship. I have administered affairs rather in spite of, than because of, his support. It has not been firm, and since, in the past two years of his father's final dying, he has become virtually sole ruler already, the wavering has been apparent in all we have done.

Kemet has continued to drift in spite of my best efforts, those of my father Aye, of the Great Wife, of Nefertiti, and of those closest to me such as Ramesses and my younger brother Nakht-Min, whom I have brought nearer to my side as the difficult months have dragged on.

Why, you might ask, does it take so long for us to move against him? Why, if we are so convinced of his unfitness, have we permitted him to remain in power until finally the inevitable day has come when he has indeed become the most high, the most holy and, in the still superstitious eye of the people, the most unassailable?

The reason, if you understand us, is simple: because for twelve years he has been Co-Regent, Son of the Sun, Living Horus, Great Bull, Good God, King and Pharaoh of the Two Lands, divinity on earth, and, with his father, co-ruler of us all. That is why. You do not topple such a

One overnight. You do not even do it in five years or perhaps even in ten, so high does he ride above us in the ancient and ongoing pageant of our history.

It takes much time and many careful plans to bring down such a One. It takes many, many errors on his part, accumulating until even the people, who go in fear and ancient awe of him, see at last what he is and determine *in their own hearts* that they must be rid of him. They are close to it now, I believe. But even then the people themselves would never rise to do it, for never have they risen against a Pharaoh, and never will they, so deep in ancient tradition and the belief of many centuries lies their worship of the wearer of the Double Crown.

It takes a small group within the Palace, close to and part of the Court, working patiently and most delicately over many years, aided by Pharaoh's errors and capable of most subtly and carefully making use of them, to finally work the people's will. And they must be very, very sure indeed that they correctly interpret the people's will, else not only Pharaoh but the people they hope to serve will turn upon them and they will be utterly destroyed.

They must also have a suitable successor who carries the blood of Ra. And what have we?

My cousin Smenkhkara is a not very bright but charming boy, swept away by the adoration of his older brother, not knowing really, at seventeen, where his true duty lies. He thinks, for various reasons, that it lies with the King—and certainly he is fortified by every tradition in that. He does what his heart and body tells him to, but in his mind he has the absolute conviction that he does it *because it is his duty to Pharaoh.* My father has told me how Smenkhkara once turned white and cried, *"I will never betray Nefer-Kheperu-Ra!"* at the lightest, most innocent suggestion that he might inadvertently do so. Now love, which I am convinced is quite genuine, has fortified that early reaction. Piled on top of it lie all the overpowering weight and tradition of centuries. Akhenaten's younger brother never will betray him, of that I am certain. (Nor would his youngest, Tutankhaten, . . . if we wait too long.) Therefore Smenkhkara would be of no use to our purposes—those "ends" with which Amonhotep, Son of Hapu, chided me so long ago in Thebes, and which have finally become clear enough to me so that they dominate my every waking hour.

We cannot use the younger brother as the instrument of his deposal.

And the youngest brother, whom one cannot overlook in the royal equation? Tut is five, still the sunny, happy child he has always been—indeed as all the children of my uncle and the Great Wife have been, except for Akhenaten. He knows nothing yet of these worrisome, unhappy concerns of his elders. We cannot use the youngest brother either . . . if we wait too long.

But here I go beyond the bounds of safety, even in my own mind. Such speculation is treason, which is why I confide it only to my father Aye, who knows and understands all things—fully as well, I am convinced, as Akhenaten says *his* "father," the Aten, knows and understands all things.

Yet even now, even after all these years, even after the judgment of time has begun to turn finally against him—at least in the minds of those of us who will have to do the things that may be necessary if he must be deposed—it is a strange thing:

I still pity Akhenaten.

I find that his "big brother" also still loves him, though the love is stretching very thin. Some tenuous tie of childhood affection—some deep, unerasable compassion for all that he has been through—old shared happiness, the uncaring innocence of the newly minted world—still holds me to my strange cousin. One does not so lightly shake the bonds of youth, and growing up, and the happy trusting years.

I find that I still hope desperately, hope against hope, that he will halt even now and turn back from the fatal course that appears to be leading him inevitably to disaster and death. I, even I, still want him to live and to be, still, a great King and Pharaoh.

Perhaps my aunt and all of us can do it when we meet in her apartments an hour from now. My intelligence and an unshakable sense of reality assure me this will not be so. But something Akhenaten can still draw upon, if he but will, tells "big brother" that he still must hope, fatuous and futile though it seems at this late date.

Aye

CAREFULLY THEY DRESS ME, clothing me in my garments of state that I may go to see my brother-in-law suitably laid at rest within his sarcophagi. Tomorrow comes the great procession, the final going beneath the ground in the Valley of the Kings. Tonight is rehearsal for Amonhotep III (life, health, prosperity!).

It is grim reality for the rest of us.

Very shortly now they will send guards and torches to show us to my sister's apartments. From all over the Palace of Malkata we will come—my son Horemheb—my daughter Nefertiti—my nephew Smenkhkara—my niece Sitamon—Amonhotep, Son of Hapu—and the Living Horus, Son of the Sun, sole King and Pharaoh of the Two Lands.

What mood will he be in? What mood will they be in? Do I understand, in fact, what my own mood is, or are so many things swirling through this close-cropped, gray-haired skull that even I, the patient, the logical, the farseeing, the all-knowing, even the Chief Steward, Private Secretary, and King's Councilor Aye, cannot make head nor tail of them?

That, however, is exactly what we all must do. This is

the last opportunity we will have to persuade Akhenaten. He has been, in a sense, lying dormant since his
father's death. He has kept his accustomed rounds in
Akhet-Aten, performed the traditional rites of mourning
there and, more recently, here in Thebes. For once he
has done what was expected of him, what the gods and
the Ancients and the people desire. But tomorrow this
all ends, and he returns again to the Aten and to all the
things that so grievously disturb his mother, the Family,
and all who love the Two Lands.

My sister thinks we can even now hold him back from
final folly. She hopes with a mother's desperate love. I
hope desperately, too, and I think like all of us, with
love. But the hope grows very dim and the love runs almost out.

Already I have tried, just before I left Akhet-Aten
to return here to take up residence until the mummification and funeral are over. It was not a satisfactory inter-
view.

I had first to separate him from Smenkhkara, who
now is almost always at his side, regardless of occasion.
It was in the throne room of the Great Palace. I do not
know where Nefertiti was. Two faces, the one long, slit-
eyed, impassive, unrevealing, the other open, fresh-faced,
sunny, innocent (in appearance, for innocence long since
died in that young heart,) confronted me.

"Begging your pardon, Son of the Sun," I said directly,
for I have ceased to dissemble with these two, "but I
would speak with you alone."

"Smenkhkara knows all my secrets."

"I am sure. But he does not know all of mine. Nor," I
added—tart, I am afraid, to the point of danger—"do I
intend him to. Smenkhkara: if you please."

This was taking great liberties, but I have become
both old and, in some areas, uncaring—or impatient is
perhaps the better word.

"I should like him to stay," Akhenaten said with a
quiet I might have interpreted as ominous had I been so
moved.

"Then I must go," I said, starting to back out.

"Uncle!" he said sharply, half rising. "You will remain. Smenkhkara will remain. Tell us what is on your mind."

"Very well," I said with equal sharpness as he resumed his seat and Smenkhkara stared at me with as much insolence as he dared. "I think it best that you go to Thebes separately, that you stay there separately, and that when you return here you live separately." I could see the eyes were slitlike no longer but open with anger. "You are the only King now. The sole burden of the Two Lands rests upon your shoulders. Much is expected of Pharaoh. You cannot betray it without dangerous consequences."

"Dangerous for whom?" he asked in an almost mocking tone. "Not for Pharaoh, surely. Pharaoh is above danger."

"Pharaoh is not above the people," I said quietly, "though fate has placed him in a position to be their god and their protector."

"The people," he said slowly, and it was the first time I had ever heard him use such a tone about them, and it made my blood run cold, "are nothing to me. *Nothing.*"

"Majesty," I said earnestly, abandoning all pretense of admonition, pleading humbly with him now, noting that even Smenkhkara was shaken by the savage tone in which he spoke, "such is no sentiment for the Good God to have. You are their god, their protector, their father. You are all things to them—"

"I am nothing to them!" he said in the same harsh voice. *"Nothing!* And they are nothing to me. *Nothing!* And if that is all you have to say, Uncle, you may go!"

"I beg of you, Nefer-Kheperu-Ra," I said, my own voice trembling with emotion and dismay, "give heed to my words, give heed to them! You must not talk so of the people—"

"Nothing!" he cried out again in a furious voice. *"Nothing, nothing, nothing!"*

So then I did leave, bowing low and backing out, for I feared to enrage him further. But when I looked up just before I stepped outside, I saw that he had clasped one of Smenkhkara's hands in his, that with the other hand Smenkhkara was gently soothing Akhenaten's forehead, and that the Good God's eyes were filled with tears and his body was wracked with sudden sobs, strangled and suppressed with a terrible, anguished determination.

And so of course tears came into my eyes, too, as I thought: how sad he is, how sad! How lost, forlorn and sad, great King and Pharaoh, Son of the Sun and Living Horus! My dear nephew, whom I have known from a baby! My *two* dear nephews, whom I have known from babies!

But it is not, of course, with tears and sentiment that one governs. And so my tears dried fast and into my heart there soon crept back the bleak desolation of what we face.

And I wept no more for lost Akhenaten, but only prayed, as I find I very often do these days, that he may not truly be lost to us forever.

Now I go to my sister's chambers. Great apprehension —yet great determination, too—fills my being.

I arrive first, am announced and go in. My sister and I exchange quick kisses and look at one another for a moment with unhappy eyes. Swiftly the others follow. Smenkhkara looks tense but unafraid; the rest of us, with trembling hearts, await his brother's arrival.

Down the hall comes the rustling of guards snapping to attention.

Silence falls.

Slowly and unmistakably, the shuffling sounds of a misshapen body being dragged along by the sheer will power of its owner reach our ears.

The door opens and he faces us, in full regalia. Dressed in our garments of state, we stare back.

It is a glittering scene.

Across it fall the ever hastening shadows of the cruel, unhappy years.

Amonhotep, Son of Hapu

THERE IS A LONG SILENCE while he stares at us, the narrow eyes moving impassively from face to face. I am standing a little behind the Family, as befits my high yet secondary station. It seems to me that his eyes dwell upon mine an extra moment. I suddenly see a happy, healthy little boy, my beloved pupil, head flung back, mouth open in generous, excited laughter, running headlong down the palm-lined pathways of Malkata. Perhaps Pharaoh sees him too, because for a split second his eyes seem to reveal, only to me, a deeply hidden anguish. He shifts position a little. As if on signal we all do the same. Quietly he holds out the crook and flail to Smenkhkara and says softly, "Brother, take these for me." The golden youth accepts them proudly and stacks them carefully against the wall. The King turns to the Great Wife, bows gravely and says:

"Mother, you wished to speak with me. Do you wish us all to speak together?"

Queen Tiye's voice trembles a little but she holds it firm, bows in return and holds out her arms.

"I do," she says, "but first may your mother have a kiss?"

"Majesty," he says, his voice suddenly hoarse with emotion; steps forward, leans down and kisses her gravely on the cheek. She hugs him with a sudden fierce hunger which, abruptly, he returns with a naked desperation that is profoundly touching. It lasts but a moment, he releases her and steps back. Their faces become formal, almost stern, again.

"Can we not all sit?" he asks then. "Are there enough chairs?"

There obviously are. The Great Wife has had them arranged in a semicircle, her small, ornate throne at its center. Facing the rest is a single chair, the small private throne occupied on so many informal occasions by Amonhotep III (life, health, prosperity!) in happier times.

Silently we all take our places flanking the Queen, Aye on her right hand, Nefertiti on her left, the rest of us, including Smenkhkara, dispersed along the half circle.

This does not please Akhenaten.

"Brother," he says, and it is as though no one else were in the room, so directly and nakedly does he speak only to him, "I should appreciate it if you would bring your chair and sit beside me."

"Yes, Son of the Sun," Smenkhkara says quickly, and quickly lifts his chair and places it alongside his brother's. Another silence falls as they stare at us calmly and without expression, Smenkhkara a little defiantly, a little on edge, but taking his cue from his brother and attempting to keep his face impassive though he does not quite look any of us in the eye. Akhenaten does, and it is obvious that he has come prepared, alerted by instinct and intelligence, for whatever may impend.

"Now," he says quietly, "you wish us to speak, Mother. Pray begin."

"My son," she says, and now her voice is as steady and impersonal as his, "tomorrow your father goes beneath the ground and you become at last beyond all challenge sole and only King and Pharaoh of the Two Lands. It has seemed suitable to me that the Family discuss with you and"—she hesitates the tiniest second, then goes firmly on—"with your brother, how you intend to conduct yourselves in the days to come. For on the answer depends the future of Kemet and of this House."

Again there is silence while we all stare at them intently, not knowing what explosion—or evasion—this may produce. But we might have known that from Akhenaten, living as always, as he fancies, "in truth," there would come an answer direct and unequivocal.

"I shall continue to conduct myself," he says quietly,

"as what I am, the Living Horus and Son of the Sun. I shall continue to conduct myself as my Father Aten directs me, to the greater glory and strength of Kemet and our House."

"And I shall continue to conduct myself," Smenkhkara says, patterning himself upon his adored older brother, "as the Good God directs, and I too shall work always for the greater good and glory of Kemet and of our House."

The Great Wife seems momentarily taken aback by the contrast between noble purpose and actual practice. There is no doubt they are both absolutely sincere, which opens vistas of rationalization that are quite appalling when one stops to think about them. To her aid comes her brother, thinner, slower, graying, seeming to gain in dignity, stature and statesmanship the older he grows.

"Is it your belief, Son of the Sun," he asks quietly, "that the course you and Smenkhkara have pursued these two years past *really* is good for Kemet and *really* reflects credit on this House?"

"What is that course, Uncle?" the King inquires, and his tone is dangerous now, and promising storms to come. But Aye is not Aye for nothing, and he proceeds, quite calmly and matter-of-factly, to spell it out.

"It is said—" he begins, but Akhenaten interrupts.

"Do not tell me what is 'said'!" he orders sharply. "Tell me what *you* think, Uncle. You have never been one to evade."

"No more will I now," Aye agrees, his voice still calm and only the whitened knuckles on his chair arms revealing the tension he feels. "I think"—and he pauses to look gravely from one end of our little half circle to the other—"and I think we all think—that you and Smenkhkara are not wise to continue this association of yours. We think it not wise in any sense, but most seriously do we think that it is not wise to continue it, and conduct it, in the public view. You cause much talk and unrest in the Two Lands, thereby. You weaken the crown, you weaken this House, you weaken"—his voice rises and so does his warning hand as Pharaoh shifts angrily on his father's throne—"the kingdom you have inherited and whose supreme head you now are. It is not necessary. It is not wise. It will destroy you both if you do not swiftly bring it to an end." His voice softens and almost breaks with sadness as he concludes. "I hope you will believe me, Nefer-Kheperu-Ra, when I say that I utter these harsh things with great reluctance and only out of eternal love for you and your brother, whom I have had about my house and playing at my knee since you both were very tiny babies, and very dear to me."

Again there is silence, which lengthens as Akhenaten studies him, while Smenkhkara, a little shamefaced but trying to show a defiant bravado, stares at the floor and plays absently with the tassel on his ceremonial belt.

"Uncle," Pharaoh says at last, and his voice is low and filled with emotion also, "I appreciate the spirit in which you speak, and the love you bear for Smenkhkara and me. I do not doubt that love. I do not doubt it"—and suddenly he looks full at Nefertiti who pales but does not change her set, unyielding expression—"from anyone. But"—and the hope that had begun to grow in all our hearts sinks away—"you do not understand about—about—everything."

"What are we to understand?" Nefertiti demands suddenly, and her voice is clear and angry. "What every sniggering gossip in Kemet understands? Or is there something higher and more mystical we are supposed to believe in?"

"*We* believe in it," Akhenaten answers very quietly. "I am sorry if you do not, for you are my dear wife, mother to my daughters—"

"Not the only mother to your daughters!" Nefertiti snaps, and Queen Tiye, alarmed, places a gently restraining hand upon her arm. But she shakes it off and plunges on. "Not the only mother to your daughters, and not the only companion of your bed! You have Kia and any girl in the kingdom you wish to command. Why is it necessary to humiliate me by turning to your own—"

"Am I not being humiliated right now?" Pharaoh shouts with an answering anger, his voice going into the croak that overtakes it when great emotion comes. *"This* is not humiliating, to be brought before the Family as before the Forty-Two Judges of the Dead, and be called to answer for my life? And this to the Living Horus, this to the King! How dare you? *How dare you all?"*

It is the greatest display of sheer anger any of us has ever seen Akhenaten show, and we are struck dumb by it and by a sudden terror of what he may do. This is increased when Smenkhkara, still playing with his tassel, still not looking up, says in a soft and deliberately mocking voice:

"You must remember he is the only Pharaoh now. You must not forget this . . . for it is the case."

Abruptly Horemheb leans forward in his chair and inquires in clear, cold, level tones:

"Shall I kill them all, O Son of the Sun? Would that solve your problem? Say the word: I am yours to command."

His eyes lock with those of Akhenaten, and for a long time, it seems, they stare at one another. But, unlike that other occasion long ago, the contest does not end with automatic victory of Pharaoh. Horemheb's eyes do not drop, he does not concede the enormity of his challenge. Akhenaten's also remain steady, it is obvious he will not yield either. Presently he speaks, more quietly. A certain contempt in his voice, for he is indeed the only Pharaoh now.

"Do not be a fool, Cousin," he says in an offhand manner that makes Horemheb flush, though now he prudently holds his tongue. "I am not a killing Pharaoh . . . unless," he adds thoughtfully, his eyes never leaving Horemheb's, "I should find myself too much provoked. . . ." His eyes swing at last away, back to the Great Wife, sitting upright and rigid on her throne. "Mother! Is this all you wished to say to me tonight?"

"We wished to plead with you, my son," she answers quietly, "for a return to sanity as you assume the full power of the Double Crown. I will concede"—and it is

obvious the concession costs her greatly, but she says it
firmly and seems to mean it—"that there may exist a
perfectly deep and genuine love between you and your
brother—even such—such a love as—as you seem to
have. But certainly you must know that it can be no more
deep and genuine than the love we all feel for you both.
Does not that give us *some* right to speak to you, *some*
right to be heard, *some* right to hope our words may
be taken as sincerely and helpfully as they are meant? I
should not like to think my sons had grown so alien to us
in their love for one another that we can no longer reason
with them, for the good of Kemet and this House . . .
and," she concludes quietly, "for *their* good, which to me,
who am still their mother, means more than all."

"We know that," Smenkhkara blurts out in an anguished
tone before Akhenaten can answer, and now he seems
not the defiant beloved but only a forlorn youth suddenly
crushed by the heavy weight of emotions in the room.
"Mother, we *know* that!"

"Then why—" the Great Wife protests, but this time it
is Pharaoh who answers.

"Because our Father Aten—"

"Forget your 'Father Aten,'" she snaps, "and remember
your responsibilities in this world!"

But now, it is clear, emotion has proved too much. She
has gone too far. She has said the wrong thing. She has
attacked the sacred name. A mother's anguish has made
her challenge the god who, in her son's mind, is unchallengeable.

To his brother he holds out a hand that visibly trembles
and indicates his wish to rise. Smenkhkara stands up, strong
and lithe, perfect features drawn and tense in the flickering
light of the wall torches, muscles rippling smoothly as he
virtually hoists the awkward body beside him to its feet.

Silence, tense, quivering, absolute, enfolds us all.

Pharaoh stares at us one by one, his narrowed eyes
moving carefully along our now frightened half circle. He
can indeed order us all killed if he so desires. Perhaps
he will . . . but of course he does not: he is still Akhenaten. But he is an Akhenaten transported out of himself

once more by such an anger as we have never seen in him.

Finally his mouth, which has repeatedly tried to form words and been stopped each time by too much feeling, steadies. His voice comes heavy and slow, at moments almost unintelligible, so great is the weight of anger it carries.

"Smenkhkara and I," he manages to grate out while we stare at him with wide, affrighted eyes, "will live in truth as we please. I shall rule this land as my Father Aten directs me. I will never—never—discuss these things with you again: *never.* Do not *ever* mention them to me again, or I will—I will—"

But then emotion overwhelms him, his voice gives out. His eyes are filled with tears of rage, his face works terribly. We are left to imagine the awful struggle between vengeance and reason that must be swirling in his heart. I am sure the thought strikes the others as it does me: *how utterly alone he is—how utterly alone we must make him feel!* And with it, finally, come the other thoughts that from now on will, I am sure, be inseparably linked with that first thought in all our minds:

But how much of it comes from him! How much of it is his own fault! Akhenaten is many things—and some are great—but how tragically, fatally flawed he is. . . .

At last Queen Tiye rises calmly to her feet. She speaks in a clear and steady voice, deliberately emptied of all emotion, deliberately returning us to the principal duty of this sad night.

"It is time to go to the House of Vitality. It is time to see the Good God placed within his sarcophagi."

She looks at me. I step quickly to the door, clap hands for servants. They come at once with torches.

The Great Wife steps forward to her sons, the one so glittering and misshapen in his regalia, the other so sleek and beautiful as he stares at her wide-eyed, looking no longer insolent now, but terribly young and uncertain in the glancing light. With great dignity she places herself between them, a hand on the arm of each.

Head held high, she takes a step. They follow.

And so our procession forms, and passes in the dancing shadows along the brightly painted mud-brick corridors of Malkata, which once knew so many happy times but now hold little but sorrow and uncertainty for the once all-powerful Eighteenth Dynasty and the haunted House of Thebes.

Kia

IT IS CHILL. The wind whips off the Nile, unseasonably cool for the final day above the ground of my father-in-law, that good, amiable and lazy man, Amonhotep III (life, health, prosperity!). He would have complained of it, asking Queen Tiye to have the servants bring him extra robes. She would have complied, with the usual half-patient, half-exasperated air with which she always assisted him to do the things he should have done himself. Now it no longer matters: he is cold beyond the coldness of the Nile, chill beyond the chillness of the winds. But soon he will be warm, for awaiting him are the myriad servants and multiple pleasures of the afterworld.

I have been in Kemet, now, for twelve years, and I have come in time to understand their religion and their funerary beliefs. The former is unique but the latter are not so far from ours in my native Mesopotamia. We, too, conceive of a happy land where all is honey, incense and abundant pleasure. May the Good God find it when he gets there, for he has not known overmuch happiness on earth in recent years.

The procession is forming on the east bank just south of Thebes. We shall move slowly north through the city to the great temple of Luxor which the Good God built, and which now is almost completed. There we will pause

for rites at the altar of Amon before proceeding down the
avenue of ram-headed sphinxes to Amon's most ancient
temple at Karnak, where we will pause for further
worship. From there we will be ferried back across the
river to the west bank, where we will pass between the
dead One's two colossal statues and pause to do worship
at his mortuary temple. We will be accompanied most of
the way by the weeping and wailing of hundreds of professional mourners, by the outcries of the people, who
genuinely loved him and are greatly worried about what
comes next, by the somber bellowing of great bronze
trumpets, the heavy beating of drums, the slow, rhythmic
shaking of a thousand sistrums in the hands of the
priestesses of Amon. Finally, alone at last save for the
highest priests of Amon, we will come to the Valley of
the Kings, and his final resting place.

In a few moments I shall be ferried across the river
in company with Nefertiti to take our places in the
baldachin that will come second after that of the Great
Wife and Naphuria and immediately after the one of Sitamon, Smenkhkara, Tut and Beketaten. Earlier this morning there was a sudden stirring in the Family, a short,
sharp argument, apparently almost a continuation of the
one Horemheb told me they had last night. I understand
that Naphuria's first idea was that his mother and all the
children should ride together in one conveyance giving
her and Sitamon the leading seats and ranking the other
children two by two behind them. This would of course
have placed himself and Smenkhkara side by side just behind the Great Wife and Sitamon.

Naphuria and Smenkhkara side by side, "living in truth"
on public display, would be exactly what Naphuria wants,
of course—and exactly what the Family does not want.
Thus the argument, settled by Aye, who suggested that
logically the Great Wife, as principal widow (Tadukhipa
is unfortunately too dim-witted to attend), and Pharaoh
should ride side by side in the first baldachin. Then the
four children in the second; then Nefertiti and myself as
principal wives of Pharaoh; then Akhenaten's five surviving
daughters; then Aye, his wife Tey and Horemheb; and

lastly, Aye's two other children, the General Nakht-Min, who is expected soon to be named Vizier by Naphuria, and his sister the Lady Mutnedjmet, an odd little character who, at twenty-six, seems already centuries older. (She always goes about accompanied by two dwarfs, Ipy and Senna, for some reason known only to her, and is becoming one of her half sister Nefertiti's closest confidants as the coolness grows between Nefertiti and Naphuria.)

Mutnedjmet may yet come to wield considerable power in Kemet—as long as Nefertiti does. How long this will be remains problematical. There are rumors the break may fast become unhealable, which could mean drastic changes in the Family, very soon.

In any event, now Nefertiti comes; and I can see, as she walks toward me with head held high and lovely face perfectly composed, that she is determined to play her role this day as though nothing threatened it. I, too, have become quite close to the Chief Wife in these recent months, though I have no such cause as she to be affronted by Smenkhkara, for my relations with Naphuria were always formal and have long since dwindled to the barest of civilities. Nefertiti has gone so far as to offer me apartments with her in the North Palace if I should ever desire them, and I have thanked her warmly and said I might well accept her kind thought if the need arises.

"If Smenkhkara moves in, I shall move out," I said matter-of-factly only last week. Her eyes flared for a second as she replied flatly, "I shall never move out unless he forces me to, and that I do not think he will dare to do."

But we both knew the bravado of that, though we did not spell it out to one another: we did not have to.

Now she steps forward, looking lovely and serene in her gorgeous sheath of gold cloth, her gleaming jewels and her favorite blue conical crown. Gravely she gives me the kiss of welcome on both cheeks.

"Be of good cheer," I counsel in a whisper as I return the gesture to the wild applause of the massed thousands waiting for us on the east bank.

"I am trying," she replies as we both turn and begin

to walk with stately tread out onto the landing stage and so into the royal barge that will take us across the Nile.

Her faithful Anser-Wossett has concealed with the cleverest of makeup all traces of strain about her mouth and eyes. She looks absolutely stunning, and I flatter myself that I too, though somewhat taller and darker and not by any stretch so beautiful, look sufficiently glamorous and royal on this solemn day.

How can Naphuria be such a fool?

But he is: and as we land on the other side and are carried high in litters to our baldachin, above the shouted love and greetings of the adoring masses, it becomes apparent that he is an even bigger one than I imagine.

But this time, he pays.

Already we see that the Great Wife is seated in the first baldachin, and that behind her Sitamon and the two youngest children are also seated and waiting. In back of Nefertiti and myself Aye and his family are ranged in the order he suggested: even today, Nefertiti and I note with a brief smile to one another, Mutnedjmet has insisted on her dwarfs. The three of them are chattering together like little magpies as they wait, while shrewd and handsome Nakht-Min, beside them, looks both amused and bored.

Naphuria and Smenkhkara are nowhere to be seen.

But then from the landing stage across at Malkata there come the military shouts and noises that indicate the approach of Pharaoh. It swiftly becomes apparent that, partially, at least, he has decided to have his way—as it soon becomes apparent that for it he will pay an unprecedented, an unheard-of, a terrible and a terrifying price.

While the thousands fall silent, and the Great Wife turns with a piercing glance that sweeps the two of us and her brother Aye and Horemheb—and says many things before she turns back and stares stiffly straight ahead—the two gleaming figures, the misshapen one leaning heavily on the arm of its straight and arrogantly challenging companion, move slowly forward to the royal barge, which has returned for them.

They walk slowly up the plank, Smenkhkara steadying his brother as they come; move to the center of the barge and stand facing the eastern bank. The boatswain shouts his orders, the heavy paddling begins, they start across the river . . . and there is no sound.

They reach the middle of the river, the brisk wind ruffling their gorgeous raiment, the oars splashing—splashing—splashing . . . and there is no sound.

The prow of the barge touches land, the waiting crewmen leap to secure it . . . *and there is sound.*

Faint and far away, starting who knows where but growing instantaneously louder until it seems to fill the world, there comes an awful, unbelievable, unimaginable greeting.

Nefer-Kheperu-Ra Akhenaten, Living Horus, Son of the Sun, Great Bull, Lord of the Two Lands, He Who Has Lived Long, Living in Truth, tenth King and Pharaoh of the Eighteenth Dynasty to rule over the land of Kemet, is being hissed.

For a long, fantastic, utterly unreal moment, the ugly sibilance continues. Then, as if by some instinctive signal that moves the body of the crowd as it would move the body of a great animal, it ceases. And once again an absolute silence falls.

The two figures have stopped thunderstruck. Their frozen immobility lasts almost beyond bearing. Then abruptly the misshapen one shakes itself, as if coming awake from some inconceivable nightmare, and starts to shuffle forward. Beside him his brother, no longer rigid and arrogant but now oddly crumpled and unsure, moves to his side. Only swift-flowing Hapi, lapping gently at his banks, breaks the silence as they are lifted carefully into litters and borne to the head of the procession, Naphuria to his mother's baldachin, Smenkhkara to that of his brother and sisters.

They are hoisted up. Queen Tiye looks straight ahead, acknowledges in no way the presence of her eldest son. In Smenkhkara's baldachin, Sitamon and the children are too shaken to speak.

In a clear, strong voice that carries forcefully through
the deathly silence, the Great Wife cries:

"Bear up the body of the Good God and let the procession begin!"

Instantly in front of her baldachin, where her husband's
mummy inside its four great sarcophagi has rested on a
wooden stand, relays of soldiers who will spell one another
every two hundred paces, so great is the weight they must
carry, leap forward to lift it high. The wooden stand is
swept away. The great trumpets begin their somber mooing.
The sistrums of Amon begin to rattle in the chilly air.
Drums beat. And the procession commences.

We wind slowly through the narrow streets of Thebes,
many of them fallen into disuse and neglect as the once
proud capital has dreamed away the years far from the
hustle and bustle of flourishing Akhet-Aten. All along
the way there is heard the weeping and wailing that
we expected. Combined with it comes an undercurrent of
discreet and loving applause for the Great Wife as she
passes. And with it also comes, furtive, fugitive, fleeting but ever present, its sources never quite perceived, its
perpetrators never quite discovered—though obviously
there are many, many of them—a steady escort for poor,
misguided Naphuria.

The hiss keeps him company, all the way.

We stop at the temple of Amon at Luxor. Doddering
Maya and fanatic, ambitious young Hat-sur-et make us
formally welcome. We pause to do suitable worship,
which Pharaoh and the Great Wife perform together, dis-
mounting from the baldachin, placing offerings on the altar, chanting (her voice clear, impervious and steady,
his emotion-choked croak barely audible) the words we
know he hates, to Amon . . . and even there, distant
on the wind, the gently ominous susurrus comes.

They remount, we move on along the avenue of sphinxes
to the great temple of Karnak and the ceremony is repeated at Amon's most ancient altar . . . and the soft,
insistent sibilance comes.

They remount, we return to the Nile, we cross, we
pass between the Colossi, we worship at the mortuary

temple, we move on through the barren rocky ravines beneath the Peak of the West, take the turning pointed out for us by the white-robed priests of Amon standing rigidly at attention, come to the entrance of the Good God's tomb, dismount and follow the enormous sarcophagi beneath the ground, down 533 steps to the final resting place . . . and still, even in the Valley of the Kings, seeming to emanate eerily even from the harsh bare rocks themselves, comes the secret, sinister, hostile sound.

In the burial chamber, finally, we hear it no more. The soldiers remove, with great sweat and grunting, the enormously heavy lids of the four interlocking sarcophagi and withdraw. Shrunken, shriveled, leathery but recognizable, the features of Amonhotep III (life, health prosperity!), still vaguely amiable even in death, stare up at us. There remain now only the Family, Maya and Hatsuret.

Maya, leaning shakily on a wooden staff, defers to Hatsuret, who intones the sacred words and hands to Naphuria the hooked iron instrument used for the Ceremony-of-The-Opening-of-The-Mouth. With a glance of pure hatred for the priests that none of us has ever seen upon his face before, Pharaoh accepts it and steps forward.

"In the name of the Aten—" he cries loudly, and as instinctively as ill-fated Aanen once did, Hatsuret blurts out, "Amon!" But this, fortunately for him, is not the time nor place for vengeance.

"In the name of the *Aten*," Pharaoh repeats angrily, voice slurred and almost unintelligible with emotion, "in the name of the *Aten*, I call upon you, Father, O great Lord Neb-Ma'at-Ra Amonhotep—*speak!*"

And taking the iron bar, he forces it with hasty revulsion between the mummified teeth (while we all shrink back instinctively in both dread and awe of the ancient ritual), and pries the mouth open. It does not open easily —there is a horrible cracking sound as the jaw hinges give way and several broken teeth rattle down the parchment throat—but it is done, as the tradition of millennia says it has to be.

He flings the instrument away with a shudder of horror and disgust—utters the ritual chant:

"You live again, you live again forever, here you are young again once more forever!"

—and so begins for his father the long process of coming to life again in the eternal afterworld.

We return above the ground, the soldiers go back down to replace and permanently seal the sarcophagi. After we leave they will seal the entrance to the tomb and cover it over with earth. Then the priests will kill them, so that no one will ever know where the Good God lies resting, and he will be safe forever from the grave robbers of Qurna who have desecrated so many tombs.

We stand at the entrance to the tomb, blinking in the sharp, cold sunlight that has now replaced the earlier scudding gray clouds, and suddenly the rigid control of the Great Wife collapses at last and she begins to cry, a hopeless, helpless, sobbing wail in which all of us women soon join, moved as we are by the loss of this Good God and the terrible tensions of the day. But swiftly we learn that her grief goes deeper than that.

As we stand closely clustered about her, Akhenaten leaves Smenkhkara and shuffles toward us. Awkwardly he stretches out his thin arms to his mother and attempts to comfort what he believes to be her lament. But he misreads it, as he does so much else nowadays, poor Naphuria.

"Mother," he says brokenly. "Mother, do not grieve for him. He rests well beneath the ground, he will be happy in the afterworld. Do not grieve too much for him."

"I do not grieve for *him!*" she cries, and her voice, too, is choked and heavy with emotion, an anguish that is almost unbearable. "I grieve for you, my poor son! *I grieve for you!*"

Abruptly we all fall silent, staring with fright at Pharaoh's face. As we do, we hear distantly on the wind, resumed, the sibilant, sinister sound. It can only come from priests of Amon hidden in the rocks, for no one else is here.

His face is transformed by an absolute bleakness—an

utter irrevocable loss—a desolation beyond desolation—a rage beyond rage.

"Re-form the procession!" he shouts, his voice in tattered chaos but its import lucid enough in the cold glittering air. "Re-form the procession! We return to visit the God Amon in his temple at Karnak!"

There is no questioning, no hesitation. We are all too stunned, he is too obviously consumed by fury. We are mesmerized. Hastily we reform the procession.

"Trumpets!" he shouts, and there is a long, shuddering blast that echoes and re-echoes, echoes and re-echoes, echoes and re-echoes yet again off the jumble of harsh forsaken crags that lie beneath the Peak of the West.

Slowly at first, then ever more quickly as his towering fury and impatience transmit themselves to our bearers, we begin to move back to the Nile.

We return to visit the god Amon, in his temple at Karnak.

And now, it is obvious, it is going to be someone else's turn to pay.

Akhenaten (Life, health, prosperity!)

I STAND BEFORE the ancient wooden doors of the temple of Amon at Karnak, and at my back the huge throng that has flocked to greet my completely unexpected and unprecedented return from the Valley of the Kings stands utterly astounded, utterly fearful, utterly still.

What, I can sense them thinking, is Horse Face up to now? What awful things will "the Criminal," "the Heretic," do this time? What dreadful wonders does the husband of his daughters, the lover of his brother, the hater of the gods, have in store for us today?

They did not expect wonders—but they have asked for wonders. And wonders such as they could never imagine are what they are going to get.

Because *I have had enough.*

I stand before this most ancient temple of Amon at Karnak and finally, irrevocably, permanently and forever, *I have had enough.*

It has not been sufficient for them to jeer and make fun of me every day of the past twelve years.

It has not been sufficient for them to despise and reject you, Father Aten, who are perfect in all ways and who have made your son Akhenaten perfect in your image.

It has not been sufficient for them to steal my people from me with sly tricks and devious words and constant opposition to all the things that you, Father Aten, have directed me to do.

It has not been sufficient for them to slander and besmirch my attempts to beget sons for Kemet who could serve the Two Kingdoms and strengthen our House—as you, Father Aten, have directed me to do.

It has not been sufficient for them to defile and degrade my union with Smenkhkara—which you, Father Aten, told us was right and good in your eyes, and which you directed me to do because it would make me happy, and thus make me better able to serve you and your kingdom.

It has not been sufficient for them to scorn you in all your beneficence and glory, and equally to scorn your son Akhenaten who has attempted always to live only in truth as you have directed him.

It has not been sufficient for Amon—it has not been sufficient for the Chief Wife—it has not been sufficient for the Family—it has not been sufficient for the people —to join in doing all these things.

Now they all must degrade and defile me yet further. Now on this day of my coming at last to total power, they must unite in a final hissing and scorning and dishonoring, so that I am made to feel totally unloved— shamed—hated—deserted—despised . . . and my mother is made to cry for me. . . .

I could not stand to see my mother cry for me. . . .

Thus have they done with their evil hatreds, their evil jealousies, their evil disrespect and irreverence for you, O Father Aten, and for your son Akhenaten, who lives in truth for you, as you direct him, in all things.

Always have I tried to be gentle and patient with them: always have I tried to be good. Always have I tried to act only for the greater glory of you, O Aten, and for the good of the Two Lands and of my House. Always have I tried to serve the people and save them from the dead weight of centuries, and to hurt no one save a few overweening priests—and even them, saving only my stupid uncle Aanen, I have never killed a one of them.

And thus have they all rewarded me. All, *all!* . . . because even my mother, though she cries for me, has become my enemy now. . . .

So be it, proud Amon and all you other hurtful gods!

So be it, ungrateful people!

So be it, jealous wife and unloving Family!

Pharaoh lies beneath the ground. . . .

Pharaoh stands before the temple of Amon. . . .

Farewell, Pharaoh beneath the ground!

Long live, Pharaoh who has lived long!

Now the world will move as you and *I* command, Father Aten.

Not one deserves my mercy—not one can say me nay.

Now it is *I* who will at last have things as *I* want them, forever and ever, for millions and millions of years.

This have you promised me, Father Aten, and in the sure knowledge of your love and support through all eternity, I now am ready to act.

At my back the Family, the troops, the priests, the people and all things on earth, in heaven and in the water are deathly still. Not a voice is raised in all the great throng that fills Karnak and crowds both banks of the river, utterly astounded, utterly terrified by my totally unexpected, totally unprecedented return from the necropolis.

Somewhere a dog starts to bark and is strangled in mid-yelps as if its master were afraid the sound might instantly bring down my vengeance.

And perhaps he is right, poor hissing fool. Because I could do it, if I would.

For the last time I look at the temple of Amon as it has existed for more than a thousand years, and then my voice rings out strong and clear. Amazingly, in the midst of my all-consuming rage, it fails me not, thanks to you, Father Aten. I hear it carrying distinctly to the farthest reaches of the crowd and even, I think, across the river, so greatly do you strengthen me in what I now must do.

"General Horemheb!" I cry. "Attend me!"

At first it is as though he does not understand. He looks at me almost stupidly and answers, "What? What—?"

"Attend me!" I cry clearly and strongly again, and evidently it finally penetrates, because, though he still looks baffled, he comes hurriedly forward to my side.

"Yes, Son of the Sun," he says quickly. "Did you want me?"

"I called you!" I exclaim angrily, and then I adopt a quieter tone, for all must be dignity now as I do what you, Father Aten, tell me I at last must do.

"General Horemheb," I say slowly, and now he seems to have come out of his fog, he watches me with an almost hypnotized intensity, "bring me a company of soldiers with battering rams. At once! At once!"

"Soldiers with—" he echoes, beginning to pretend again that he does not understand—as if that could deter me! I seize his arms so sharply and fiercely that even Smenkh-kara, standing beside me, shrinks back a little at my vehemence.

"Battering rams," I repeat, trying hard to maintain my dignity as you advise, Father Aten, but finding it hard to do in the face of his deliberate incomprehension. *"Battering rams."*

Now he focuses on me sharply, now he stares at me as he did in my mother's room last night, as he did so long ago in Akhet-Aten when I had him kill our uncle Aanen. Once again our eyes lock, but this time I know it will be the last time, for I will never again accept from him or anyone such insolence, never again for even a single moment, ever.

Furiously I glare at him: with troubled, wide-staring eyes, he looks back.

No sound comes from anywhere as we pursue our contest to the end.

At last, just as I am about to explode in terrible anger —but you keep me from it, bless you, Father Aten, I remain icy calm—his eyes finally drop, and as if to put a good face on it and pretend that he is still in command, he whirls sharply about and cries:

"Two detachments of soldiers with battering rams! To my side at once!"

And abruptly, like little puppets—*my* little puppets, now, forever and ever—two detachments of twenty soldiers each hastily separate from the rest, run to the barracks that guards the temple and return as fast as they can with the battering rams.

"Now!" I cry, and nowhere in the world anywhere is there any sound but my voice, so still and terrified is everyone. "Batter down the doors of evil Amon!"

There is a great gasp from the crowd and the soldiers pause uncertainly, terrified of the god and terrified of me, not knowing which to be more afraid of. They will learn.

"Batter them down!" I shout, my voice now choked with emotion but sounding clearly enough, I gather, for another irrepressible gasp of disbelief comes from the throng and seems to fill the world for a second before I turn around and wither it instantly to silence with my fierce, implacable gaze. (In that moment I look into the eyes of my mother, Nefertiti, my uncle Aye, my children, but I know not them and they know not me. We no longer exist for one another. They are only a pathetic little huddle of people, as terrified and indistinguishable to me as all the rest.)

"General Horemheb—" I shout, permitting my voice to rise ominously as you, Father Aten, now instruct me to do.

And Horemheb yields to me completely at last.

"You have heard the King!" he shouts. "Batter down the doors of the temple of Amon!"

The soldiers draw back, shift the heavy iron-tipped timbers for a firmer grip, tense themselves to hurtle forward—when suddenly from the side hasten two white-robed figures. One moves shakily with a wooden stick, the other assists at his elbow. It is Maya and Hatsuret, of course, and before the soldiers can move, they have spread-eagled themselves across the two great doors, hands linked.

A groan goes up from the crowd, but for you and me, Father Aten, it is the opportunity of a lifetime. I shall get them both, the ancient fool and the younger one who now sparks Amon.

"Strike!" I shout, the word bursting clearly from my emotion-choked throat, so great is my determination. "Strike NOW!"

And as if mesmerized and terrified beyond thinking, as indeed they are, the two companies of soldiers hurtle forward.

There is a great crunching and grinding, a terrible agonized shriek from the crowd—and the ancient doors collapse in a welter of splinters and dust and blood.

Then all is quiet again as I cry loudly so that all may hear:

"Brother! Cousin! Accompany me and witness the end that will come to all who defy Pharaoh!"

We advance slowly through the dazed soldiers, who have let the battering rams drop to the ground now that they have done their work and are staring in blank-faced horror at what remains. It is Smenkhkara who is the first to see what has happened.

"But where," he asks stupidly, "is Hatsuret?"

He is right. Only one flesh-stripped pair of legs, one set of shattered arms, one bloody ripped white robe, one crushed and spilling skull, can be seen among the splintered shards. Hatsuret, that clever one, has left old Maya to die and has slipped aside just in time. He is lost now among the sheltering crowds. But he will not escape my vengeance.

"Be it known," I shout, swinging about as fast as I can to face the terrified mass, "that from this day forward there rests upon the head of the traitorous priest Hatsuret a bounty of a thousand in gold. Whosoever brings him to me dead or alive will receive still further rewards and the assurance of a peaceful and happy life for himself and his family, so long as they all shall live!"

I wait for a moment, but of course there is no immediate response: Amon still has too many friends. Hatsuret is well hidden and sure to remain so, for a while. But I will have him yet.

"General Horemheb," I command, still facing the crowd, "take with you sufficient soldiers to accomplish the task and go you in to the altar and bring to me the Sacred Barque and the statue of the god Amon-Ra!"

Once again the crowd utters a deep, shuddering gasp, once again our eyes lock in furious combat, until suddenly once again his rigid gaze collapses and I see that he is finally broken completely to my will. For this I shall worship you forever, Father Aten, for now I know that I need worry no longer—as secretly I often have—about the loyalty of my cousin Horemheb. He is my liege, and yours, forever.

In a dazed voice he gives the order. In a dazed fashion he and the soldiers stumble into the dark recesses of the temple—always dark, always secret, always hidden and evil, that is you, O Amon! But no longer, my vicious friend! No longer!

A heavy, waiting silence settles over all. Once again my glance crosses those of my family, but it is as if we are dead to one another: we do not really see one another at all.

Presently behind me comes the sound of stumbling footsteps. In front rises a strange, agonized murmur. These are the mourners for Amon, who do not know what I intend, but fear, quite accurately, that it will be something awful for their evil god. They are deathly afraid of me now—at last Horse Face has their respect, Father Aten, and we know how amusing and satisfying that is, do we not?—and they dare do nothing more than offer this ago-nized animal groan.

Horemheb and the soldiers come around slowly and stand at attention before me. Uplifted above the soldiers' heads is the Sacred Barque, that frail, ancient little wooden boat, perhaps no more than five feet in length, which is so infinitely old that its sides are papyrus-thin with the polishings of centuries.

In it, attached at the base so that he is rigid and upright, his face stern, unfriendly and fierce as it has been through-out our history, there stands, perhaps three feet tall, your antagonist and mine, O Aten, the solid gold figure of the god Amon-Ra.

"General Horemheb," I command, "remove the statue of Amon-Ra!"

Again the animal groan from the crowd. The soldiers lower the barque to waist level so that Horemheb can reach the god. He removes him carefully, staggering a little under his weight, and hands him to three of the sturdiest soldiers. They make a sling for him with their hands, trembling in awe and fear but doing my bidding, as they must.

Again the animal groan from the crowd. But they have not seen all my wonders yet, have they, Father Aten?

"Place the Sacred Barque here at my feet," I command, and as they do so, Smenkhkara instinctively starts to step back. But I hold out a restraining hand and say:

"Brother, join me!"

And lifting first one foot and then the other, I trample on the Sacred Barque, whose ancient fragile sides begin to crack and crumble beneath my blows. At my side Smenkhkara begins to trample also in a frenzied, mindless, almost terrifying fashion.

And over all the animal groan rises and is broken now by horrified, anguished shouts and protestations that can-not be restrained.

But you are with us, Father Aten, and we do not falter or hesitate.

We trample and *trample* and TRAMPLE until we al-most forget to stop, so furious do we become in expressing

our hatred and our final triumph over this cruel, vindictive, venal god.

It is only when Horemheb ventures to say at last in a
broken, desolate voice, "It is done, Majesty. Son of the
Sun, desist, the barque of your enemy is no more!" that
I finally return to myself and realize again where I am
and what I am doing, and what I still have left to do.

"Now, citizens of Kemet," I shout, contemptuously
kicking the superstitious dust of centuries off my golden
sandals, "follow me to the banks of the Nile and witness
the fate of Amon, which shall be final and forever, and
will last for millions and millions of years!"

I gesture to the soldiers holding Amon to precede me.
Horemheb falls into step at my right hand, on my left
Smenkhkara offers me his arm. I begin to shuffle forward
slowly and painfully toward the river, some four hundred
feet from the ruined temple. The crowd parts before me,
fear and terror in its eyes. I no longer see my family,
or anyone: I go now to keep my final appointment with
the eternal enemy of my life.

Halfway there, as I start to pass through the great pylon
gates erected by my father, his cartouche confronts me
and a sudden inspiration strikes.

Abruptly I stop.

"Bring me a chisel and hammer!" I cry; and from
somewhere in the crowd, his face white and tense but
still obedient to my command as he has always been,
steps the chunky little figure of my faithful Bek. In his
hand he carries the chisel and hammer with which he
was working when I returned so unexpectedly from the
Valley of the Kings to shatter forever the world of Amon.

He bows low and with a trembling hand extends them
to me. Once again the deathly silence falls, as all wonder
what I will do next. I do not keep them in suspense. I
step forward at once and awkwardly begin to chip away
at the hieroglyphs for "Amon" in my father's name of
Amonhotep.

I do not do it very well, but it is enough to show my
intent. Then I hand the chisel and hammer back to Bek.

"Continue," I command, "until the name of Amon is

completely gone from my father's name. And gather you
all your company of sculptors and artisans from everywhere in the Two Lands, Bek, and do you similarly remove the name of Amon wherever and whenever you find
it, through all the length and breadth of Kemet. This do I
decree!"

With a sigh that seems to come from the very depths of
his heart, my faithful Bek bows and whispers, very low,
"Yes, Your Majesty."

And again the great groan comes from the crowd.

But they are human, they are curious, the show is
still going on: they jostle along as closely as they dare
behind the cordon of soldiers that has instinctively formed
itself around me.

We resume our walk to the river, under skies that now
have entirely cleared of the gray clouds that earlier de-
pressed the day. It has become noticeably warmer, too.
It seems to me that Ra in his form of Amon, cold and
sinister, has slunk away. Ra in his form of the glorious
Aten now stands bright and beneficent over all the world.

Suddenly I feel very happy, Father Aten. What I am
doing is just and right. You are with me, and all is well
with your son Akhenaten as he does what you direct him,
living in truth this day as he has never in all his twenty-
seven unhappy years lived in truth before. Those unhappy
years are over: the happy years are about to begin. This
do you tell me now, O Aten, and this do I believe.

We come to the bank of the river. Hapi sparkles in the
sun as he races swiftly away north past Akhet-Aten to
the Delta and the Great Green. He does not know the
gift I am about to give him, but he will receive it and
keep it well, for he is very secret and, in many places,
very deep.

I hold up my golden crook of office. All stop. The
heavy, terrified, watching silence falls again.

"Soldiers!" I command. "Do you hurl the statue of him
who is no longer a god, the evil impostor Amon-Ra who
has for so long plundered and disgraced the land of Kemet,
do you hurl him into the farthest reaches of the Nile!"

They tremble—they give me horrified glances—they

hesitate—they mutter to one another—the crowd begins
to groan again.

"AS I COMMAND YOU!" I shout at the top of my
lungs. "NOW!"

They start as if stabbed, which they would certainly
be did they not obey—step back three paces from the
water's edge—hesitate for one last second—draw back
their arms in unison—encourage one another with their
own shout of *"Now!"*—run forward to the very edge of
the bank—and hurl the golden statue of my enemy far,
far up and out, into the bosom of the Nile.

It rises—hurtles forward—twists and turns—glitters and
gleams in Ra's rays as though it had a life of its own—
and then with a heavy splash disappears into the arms of
Hapi, nevermore to be seen by mortal man.

A last great, dreadful sighing sound comes from
both banks of the river, as though all the deaths in all
the world were being mourned at the same time. I perceive that I must make sure that the impostor really *will*
nevermore be seen by mortal man.

I raise my golden crook again. Instantly, obediently—
for now, I think, they are truly and permanently terrified
of me, which I regret, but I offered them love and they
would not have it—they stop their silly noise and listen.

"Be you all aware," I cry, and my voice carries clearly
over Hapi's steady lapping, "that if any man or any
woman or any child shall attempt to recover the statue of
the impostor, then that man or woman or child, be they
high or low in this land, will be slain with the most horrible of tortures as befits a death-enemy of Pharaoh. Be
you all aware that this ban lies upon you all, forever and
ever, for millions and millions of years. I, Nefer-Kheperu-
Ra Akhenaten, so decree it in the name of my Father
Aten! You are warned!"

I wait a long moment to let this sink in; and then I
proceed to the further final business of this day, for I
have decided that it were best to conclude it all now
that I have begun. My mother and father told me long
ago—my uncle Aye reaffirmed it—my own experience
has borne it out—and you, Father Aten, have finally con-

vinced me of it—that if you would strike at all, you must strike fast and strike completely. This I have finally learned, thanks to you, Father Aten, and to my family who hurt me so last night, and to the priests and people who hissed me on my way this morning. It has been a long time coming, but now I shall not look back. I have suffered enough. And so today I shall do it all.

"And furthermore!" I cry, and this time the groan is almost desperate, I have shocked and battered them so already. But they have asked for it and there is no turning back.

"Furthermore, from this day forward all the temples of Amon everywhere in Kemet and in all friendly lands along its borders shall be closed entirely, forever and ever. All their goods and treasures shall be returned to Pharaoh at once to be placed in the temples of the Aten, and all their priesthoods shall be utterly and forever dispersed."

More groans and outcries, more weeping and wailing, quite open now. But I proceed regardless, as you know I must, O Aten.

"And all the temples of all the other gods, who have aided and assisted Amon in his attempts to conquer Kemet and ruin my House and subvert the great god Aten, shall also be closed immediately, forever and ever, and all *their* goods and treasures shall be returned at once to Pharaoh to give to the Aten, and all *their* priesthoods shall be utterly and forever dispersed.

"And there shall be no other god but Aten."

More groans, more wailing. Why will they persist in these stupid, pointless sounds? It will do them no good and may only make me angry. And for the moment, at least, I am not angry at all. I am simply rendering judgments too long delayed.

"There shall be no other god but Aten," I repeat firmly into their disrespectful clamor, and it does abate abruptly to hear my final word on the gods, none of whom has ever been as powerful as Amon, but all of whom have had many adherents among the ignorant. "And all temples and all treasure and all things in the land of Kemet shall belong to him and to me, his son Akhenaten, whom he loves and commands you to worship from this day forward, forever and ever.

"I, Nefer-Kheperu-Ra Akhenaten, Living Horus, Son of the Sun, King and Pharaoh, so decree it!"

I think, now, that I have done enough to complete this day. Yet as I turn to leave the riverbank, the crowd falling back in awe and fearful whispering at my advance, I stumble on a rock and clutch my brother's steady, loving arm. And as I do, there suddenly comes into focus before my eyes the deathly pale, desperately strained, but still perfect face of my wife. Always, always, *always* perfect! Does she never have a human reaction?

And I realize that there is one more piece of business left that I must do. And I decide that it, too, might as well be accomplished, once and for all, this day.

"Stop!" I cry, and obediently they shrink to frozen silence before me—all, all, all but my stout Smenkhkara, who stands steady, loving and strong at the right hand of his King.

"Help me to that pedestal," I say to him, pointing to the great stone platform on which stands a colossal statue of our great-great-grandfather Tuthmose III (life, health, prosperity!). Tenderly, but how strongly, he lifts me up. I face the crowd, I stare down upon Nefertiti.

"Come to my side," I say to Smenkhkara, and her face suddenly becomes completely white, drained of all color, as he rises to me in one lithe, lovely leap—such a leap as I could once accomplish, long ago before my illness came and loveliness vanished from my life . . . until he returned it to me, with your blessing, O Aten.

"People of Kemet!" I say, and in the awful stillness the rest of my family comes in focus, too, and I see that they, too, like her who has been my wife, are seeing ghosts and death's-heads—or so they look, ghastly, strangely shriveled and sadly pathetic as they appear to me.

"People of Kemet"—and now, in spite of myself, my voice does thicken with emotion, for I must confess I am not completely happy with what I do, I like to hurt no

one, but I must do what is right and just—"People of
Kemet, you all know that the Chief Wife of Pharaoh has
failed to give him sons. You all know that in recent
months she has spent increasing time away from him,
having decided, apparently, that she prefers the company
of others to that of him whom she has so sadly failed in
this regard. You know that she has become, thereby, no
longer a fit mate for the Living Horus, to whom she gives
neither sons, nor comfort, nor happiness. Therefore she
must be cast out."

Abruptly there is a shrill, high keening whose source I
cannot for a moment perceive. Then I see that it comes
from my wives, my mother and my sister Sitamon, who
are clinging together, weeping as though their hearts
would break.

All else is still with a stillness like death as the horrid
sound continues. They are shameless about it. It is gross
discourtesy and disrespect to me. How can they forget
their royal dignity so?

For just a second, I will confess to you, Father Aten,
this shakes me and I find myself almost unable to continue.
But I harden my heart as you and I know I must; and
presently, though my voice still shakes a bit with emotion no matter how just I know my action to be, I continue.

"Fortunately, people of Kemet, the Living Horus is
not alone, though he no longer has the loving company of
the Chief Wife, or the comfort of her presence at his
side. He is not alone, nor will he ever be again! The
great god Aten has brought to him a companion of his
heart to love and comfort him forever, to work with him
for your good, my people of Kemet, to do all things right
and glorious for the Two Lands, and to be unto him a
right arm, a left arm, a right leg, a left leg, a head, a
heart, a body, a *ka* and *ba* to love and tend the Living
Horus in all things, for all the days of our lives until we
shall both return to the Aten, to live together forever
and ever in the afterworld.

"Therefore on this day do I put aside the Chief Wife
Nefertiti, leaving her, for the love we once bore for

one another, the North Palace at my capital of Akhet-Aten and sufficient of gold and staff to conclude her days in dignity—"

Now the terrible keening of my female relatives is joined and overwhelmed by a great wailing from the crowd which not even my fiercest glances can suppress. I had no idea she was so popular. But in due time, of course, curiosity quiets the unseemly clamor enough that my closing words can be heard.

"—and take unto my side my brother, the Prince Smenkhkara, whom I declare to be, now and hereafter, forever and ever, Ankh-Kheperu-Ra, Co-Regent, Living Horus, Son of the Sun, King and Pharaoh of the Two Lands of Kemet, one with me in our hearts, bodies and all things.

"And from the former Chief Wife Nefertiti I take her title of 'Nefer-Neferu-Aten'—'Fair Is the Goodness of the Aten'—and I hereby give and bestow it upon my brother, the King and Pharaoh Ankh-Kheperu-Ra Smenkhkara."

The wailing rises again but I shout above it, and curiosity, of course, again subdues it.

"And to him I give the right and permission, forever and ever, to style himself 'The Beloved of Akhenaten,' for so"—and here my voice does openly tremble, because of the great gratitude and love I bear for him, and because of the great triumph I feel within me that we are at last free to live in truth before the world as you, O Aten, would have us do—"for so he is, and will ever be, to me. . . .

"Thus do I, Nefer-Kheperu-Ra Akhenaten, Living Horus, Son of the Sun, King and Pharaoh of the Two Lands, decree it! People of Kemet, I give and commend to you the Co-Regent Ankh-Kheperu-Ra, who will be your true liege lord and will love and comfort me forever!"

And turning to my brother, I kiss him full upon the lips. And taking his hand, I lead him forward upon the platform and present him to our people.

And now, suddenly, there is no more wailing from the crowd, neither is there any applause or greeting. Nothing but a deep and absolute silence, broken only by the gradually diminishing sobs of my women. And presently even those are stilled, and only silence—only nothing— only nothing beyond nothing—prevails in all the world.

Smenkhkara stands looking out, at first calmly, bravely and defiantly. Then when there is no response from any-where his straight back begins to slump a little, the proud carriage of his head diminishes. He flings me a sudden frightened glance, and at once I step forward beside him and speak in clear, untroubled tones to our people, who seem temporarily to love us not—but we do not care, for we love one another, and they will come to under-stand this, and to love us too.

"We return now to Akhet-Aten," I say. "May the great god Aten keep and comfort you. This do we, King Akhen-aten and King Smenkhkara, desire for you. We leave you now, secure in his love for us, in which we know you join."

But still there is only nothing, and nothing beyond noth-ing; and so in a moment I say quietly to my brother, "Help me down." And with a convulsive grasp that shows how shattered he is by our people's apparent hostility, and how much he welcomes the opportunity to do something active in the face of it, he assists me down.

I think they do not love us yet, but I think they will. For now they have no choice. We are King and Pharaoh, one heart, one mind, one body, and they must.

Not looking back at anyone, not even the Family or anyone, we walk slowly, my hand upon his strong, sup-porting arm, through the motionless crowds to the landing stage. Silently and without expression the crewmen help us aboard. I raise my voice and cry:

"Lift anchor and set sail for Akhet-Aten!"

Slowly the barge pulls away and swings out into Hapi's swift-flowing tide.

We take our positions in the prow and we do not look back.

Ahead lies a glorious future with you, O Aten, as our strength.

Behind lies—for the moment—nothing, and nothing beyond nothing.

But it will change.

It must.

They have no choice.

Tiye

MY SONS, *my sons* . . . my heart is dead within me. The Two Lands cry out . . . and now, as always, the Great Wife must answer . . . though my heart is dead within me at the thought. . . .

Nefertiti

I CANNOT THINK . . . I cannot think. We loved each other once . . . I cannot think . . .

Kia

I MOVE to the North Palace also on my return. We will take Tut with us, and the girls. I have learned how the game is played, in this strange land. Poor Naphuria is too besotted to see it, but we will hold the pawns. I shall be useful at last, to Kemet. . . .

Aye

IT IS LATE: Ra sinks in the west. We met once more an hour ago, in Malkata—just the three of us this time, my sister, Horemheb, myself. Certain things were discussed, certain plans were made. We three are not made of iron for nothing . . . though, may the gods help us, we pity and love him still, poor, lost Akhenaten. . . . If only his life had moved differently. If only . . . *"If only!"* The plaint of sentimentalists and fools—coming from us who, for Kemet's sake, can afford to be neither, any more. . . .

Amonhotep, Son of Hapu

HOREMHEB TELLS ME that he has ordered a boat and divers to take the river as soon as night falls. They will recover Amon and Horemheb will know where to hide him and keep him safe until he is needed again.

Which, I think, will not be too far off.

Horemheb

AKHENATEN IS GONE, insane, beyond recapture. He has humbled me for the last time, though for yet a while I must do his bidding as the gods fall—for they will fall. He has decreed it, and he is the Living Horus.

They will fall.

But so, I think, will he.

Amonemhet

I, THE PEASANT Amon-em-het, would tell you what I saw this night as I watered my cattle some fifty miles north of Thebes upon the River Nile.

It was dusk. The river flamed to gold, then, as always, quickly faded. In the west the barren, low-lying hills that guard the length of Kemet on both sides softened from rose to purple to the start of black. My cattle lowed their thanks and went to sleep. Thoth and other night birds murmured to their young among the reeds. Hapi flowed silently, Nut claimed the earth and great stars shone. I was ready to go back to my hut, my sleeping children and my eager wife. All was at peace.

Suddenly far to the north I saw a glow of light. Someone was on the river. What fool travels at night through Hapi's treacherous shoals? I wondered. I turned and waited while the light drew closer. Presently a sight you will not believe surprised my eyes.

It was the King's barge, this I know, for I have seen it pass many times when he has gone up and down the river. And standing in the prow was the King himself, and beside him another I have often seen, his brother the Prince Smenkhkara. Great torches flared along the sides and fore and aft careful oarsmen with long polls probed the currents to guard against floating logs and hidden bars of sand. I shrank back among the reeds and stared in awe at the dazzling sight.

They were dressed all in gold, and as the barge moved swiftly on Hapi's bosom I heard their voices, at first faint, then becoming louder as they came abreast of me, then still louder, then gradually becoming weaker and

fading away as they passed on north. They were chanting
a song of some sort, which I had never heard before. I
suspect it was the King's hymn to his god the Aten, whom
he would place above Amon, though he never can, for the
people will not permit it.

I suspect that is what it was, but I am not sure; because,
though it is carved in many places in Kemet, even in our
tiny village where no one from outside ever comes except
to collect taxes, I cannot read, and so I am not sure. But
I believe it was. And it was quite pretty, I thought, as
they sang it while they gleamed and glittered with gold
in the light of the great flaring torches dancing on Hapi's
dark bosom, in the soft desert night.

Together, as with one voice, they chanted and I heard
their many words:

*"Thou arisest fair in the horizon of Heaven, O Living
Aten, Beginner of Life. When thou dawnest in the East,
thou fillest every land with thy beauty. Thou art indeed
comely, great, radiant and high over every land. Thy rays
embrace the lands to the full extent of all that thou hast
made, for thou art Ra and thou attainest their limits and
subdueth them for thy beloved son, Akhenaten. Thou art
remote yet thy rays are upon the earth. Thou art in the
sight of men, yet thy ways are not known. . . .*

*"The earth brightens when thou arisest in the Eastern
horizon and shinest forth as Aten in the day-time. Thou
drivest away the night when thou givest forth thy
beams. . . .*

*"Thou it is who causest women to conceive and maketh
seed into man, who giveth life to the child in the womb
of its mother. . . .*

*"How manifold are thy works! They are hidden from
the sight of men, O Sole God, like unto whom there is no
other! Thou didst fashion the earth according to thy desire when thou wast alone—all men, all cattle great and
small, all that are upon the earth that run upon their feet
or rise up on high flying with their wings. . . .*

*"Thou makest the waters under the earth and thou
bringest them forth as the Nile at thy pleasure to sustain
the people of Kemet. . . .*

"All distant foreign lands, also, thou createst their life. . . .

"Thy beams nourish every field and when thou shinest they live and grow for thee. Thou makest the seasons in order to sustain all that thou hast made, the winter to cool them, the summer heat that they may taste of thy quality. Thou hast made heaven afar off that thou mayest behold all that thou hast made when thou wast alone, appearing in thy aspect of the Living Aten, rising and shining forth. Thou makest millions of forms out of thyself, towns, villages, fields, roads, the river. All eyes behold thee before them, for thou art the Aten of the day-time, above all that thou hast created.

"Thou art in my heart, there is none that knoweth thee save thy son Akhenaten. Thou hast made him wise in thy plans and thy power!"

Many, many words did they sing, all the words of their song, and three times they sang it, from beginning to end, as they passed me, starting with the first moment I saw them in the twilight to the south until they faded from my sight in the darkness of the north; so that I was able to understand quite well what they were saying. It was pretty, as I say, and you would not believe the splendid sight they made, standing in their golden clothes with the great torches flaring out upon the dark water on both sides.

I swear to you this is what I saw, but I cannot say it convinced me, now that I know what the writing in our village means. I still like the old ways of Amon, myself. But it was something, to see the King and the Prince Smenkhkara, so golden and chanting in the night. I went back and told my wife about it before we fell upon one another with happy cries that finally wakened both the children, so that we had to draw the old camel's-hide blanket over us to finish the business.

I don't know whether she believed me or not, or whether it matters, really. We have two mouths to feed already, and likely to have a third if we keep on like this. Amon has always understood such things, we feel easy with Amon. I am not so sure the Aten does, and anyway, I do not intend to bother my head about it, or with what happens in great cities.

It was pretty, and I loved to see them pass, because of course we are far from the great ones, here. But it really doesn't matter much to me, my wife, or anyone I know here in the village.

Akhenaten (Life, health, prosperity!)

WE GLIDE ON THROUGH the magical night, chanting as we go. All we have left behind are forgotten: it is as though they had never been.

I have never known the world to be filled with such happiness, for I am with the One who understands and loves me, and we worship you, O Aten, as one body, one heart, one mind.

Now all things will at last come right for your son Akhenaten. His sad, unhappy days will end. Now Kemet and all will finally worship you, my Father Aten, and your son Akhenaten, whom you have directed in all things, to your greater glory, and to his . . .

I smile at Smenkhkara and he smiles at me, strong and beautiful in the flaring torchlight as we speed over the swift dark river.

Together we will be happy and together we will make Kemet happy.

I so decree it and it will be so:

For I am Akhenaten, he who has lived long, and I will live in truth forever and ever, for millions and millions of years.

October 1974–August 1975

FOR FURTHER READING

Aldred, Cyril. *Akhenaten and Nefertiti.* New York: Brooklyn Museum and Viking Press, 1973.

Akhenaten, Pharaoh of Egypt. London: Abacus, Sphere Books Ltd., 1968.

Egypt: The Amarna Period and the End of the Eighteenth Dynasty. The Cambridge Ancient History, Vol. II, Chapter XIX. Cambridge University Press, 1971.

Breasted, James H. *Ancient Records of Egypt,* Vol. 2; *The Eighteenth Dynasty.* New York: Charles Scribner's Sons, 1906.

A History of Egypt. New York: Charles Scribner's Sons, 1909.

Budge, E. A. Wallis. *The Egyptian Book of the Dead.* New York: Dover Publications, 1967.

The Mummy. New York: Collier Books, 1972.

Carter, Michael. *Tutankhamun.* New York: David McKay Co., Inc., 1972.

Champollion, Jacques. *The World of the Egyptians.* Geneva: Editions Minerva, 1971.

Cottrell, Leonard. *The Lost Pharaohs.* London: Pan Books, 1956.

Desroches-Noblecourt, Christiane. *Tutankhamen.* London: Michael Joseph, Ltd., 1963.

Erman, Adolf. *The Ancient Egyptians: A Sourcebook of Their Writings.* New York: Harper Torchbooks, 1966.

Life in Ancient Egypt. New York: Dover Publications, 1971.

Forman, Werner, and Kischewitz, Hannelore. *Egyptian Drawings.* London, New York: Octopus Books, 1972.

Frankfort, Henri. *Ancient Egyptian Religion.* New York: Harper & Row, 1971.

Grayson, A. K., and Redford, Donald B. *Papyrus and Tablet.* Englewood Cliffs, New Jersey: Prentice-Hall, 1973.

Harris, James E., and Weeks, Kent R. *X-Raying the Pharaohs.* New York: Charles Scribner's Sons, 1973.

Hawkes, Jacquetta. *The First Great Civilizations.* New York: Alfred A. Knopf, Inc., 1973.

Hayes, William C. *The Scepter of Egypt, Part II: The Hyksos Period and the New Kingdom.* New York: Metropolitan Museum of Art, 1959.

James, T. G. H. *Myths and Legends of Ancient Egypt.* New York: Bantam Books, 1972.

Johnson, Irving and Electa. *Yankee Sails the Nile.* New York: W. W. Norton & Co., 1966.

Kaster, Joseph. *Wings of the Falcon.* New York: Holt, Rinehart and Winston, 1968.

Lons, Victoria. *Egyptian Mythology.* London: The Hamlyn Publishing Group Ltd., 1963.

Meade, N. F. Mansfield. *Egypt: A Compact Guide.* Luxor: Gaddis, 1973.

Mertz, Barbara. *Red Land, Black Land.* London: Hodder and Stoughton, 1966.

Murray, Margaret A. *The Splendor That Was Egypt.* New York: Hawthorn Books, Inc., 1963.

Niebuhr, Carl. *The Tell el Amarna Period.* London: David Nutt, 1910.

Petrie, Flinders. *Wisdom of the Egyptians,* Vol. LXII. New York: Rinehart and Winston, 1968.

Steindorff, George, and Seele, Keith C. *When Egypt Ruled the East.* Chicago: University of Chicago Press, 1957.

Weigall, Arthur. *The Life and Times of Akhnaton.* London: Thornton Butterworth, Ltd., 1910.

White, Jon Manchip. *Everyday Life in Ancient Egypt.* New York: Capricorn Books, 1967.

Wilson, John A. *The Culture of Ancient Egypt.* Chicago: University of Chicago Press, 1951.

Zayed, Dr. Abd el Hamid. *The Antiquities of El Minia.* The Society for the Promotion of Tourism in El Minia.

Two other books deserve mention. It was through Evelyn Wells' *Nefertiti* (New York: Doubleday & Company, Inc., 1964), picked up casually some years ago for idle reading, that I first became intrigued with the period and decided to read further. In her version both Akhenaten and Nefertiti emerge as superhuman beings perfect in every respect—which Akhenaten in particular certainly was not —but it is an entertaining and enjoyable account. And to that eternally amusing gentleman, Immanuel Velikovsky —who on Egyptology, as on all other subjects, jumps on his horse and rides wildly off in all directions—we owe *Oedipus and Akhnaton* (New York: Doubleday & Company, Inc., 1960). Like all his books, it contains just enough of a shred of possibility so that it makes the reader stop and think. And this, it seems to me, is sufficient to warrant its inclusion on anybody's list.

REMEMBER IT DOESN'T GROW ON TREES

ENERGY CONSERVATION -
IT'S YOUR CHANCE TO SAVE, AMERICA

Department of Energy, Washington, D.C.